Books by Deb Stover

SHADES OF ROSE
A WILLING SPIRIT
SOME LIKE IT HOTTER
ALMOST AN ANGEL
ANOTHER DAWN
STOLEN WISHES
A MATTER OF TRUST

Published by Pinnacle and Zebra Books

STOLEN WISHES

Deb Stover

Zebra Books
Kensington Publishing Corp.

http://www.zebrabooks.com

ZEBRA BOOKS are published by

Kensington Publishing Corp.
850 Third Avenue
New York, NY 10022

Zebra, the Z logo and Splendor Reg. U.S. Pat. & TM Off.

First Printing: October, 1999
10 9 8 7 6 5 4 3 2 1

Printed in the United States of America

*This book is for our Bonnie—our Sunshine—
and her band of outlaws, Barbi and Ben.*

*Special thanks to Carol, Karen, Mo, and Paula.
You're the best.*

Dear Readers:

Stolen Wishes is a book with some *very* special characters. I hope you love them as much as I do. This story is about love, honor, and commitment—the bonds that forge a family that are far more powerful than mere genetics.

Though *Stolen Wishes, Another Dawn,* and *A Willing Spirit* are all books that stand alone, they are related through U.S. Marshal Sam Weathers. Many of you may remember Sam from *A Willing Spirit* as the spirit in question. *Another Dawn* and *Stolen Wishes* are actually prequels to *A Willing Spirit.*

I hope you enjoy my work. I love to hear from readers. Please write to me at:

PO Box 1196
Monument, CO 80132

You can also E-mail me at deb@debstover.com, or visit my Web page at http://www.debstover.com. I'm definitely an on-line junkie. See you in cyberspace.

May all your days include a bit of magic!

Love,
Deb

Prologue

Southern Kansas—1888

The relentless north wind sliced through Mary Goode's threadbare coat as she trudged along the narrow trail. An image flashed through her mind of a warm fire and sweet tea with hot milk. Ah, but England was a far better place than this godforsaken land, where parents died of mysterious fevers and left their children homeless orphans.

Tears pricked her eyes, but she blinked them into submission. Now was not the time, and if all went as planned, she would never succumb to tears again. Crying was for children, and fate had decreed that at thirteen, Mary was no longer a child.

Huge snowflakes floated down from the blue-black canopy until whiteness nearly obliterated the dark sky. She paused and pulled her coat closer, wishing she still had the warm muffler her mother had knitted last winter. Alas, her guardians had taken everything.

Including Robin.

Her breath caught in her throat at the thought of seeing her brother again. Soon, she promised herself. Very soon.

Turning her face into the wind, she continued her journey, pausing at the top of a slight hill. She tucked a stray curl beneath her hood and blinked several times. At last, the massive brick and stone structure came into view.

God, please let him still be here.

Three months had passed since their parents' deaths, when the sheriff had taken her brother to this dreadful place. Though they called it an asylum, in truth it was a prison where people like Robin were locked away until they died and were no longer a burden to anyone.

Mary would never forget that horrible day when they'd dragged Robin from her side. Weak from the same fever that had killed their parents, she'd been unable to run away and hide her brother. But now she was strong, and she would take Robin across the border to Indian Territory, where they would hide until their grandfather came for them.

What horrible things might these people have done to her smiling brother, whose laughter brightened even the most dreary days? Her mother had often called him one of God's special angels, and their father had raised Robin with patience and love. Not once could Mary recall having heard her father refuse to read his son the same bedtime story. Every night until that horrible fever had rendered their father unconscious, he had read from *The Merry Adventures of Robin Hood.* Of course it was also his favorite, which was why Lawrence Goode's only son bore the name Robin.

Mary knew the entire story by heart, though she no longer had the book. That, along with everything else she'd loved, was gone. But no one could take her memories. Those were hers to cherish, and soon she would have her brother to share them.

She blinked, certain no one in this place had ever read

Robin his favorite bedtime story. She would recite it to him herself once they were safe, but first she had to find him.

"Please, God, make it so," she whispered into the snowy night. "Please."

Her mother's last words echoed through Mary's mind, as they often did. *Look after your brother, Mary. He will always be a child.*

Mary stumbled and her throat worked convulsively, her vision blurred. *I will not cry.* She drew a shuddering breath; the icy air cleansed her lungs and purged her mind.

Stealthily, she crept around the building, searching for a window without bars. There had to be a way for her to get inside to Robin. Soft light streamed through a ground-floor window, spilling onto the freshly fallen snow in a square of gold. Peering into the room, she determined it was the kitchen and, more importantly, unoccupied.

She widened her stance and gripped the window, easing it open very slowly. The old wood creaked and her heart pressed against her throat, a tight fist of trepidation.

And hope.

Within a matter of moments, she was inside. At first, she thought to leave the window open to aid their escape, but in this weather that would surely draw unwanted attention.

After closing the window, she rubbed her arms, savoring the kitchen's warmth. Without knowing where in this huge building she might find her brother, she resigned herself to searching every room on every floor if necessary. A narrow staircase drew her attention, and she decided upstairs made the most sense this time of night.

Her eyes readjusted to the darkness by the time she reached the next floor. She stood with her back pressed against the wall, waiting and wondering, listening to her heart pummel her ribs and echo through her head.

A lone lamp burned at the far end of the hall, and she

inched along the wall until she came to the first closed door. With sweaty fingers, she turned the handle and peered inside. A lamp burned near the window, illuminating the room enough for her to see several cage-like iron cribs lined up against the far wall. Most of them were occupied by small bundles.

Oh, dear God. She held her breath and her throat burned with the need to vent her rage at this injustice. If she were rich, she'd take all the babies home and raise them herself. With a shudder and a powerful sense of futility, she left the room and proceeded to the next door.

On the fourth floor, she noted one door slightly ajar with light overflowing into the hall. She heard someone talking from inside, though the words were muffled. Still, something about the voice's inflection and tone beckoned her.

Holding her breath, she peered through the open door. Joy surged through her when she recognized Robin sitting cross-legged on a narrow bed near the window. He clearly didn't see or hear her as she stepped into the room, for he continued moving his hands and talking excitedly, reciting his favorite story.

He remembers. Mary's determination renewed itself. She would find a way to take Robin away from here, to a place where they could live together again as brother and sister. Though he was six years her senior, he would always be her little brother in so many ways.

Her eyes blurred as she searched the stark room until her gaze came to rest on two men seated on the floor near Robin's bed. They were staring up at him, hanging on his every word. One of them was very tall and dark, obviously an Indian. The other man was the complete opposite, and she knew if he stood he wouldn't even reach her shoulder. She'd seen a man like him once—a midget, her father had called him.

At first, she remained in the shadows near the door,

wondering if the men would try to stop her. But the expressions on their faces told her of the trust and adoration they obviously felt for her brother.

Robin continued the story, pronouncing some words in ways she knew most people wouldn't understand. However, Robin's audience, whoever they were, obviously understood.

Knowing she could delay no longer, Mary stepped into the lamplight. "Robin," she said quietly. "It's me, Ma—"

Robin leapt to his feet and rushed into her arms. "Maid Marian," he whispered.

Hearing her father's pet name for her made Mary's heart flutter. "Yes, Robin. I've come for you." She cast a furtive glance at the men, who now rose.

"This is Little John," he indicated the towering Indian, "and that's Friar Tuck." He patted the smaller man on the shoulder.

Mary swallowed hard. "How nice. I'm pleased to meet you both." She looked at her brother again. "We must hurry, Robin."

"All right." Obediently, he went to the corner and pulled on an old coat, several sizes too large. "Make haste, men."

As Mary stared in surprise, the mismatched pair imitated Robin's actions. The small man donned a coat far too large for his short frame, while the Indian wrapped a blanket around his shoulders.

"We go," Little John said.

Friar Tuck put a fist on one hip and glowered up at Mary. "You're but a child," he said, shaking his finger at her. "But that's all right, Maid Marian. I shall take care of you all."

Mary realized that if she refused to allow the men to accompany them, they might alert the staff to Robin's escape. "Very well then, follow me."

"Where we going?" Robin asked, his eyes wide and filled with unconditional trust.

Praying for a miracle, Mary reached up to push a stray dark curl from her brother's brow. With a smile, she said, "Why, to Sherwood Forest, of course."

Chapter One

Indian Territory—1896

SHERWOOD FOREST
NO TRESPASSING

Shane Latimer read the crude sign attached to a gnarled hickory and chuckled. He shook his blond head and rubbed the back of his aching neck. Though rain had made the trail almost impossible to follow, he'd made it.

Why had the outlaws marked their hideout with a sign? Either they were even more cunning than Shane had thought, or they were fools. Their reputation indicated the former.

He looked around, marveling at how drastically the terrain had changed once he left southern Kansas and entered the northeastern corner of Indian Territory. Some would deem the lush countryside paradise. Considering the amount of rain that had fallen on him since yesterday, the abundant foliage was understandable. But right now he'd trade his last strip of jerky for the hot Texas sun baking through his bones.

He had to give the Merry Men credit, though. They'd chosen the location for their hideout wisely. Missouri, Arkansas, and Kansas were each less than a day's ride from here, giving the outlaws a wide and varied area in which to practice their thievery.

Watery sunlight broke through the clouds as a mockingbird sailed past, distracting Shane from his daydreams. "Get your hide moving, Latimer," he muttered to himself, peering beyond the sign and into the dense forest.

After all this time, he knew his backside wouldn't part company with the saddle willingly, so he decided to remain mounted for now. With a sigh, he retrieved his canteen and took a long drink. Then, as he secured it to his saddle horn again, he saw him.

Half-naked and motionless, the man blended with the trees as if part of the forest. Shane swallowed hard, taking in the long black hair, the buckskin breeches, and the feathers adorning the man's lance and headband.

An Indian in Indian Territory—no surprise there. However, the brave was as tall as many of the surrounding trees. Shane wasn't exactly short, standing well over six feet himself, but he knew the giant would dwarf him.

And beat the hell out of him in a fair fight.

Of course if it came to that, he'd manage somehow to swing the odds in his favor. With the reins laced through his gloved fingers, he allowed his hands to rest on his thighs, never shifting his gaze from the silent brave.

He could think of only one way to determine the man's intentions. Slowly, Shane moved both hands to the pommel as he shifted his weight in the saddle. The contrast between creaking leather and dead silence gave him pause, but the brave didn't even blink.

Shane raised a hand in greeting. "Nice day," he said and touched the brim of his hat.

Silence.

"Well, I'll be on my way then," he said, gathering the reins.

The brave widened his stance and gripped his lance with both hands. "Who goes there?" he asked in a booming voice that sent birds fluttering from nearby trees.

Shane figured he had three choices. One, he could draw his gun and get rid of the problem, though killing was something he didn't take lightly, and the brave hadn't done anything to warrant killing. Yet. Two, Shane could turn and ride away in silence, or three, he could try to bamboozle his way past the brave. Maybe.

"Who goes there?" the Indian repeated.

"Well, who are you?" Shane grinned. *No harm in trying.*

"I am called Little John."

Perfect. "Little?" Shaking his head, Shane chuckled. "I'm looking for someone. Maybe you've see—"

"Who goes there?" Little John asked again.

"I told you, I'm looking for—"

"You go." The brave's voice left no room for argument. "Leave Sherwood Forest."

Shane stared long and hard at Little John, weighing his options and his chances. *Damn.* The giant's stance and expression remained unwavering. Shane's element of surprise was lost no matter what. Either the brave would warn the others, or a bullet fired from Shane's gun would reveal his presence.

His decision made, Shane nodded and urged his horse to turn north. He'd have to circle back and ford the Verdigris. A menacing whir caught him by surprise.

His horse reared, throwing Shane from the saddle. He hit the ground hard and rolled away from the flailing hooves. Somehow he maintained his grip on his pistol.

Squinting, he managed to fire two rounds, but missed the coiled snake.

The gunfire sent the mare into even greater panic just as the snake struck, impaling pearl-white fangs into the horse's fetlock. The bucking frenzy would pump the snake venom through her large body that much faster. Shane had no choice but to end the animal's suffering. God knew he didn't want to do it.

Clutching his pistol, he rolled onto his hip to rise, but another eerie rattling turned his blood to ice. He swallowed hard knowing the snake was close. Too close. He shifted his gaze to one side without moving his head, searching until he found the small rattler coiled, ready to strike. Again.

Stealthily, he cocked the hammer of his pistol, praying the metallic click wouldn't prompt the snake to strike. Sweat dripped from Shane's brow and pooled in his eyes, but he didn't even blink.

The mare moved closer, still bucking but with less vigor. Fearing the horse would prompt the snake to strike, Shane pulled the trigger.

The mare's hoof glanced off Shane's temple and his shot went wild. Pain exploded through his head. Knowing what he had to do despite his blurred vision, Shane turned his gun on the mare and pulled the trigger. This way would be far more merciful than death by snakebite.

And where was that damned snake?

The mare went down instantly—Shane's shot had been clean. She suffered no more. "Damn shame," he whispered, gnashing his teeth.

As if from nowhere, Little John appeared, staring down at Shane like an indulgent parent. "Good horse. Great loss."

"Yeah." Shane tried to nod, but his head threatened to split with the slightest movement. He pressed his glove to his temple, then pulled it away bloodied.

The brave extended his large hand. Hesitating only a moment, Shane allowed the giant to haul him to his feet. He sensed he was in no danger—at least no immediate danger.

Little John had to be nearly seven feet tall, with silver streaks glistening in his blue-black hair. Barely reaching the Indian's chin, Shane wondered how the hell he was going to get out of this mess.

"I need to see to my horse," he said, tightening his grip on his pistol as he took two dizzy steps toward the mare. She lay on her side, unmoving, but he had to make absolutely sure. If there was one thing he couldn't do, it was walk away from a suffering animal.

"Snake."

Little John's voice startled Shane, making him turn in midstep. Twin probes of fire pierced his calf, sending Shane immediately to his knees.

He'd forgotten the damned snake.

Stunned, his fingers went limp and his pistol fell impotently to the ground. Little John shot past him and grabbed the snake and sent his knife through it. It sure as hell wouldn't bite anybody else.

But that wouldn't save Shane or his horse.

Fire sizzled in his calf. Looking down, he saw the snake's deadly yellow venom, tinged with streaks of his own blood, oozing from the twin holes in his jeans. The pain in his leg rivaled the constant throbbing in his temple.

Stiffly, he lowered himself to the ground and yanked a knife from his boot. Ignoring the blood trickling down the side of his face, Shane ripped the blade through his jeans until the fang marks were revealed.

The rattler had been small, comparatively speaking, but little ones had more potent venom. Still, after biting the mare it couldn't have had much left. Maybe Shane had a chance, but he had to act fast. The wound on his head wasn't helping matters any. His vision blurred and cleared.

Little John's shadow loomed behind him as the sun again broke through the clouds. The brave reached down with his huge hand, holding it out for the knife.

"Help," Little John said.

Indecision slashed through Shane. What choice did he have? With a sigh, he placed his knife, his trust, and his life in the Indian's hand. "There's whiskey in my saddlebags."

While Little John retrieved the nearly full bottle of whiskey, Shane loosened the bandanna from around his neck and wound it tightly, just above his knee. He grabbed a sturdy stick and slipped it beneath the bandanna, then gave it a decisive twist. Then another.

Little John handed the whiskey bottle to Shane, who splashed some over the snakebite. He sucked in a sharp breath as the fiery liquid burned his wound. Then he tipped his head back and swallowed a generous amount. A far more pleasant warmth seeped through his veins, and he took another pull of the potent, numbing—at least he sure as hell hoped so—liquor.

With the bottle still clutched in his fist, he met Little John's curious gaze. "Do it," Shane urged. "Now."

Grunting, Little John made two clean slits on Shane's leg, crisscrossing between the wounds left by the snake. Without speaking, the Indian sucked the poison from the cuts and spat on the ground repeatedly.

A wave of dizziness swept through Shane and he shuddered, knowing at least some of the venom had crept up his leg and into his blood. Only time would tell if he lived or died. He touched the side of his head again. Hell, he might survive the snakebite and still die from the blow to his head. That would make the snake victorious either way. Dead but victorious.

His vision blurred again as Little John continued his efforts. Shane fell sideways and hit the ground hard, his head landing in a mound of damp leaves near Little John's bare feet. The earthy scents of mud and rotting leaves filled Shane's nostrils, assuring him he was still alive. For now.

"Little John help more."

The brave's voice sounded far away, though Shane was vaguely aware of the giant's strong arms sliding beneath his knees and shoulders. A moment later, Little John lifted him as if he weighed no more than a small child.

Swirling darkness, waves of dizziness, and unbearable nausea spiraled through Shane. His gut clenched and he retched, then swallowed great gulps of air to calm his gut. The snake's venom couldn't have worked this fast. It looked as if the blow to his head might prove more deadly than the snake.

But there was one problem that snake hadn't taken into consideration. Shane Latimer was nowhere near ready to die.

Little John took a few jarring steps, then broke into a full run, sending shards of pain splintering through Shane's head.

"Maid Marian make better," Little John said forcefully, never slowing his pace.

Wondering what sort of insanity awaited him, and if he would live long enough to see for himself, Shane slipped into blessed oblivion.

Mary stepped outside the door and looked up at the sky, where patches of blue broke through at long last. For three weeks it had done nothing but rain.

Her gaze rested on her brother's dark head bent over the task of restringing his bow. At twenty-seven, Robin Goode still possessed the mind of a boy, filled with mischief and fantasy.

With a sigh, Mary looked around the area surrounding their isolated cabins in the woods—home for the past eight years. Sometimes, when she permitted herself to remember her parents and their life in England at Briarwood, she found herself yearning for something more.

But her parents were gone, and here she had a home and what remained of her family. What else was there? *A husband and children.*

No. Drawing a deep breath, she banished such thoughts. Dreams and tears weren't for her. She had responsibilities, and no time for daydreams or crying.

After all, this was a good place to live, with an abundance of game, water, and fertile soil. *Eight years.* She and Robin were both grown now. They could probably return to civilization, but what if something happened to her? What about Robin? There was no doubt in her mind that the authorities would put him back in that asylum, or another one just like it. Or worse. No, she had to stay here with her brother and their haphazard family—misfits one and all.

Perhaps Little John was a little slow, but Mary knew he would do anything to protect Robin. The tall Indian was loyal and good-hearted.

Friar Tuck was a fussy little old man now, who'd appointed himself in charge of them all. He was a dear, sweet man, though sometimes a trifle on the bossy side. He'd never shown any signs of instability, other than his random recitations of Shakespeare and some strange scientific ranting no one understood.

They had no clue about his earlier life. According to both Little John and Robin, Tuck had arrived at the asylum shortly after Robin, so he hadn't been there long before Mary came for them.

Yes, *them.* She smiled to herself, for fate had surely played a role in their situation. Though she'd gone to that dreadful place with only Robin in mind, now she couldn't imagine their life without Little John and Tuck. Yes, fate . . .

Mary picked up her egg basket and headed toward the henhouse, inhaling deeply of the rain-washed air. Except for one unwelcome serpent that appeared from time to time, their Sherwood Forest was truly a Garden of Eden, especially in spring. A sweet profusion of honeysuckle bowed the fence around the henhouse—a startling contrast with the chicken yard's typical stench.

She bent down to enter the squat log structure, but a shout stayed her.

"Maid Marian."

Recognizing the urgency in Little John's voice, Mary dropped her basket and hurried to where Robin had set aside his bow. They both stared into the woods from where the voice had come.

"Maid Marian," the call came again. The sound of him crashing through the trees and underbrush heralded his arrival. "Need help."

Winded, Little John paused before them with his burden. "Snake," he said.

"Oh, no." Cringing, Mary turned toward the cabin. "Bring him inside," she ordered. "Robin, get my herbs from the shed. Quickly now."

Little John ducked to enter the cabin and dropped to his knees beside the straw tick in the front room. Carefully, he deposited the unconscious man, then stepped away.

Mary's attention was riveted to the man's bare leg, red and distended below the tightly wrapped bandanna. "How long ago was he bitten?" she asked.

Little John looked out the window, tilting his head to see the sky. "Two—no, one hour."

She smiled, realizing how hard he was trying to understand. For years, she and Tuck had tried to help both Robin and Little John with the concepts of time. They both grasped the passing of days, but they struggled with shorter intervals.

Turning her attention back to her patient, she looked

at his face. Burnished golden hair curled around his handsome face and nearly touched his shoulders at the sides and back. A heated flush crept up her neck to her face as she noted the profusion of curls peeking from his open collar.

Ashamed for failing to concentrate on the man's injuries, Mary followed the trail of dried blood on his cheek to the massive discoloration at his temple. She had no way of knowing which of his injuries was more serious. If the snake had bitten him only an hour ago, a man his size shouldn't have been unconscious.

"Horse kicked," Little John explained.

Robin rushed in, depositing a basket of herbs and bandages beside the bed. Mary knelt on the floor beside the wounded man to examine his leg more closely. Little John had thoroughly siphoned the venom. She squeezed the inflamed flesh around the fang marks gently but firmly. The man moaned in pain, but only clean blood oozed from the wounds—no trace of the noxious, straw-colored venom.

"You did well, Little John," she said, reaching into her basket for a few items. "Bring the kettle, please. Careful, it's hot."

After Little John returned with the kettle, Mary stirred hot water into a wooden bowl filled with herbs until she had a thin paste. Adding a generous glob of red clay from the riverbank, she soon had the necessary consistency for a good poultice.

Fragrant steam wafted up from the mixture as she spread it thickly on the man's leg. With any luck at all, the poultice would draw any lingering poison from the bite. "Robin, we'll have to cut away his boot. His foot is too swollen to remove it any other way."

Nodding, her brother grabbed a huge pair of shears from a shelf near the window. Mary watched him carefully cut through the soft leather, far enough for the boot to fall to the floor with a solid thunk.

"Thank you," she said, and removed the man's sock. His bare toes were icy, and the little one was already turning blue on the outer edge. She had no choice but to loosen the bandanna. And pray she wasn't releasing more poison.

"Who is he?" she asked Little John as she turned the stick that held the twisted bandanna in place.

"Don't know."

Merely nodding in response, Mary rinsed a cloth in cool water and bathed the dried blood away from her patient's face. Even with the discoloring and swelling, she could see he was a handsome man. He moaned again, and his eyes fluttered open for an instant. They were green and glazed with pain.

"Thirsty," he whispered.

Excessive thirst was an expected consequence from a rattlesnake bite. Mary took the cup Robin handed her and dipped it into the pail of fresh water. Holding the back of the man's head in one hand, she lifted him and held the cup to his lips. He drank greedily, then fell back against the bedding.

She felt his toes again and noted their color. They were still cold, but healthy pink had replaced the blue tinge. She could only hope that by saving his leg she hadn't cost him his life. Biting her lower lip, she loosened the bandanna a little more.

She bathed his face again, noting the cut wasn't serious, but the bruising was massive. All they could do now was keep him comfortable and try to satisfy his thirst. And pray.

Rising, she faced Little John. "What happened?"

Tuck came in during Little John's recitation of the morning's events. With a sigh, he shook his bald head and faced Little John. "Well, did he have anything with him? We need to know who he is in case he doesn't make it.''

"Had a horse," Little John said clearly. "Horse dead. Snake.''

Tuck rolled his eyes and shook his head. With an indulgent sigh, he tilted his head back to stare up—way up—at Little John. "Did the man have a saddle? Hmm? With saddlebags, perhaps?''

"Whiskey." Little John nodded. "Yes.''

Mary stood beside Little John and took his hand. "You were very strong and brave today, my friend," she said with complete sincerity, smiling when the Indian blushed with pride beneath his bronze complexion. "This man owes you his life.''

"*If* he lives." Tuck folded his arms across his pudgy belly.

"True." Mary could hardly argue that point, though she desperately wanted the stranger to live. She didn't take time to ponder her reasons as she returned her attention to Little John. "Can you take Robin along to help you retrieve the man's saddle and any other belongings?''

"Make haste, Little John," Robin said, turning toward the door. "Lead me to saddle.''

Grunting in acknowledgment, Little John followed his friend and self-appointed leader toward the door.

"Be careful," Mary called after her brother, as always.

Robin paused at the door. Wrinkling his brow, he stared at the injured man. "I wonder . . .''

"What?" Mary looked at the stranger again, then back to her brother. "What is it, Robin?''

"Will Scarlet.''

Chapter Two

Shane struggled against the pressing darkness. He wanted to see as well as hear what was happening around him, but no matter how he tried, his eyelids refused to cooperate.

The fact that he was still breathing was a very good sign. He couldn't be dead, because his head hurt too damned bad. He couldn't even defend himself. If they searched his saddlebags, he was a goner, because they'd probably find the badge rolled inside his clean shirt. He often hid it when entering an unfamiliar area or facing people he didn't know. No reason to advertise his identity until he knew exactly what—and who—he was up against.

His leg burned like the fires of perdition, and his head felt as if the devil himself was dancing a jig across his scalp. Footsteps approached the bed, or whatever he was lying on, and he heard a chair scrape against a bare floor.

"Still not awake?"

There it was again, the angel's voice—soft and melodic, with an unusual accent. Despite his pain and wariness,

Shane relaxed into the soft bedding. He remembered her voice calling him up from the pain again and again, though he had no idea how much time had passed. For all he knew, he could have been here for days.

His throat was so dry he couldn't swallow, but he knew that was from the snake venom. "Water," he croaked, and within seconds, he felt her cool hand behind his neck and precious moisture touched his lips. He drank greedily until she pulled the cup away.

"Not too fast," she said quietly. "I'll give you more in a few minutes."

Shane brought his hand to his temple and found a bandage where his horse had kicked him. "Thank . . . you."

"You're welcome," she said and offered him more water. "I wasn't sure you'd make it."

"Wouldn't have without . . . help." Drinking the water exhausted him, and he was grateful when she let his head rest against the bed again. "Who . . . ?"

"Little John saved your life," the angel said matter-of-factly. "If he hadn't been there . . ."

"I know." Shane was beholden to an outlaw, stranded without a horse, and he couldn't defend himself against a stiff breeze, let alone a band of outlaws. Yet, for some reason, he didn't feel threatened. Even in the forest after the snake struck, he'd known Little John meant him no harm.

"Rest."

He heard a chair slide across the floor, and panic struck. "Don't go," he whispered, mortified the moment the words left his lips. He hadn't cried for his mama since the age of seven, and here he was begging a stranger to stay at his side. "Sorry."

"Nothing to be sorry about." She slipped her hand behind his neck again. "More water?"

Shane drank, feeling somewhat stronger now. "Thank you."

"If this stays down, we'll try broth next." She sighed, and her chair creaked.

He tried again to open his eyes and realized they were stuck shut. "My eyes," he whispered.

She leaned over him and he felt her warmth almost touching his torso. She smelled of nothing but sunshine—he liked that.

"Forgive me," she said, and he felt a cool, damp cloth gently bathe his eyes. "I was so worried about your head and leg, I didn't realize . . ."

Blood? Of course, Shane remembered blood running into his eyes. Gradually, the dampness loosened his stuck lashes and he pried open his eyes. Blinking several times, his eyes teared and stung.

The first thing he saw was a blur of gray; then he realized it was the angel's clothing, because she was leaning across him to check his bandage. She bent closer and looked at the side of his head, her breasts staring him in the face.

Last time a woman's breasts had hung in his face, the circumstances had been a lot different. He was so weak now he couldn't even summon the desire for a woman, much less act on it. But he wasn't too far gone to notice that this angel had nice, full breasts, though her loose clothing did its best to conceal them.

"No more bleeding," she said, straightening. "I think you're going to make it."

She was smiling when he first saw her face, and he'd never seen a more beautiful sight. Her hair was dark reddish brown, and her eyes were the bluest of blues. She wore men's clothing that hung in baggy folds from her slender frame, almost as if she were trying to hide herself from prying eyes.

She was flesh and blood, and the sooner he banished

that angel notion, the better. After all, she was living with outlaws. She could *be* an outlaw herself. Or married to one . . . A sinking sensation hit him in the gut as he pondered the significance of her presence here.

He moistened his lips and continued to study her. Two thick braids were wrapped around her head like a crown, and he suspected her hair would hang past her waist when loose. *Not an angel, but still beautiful.* "Who . . . are you?"

"Mary Goode," she said, meeting his gaze. "Who are you?"

Shane cleared his throat, realizing the outlaws had not yet discovered his identity. Lies didn't fall easily from his lips, but right now survival took top priority.

Then he remembered a very special lady doctor he'd once known, who'd lost her memory from a blow to the head. They'd called her Dr. Sofie, because all she ever remembered was her first name. "I . . . I don't remember." Maybe that would buy him some time.

"Oh, dear." Mary leaned closer and stared into his eyes. "Your head injury, I suppose. I'm sure you'll remember later, though. Can you see clearly?"

Shane nodded, immediately regretting the action as pain tore through his skull. Every muscle in his body ached, throbbed, or burned. He was in sorry shape.

"My brother should be back with your saddle soon."

Shane swallowed hard. "Your brother?" If anyone searched his saddlebags . . .

"Yes, Little John took my brother Robin to—"

"Robin?" His heart thundered against his aching ribs. The angel was the notorious outlaw's sister. Shane drew a deep breath and shifted slightly to watch Mary's expression. "Your brother's name is Robin?"

"Yes." Mary tilted her head to one side, her expression quizzical. "Why?"

Shrugging, he tried to smile, but his lower lip cracked

right in the middle. He dabbed at it with his fingertip. "Just curious." That was an understatement.

"You must be feeling better then." She held the water toward him, and he raised up on his elbow, gripping the cup with one hand. He was weak, but he managed to get it to his lips and drain it. "Yeah, I feel better. Thanks."

"I'll get that broth." She reached for the cup, covering his fingers with hers for a brief moment. Her eyes widened as if the physical contact shocked her; then she quickly recovered and took the cup from his grasp. "Don't try to get up."

Shane had to chuckle as he let his aching head fall back against the pillow. He was nowhere near ready to stand.

He watched her bend over the open hearth and ladle the broth. Despite her baggy clothes, her curves were obvious and appealing to the eye. Her gray shirt was tucked into the belted waistband of a pair of patched brown trousers. Rags at best, and hardly the sort of attire he'd expect a successful outlaw's sister to wear.

Shane scrutinized the cabin. It was clean and well built, and the wood floor would be considered luxury to many in the Territory. Dirt floors were the usual for small cabins. Here, someone had taken great care to fit the boards into place.

For Mary?

Her brother might not provide pretty dresses for her, but at least she had a clean, dry floor beneath her feet. Shane was glad Mary didn't have to live on a dirt floor. Outlaw's sister or not, she'd shown him nothing but kindness.

A small clock ticked away on the mantel, though Shane couldn't quite make out the hands in the shadows. It had the look of fine craftsmanship, obviously booty from one of the Merry Men's raids.

Shane's holster and pistol hung from a hook near the door, too far to do him any good. His boots sat on the

floor beneath, but he could tell from here that one of them
had been cut. Wiggling his toes, he reminded himself
why that had been necessary.

The rest of the cabin's sparse furnishings were homemade, mostly of bent willow and oak, both plentiful in
the area. Why would Robin and his Merry Men furnish
their hideout with homemade furniture and dress Mary
in rags? It made no sense—none at all.

Too much thinking, Latimer. Shane's head pounded,
but he turned his attention to the rest of his body, pulling
the covers back to reveal his toes. One foot was swollen,
but the color was good. He owed Little John and Mary
more than his life. They'd also managed to save his leg.

Breathing a sigh of relief, he lifted up on both elbows
and turned his injured leg to the inside. His calf was
covered with a poultice, shielding the snakebite from
view. Then he realized another truth.

Someone had undressed him. He looked at Mary again,
and his ability to breathe vanished in a powerful hurry.
The thought of her looking at his naked body made him
arch a brow, sending pain through his wound again. Had
she seen anything of interest?

As if he could act on her interest, if it existed.

No, he decided, her concern was purely medical. Mary
had taken very good care of him, and for that he was
grateful. Still, he couldn't let his gratitude cloud his judgment.

He was trapped naked in a den of thieves.

Mary's hands trembled as she dipped broth from the
soup that would be tonight's supper. Though she'd lived
among men all her life, exclusively for much of it, none
of them had ever made her feel the way this stranger did.
Even while he'd been unconscious, the feel of his hard
muscles beneath her hands had made her warm all over.

She rose from the hearth and turned. He was watching her, his narrowed gaze intense and unwavering. Her heart fluttered in her chest and her hands trembled again, threatening to spill the hot broth. Drawing a deep breath, she steadied her hands and approached the bunk, reminding herself that he would soon be gone.

Why was he staring at her? There was little to see that might appeal to a man. She'd made certain of that.

He's hurt. She could have kicked herself. This man had been badly hurt and couldn't possibly have anything in mind beyond his recovery. She was safe.

For now . . .

And once he was on his feet again, Robin, Tuck, and Little John would send him away. Then she wouldn't have to worry about him any longer.

Or remember the way his sleek muscles had felt beneath her ministrations.

Stop. She was wicked to think about his body at all, other than his injuries. *Wicked, vile, wanton.* She was a good girl and she mustn't dwell on such things. *Double Scripture for you tonight, young lady.* She remembered her mother's admonition well, and would inflict it on herself without delay.

Because her single transgression had happened against her will. Drawing a deep breath, she pushed the memory aside, unwilling and unable to address it now. Or ever.

"The broth will strengthen you," she said, holding the cup steady as he pushed himself to a sitting position. The quilt slipped from his shoulders, revealing a broad expanse of chest. He was a beautiful man, she allowed, for there was no point in denial.

She held the broth toward him. While he'd been helpless, tending him hadn't seemed at all awkward, but now that he was sitting up and watching her with those beautiful green eyes . . . "Do you think you can manage this?"

she asked, praying he wouldn't burn himself because of her cowardice.

"I think so." He eased himself around so that his back leaned against the rough log wall, pausing to breathe heavily for a few moments. "Now I think I can at least keep from falling out of bed." A mischievous grin followed by a wince of pain made her heart melt.

"Forgive me, it's too soon for—"

"No, I'm fine." He grabbed a handful of blanket and shoved it weakly behind his back. "There."

Mary swallowed hard and handed him the cup with quivering hands. *You're a coward, Mary Goode.* She tried not to look at his chest, but the muscles that rippled in his arms were just as disconcerting. "Careful, it's hot."

Though she wanted to turn and run the moment his hands closed around the cup, she forced herself to remain. This man wasn't here to attack her, and it was time for her to forget that incident. She had to.

For Robin's sake.

If her brother ever learned what that horrible man had done to his sister . . . The mere thought made her throat constrict, and sweat pricked her skin beneath the heavy shirt. Remembering the vile man's taunts made her physically ill, but she drew a deep breath and brought her fears under control.

Her patient wasn't that evil man, and she had no reason to believe he meant her, or Robin, any harm. As she met his gaze again, she found him staring. Even with dried blood caked around his eyes, he was handsome, and he didn't have the crazed look that other one always did.

He lowered the cup, balancing it on his knee. "Good broth, thanks." He shifted his weight, though his gaze never strayed from hers. "I feel better already. Stronger."

"Good, it's empty. Would you like to try a little more?"

He nodded. "But I have a question first," he said,

keeping hold of the cup even after her fingers closed around it.

Mary stared at his hand next to hers, willing herself not to stammer as she waited for his question. "What?"

"Why do you look at me as if you think I'm going to eat you?"

Stunned, Mary jerked back and the cup fell to the floor with a clatter. She bent to retrieve it, cursing herself all the while for reacting so. She probably *had* been looking at him that way, and she couldn't blame him for wondering why. Of course, she couldn't possibly explain without disclosing secrets better left buried. The fewer people who knew, the better.

"I'm sorry," she whispered, willing herself not to run. Steeling herself, she met his gaze. "I'm not accustomed to strangers." That was certainly true.

"I thank you kindly for your hospitality and your doctoring, ma'am." His expression was warm, unthreatening. "You should know—er, I should tell you I would never hurt a woman. I might not remember my name just now, but I know my mama raised me right."

Mary stared at him for several silent moments, gripping the cup so tightly her knuckles turned white. "I believe you," she said, though she had no idea why. "Thank you for that."

"Thank *you*." He smiled, and his eyes twinkled.

She nodded and hurried to the hearth. Robin would return soon; then she wouldn't be alone with her patient any longer. In the meantime, she had to regain control of herself before Tuck saw her discomfiture and cross-examined her again. The little guy was far too wily to fool for long.

Mary returned and handed the broth to the stranger just as a knock sounded at the door. She peered through the slit Little John had fashioned in the wood and sighed with relief. "Robin. I was starting to worry," she said, opening the door.

Her brother walked in, removed his feathered cap as he'd been taught, then hung it from a hook near the door. Little John followed with the stranger's saddlebags slung over his shoulder.

"We had to barter," Robin said, raking his hand through his shaggy dark hair. "Sassy Sally had saddle."

Mary's face flamed with heat at the mention of the notorious Sally. Everybody in the Territory knew she was a harlot, though Mary couldn't imagine any man wanting to get within ten feet of Sally's lice-ridden body, let alone paying for the privilege. "So you had to—"

"He's awake," Robin said, going immediately to the bunk, where the stranger still leaned against the wall with the cup in his hands. "Will Scarlet, welcome."

Mary covered her face and groaned softly. Robin's obsession with *The Merry Adventures of Robin Hood* grew wearisome. "Robin, this man isn't Will Scarlet."

Robin stood beside the bunk, his stance wide and his hands clasped behind his back. His homespun tunic had been dyed a faded green with hedge apples, leaves, and grass. Though it was a lot of work to turn the rough fabric green, Mary did it because she loved her brother and it made him happy.

And, God help her, she'd do anything to keep him safe and happy.

"Then what name?" Robin asked, still staring at the stranger. Little John and Tuck flanked Robin until they formed a semicircle around the injured man. "Well?"

Tuck put a balled fist on each hip. "You look healthy enough," he said. "Answer Robin, man. What's your name?"

"Who goes there?" Little John boomed.

The stranger stared at Robin long and hard, then covered his face in his hands. He shook his head and groaned, then raked his fingertips down both cheeks. "You're Robin? Er, Mary's brother?"

"I am." Robin thrust out his chest and stood as tall as possible, which made him almost exactly Mary's height, and a head or two shorter than the stranger.

"Robin," the stranger pointed to the hat by the door, then to her brother's clothing, "Hood?"

"There, I told you," Robin said, shooting Mary a victorious glance. He waved his hand toward the stranger. "Will Scarlet."

"Goode," Mary said, rushing toward her patient. "Robin and Mary *Goode.*" Sometimes Robin went too far . . .

"Robin," her brother said, pointing to himself. Then he pointed at his companions. "Little John and Friar Tuck."

The stranger's eyes widened as his gaze took in the threesome surrounding him.

Mary groaned.

"And you think *I'm* Will Scarlet?" the stranger asked, setting his empty cup on the bunk beside his hip. His expression was unfathomable as he placed his hand across his chest. "Me?"

A sinking feeling oozed through Mary as she watched this exchange. All three heads nodded at the stranger.

"No," she said, knowing even as she spoke that they wouldn't hear her. They were too lost in their make-believe world. "No, please, no."

Tuck stepped closer to the bunk. "Your hair isn't red—it's gold. Still . . ." He rubbed his chin thoughtfully and gave Robin a solemn look. "It's possible. I do believe you could be right. Yes, indeed."

Mary couldn't let them bring this stranger into their midst. He made her feel things she shouldn't, and they didn't *know* him. He could be a gunslinger for all they knew. "But—"

"Do you have another name?" Tuck demanded. "Speak it now and be done with this, or admit you're Will Scarlet."

The stranger looked at each of them. Mary held her breath as his gaze lingered on her. Did he truly believe this nonsense? Surely the three men she loved more than any others were the only ones who could—or would— live their lives pretending to be men of legend.

"I don't know my name," he admitted, his gaze still locked with hers.

"If you don't remember, then you could be Will Scarlet," Robin persisted. "Why else would you be here?"

The stranger shifted his gaze from Mary to Robin. "I don't remember." He gave a shrug. "But I thank you all for helping me. You say those are my saddlebags?"

"Yours." Little John held the leather bags out to the stranger. "Yes, but horse gone. Dead."

The man nodded and pulled the saddlebags closer to his body. "Thanks for getting this for me."

"Maybe there's something in there that will tell us who you are," Tuck suggested, tapping his bearded chin with his forefinger. "Hmm?"

The man shrugged and opened a bag. He dug through both pouches, then sighed. "Nothing with a name."

"Be reasonable," Mary said, stepping in front of her brother. "For all we know, he could be the . . . the Sheriff of Nottingham."

"No, Maid Marian." Robin shook his head. "This our friend Will Scarlet."

Mary threw up her hands in defeat and whirled around to face the stranger. His eyes were hooded, but she could tell he was watching Tuck closely. Why?

"I suppose we have to call you something while you're convalescing," she said, praying that would be a very short time.

"I guess Will Scarlet is as good a name as any," he said, looking directly at her. "In fact, I kind of like it."

"Aha, I told you." Robin thrust his hand toward the stranger. "Welcome to Sherwood Forest, Will."

The man shook hands with her brother, but his gaze kept shifting back to Tuck, then to Mary. His eyes twinkled and his coloring was much better now. He smiled at her again, and her knees grew weak and her palms sweaty.

He had to remember his identity soon so he could leave them in peace. She couldn't bear to have him around, reminding her of what he made her feel.

And want.

Chapter Three

Shane awoke to watery sunlight streaming through the open cabin door. A quick survey of the room confirmed he was alone. Thank God his gunbelt and saddlebags were still where they'd been last night.

He had to hide his badge where no one would find it. Then he had to concentrate on recovering from his injuries and regaining his strength. Later, he'd decide what to do about the notorious "Robin Hood."

Chuckling quietly, he pushed himself to a sitting position and leaned against the wall. He knew better than to get up too fast. Besides, there was no hurry, because he had no idea what to do about Robin and his Merry Men.

This place was like some sort of asylum, where grown men believed they were fictional characters. And he'd heard Robin call Mary "Maid Marian." Shane shook his head and remembered Robin's solemn expression when he'd announced that Shane was Will Scarlet. Shane had read *The Merry Adventures of Robin Hood* in college, and it was a fine story—one of his favorites, in fact. But this was ridiculous.

How could Robin and Little John, who were like overgrown children, be the clever outlaws who'd pulled off heist after heist around the borders of Northeastern Indian Territory? Simple. They couldn't. Someone else had to be the brains behind the Merry Men.

Tuck . . . or Mary?

Shane closed his eyes for a moment. He hoped it wasn't Mary, but he couldn't omit the possibility. Women made very clever outlaws, too. Belle Starr had proven that countless times before her death. And she wasn't the only one. Was Mary Goode the brains behind this gang of thieves? He sure as hell hoped not.

Shane swung his legs over the edge of the bunk, wincing as blood rushed to his feet and set the snakebite afire all over again. "Slow and easy," he whispered, easing his bare feet to the cool floor.

The sooner he had clothes on and his gunbelt strapped around his hips, the better he'd feel. He shoved farther from the wall, putting more and more weight on his feet as he eased himself up. The pain in his calf was excruciating, but he'd felt worse. *Yeah, right.*

If not Mary, then Tuck, he decided, pulling the quilt around his waist before he pushed completely to his feet. Liquid fire shot through the veins in his leg, past his knee and into his groin. Gasping, he pulled the covers aside to examine his leg again. Angry red streaks traveled up from the poultice, angling inward.

Blood poisoning. *That sonovabitching snake might win yet.*

A wave of dizziness assaulted him and bile lurched to his throat. He leaned on the heels of his hands and lowered himself down to sit on the bunk. Common sense told him he had to get his leg stretched out again fast.

After a moment, he summoned the strength to swing

his legs back onto the bunk, but he couldn't manage the quilt just yet. He just sat there, staring at his bare toes and feeling like a danged fool.

He had a job to do, but first he had to stay alive to do it. His orders said to bring Robin Hood and his Merry Men in to face Judge Parker in Fort Smith. But Robin Hood was like a boy playing some kind of game.

Could Robin's game be a ruse to fool others—could he be that clever? Or was he really as slow and innocent as he seemed?

Shane sucked in a breath to steady his gut, and tried to jerk the bedding from beneath him at the same time. Pain sliced through his leg and he fell back, the quilt still trapped beneath him, and his body exposed to the chilly morning air.

A shiver chased itself through him and he realized another terrible truth. He had a fever—a pretty high one, from what he could tell. No wonder he felt so puny.

He closed his eyes and concentrated on taking slow, steady breaths. Thinking about how sick he was wouldn't help, so he turned his thoughts back to the Merry Men.

Summoning an image of Robin's face, Shane remembered the man's vacant, innocent expression, his slightly protruding tongue, his small ears and head. He'd seen a man like Robin before, and he'd been even slower and more backward. No, Robin Goode, or Hood, wasn't pretending.

And neither was Little John. Though the big Indian had saved Shane's life, his slowness had been obvious. No way could Little John be plotting and executing the raids.

That left Tuck and Mary. One of them had to be the brains of the outfit, or there was another member of the gang he hadn't met yet. Shane's instincts pointed straight at Tuck. A midget. A familiar one. Where had Shane seen that face before? On a wanted poster?

Shane lifted his hips and tried again to pull the bedding from beneath him. He had to get covered before he made himself any sicker. The quilt edged out some, and he lifted up on his elbows and scooted toward the wall. Again, the flexing muscles of his leg protested. The pain made his belly roil and he grabbed it with both hands.

"What on earth . . . ?" Mary's alarm was obvious in her tone, and Shane didn't even have the strength to make himself decent as she hurried into the cabin.

He rolled his head enough to see her place a basketful of eggs on the floor near the rocking chair. She turned back to the bunk, her expression reflecting shock at finding him like this. Naked.

"You . . . you tried to get up," she accused, reaching toward him, but hesitating.

Another chill raced through him and he shuddered from head to toe. "Stupid," he whispered.

"Yes." She set her lips into a tight, thin line and grabbed him under his arms. "Help me scoot you up in the bed if you can."

Shane braced himself on his elbows and pushed with all his strength. Again, the searing pain shot through his leg, but between his and Mary's efforts, they managed to move him enough for her to pull the quilt from beneath him.

"You're on fire." Her voice no longer sounded angry. The gentle angel's voice had returned, thank goodness. "Feverish. I'll have to get some more herbs."

His teeth chattered as she covered his burning, shivering body. Whatever was happening inside him was happening danged fast. She smoothed the warm patchwork beneath his chin and across his shoulders, tucking him in the way he remembered his mama doing when he was a youngster.

"Leg," he muttered. "Poisoned blood." He tried to focus on her face as she bent over him, but all he saw was a blur. Pity, he would've liked to see her pretty face once more. "I'm a goner."

"Don't talk that way." She moved to the end of the bunk and exposed his foot. Her fingertip traced the angry red streaks up his leg. "I'll have to cut this poultice away and make another."

Her voice trembled, and he knew this was bad. He couldn't die without telling her who he was so she could let Jenny know what had happened to him.

But it was too soon to start confessing. What if he didn't die? He was on the verge of solving the Merry Men case, and he knew that would make Sam proud.

Shane looked up to that man. Marshal Sam Weathers had saved Jenny back in Colorado after their folks died. He'd saved Shane, too, from the business end of a rope. Hell, Sam was the reason Shane had left the Texas Rangers to become a United States Marshal.

Well, then he couldn't tell Mary who he was yet. He'd bide his time and pray for a miracle. And he had a hunch a miracle was exactly what he needed. Mary pulled away the dried poultice, moistening it where it stuck. Her gentle touch reminded Shane what a good woman she was, and he regretted ever suspecting her of running the Merry Men.

Tuck was the key. Now to remember why that little man looked so familiar . . .

If Shane lived long enough for it to matter.

Mary mixed the poultice thoroughly and added additional herbs. Little John often took her to a neighboring Indian village, where she did what she could for the ill. Sometimes she helped, but sometimes she failed.

She hated to fail.

She'd seen wounds like his before, and it usually meant loss of limb. Or life. Her breath caught in her throat as she applied the still steaming concoction to her patient's inflamed wound. *Please, let this help,* she prayed.

His eyes drifted closed, then flew open to look around with a crazed expression. *The fever.* She tied the ends of the fabric strips together, then left his leg uncovered so the poultice could dry and draw out the poison. She hoped.

She made another mixture with fresh water and slipped her hand behind his burning neck to lift his head. "Drink this."

He gulped the medicine Mary hoped would diminish his raging fever. Her hands burned wherever they touched his bare skin. "This will make you feel better," she said with far more conviction than she felt.

"Thanks." He let his head fall back against the bunk the moment her hand slid from behind his neck. In the few moments since she'd walked in and discovered him, he'd grown much weaker.

He could be dead by nightfall.

Her throat constricted and her eyes burned with unshed tears. She'd seen death many times before, but each one was an excruciating tragedy for her. Often she longed for civilization and real doctors, but the risk was too great. What if someone tried to take Robin away again? Without her grandfather's protection, she couldn't be certain of anything.

A shudder swept through her. She would never let anyone take Robin away again. *I promised.* Her mother's last words returned to remind her again.

Look after your brother, Mary. He will always be a child.

And she had—she always would, no matter what.

Unfortunately, living in isolation meant more than loneliness. Indian Territory was a haven for outlaws, too, though the United States government had some jurisdiction over the area. An outlaw's unwelcome attention was the reason Mary dressed as she did. Though Robin often traded for yard goods from which she could make dresses, she opted to wear the same type of clothing her brother wore to shield herself from unwanted attention.

She sighed and glanced at her patient again. He was resting quietly now, though his color was still flushed and his skin dry. Neither were good signs. She would get some cool water and bathe him. Though the Indians advocated sweat for fevers, Mary believed cooling the skin was more beneficial. As long as her patient didn't get overly chilled, it couldn't hurt, and it *might* help.

She stooped to retrieve her pail and straightened, but a soft scraping sound alerted her to someone's presence. She turned slowly, hoping to find Robin, but another man hovered in the open doorway.

A most unwelcome one.

Terror and hatred oozed through her, making her blood pound at the temples. "Go away," she whispered, her voice trembling despite her best efforts. "You aren't welcome here."

Angel Rodriguez shot her a lopsided grin and lounged lazily against the doorjamb. "You are not glad to see me, *querida?*" He placed his right hand over his heart. "I am hurt."

"Go." If Robin saw how much Angel's presence upset her, he might suspect . . . "You're not welcome here," she repeated carefully.

He arched an eyebrow and flashed her a slow, easy grin, much like a fox at the henhouse door. The feigned innocence on his face infuriated her even more. "Why, *querida?* I thought you would be eager to see me again."

Mary's laughter erupted, surprising even herself with the madness lurking just beneath its surface. Yes, this man could easily drive her mad, but she couldn't allow that. She had to stay strong for Robin. Mustering her self-control, she said, "Go."

"No." Angel walked across the room, his spurs jingling

with every step. As always, he wore all black, with a huge silver buckle on his belt and silver braid around his hat brim. Pistols flanked his lean hips, pearl and silver handles gleaming with menace.

He was a deceptively beautiful man, groomed to perfection, bathed in a peculiar blend of perspiration, bay rum, and trail dust. Scents she would always associate with him. With terror.

With hell.

Angel Rodriguez was the farthest thing from an angel Mary could imagine. As he drew closer, she clenched her fists at her sides, wishing she still held the long scissors she'd used a few moments ago to cut the cloth strips for the poultice. She would run the points through this beast's heart. Yes, she would. Taking human life appalled her, but this man was the exception.

"Ah, what have we here, *querida?*" He paused and looked down at the feverish man, then leveled his gaze on Mary, his obsidian eyes narrowing. "Yours?"

"Don't be ridiculous," she snapped, immediately regretting her words. Perhaps she should have let Angel believe the stranger was her husband. "He's injured."

"His *nombre, querida?* Name?" Angel looked down at the patient again. "I don't recognize this gringo."

Mary refused to give the outlaw any additional information, not that she had any. Then she recalled that Robin had decided he knew their uninvited guest's identity. Why not? It might get rid of Angel sooner. "His name is Will Scarlet."

The legendary name obviously held no meaning for Angel, who merely shrugged. "He is a big blond one." His leering gaze swung back to pin Mary. "But you like them dark, eh, *querida?*" He reached out and touched her collar. "Why do you hide your beauty so? Such a waste."

Mary's blood roared. Her stomach churned in protest

and an icy chill shot through her veins. She froze—couldn't move. This man's touch was the most vile experience she'd known. Hell would be far preferable.

Angel trailed his fingertip to the inside of her collar and up the side of her throat. Mary dug deep within her and summoned every ounce of strength she could muster. Angel Rodriguez would never have his way with her again. *Never.*

"Don't touch me." Her voice no longer trembled, and she slapped his hand away. "Don't *ever* touch me."

"What happened to his leg?" Angel asked, still staring at her as if he hadn't heard her protests.

"Rattlesnake." *Like you.* Mary looked down at Will, then met Angel's taunting gaze. "Leave here."

His eyes darkened to twin black pools and he glanced from her patient back to Mary. "He's as good as dead, *querida.* Why do you bother?"

"You couldn't possibly understand human decency." She squared her shoulders and lifted her chin. "Now get out of here."

Something sinister flickered through his eyes; then he shrugged as if unaffected by her demands. "I will go, *querida,* but I shall return." He chuckled, a dark evil sound that filled the cabin and made Mary's skin crawl. "Never forget that."

He turned and slithered out, his heels striking wood, his spurs jingling with false merriment. Mary shook convulsively, unable to move. She stood staring through the now empty doorway, gulping air and willing her trembling to cease. She couldn't let Robin see her this way.

A cold sweat beaded her skin as a breeze wafted through the open door. She shivered and closed her eyes, then rubbed the back of her sweaty neck, forcing herself to move again. She had work to do. But first, she closed and bolted the door.

Returning to the bunk, she looked down at her patient,

surprised to find him staring at her through fever-glazed eyes. "Who was that?" His voice rasped. "Did he . . . hurt you?"

Mary forced herself to smile. "No." *Not this time.* "More water?" She bent over her patient and lifted his head again. "You're not as hot now." Maybe the herbs were working. "Here." She held the tin cup to his lips and he drank, closing his eyes as he swallowed every drop. His golden lashes rested against his flushed cheeks, and a protective surge washed through her.

She wanted this man to live. The intensity of her feelings stunned her, but she didn't take time to analyze them. All that mattered was helping Will recover, and protecting Robin from harm.

Remembering Angel's mockery, she shivered again and eased Will's head back to the bunk. Angel would return to see if Will was still here. She knew that, and she knew *why*.

Mary straightened and watched her patient's eyes open again. A weak smile widened his mouth, then he dozed off again. Yes, she *desperately* wanted this man to recover. Another truth slammed into her as she watched his face relax in slumber.

She wanted him to stay.

He's a stranger. An ache began in her chest and spread as the now familiar longing took control. She wanted so many things life had denied her. A husband and children. If this man never remembered his name, could he remain here as Will Scarlet?

"Jenny," he mumbled in his sleep. "Jenny."

Was Jenny his wife? Disappointment pressed down on her, followed immediately by shame and regret. What was she thinking? This man deserved to recover, yes, and to regain his memory, to return to the life he'd left behind.

To someone named Jenny.

His wife was a lucky woman. Mary had seen every

inch of this man and knew he was strong and virile. A heated flush flooded her cheeks as she remembered how he'd looked when she walked into the cabin earlier. Sprawled across the bed in all his naked glory . . .

A man like Will Scarlet would father many children. Fine, strong boys and girls. Mary's hand fell to her belly, her empty womb, and the ache intensified. The thought of carrying a child, of giving birth, of holding that baby to her breast tore a sob from her throat.

She brought her knuckles to her mouth and bit down hard, forcing her tears away. Though she didn't live alone, she often felt alone. Tuck was the only one she could talk to about anything important or complicated, but he was a man. He couldn't possibly understand her fierce desire for a baby. Only another woman could understand something like this.

Her mother would've understood. "Mother," she whispered, allowing herself to picture her mother's beautiful face and warm smile, but for only a moment.

No, stop. Thinking about what could never be only made it hurt more. Resolutely, Mary scrubbed her eyes dry, banishing the scalding tears and her futile dreams. She had work to do and a patient to tend. Dwelling on the impossible wouldn't do either of them a bit of good.

Again, she looked down at her handsome patient. Will Scarlet.

What if he never remembers?

Tuck watched Robin and Little John wrestle in the grass. John was easily twice Robin's height, and Robin towered over Tuck. They made an interesting trio.

A smile tugged at Tuck's mouth as he folded his arms behind his head and leaned against the trunk of a tall oak. Life here was good. Peaceful. So much more pleasant than the one he'd left behind. The secret life no one knew about . . .

But since he'd regained his memory, there were things he missed and longed for, like books, theater, his research. Yes, he missed even that, but not enough to surrender his solitude in this paradise. Not to return to the demands of the society he left behind, where everybody wanted something, and he was expected to give at will.

The only thing he missed enough to give up this life for was Fatima. And she would want nothing to do with him after so much time. If only he'd remembered sooner . . .

He sighed, deciding it was time for another sojourn into either Missouri or Arkansas, where they might find a greedy rancher with a well-stocked library. Yes, he was in dire need of new reading material, and more diaries for his notes. He had many volumes now, and someday the world would be shocked to discover that the brilliant scientist Ichabod Smith had lived and worked for many years in this wilderness.

Yes, indeed.

While the world canonized Thomas Alva Edison, Ichabod Smith would continue his extraordinary research. He needed more paper for his notes and formulas. His haphazard laboratory served its purpose, and was all he could hope for in the small cabin he shared with Little John. It sat back in the trees behind Robin and Mary's, and Tuck knew his cabin-mate would ask no questions.

Mary would, but she needn't know about Tuck's experiments. He smiled, then sighed as he thought of the lovely, lonely girl. This wasn't the kind of life she deserved, yet the vow she'd made her parents was sacred to her.

Glancing at Robin, who laughed joyously as he tackled Little John from behind and spilled them both onto the ground, Tuck smiled again. Robin was a joy, and Mary's devotion understandable. Still, Tuck felt certain the girl's mother hadn't intended for her to live as a martyr to protect her brother.

Mary needed a husband and children of her own, but

the only men who came to their Sherwood Forest on the Verdigris River were Indians, married ranchers, and outlaws. Though she could have involved herself in the ranch families' social circle and even attended church, Mary opted to remain sequestered with her brother, fearing someone would steal him away again.

"Aha, I win," Robin shouted. Little John had let him win, of course. He always did.

And what about Will Scarlet, or whatever his name was? If the lad never remembered who he was or where he was from . . . But he could be an outlaw, or married, or—

The Sheriff of Nottingham?

Tuck knew Mary was teasing when she'd said that, desperately trying to make Robin abandon his insistence that the stranger was Will Scarlet. Still, after searching through the stranger's saddlebags, Tuck knew enough to proceed with caution.

The United States government had cracked down on crime in Indian Territory during the past few years, and there were those who considered Robin, Tuck, and Little John outlaws—*preposterous notion, of course*. The Merry Men always gave far more than they kept from each raid, and they never harmed a soul. Never.

Well, as long as the stranger couldn't remember, it didn't matter. And the poor lad was probably too young to remember Ichabod Smith.

Yes, it was time for more books, and they would give most of them away, Tuck decided, pushing to his feet. The Indian School could always use more books.

"Robin, Little John," he called, approaching his friends. They were exhausted and panting from their boyish romp, each sprawled out on the damp ground a few feet apart. "I think it's time to give to the poor again."

Robin's expression grew solemn and he stood, slinging his bow and pouch of arrows over his shoulder. With a flourish, he straightened his hat, firmly in his role again. "Make haste, men."

Tuck smiled as Little John hoisted him onto his pony. All would go well, they would obtain more books for Tuck and Mary, writing utensils and paper, and give much, much more to the Indian School.

A fine day's work for a band of misfits.

Chapter Four

It had to be a dream.

Something slightly cool and damp brushed across Shane's shoulders and down his arms—one, then the other. He heard a splashing sound; then someone—a woman—touched his cheek. Savoring the feel of her soft hand against his burning cheek, he turned into the caress.

"You're so hot," she whispered, then she washed his chest and midriff with the damp cloth. He shivered slightly as she wiped lower, moving the quilt so he lay nearly naked beneath her soft hands.

He struggled to open his eyes, trying to determine where he was and, more importantly, who she was. Maybe Sam had taken him to that saloon in Coffeyville again. That had been some wild time. The memory oozed through him as he remembered the buxom redhead he'd spent two days and nights with there. Older and much more experienced than Shane, she'd turned him every which way but loose. What was her name? *Lenore.*

Yes, that must be where he was. He'd had too much

bourbon and Lenore was cleaning him up so she could have her way with him. Why the hell did his leg burn like the fires of perdition, though? Well, remembering Lenore's talents, he figured she'd take his mind off the pain in no time.

He heard her rinse the cloth again, and she washed his other leg. The coolness made him tingle and shiver as his body responded as she must've known it would. This was obviously another of Lenore's little games. Well, it was working. Drunk or not, he was harder than the barrel of one of his Remingtons.

She spent more time with his foot than he'd have liked, though when she set the cloth aside and massaged it, he heard himself groan. A moment later, she very gently bathed his other foot, then skipped the rest of that leg. She eased the quilt upward and trailed her fingertips along the burning skin of his inner thigh.

"Mmm," he said, wishing she'd give the rest of his anatomy its fair share of attention. Lord knew he was ready. If it weren't so damned dark in here, he'd be able to see her and tell if she was as naked and ready as he.

"So hot," she said.

The quilt moved a little and he throbbed in anticipation of her introducing the rest of him to her bathing technique. Well, he'd just help things along a little. His hand felt unbelievably heavy as he groped in the dark for the edge of the quilt and flung it away.

"Wash this," he whispered, wondering if she'd use her mouth on him first like she had before. Her gasp was loud enough to be a shout. Then the quilt settled over him again and he shivered so hard his teeth rattled in his head.

"You're . . . you're just delirious." She slipped her hand behind his neck and lifted his head. "Here, drink this."

Confused, he forced open his eyes and saw her shape,

though the edges of his vision were blurred. Not Lenore, he realized. The hair was the wrong color. Even so, the woman had stripped him and had her way with him while he was drunk.

Now it was his turn.

He reached behind her head, wondering again why his arm felt so damned heavy. *Must be the bourbon.* She didn't resist as he pulled her face toward his and claimed her lips. Soft, warm, moist. He wanted more, but she had her lips pressed together so tightly, he couldn't taste her the way he wanted.

Suddenly, she reached up and pinched his nose. Of all the infernal things . . . He had no choice but to break their kiss. Next thing he knew, she had a cup against his lips and was pouring some devil's brew down his throat so fast he nearly drowned.

Exhausted and sputtering, he let his head fall back against the bedding as she moved away. He peered through one eye and saw her standing beside the bed, wiping her hand across her mouth furiously. Definitely not Lenore.

Breathing heavily, she glowered down at him. ''Mr. Scarlet,'' she said sternly, ''the only reason you didn't find my knee between your legs is because of your wound.''

''Mr. Scarlet?'' he echoed, even more confused than before.

''However, touch me again and you'll find me far less tolerant.''

Weariness battled against confusion and curiosity, pressing him deeper into the blackness. He no longer saw the woman, even when he thought his eyes were open. She touched his forehead once more, then whispered something soft and comforting before the black void drew him in completely.

Mary told her heart to stop pounding so wildly as she stared down at Will Scarlet. Her cheeks flamed again, remembering how he'd jerked the quilt away and invited her to wash him.

There.

Good Lord, but he was huge. She knew all too well how much the male body could grow, but *this* was . . . well . . . shocking. It reminded her of the one time in England when she'd seen her grandfather's stallion cover a mare. Well, perhaps not *that* huge, she decided as her trembling ceased.

He was asleep now, thank heavens. Wearily, she slumped into her rocker and rested her chin in her hands. Bathing Will had exhausted her emotionally and physically.

When he grabbed the back of her neck, she'd relived a nightmare she wished never to experience again. Only her sense of reason had prevented her from thrashing and kicking out wildly. Calm logic in the face of terror. She'd summoned that by reminding herself of his condition. He didn't have the strength to harm her, even if he tried. More importantly, she knew in her heart that this man meant her no harm, unlike that other man.

But if she ever truly encountered that nightmare again, she would use calm and logic again.

To kill the man.

Shane had to break free. Jenny needed him. Images from the past flashed through his mind—Jenny, Redemption, Sam Weathers, his mother's smiling face, his father's drunken snarl, his uncle's murderous acts. He had to survive for Jenny.

Then the images shifted from past to recent events. The last time he saw Jenny, she announced her engagement. Shane asked her to wait until Thanksgiving, right after her next birthday. And . . . he promised to be home by then. He had to keep that promise. He had to.

I promised, dammit.

Groaning, he urged his eyes open, struggling to focus on his surroundings. Blurry waves of color blended together, then one shape moved toward him.

"You're awake," the angel whispered, touching her hand to his forehead. "Still feverish, but cooler." She slipped her hand behind his head and held the cup to his lips until he drank the bitter concoction. "But I wish we had a real doctor around here."

"No," Shane muttered as his head fell back against the pillow. "No." He might be delirious, but he knew what a doctor would do, and Shane wasn't about to go through life with one leg.

He'd rather die.

But his sister would want him to come home—whole or not. Yet what good would he be to anybody with only one leg? His eyes burned and he blinked rapidly to clear them. Mary's pretty face finally came into sharp focus. "No doctor," he repeated.

She nodded and bathed his face with a damp cloth. "Don't worry, Will," she said clearly. "Rest."

Will? Shane licked his lips and continued to study her, remembering their proclamation regarding his identity. Well, what else was she supposed to call him? It wasn't as if he'd volunteered any information, and he wasn't about to now. He *would* get well.

A vague memory nagged at him. Had Mary bathed him? All of him? Heat flooded his cheeks and it wasn't from his fever. Even if she had, he knew it was only because she'd been taking care of him. Good thing. He'd be dead two times over if she hadn't been here to pull him through.

Yeah, he remembered her washing him, and—dammit—he remembered liking it. A lot. *Think about something else, Latimer.* He released a long, slow breath and salvaged his sense of decency.

"Talk to me," he said, clearing his throat. "Tell me about you and . . . your brother."

Maybe he couldn't stand on his own two feet, but he could ask questions. Besides, the answers might come in handy when he was strong enough to make some arrests and head back to Fort Smith.

"What do you want to know?" Her voice sounded strained. Pensive.

"Your accent." He drew a deep breath to quiet the churning sensation in his empty gut. "You aren't from here." Talking sapped what little strength he still possessed, but he willed himself to remain alert.

"We were born in England." The coolness touched his face again. "But we've been here a long time now."

"How . . . how long?" He swallowed, his throat burning in protest.

"You ask a lot of questions." She removed the cloth and he heard her rinse it before placing it against his forehead again. Her touch soothed him, just as the softness of her voice always did. "Why?"

"Nothing . . . else to do." He tried to smile, but suspected it more closely resembled a grimace. If only he could forget her bathing him so thoroughly before. . . . "Thanks for helping me."

"Anyone would've helped under the circumstances." She shrugged and looked away, but not before Shane saw the expression in her eyes. She'd been looking at him with an intensity he hadn't expected. Why? She couldn't know his identity. Could she?

"No, not just anyone." He closed his eyes as she wiped his neck with the damp cloth. No one else's touch could possibly be as gentle as Mary's. Under different circumstances, her touch would've evoked something a lot less restrained than what he felt now. "I'm right grateful, ma'am."

"You're welcome." She fell silent for several moments. "You talked some in your sleep."

Shane's heart lurched upward to press against his throat. He couldn't admit anything yet. "Did I? What did I say?"

"Nothing, really." The shrug came again. "Maybe you have a wife somewhere."

"Wife?" Shane blinked, hoping his expression wouldn't give him away. "I . . . I don't think so."

"Well, if you can't remember your own name, it isn't likely that you'd remember anyone else in your life." She smiled gently and patted his hand. "Get some rest."

"What time is it? What day?" Shane had no idea how long he'd been here.

"You've been here since yesterday morning, but it's late now," she said. "Nearly eleven."

Shane shifted his gaze toward the shuttered window near the door. No light filtered in around the frame. "Where's your brother?"

She tensed, dropping the cloth into the basin. "I don't know."

Shane felt less shaky now. Was his fever waning at last? He reached for her hand. "You saved my life, Mary."

She looked right at him, that mysterious longing present again. He held her gaze for several moments, wondering what thoughts coursed through her mind as he held her soft hand. She made no effort to pull away, and he certainly didn't have the strength to stop her.

"Little John is the one who saved you," she said, breaking eye contact. She pulled her hand from his grasp and stood. "He brought you here."

"Yes." Shane missed the feel of her hand in his. *Foolish, Latimer.* Besides, he still couldn't be sure she wasn't an outlaw herself. The thought distressed him more now than it had the first time it had crossed his mind. "Is Little John gone, too?"

Are the Merry Men on one of their infamous raids?

"I haven't seen my brother, Little John, or Tuck since this morning." Mary went to the door and opened it, emptying the basin outside.

A gentle breeze carried the soft nocturnal sounds through the open door. Frogs—hundreds of them—sang their peculiar tune into the night.

Mary stood at the open door, gazing out at the darkness, undoubtedly wondering about her brother's whereabouts. *So am I, pretty lady. So am I.* Pity Shane hadn't been strong enough to follow Robin and his gang this morning.

With a sigh, she closed the door and refilled the basin from a pail near the hearth. "I can't imagine what's keeping them tonight."

As she crossed the room, the gentle sway of her hips met with his approval. Though her clothing was anything but feminine, everything else about her was soft and delicate. He would love to see her beautiful hair down, to touch it—

Whoa. He drew a slow breath and waited for her to sit at his side again. She smiled as she lowered herself into the rocker, transforming her pretty face into one of incredible beauty.

"You're very . . . beautiful," he muttered, unable to keep his opinion to himself.

Redness crept up her neck to blossom in her cheeks. "I'm not." She looked away and wrung out the cloth, then placed it gently against his forehead. "You must still be delirious, though your fever is down. How do you feel?"

"Better, I think." He smiled. "Thanks to you."

"I'm glad."

She smiled again, and Shane knew she meant those words. She really was pleased about his improvement. And why did that make him warm in a far more pleasant manner than his fever had?

He watched her rinse the cloth again, and when she

brought it back to his face, he reached up to cover her hand with his. "I meant what I said earlier," he whispered. "You're a beautiful woman, Mary Goode."

Mary blushed again, but her bright blue eyes snapped with something belying that. "I don't want to be," she whispered.

Shane burned to protest, to demand she tell him why, but the expression in her eyes stayed him. This was obviously territory his angel of mercy didn't want to cross. "I'm sorry, I didn't mean to upset you."

She nodded, and her eyes glistened as if she might cry. But she didn't. The woman swiped at her eyes with the cuff of her sleeve, deepening Shane's concern, but he held his tongue. For now. Maybe later, after he learned the depth of her involvement with the Merry Men, he would discern the reason for Mary's refusal to cry. Seeing her try so hard not to cry made him ache deep inside, and he wanted desperately to make her laugh and smile, to take away anything the least bit painful.

Damn. Those herbs of hers must've addled his brain. Once he regained his strength, his common sense was sure to follow. He hoped.

Change the subject, Latimer.

"Does Robin, uh, go off like this often?" All right, so it wasn't exactly subtle, but at least it was safe.

Mary lifted one shoulder and wrung out the cloth again. "The three of them take off hunting or visiting pretty often, but as long as they're together, I try not to worry."

"Visiting?" *Stealing.*

She smiled, and the transformation made Shane's heart stutter. Beautiful wasn't enough to describe this woman. She was perfect. An angel's smile.

An outlaw's sister.

"Little John's family lives in the village a few miles downriver," she explained. "In fact, they're all that's left of the village. He takes Robin and Tuck there to visit, and they often stay overnight if it gets late.''

"But you worry anyway.''

She lowered her gaze for a moment, then looked right at him. "I'll always worry about Robin. You met him. Saw . . .''

Shane nodded. "He's slow.'' No point in beating around the issue. "So's Little John.''

"Yes, but not as slow as Robin. Little John looks after him.''

Shane remembered when he'd first seen the giant brave standing in the trees. Yes, Little John was big enough to protect Robin from just about anything. "Together,'' he said, thinking aloud, "they sorta make a whole.''

She looked surprised, and he thought for a moment she might take offense, but after a while she smiled again. He'd do or say darned near anything to make her smile. *Dangerous thinking, Latimer.*

"I've never thought about it that way, but I suppose that's true. At least I know Robin will be safe when he's with Little John and Tuck. One is strong and the other smart.'' She met Shane's gaze. "Robin isn't strong or smart.''

"I reckon that's so.''

She sighed, staring toward the door. "I honestly think Robin's sweet on Little John's sister.''

"Really?'' Shane lifted one corner of his mouth, feeling stronger by the minute. "How's that?''

Red bloomed in her cheeks again. "Well, I don't know for certain, but . . .'' She cleared her throat. "He takes long walks along the river with her whenever we visit the village. She's . . . like Robin, if you know what I mean.''

"Ah, but I thought the Indians didn't—er, I thought . . .''

Mary's lips pressed into a thin line and anger snapped in her eyes. "Some tribes believe children like Robin shouldn't . . .'' She bit down on her lip until it turned white, then drew a deep breath. "Some tribes kill any child who's born imperfect, but Little John's people consider them special." She smiled wistfully. "They consider people like Robin and Walks in Sunshine blessings. I agree."

Shane nodded. "That's good." He'd heard stories of deformed babies taken into the wilderness and left to die. Thank goodness Little John's tribe saw things differently. "Real good."

"Yes." She smiled again. "Sunshine's mother once said something very wise. She said, 'Walks in Sunshine was born without evil.' " Mary nodded matter-of-factly. "That's why they call the girl Sunshine. I think that's true of Robin, too. Not a mean bone in his body."

Except he's a thief. Guilt pressed down on Shane. He was here to arrest Mary's brother, and possibly Mary herself. Hearing about their private affairs made it damned difficult to stay focused. Even so, he wanted to know as much as possible about these perplexing people. Though he knew better, everything about the Merry Men indicated they weren't outlaws. *Damn, am I ever discombobulated.*

She pressed the back of her hand against his forehead. "You're much cooler now."

Dragging himself from his conflicting thoughts, Shane said, "Yeah, I can tell." The chills and fever had passed, leaving him weak as a newborn but confident he wouldn't die. Finally. "I'm gonna make it." It was his turn to smile.

"Yes, I believe you are."

Shane captured her hand in his and held it to his lips, delivering a kiss to her knuckles. "Thank you, pretty lady."

Mary appeared stunned. The brilliant blue of her eyes darkened and her cheeks turned even pinker than before. "Will, please . . ."

Reluctantly, he released her hand, but he held her gaze. "I reckon Will Scarlet will do." He shot her a crooked grin. "For now."

"Yes," she whispered, her voice taking on a huskiness he hadn't noticed before. "For now."

Mary kept watch from her rocking chair, forgoing the pallet she'd made for herself near the hearth. She dozed off, then jerked awake. *Robin.* A quick glance at her brother's empty bunk confirmed his continued absence. "Robin, where are you?" she whispered, rising to check her patient. His sleep was natural now, thank goodness. Fever no longer flushed his cheeks, and the red streaks on his leg had miraculously vanished.

Will Scarlet would live. But would he stay once he remembered his true identity? *No, of course not. Why should he?* Remembering the feel of his warm mouth against her knuckles, a tremor swept through her.

Why, indeed, Mary? Even though he made her feel almost . . . untainted, she could never allow a man into her life after . . . She'd been foolish to ever consider keeping him here. With her. *For her?*

With a sigh, she pushed aside her folly and opened the shutters, staring out at the pinkening sky. She might as well stay awake, because she'd get no real rest while worrying about Robin's absence. Besides, she had plenty of chores to keep her busy while she sharpened her tongue for her brother's return. Robin, Little John, and Tuck would all get a fierce scolding. How many times had she pleaded with them not to leave her here to worry like this? All they had to do was tell her they'd be away overnight hunting, or visiting Little John's family.

Anger replaced her worry, for she knew in her heart that her brother and his friends were fine. They would return sometime today bearing gifts and supplies. She breathed a sigh of relief, but kept her anger near the surface, where she could resurrect it the moment she heard their approach.

Mary poked the dying embers of last night's fire and added several small pieces of blackjack. Once the flames licked merrily at the dry tinder, she added a larger log and hung the kettle. She needed tea and plenty of it this morning. Though she'd learned to drink coffee, she much preferred her tea.

Smiling, she remembered her mother's tea, served sweet with hot milk. Nothing had been as fortifying or as tasty. How she missed her mother.

Mary left the kettle to heat and glanced at Will again. He was resting peacefully still, free from the fevered restlessness that had made him grab her last night. And kiss her . . .

Her heart shoved upward against her throat as she remembered his kiss. Pressing her fingertip to her lips, she closed her eyes, feeling the warmth of his mouth against hers, the pressure of his hand at the back of her neck. He'd been gentle but urgent in his quest.

Then another man's face leapt to the forefront of her mind, and her belly heaved in protest. Trembling, she opened her eyes and drew a deep breath. Her memory of what Angel Rodriguez had done to her would plague her for the rest of her life.

She lived with the terror he'd inflicted on her every day, and many nights the nightmare played again in her slumber to remind her. She'd never be free. Never.

With a sigh, she stilled her trembling and swallowed hard. In truth, each time her brother, Tuck, and Little John left her here alone, her fear grew more daunting. To leave the safety of the cabin to visit the necessary house took every ounce of courage she could muster. If Angel found her alone and vulnerable again . . .

A shudder rippled through her, and her belly heaved

until she drew several calming breaths. She had to believe that Angel was far from here now, since she'd seen him only yesterday. He never remained long in the area, thank heavens.

Besides, she couldn't delay visiting the outhouse another moment. Squaring her shoulders, she slipped quietly outside, leaving the cabin door open to the mild morning air. She paused to stare at the clear sky. The endless days of rain seemed to be at an end. Two days now of sunshine—a good sign.

Her ornery old rooster crowed as the sun peeked over the eastern horizon, spreading its golden rays across the forest and prairie beyond the river. The river itself was a silver ribbon, winding its way through the trees on its way to the Mississippi.

Loneliness pierced through her and she swallowed hard. Some days she ached to throw herself into that river and swim with its current as far as she possibly could.

To civilization. To people.

Loneliness was the worst part of this life. She desperately missed having another woman to talk to, parties to attend, a church where she could worship. She missed it all.

But she had Robin and he was safe.

The rooster crowed again and Mary shook herself from her reverie and hurried to the outhouse. When she exited the narrow building, the sun had risen fully and she looked in the direction of the Indian village.

"Come home, Robin," she whispered, walking toward the cabin and her tea. "Come home soon."

Just as she reached the cabin door, a clattering sound emerged from the road that wound through the trees. Mary's heart skipped a beat—or several—and she froze. Gradually, she recalled that Angel always rode a white horse. The racket she heard now had to be a wagon. Breathing a sigh of relief, she waited. After a moment, a buckboard pulled into the clearing and stopped before the cabin.

"Good morning, Miss Mary." Henry Runningwolf, Little John's youngest brother, leapt down from the wagon seat and offered his hand to his wife, Ruth.

"Good morning." Mary patted her hair self-consciously. She so seldom had callers. Why couldn't they have come later in the day, after she'd made herself decent? Then she recalled her brother's continued absence, and alarm shot through her. Had Little John's family sent Henry here with bad news? "Have you seen Robin?"

"No," Ruth said warily. "Is he missing?"

Henry stepped forward with an urgent expression. "Want me to go to the village and check?"

"No," Mary said more harshly than she'd intended. "I'm sorry. I'm sure they're at the village."

Ruth adjusted her bonnet as the sun rose higher. "Those men run wild. It's time they all settled down and took brides."

Mary laughed, though she knew Ruth was quite serious. "Forgive me, but it's hard for me to think of Robin and Little John as anything but children."

Henry shook his head slowly, his expression somber. "Miss Mary, they aren't children. They're men, full growed."

Dismissing the notion, Mary turned to Ruth again. "What brings you out this far?"

"Well, we promised you we'd stop by next time we headed to Tahlequah," Ruth explained, her hand dropping to her swollen belly. "With the little one on the way, I need some yard goods, and the selection in Bartlesville is poor."

"Oh." Mary smiled knowingly. Henry and Ruth Runningwolf were the closest thing to friends she had, though she only saw them a couple of times a year. They lived in Bartlesville, many miles upriver. "I'm so happy for you both." She *was* happy, but their good fortune intensified the longing ache in her own heart for what could never be.

Henry cleared his throat, obviously uncomfortable with women talk, and turned his attention to the back of his wagon. He lifted a basket and brought it to Mary. His gap-toothed grin was endearing and genuine. "A present."

A lightweight blanket covered the basket. Curious, Mary lifted one corner and peered inside. A pair of eyes glowed back at her through the semidarkness. "What . . . ?" She looked at Ruth and Henry, who were still smiling. Suddenly, she knew, and a soft meow confirmed her suspicions.

"We promised you one of Agatha's next litter." Ruth patted Mary's arm. "She's a beautiful calico, Mary."

Overcome with joy, Mary removed the blanket and reached in to retrieve the tiny kitten. "She's perfect." The kitten stiffened in her grasp, but she held it close to her heart and rubbed her cheek against its soft fur. Something warm and small to love at last—not a baby, but this would have to do. "How can I ever thank you?" Her throat filled and her vision blurred. "Thank you so much."

"You're most welcome, Mary." Ruth reached for her husband's hand. "We'd best be on our way."

"Of course." Still holding the kitten, Mary walked to the wagon with them.

Once they were settled and Henry had the reins in hand, Ruth gave Mary an almost scolding look. "I've never understood why you stay here alone so much. You don't have to." She drew a deep breath and rushed on before anyone else could utter a syllable. "Come for a visit sometime. Soon. My brother is back from college, and he's set up his practice in Bartlesville. He's a real doctor now, Mary."

Ruth hadn't been shy about her wish for Mary and William to meet. "How nice, especially with the baby on the way." Mary forced a smile, resisting the urge to beg Ruth never to mention her brother again. "Have a safe journey." She stepped back from the wagon with the purring kitten in her arms.

Ruth shook her finger at Mary. "There's no reason for you to live out here like outlaws. No reason at all."

Coming to her rescue, as usual, Henry gave Mary a sympathetic look. "They opened the border to more settlers, Miss Mary," he said. "The soldiers have been runnin' some folks off land they've lived on for years, sayin' they're here against the law. Foolishness, if you ask me."

"Yes, foolishness," Ruth agreed, casting Mary a sad smile. "We'll check again for an answer from your grandfather, Mary."

Mary nodded, unable to speak. Over the years, her trusted friends had posted no less than a dozen letters to her grandfather in England. He could be dead by now, leaving her and Robin stranded here forever. But what about their Uncle Bartholomew? Surely he would have seen the letters, too.

Of course, he would've sent someone after them by now, if he intended to at all. Wouldn't he? "Thank you," she murmured at last.

"We'll stop at the village and tell your ornery brother to come home." Henry tipped his hat, then put the team into motion. The wagon lumbered down the rutted trail that passed for a road.

Mary stood frozen for several minutes after the wagon had vanished into the trees. Yes, she had reasons to remain hidden away with her brother. Good reasons.

And God help her if the soldiers tried to run them out of Sherwood Forest. God help *them*. The thought of losing this safe haven terrified her. But Little John's father had given them permission to build their cabins here. Surely no one would make them leave. Where would they go if they lost their home?

Would the soldiers take Robin back to the asylum?

A shudder rippled through her, and she turned toward the cabin, stroking the kitten absently. She wouldn't let anyone take Robin again. No. If the soldiers came, then she and Robin would go away, but they'd go together. Somewhere.

Sometimes life was horribly unfair, but it was the only one she had. But her life wasn't hers, really. It belonged to her brother and to the promise she'd made their dying mother.

No point in worrying about soldiers who probably wouldn't come anyway, she decided.

"Soldiers." If they came, she'd do what she must.

Soldiers? Bracing himself against the wall, Shane backed away from the window and lunged across the small cabin to his bunk. A cold sweat popped to the surface of his skin, and his gut recoiled in protest.

He should never have tried to get up, but once he heard Mary talking to someone other than her brother and the Merry Men, he had to hear the conversation. Something important might've been exchanged. The threat of soldiers and Mary's reaction had been the only thing that might relate back to the case.

"Damn." Shane made sure he didn't land on top of the quilt this time as he flopped into the bunk. He felt like hell itself and knew his adventure across the room would set him back a spell, but only temporarily. He was already much better than last night.

He heard Mary's approach and tugged the quilt up to his chin, mopping his face dry with the corner. Concentrating on his breathing, he quieted himself and struck what he hoped was an innocent pose. Well, how guilty could a man in his condition look anyway?

After closing the door behind her, Mary walked to the

bunk. "Oh, you're awake," she said, cradling the kitten in her arms. "Look. Isn't she beautiful?"

"Cute little mite," Shane whispered, hoping his voice didn't betray his recent exertion.

"I'll have to keep her inside so the owls won't get her."

"And so she won't eat your chickens later." He tried to grin, but figured it was a poor effort.

Mary laughed and it was a glorious sound. Shane stilled, watching her beautiful face and savoring every syllable of her musical laughter. Something swelled in his chest and pressed against his aching throat. His breath caught, then started again at a more rapid pace.

"Are you all right?" She tucked the kitten under one arm and reached down to touch his forehead.

He managed a nod and a weak smile, then licked his lips as another memory surged to the surface. He'd heard that woman mention her brother the way women do when playing matchmaker. Lord knew he'd seen his sister in action often enough, and he was usually right in the line of fire.

Was Mary Goode husband hunting?

Chapter Five

"Maid Marian!"

The words echoed from outside, reminding Shane why he was here. Mary rushed to the door, the kitten still clutched to her breast. *Lucky cat.* Whether or not Mary Goode was after a husband made no difference to him. That was her business.

But her brother was *his* business. And he'd best not forget it again.

"Maid Marian!"

The sound of hoofbeats grew louder, then stopped altogether. Still carrying the kitten, Mary stepped outside. "Robin Goode, *where have you been?*"

Shane chuckled quietly, imagining the expression on her face as she gave her brother and his cohorts the sharper side of her tongue. Mary Goode was someone he wouldn't want to anger—his humor faded—but he knew he would before all this came to an end. After all she'd done for him, he truly regretted that, but it couldn't be helped.

"Ah, sis, don't be—"

"Mad? *Mad?*"

She backed into the cabin, offering Shane a perfect view of her backside. *Pity her britches are so dang baggy.* Still, a man could tell when a woman was worth looking at.

And Mary was definitely worth looking at.

A stirring low in his belly, followed by a tightening right between his legs assured Shane he was definitely recovering. He cleared his throat and turned onto his hip to hide his body's enthusiasm. The movement caused only a slight twinge in his leg—further evidence that the worst was behind him.

"Now, Mary," Tuck said, "don't be angry with the boy. It's all my fault, I'm afraid."

Yep, I'll bet it is, little man. Shane narrowed his eyes as the guilty trio followed Mary into the cabin and she closed the door.

They looked even more bedraggled than they had yesterday. The green feather in Robin's hat drooped, food matted his scraggly beard, and his shirt sported some kind of dark stain. Tuck stroked his neat, silver beard into a sharper point, and Little John lowered his head in apparent shame.

"Sorry, Maid Marian," Little John said with a sigh. "Went to Father's village."

"I see." Mary turned on Robin, shaking her finger in his face. "And you never once thought I might be ... be worried?" Her lower lip trembled, but she didn't shed a single tear.

A crazy urge to take her in his arms slammed into Shane. He released his breath very slowly as he watched Robin do just that.

"Sorry, Mary," Robin said quietly.

This was the first time Shane had heard Robin call his sister by her given name. It made him seem more real. More human.

More vulnerable.

Though Robin still wore his costume, at this moment he was very much Robin Goode—not Hood. A man who wasn't exactly all there. A man who loved his sister.

As Shane loved his.

Dammit, Latimer. He's an outlaw. But at this moment, Robin was nothing more—or less—than Mary Goode's brother. His hat fell to the floor as he continued to hold his sister, and sunlight glinted off several silver strands in his dark hair. Surprised, Shane looked from Mary's shiny hair to Robin's and realized her brother was the older of the two.

Robin seemed younger, so Shane had mentally put Mary in the role of big sister. He shook his head now, watching her step away from Robin and show him the kitten.

"If you promise never to stay away overnight again without telling me first, I'll let you hold my kitten," she said with a smile, though Shane suspected she was deadly serious. "Isn't she beautiful?"

Tuck gave the kitten a cursory glance and folded his arms across his chest. "It'll be a long while before she's big enough to be a good mouser."

Mary shot Tuck a mischievous glance. "You're a fine one to hold size against her." Her smile and soft laughter took the sting from her words.

Tuck blushed fiery red and ducked his head. When she bent and kissed his cheek, he cleared his throat. "She'll grow," he said, his voice husky with embarrassment.

Little John gently stroked the tiny kitten with the backs of his giant fingers. "Soft," he said.

Robin put his finger to his chin and circled his sister and the cat. "Dog be better," he said at last. "Where'd you get her?"

"Ruth and Henry brought her on their way to Tahlequah." Mary rubbed her cheek against the kitten's head.

"Why they go to Tahlequah?" Robin asked.

Shane was growing accustomed to Robin's speech and understood almost everything now. Of course, *he* was more interested in why Robin and his Merry Men had gone to Tahlequah, if they had at all.

Mary's cheeks flamed. "Well, you know Ruth is . . . expecting a baby, and they needed to buy some things they couldn't get in Bartlesville."

"Indian Territory has to be the most diverse place in the world," Tuck said.

"Huh?" Robin asked, scratching his head.

Tuck chuckled. "Think about it, Robin. There are cities like Tahlequah with colleges and nearly every luxury a person could want." He cast Mary a solemn glance. "And there are places remote and wild . . . like this."

"Sherwood Forest nice," Little John said, giving a quick nod.

"Yes, it's lovely, and I understand why you chose to stay here, rather than move to the city like your brothers." Tuck sighed, inclining his head toward Mary. "But even a prison can be beautiful."

Mary's expression hardened and she pressed her lips into a thin line. She and Tuck stared at one another as if sharing some great secret.

One Shane needed to know.

After a moment, Mary cleared her throat and turned to her brother again. "The kitten needs a name."

"Dog. D-A-G," Robin said with a firm nod, reaching for the furry bundle.

Mary shook her head and waited.

Shane didn't want to witness all this. Every word, every gesture of affection, every impish grin, just reminded him that he would soon tear this strange little family apart.

"I promise," Robin said quietly. He took the kitten and held her near his chest, gazing down at her. "D-*O*-

G?'' He looked up for his sister's nod of approval, then his chest puffed up with obvious pride. "Call her Dog."

"Silly, Robin, she's not a dog. Save that name for your next hunting dog." She looked down at the furry kitten. "As for this little one, how about Katie? Katie Calico."

"Well, Aphrodite would be better, but I suppose that's a fine name for a cat." Tuck pulled out his pipe, but a stern look from Mary had him pocketing it again in short order. "I know. Outside."

"Yes, but don't let Katie out."

"Indeed, the chickens might mistake her for a worm," Tuck said, sending Robin into a series of deep guffaws. Little John merely chuckled quietly, though his grin was huge and genuine.

Shane couldn't prevent his own feeble chuckle from joining in. These *merry* men and Mary had saved his life, and he would repay them by destroying theirs. His laughter died a quick death. Just like he would have after that snakebite without their help.

Damn. Guilt oozed through him as he quietly watched the group tease and hug like a real family. Like his own family back in Texas.

He was getting soft. *Buck up, Latimer.* He drew a deep breath as Robin turned toward the bunk. His eyes widened in recognition, followed by a genuine smile.

"Will Scarlet lives." Robin strode toward the bunk with the kitten in tow. "Better now, Will?"

"Some." Shane pushed up onto his elbows as Mary and Little John appeared beside Robin. "Got a whole lot worse while you were gone, but your sister here managed another miracle."

"Maid Marian good." Robin nodded and grinned at his sister.

Shane looked from Mary to her brother. "Where'd you all go? Your sister was mighty worried."

Robin shot Little John a sideways glance that stoked

Shane's suspicions to full steam. More convinced than ever that the Merry Men had performed another of their notorious raids, he repeated the question.

"We traded some hides downriver," Tuck offered, appearing at Robin's side. "We obtained a fine collection of books from an estate auction in—"

"Books?" Mary's mouth formed a perfect circle and her eyes glittered.

"Yes, and we took several to the Indian School. The rest are for you, dear Mary," Tuck announced with a flourish. "I hope you'll be pleased with the selection. I may want to borrow a few myself."

"Obtained" must be a new word for "stole." Shane bit the inside of his cheek to silence the building accusations. At least he no longer doubted who ran the Merry Men Gang. Tuck had just confirmed his role and proven Mary's innocence. *Thank God.* Now all Shane had to do was catch them in the act.

And make Mary hate his guts.

But he couldn't let that matter. He had a job to do, and he'd need a new horse to do it. "Know where I can get a decent horse around here?" he asked no one in particular.

"Village," Little John said. "Trade."

Trade what? Shane didn't have anything but his saddle and personal belongings. "I don't think I have anything much to trade."

"When you're stronger, you can go hunting with Robin and Little John," Mary said quietly. "Then you can trade hides for a horse."

Shane didn't have that kind of time if he planned to follow the Merry Men on their next raid. "Is there anything else the chief might take for a good horse?"

"Music," Little John said, smiling. "You sing good and Father give horse."

Shane arched a brow and rubbed his whiskered chin.

"I'm no Alan-a-Dale, but I can sing and play the guitar some." He grinned at his own wit. How had he managed to pull that character's name from his foggy memory?

"I thought you couldn't remember anything," Tuck said quietly. Calculatingly.

Shane met his gaze for several seconds, then shifted his glance to Mary. Her eyes were wide and she held the tips of her fingers to her lips. Waiting.

"Yeah, I wonder where that came from." He gave a nervous laugh. "Wish I could remember as much of the real world as I can of books."

Mary smiled and nodded, as did the others. All except Tuck seemed to accept Shane's explanation. The little man's eyes narrowed and he folded his arms across his belly.

"Wait," Robin said, breaking the stare-down between Shane and Tuck. Robin handed the kitten to Little John and hurried away, returning a moment later with a guitar, minus one string. "Here."

"Robin, it's too soon." Mary reached for the guitar and wrapped her hand around its neck, but Shane's hand closed over hers. They stared at each other for several moments until she blushed and slipped her hand from beneath his. "It's old and out of tune, I'm afraid. Robin brought it home from one of his trading trips, but none of us knows how to play."

Probably stolen. Shane nodded and ran his hands over the neck and strings, knowing the instrument would play fine, even with the bass string missing. He needed to sit up in order to strum it, but he'd tuckered himself out from his adventure across the cabin this morning. "Leave it here and I'll see to it later," he whispered, exhaustion making his hands and voice tremble. The simple act of talking, on top of his trip across the cabin earlier, made him so tired he could barely speak.

Mary took the guitar and propped it against the wall

near the bunk as Shane's head fell back. "You've overdone," she said, feeling his cheek with her cool fingers.
"No fever, though."

"Just a mite tuckered," he said, savoring her touch.
"That's all."

Tuck shoved his way in front of Robin and put both
hands on his hips. "I think our Will Scarlet needs nourish-
ment and rest," the little man said matter-of-factly.

Shane held Tuck's gaze for several seconds, struggling
to remember why the man tugged so at his memory. It
was an old memory, long forgotten. *What?* Tuck's eyes
narrowed, but his gaze remained unwavering, as if chal-
lenging Shane to remember.

"I'll warm the broth and start the beans." Mary
retrieved her kitten and turned toward the hearth. "I had
to do all your chores plus mine yesterday, Robin."

With a sigh, Robin grabbed his hat from the floor and
jammed it onto his head. "Robin Hood doesn't feed chickens and milk cow."

"But Robin *Goode* will if he wants to eat." Mary's
smile was clever and false, but her laugh that followed
was genuine. "Be off with you, Robin, and let me cook
in peace. But don't let Katie outside."

Chuckling, Tuck followed Little John and Robin to the
door. He paused and looked back over his shoulder at
Shane. "Mend quickly, Will Scarlet."

Shane gave a curt nod, sensing that Tuck had something
in mind for Will Scarlet.

But what . . . ?

Confident now that her patient would fully recover,
Mary breathed a sigh of relief. He'd downed two cups
of broth before falling into a deep, peaceful sleep. The
feverish thrashing no longer plagued him, thank heavens.

She watched him for several minutes, noting that the

bruise at his temple was already turning yellow and the swelling was completely gone. Will Scarlet was an incredibly handsome man—every inch of him—all golden and warm.

Yes, warm. Recalling how he'd looked last night when he'd thrown aside the quilt, her cheeks flooded with heat. She shouldn't want him or any man after the horror she'd suffered, but there was something about this one. Something special, she decided. He touched her deeply, though she had no idea why. She pressed her hand over her heart, feeling its steady thrum against her palm.

Impulsively, she bent over him, brushing a golden curl from his forehead. He looked younger asleep, she noted, and her heart swelled with a protectiveness that stunned her. She *cared* about this man.

Straightening, she drew a deep breath and gripped the handle of the cup so tightly her knuckles turned white. Her throat went dry and something coiled low in her belly—a tight knot of longing she didn't want to feel. It didn't matter what she wanted or whether it was right or wrong. Swift rivers of heat spiraled through the rest of her body, and this current had but one name.

Desire.

But she couldn't feel desire. She *couldn't.* To want a man in that way now, after what she'd suffered, made her disgusted with herself. Shame pressed down on her as she trudged across the room to rinse the cup. After hanging it on a hook near the hearth, she lifted the lid from the simmering pot and stirred the beans with a long wooden spoon.

Fortunately, her men were easy to please. Give them fresh hot food and plenty of it, and they were happy. A smile tugged at her lips as she shoved a pan of cornbread into the makeshift oven Little John had concocted for her. The rock ledge often grew too hot if she let the fire get away from her, but she'd learned over the years to let it burn down to glowing embers before baking.

With the men outside and Will sleeping, she released a sigh and saw Katie stretch from her nap and waddle toward her. The kitten had consumed enough cream to lull her into a nice long nap. Smiling, Mary scooped up the kitten and sat on a bench at the table.

Tuck had promised to bring the books this afternoon. Maybe that would take her mind off Will. And the thought of having something new to read brought her more joy than she'd had in ages. She could hardly wait.

But a pall shadowed her excitement, because she had to tell Tuck about Angel. She couldn't risk being here alone without protection anymore. Mary would rather die than have that man's mouth and hands on her again.

Never again.

The familiar terror clogged her throat, and bile rose quickly in its wake, but she forced a deep breath and quelled it. Fear would do her no good. She needed strength.

She needed a *gun.*

They didn't own a single shotgun or rifle, because Mary always feared Robin would get hurt. All their hunting was done with bows and arrows, which Little John had shown them how to make and use when they first came to Indian Territory. Mary truly hated that they killed animals, but they'd assured her they only hunted what they needed, and that Little John had taught them to kill quick and sure. No suffering. Still, she hated it, though having meat through the winter was important enough to make her accept it.

But, God help her, Mary needed something more than a bow and arrow to fight Angel Rodriguez. She knew Tuck had a derringer, which he'd tried to give her once before. She'd adamantly refused then, but now she knew that had been foolish. When the men went hunting or trading, she became a woman alone in the wilderness. Vulnerable. If she'd had a gun that other day, she wouldn't be living in fear now.

Yes, she would learn to defend herself. That was that.

The door opened and Tuck slipped inside. She pressed a finger to her lips and he nodded in understanding, casting a quick glance at Will Scarlet.

Tuck tiptoed across the room and placed his saddlebags on the table. They were near bursting, and Mary's heart fluttered in anticipation. *Books!*

He grinned at her as he unloaded the beautiful leather-bound books, stacking them in front of her on the crude wooden table. Mary's mouth literally watered at the sight.

"All for you," Tuck whispered, his eyes twinkling as he produced one more volume. This one had an illustration on the cover. One that brought tears to her eyes—tears she would never shed.

"Oh, Tuck." With trembling hands, she reached for the precious copy of *The Merry Adventures of Robin Hood* by Howard Pyle, exactly like the edition her father had read to them. After she'd recovered from the same fever that had killed their parents, Mary had found all their belongings gone. Stolen. Remembering the terror of finding Robin stolen from her as well, she first thanked God for the gift, then Tuck. "Thank you for this. Thank you, my friend."

She reached out and hugged the little man around the neck. After returning her embrace, he sat beside her on the bench and patted her hand. "When I saw the book, I hid it from Robin." He kept his voice low, and his expression was warm. "You've given me a home here with you, and I wanted you both to have this remembrance of your parents."

Mary nodded, overcome with bittersweet memories. "Thank you." She dabbed at her eyes with the edge of her apron, then opened the book's cover and gazed at the familiar words on the title page. "We'll read this tonight after supper."

"Every night, I imagine." Tuck's eyes twinkled.

Mary set the book aside and cleared her throat. Now was as good a time as any. "Tuck, I . . . I've changed my mind about the derringer."

Tuck's eyes narrowed and he tilted his head to one side. "Something's happened." He took both her hands in his and leaned closer. "Will Scarlet?"

"No, of course not." She swallowed hard and summoned her wayward courage. Releasing a long sigh, she said, "Angel Rodriguez was here again."

Tuck closed his eyes and gave her hands a squeeze. When he reopened his eyes, Mary saw that he knew the truth. Shame slithered through her, insidious and powerful. She couldn't bear for him to know, yet she couldn't prevent what had already happened. How had he learned her most dreaded secret?

"I . . . I want the gun, Tuck," she whispered fiercely, unable and unwilling to acknowledge his knowing expression. Her fury would protect her from weakness. For now. "I *need* the gun."

Tuck's lower lip trembled, and she thought for a moment he might talk about her nightmare. It was painful enough to have him know at all, but to actually hear him give voice to it . . .

Never.

Mary squeezed her eyes closed for a moment, then drew a deep breath. "Please, Tuck?"

"Anything for you, dear Mary." His tone was kind and gentle, though it crackled with an undercurrent of emotion. "I'll bring you the derringer and all the bullets I have."

"Thank—"

"But know this, Mary Goode. You and Robin are like my children in every way that matters. I know you don't

think of me as a father, but there it is. I can't help myself.''
His expression hardened, and an ominous light entered
his faded eyes. ''You'll have my derringer, but if I ever
see Angel Rodriguez here again . . . I'll kill the bastard
myself.''

Mary's breath caught on a sob and she bit the back of
her knuckles to quell it. A moment later, Tuck's arms were
around her shoulders and she wept bitterly and silently,
feeling her father's presence in spirit.

Shane held his breath, hanging on every whispered
word, every revelation. He closed his eyes when he heard
Mary's sob, dredging up a fuzzy memory. It must have
been yesterday. Yes, now he remembered seeing the
black-clad man. Here. In this cabin.

Touching Mary.

Angel Rodriguez. Shane knew the name well from
wanted posters and gossip he'd overheard in saloons. A
killer, a con, a thief. Rodriguez had sweet-talked dozens
of women out of their land, then left them heartbroken
and penniless. What he hadn't wooed he'd taken. Both
the United States and Mexican governments had huge
bounties on the bastard's head.

Dead or alive.

Shane didn't give a damn about the bounty, but he did
care about the women who'd fallen victim to that devil's
charm. Rodriguez had stolen hearts along with property,
then left his victims destitute. Sometimes dead. He'd
never committed any crimes in Indian Territory that Shane
knew of, but many women in Texas and California had
been victimized by his villainy.

Sam had once told Shane that he believed Rodriguez
sometimes ventured into the Territory after one of his
cons. Probably hiding out until his victim's irate family
had calmed down a little, and the law wasn't in such hot
pursuit. The bandit always worked alone.

Rodriguez's crimes were far worse than any the Merry

Men may have committed. Shane suddenly realized that remaining here and pretending to be Will Scarlet could prove far more valuable than he'd originally planned.

But what was Rodriguez's interest in Mary Goode? Shane opened his eyes and watched Mary cry against Tuck's shoulder. She had no money, no land, nothing of value. It made no sense. What could Rodriguez want from—

No! Tuck's reaction to that man's name had said it all. Realization ripped at Shane with razor-like talons.

The thought of anyone hurting Mary—especially in *that* way—made Shane physically ill. For a moment, he thought he might retch. Deep, cleansing breaths calmed his roiling gut, but his rage remained just beneath the surface. Lurking. Ready to strike fast and sure.

Dead? Or alive? He clenched his fist at his side.

Dead.

Chapter Six

"Thank you, Little John," Mary said as the brave finished helping her carry hot water to the large washtub.

"Welcome, Maid Marian." Little John turned toward Shane. "I carry Will Scarlet out now."

Mary shook her head. "No, he's asleep and I hate to move him. He's so much better now . . ."

Asleep? Guiltily, Shane swallowed hard and closed his eyes to mere slits, watching Little John duck through the door and close it behind him. He really should've let Little John take him outside, but it was too late now.

He was very much awake . . . and alone with Mary. *Damn.* Since the cabin had only one room and Mary shared it with her brother, she'd probably always had that curtain across one corner for privacy. But *he* wasn't her brother, and that curtain was *way* too flimsy.

Now the woman was hell-bent on stripping to her birthday suit and taking a bath right here in the same room with him.

After three days, boredom had made him count every

beam in the ceiling. However, boredom was far preferable to the humiliation of being bathed like a baby. Yes, he was certain now he hadn't dreamed that experience, but he sure as hell hoped he hadn't actually enjoyed it as much as he remembered.

Who was he fooling? Hell, yes, he'd enjoyed it. What man wouldn't like having a beautiful woman rub him down with a damp cloth? All over? Well, almost all over.

Oh, yes, he definitely remembered *that*.

Shane drew a shaky breath, then released it slowly. Mary Goode would be the death of him yet. And very soon he would have to endure the sound of every drop of water splashing against her bare skin.

Bare skin.

He swallowed the lump in his throat as his blood headed for his groin like a bear after a honey tree. Wounded or not, he grew hard—hot, tight, and fast. He groaned quietly as Mary hummed, gathering her soap, clean clothes, and other odds and ends no normal man could've identified. And Shane was pretty normal, especially when it came to his appreciation *and* ignorance of beautiful women.

If only he could get up, get dressed, and go outside with the others until she was finished. *And find me an ice-cold spring to soak my privates in while I'm at it.* With a sigh, he accepted defeat. Another day or two and he'd be able to do just that, but not yet. He was still too weak.

She looked toward him and held the lamp higher. Shane squeezed his eyes shut and forced himself not to grimace.

Or peek.

The least he could do for the woman who'd given up her bed and her time to save his pitiful hide was to let her think he was asleep so she could enjoy her bath. Reminding himself of his noble motives, Shane didn't look again until he heard her slide the curtain into place.

His heart gave a serious lurch when he realized she'd

taken the lamp behind the curtain with her. He had a clear view of her silhouette through the white muslin.

Lord, give me the grit I'll need to survive this, he prayed. *But make tracks.*

Why couldn't she take a bath during daylight when she wouldn't need a lamp? He should turn his back to her. Face the wall. He should.

But he didn't.

No, sir, a herd of wild mustangs—all stallions—couldn't have dragged Shane's gaze from that wretched excuse for a curtain after he saw her start unpinning her hair. The silhouetted tendrils fanned out around her head and shoulders, holding him captive. For three days, he'd fantasized about how her tightly braided hair would look long and loose, and now he could almost see it.

He rubbed his fingers together, imagining the feel of her reddish brown curls sliding between them. The strands would be silky soft. He knew that, because of the way her hair shined. Shiny meant soft. He'd heard Jenny say that a hundred times, and his grandmother five hundred. They both rinsed their hair in rainwater and sometimes vinegar, insisting that was what made it soft and shiny.

Rainwater. Was Mary going to bathe and wash her beautiful hair in rain or springwater? He could almost see her standing beside the spring-fed pond on his grandma's ranch, her hair cascading down her bare back and barely hiding her breasts. . . .

The heaviness between his legs intensified, tugging until he knew he was as hard as he'd ever been. *Down, boy.* But his body was having none of that and gave an insistent throb to prove its point. *Well, it won't do you one iota of good.*

Glancing down the length of his body, he noted the conspicuous tent in the patchwork quilt. At least Mary wouldn't see him being indecent. Again.

She started that infernally sweet humming again, dragging Shane's attention back to the curtain. He sucked air between his teeth and held it, his gaze riveted to her shape behind that threadbare piece of muslin.

Mary slid her baggy shirt from her shoulders and shook her head, making her hair swing to and fro again. This time, he suspected, over bare shoulders. Softness sliding over her perfect flesh . . .

You've been without a woman too dang long, Latimer.

He was practically making love to her shadow, but he couldn't help himself and she'd never know. He would, though, and shame pressed down on him.

His cock answered with a mulish tightening.

Damn you.

He blinked as she turned her back to the curtain and bent over to remove her breeches. Her round bottom brushed against the muslin, creating a life-threatening distinction between light and shadow. She straightened and reached over her head, displaying her full length for his entertainment.

And torment.

He had to breathe soon or she'd find him dead by the time she ended this torture. Be just his luck he'd go through eternity hard enough to hammer nails. Then Mary'd know his cause of death.

Here lies Will Scarlet, who died from too dang many impure thoughts and not enough deeds. . . .

She turned to one side, displaying her firm breasts in such detail, Shane figured death was imminent. His heart gave a sudden lurch against his ribs as she bent over at the waist to trail her hand through the water. The sound of gentle splashing, the sight of her slender body, and his lengthy spell without a woman made all this a powerful aggravation.

Pity he had such a good imagination. Ma and Grandma had always praised him for that when he made up tall tales as a boy, but now Shane recognized it as the curse it truly was. *Yessirree, a curse.* His mind's eye filled in every delicious detail suggested by Mary's shapely silhouette.

Her skin was all pink and white, smooth as silk. Her neck was slender, sloping to strong shoulders and arms. All her hard work would make her firm and hardy, rather than soft like some women. Of course, he knew without a doubt that she was soft in all the right places. Lord help him. Her breasts were high and firm, with—

He caught his breath on a gasp that almost gained fruition as she lifted a long, shapely leg and stepped into the tub, slowly lowering herself until all he saw was her head and too much of her upper body. Those pert breasts of hers could drive a man to desperation.

No doubt about it—the woman needed a deeper tub.

Humming softly, she poured water over her head and soaped it. Shane heard her blowing bubbles through the water as she poured several more pitchers over her head. Her lips were probably puckered just right for a kiss. A shudder rippled through his body and a cold sweat popped to his skin's surface, as an impossible notion burst to the forefront of what was left of his mind.

Had he kissed Mary? The recollection nagged at him. No, it must've been a dream. If he'd really kissed Mary Goode, he'd damned well remember it. In detail.

Her bath seemed to take forever. The water must've been downright frigid by the time she finally stood. He licked his lips as she stepped from the tub. Water droplets would be trickling along her skin, over hills and valleys, vanishing into crevices he burned to explore. The tips of her pretty breasts would be hard little nubs, just begging a man to—

Shane groaned and turned onto his side—facing the curtain, of course. She rubbed her head and body vigorously, probably giving herself an all-over pink glow. His mouth went dry and his body screamed for release.

He hadn't relieved himself with his hand since he first learned how pleasant the real thing could be, but as his need became more dire, he actually considered it. But what if Mary came out and caught him?

He was damned if he did and damned if he didn't.

No, he'd just suffer, which was just what he deserved for spying on her. She had no idea that he watched her every move, or that her shadow revealed every curve of her luscious body. She pulled an article of clothing over her head, putting an end to his first experience as a voyeur.

He should be—*was*—ashamed of himself, but the tension between his legs was punishment enough. As Mary moved about behind the curtain, combing out her long hair and continuing to hum, Shane heard a soft meow beside his bunk.

Mary's kitten was climbing up a loose corner of his quilt. He chuckled softly, simultaneously aggravated and relieved to have something distract him from watching his hostess. He was about to reach down and pluck the kitten up onto bed with him when the curtain opened and Mary stepped out.

Shane's breath froze in his throat. Her hair was down, hanging past her waist in deep, damp waves, just as he'd imagined. The urge to touch it, to taste her, to kiss her consumed him. In all his days, he'd never wanted any woman with the fierceness he did now. This naive young creature possessed powers she couldn't possibly realize.

A siren in an outlaws' hideout.

He should close his eyes. If she saw him awake, she might realize he'd been watching her. But he couldn't stop staring at her angelic face surrounded by all that glorious hair. As she approached him, he noticed her long gray robe. It was tied at her waist and concealed her beauty from roving eyes. *His* eyes.

"Will, I'm sorry if I woke you," she said quietly, pausing a few feet from the bunk.

He was right—her skin glowed.

"You didn't," he croaked, his throat as dry as Texas in August.

"I'll call Robin and Little John to empty my water then." She shook her head, making her hair swing and ripple around her. "I promised them a story."

She has no idea.

Shane felt he should be punished for taking advantage of Mary's innocence this way. His remorse ran deep, but he couldn't say he actually regretted his transgression. It had been an incredible experience—frustratingly so.

As she turned to go to the door, Katie Calico gained purchase and propelled herself the last few inches onto the bunk. Shane glanced down at the furry critter as he rolled onto his back, his body re-creating the tent beneath the quilt. He flinched from the weight of the covers, wishing he were surrounded by a different sort of weight—something soft and tight. No, not something. *Someone.* Dammit, he had to stop thinking about Mary.

Releasing a long, slow breath, he looked again at the cat. *Cute little mite.* The kitten hissed and extended her tiny claws, crouching as if after a mouse . . .

And attacked the flinching tent pole.

Mary held the precious book in her lap, blinking back the stinging behind her eyes. The illustrations were faded and the pages worn, but this gift meant more to her than all the other books combined.

She sat in her rocking chair, looking around at the expectant faces. Little John sat before the fire, cross-legged. Tuck and Robin shared the wooden bench, and Will Scarlet looked on from his bunk in the corner. Her bed, actually, but the pallet near the hearth would do for a few more days.

Gingerly, she turned the page and read, *"The Merry*

Adventures of Robin Hood by Howard Pyle.'' She looked at her brother before turning another page. Their father had read this version of Robin Hood's legend to them more often than any other, though he had owned several older versions from his childhood. Robin's rapt attention made Mary's heart ache for all the years they should've had with their dear parents. But mourning their loss forever would do none of them any good.

Putting as much emotion into her voice as she possibly could, Mary read until her voice began to crack. "We'll read more tomorrow evening," she said, stroking the book's spine as she closed it. "No need to read it all at once."

Robin continued staring at her, his eyes moist and distant. *He'll always be a child,* her mother had said, but so many times, Mary saw the wisdom of a grown man lurking just beneath the surface. Like now.

Little John and Tuck murmured their thanks and good nights, then left quietly to go to their cabin. When Robin didn't move from the bench, Mary rose and put the book on a crude shelf near the window. She looked back and saw her brother's shoulders slumped, and her heart broke. She glanced quickly at Will Scarlet, noting he also watched Robin.

"I miss them, too," she said, rubbing her brother's shoulder.

Robin patted her hand as she sat on the bench at his side. "I know." He met her gaze, his expression thoughtful. "Something else."

Did he mean something else was bothering him? Mary studied him thoughtfully, still wishing he'd shave off the scraggly beard he'd grown after they came to Indian Territory. Sometimes it was hard to think of him as a child with all that hair on his face. Jerking her attention back to his eyes, she noted the tiny lines at the corners, the silver strands mingled with his dark hair across his brow. *A child, Mary.*

"What is it, Robin?" she asked quietly. "What's bothering you?"

He blinked, then met her gaze steadily. "I love Sunshine," he blurted, looking down at his lap. His cheeks reddened above his beard.

"Of course, I love her, too. She's a very nice girl."

"Not that way." He paused, obviously struggling for the right words. "Different. Like . . . like Father loved Mother. Like Little John's father and mother."

"Oh." A knot formed in her throat as Robin's expression grew more intense. He couldn't love Sunshine *that* way. The mere notion was ludicrous. Robin was a child in a man's body. A child! Pure, sweet, innocent . . .

A child with whiskers and graying hair, Mary? No, she couldn't listen to those doubts. They would ruin her image of Robin. Her mother had said he would always be a child, and so he would.

"I like to . . . to walk with her." Robin met her gaze again, his expression solemn.

"Walking is nice," she whispered, clinging to the fact that all her brother's Rs still sounded like Ws and his Ls were nonexistent. Nothing had changed. He was still a child in a man's body.

"I kissed her." He lowered his gaze again, then stared right at her. "I liked it. A lot. I . . . I want to kiss more."

"I see." *Dear God, but I don't see.* There were no words. Pressing her lips into a thin line, she forcibly quelled the voices. Surely Robin's physical urges equaled his mental abilities. God couldn't be so unfair as to give him *those* needs. Did her brother lie awake nights thinking of kissing Walks in Sunshine? And more? Did he have the same darkly erotic dreams Mary used to suffer herself?

Before Angel Rodriguez had turned all her dreams to nightmares?

"I go see Sunshine soon." The sound of Robin's voice jarred his sister back to the present. "Soon."

Mary forced a smile and drew a deep breath. "Soon, Robin." She cupped his cheek and kissed the other. "Get some rest now." *And please stop talking.* She had to think about this. The thought of Robin having . . . urges was too new and bizarre to deal with easily. And maybe it wasn't like that at all. Perhaps a good night's sleep would make it all better.

Robin went to his bunk and stripped off his shirt and removed his boots. Mary looked away before he dropped his breeches. She didn't want to think of him as a grown man. She *couldn't.*

Wearily, she banked the fire, then picked up the lamp from the table where she'd been reading. She looked across the cabin toward Will, noting the somber expression in his eyes. He looked at her with something resembling pity.

Her heart fluttered and raced away. He couldn't know about Angel, she reminded herself. No, he must've overheard Robin. Will Scarlet pitied the woman whose brother would always be a child, though he wanted to be a man. Stunned by that realization, Mary glanced over at Robin, who lay with his back to her and the quilt pulled up to his chin.

Of course, Robin wanted to be a man, and having someone like Will around must've brought all those feelings to the surface. Somewhat more at ease, Mary faced her patient again. She would accept pity from no one.

Yet he looked at her with such a quiet intensity, it unnerved her. Those green eyes of his seemed wise beyond his years, as if he'd suffered a great deal. But what could a handsome man like him know of suffering?

"Good night, Will," she said.

" 'Night, ma'am."

His husky whisper poured over her like warm honey,

making her limbs heavy and boneless. That nagging ache
began low in her belly again, crawling upward until it
encased her heart as well. She swayed slightly, then caught
herself and turned abruptly away before his fervent
expression crawled any deeper into her heart and soul.
Her thoughts toward Will were wanton and uncalled for.
He'd done nothing to suggest anything inappropriate, after
all.

Then she remembered how he'd responded to her bathing his feverish body. A relentless liquid fire surged
through her. She froze and glanced back over her shoulder.
He still watched her, his expression even more intense
now, his eyes hooded.

Was his body engorged now as it had been when he'd
thrown back the quilt during his delirium? *"Wash this,"*
he'd said, and she again saw every explicit detail of his
very male body. She quivered from somewhere deep in
her women's core. Somewhere dark.

Somewhere dangerous.

If only her dreams could remain on the present, and
the fair-haired man who'd held her attention since his
arrival. Unfortunately, old memories—nightmares—
plagued her slumber.

*Mary stooped at the riverbank, scrubbing the wash and
beating the worst of it with a flat rock. The sun was high,
the sky crystal blue.*

*She didn't sense danger until Angel Rodriguez came
up behind her. Above the sound of rushing water, it was
no surprise she hadn't heard his approach. He didn't
come to Sherwood Forest often, but each time he did
Mary grew more wary. She'd seen the way he looked at
Robin. And at her. She had no doubt he would stoop to
cruelty if it would offer him a moment's sadistic pleasure.*

Angel's smile was false, but might seem charming to

*some. Mary saw him as the snake he was. As usual, he
tried to coax her into a kiss, promising to take her away
to Mexico with him, where servants would do her bidding.
He promised her jewels and luxuries Mary'd never imagined. Treasure that held no appeal to her. The only thing
she'd ever wanted besides a safe home with her brother
was a husband and family, but not with the likes of Angel.
Not that he was offering anything even remotely honorable.*

*"No," she said for at least the fiftieth time. "I must
stay here for Robin." But this time her answer angered
him and he grabbed her hard and dragged her into the
trees.*

*He shoved her to the ground, then used a knife to slice
away her clothing. When he tried to kiss her, she bit his
tongue, tasting the metallic tinge of his blood. Angrily,
he jerked away and slapped her, then pressed his hand
to her mouth. "Fight me again,* querida,*" he whispered
menacingly, "and I will* kill *your precious brother.*

"You made me do this. You made me . . ."

Chapter Seven

No matter what, Shane Latimer was hauling his butt out of bed today. He couldn't take another day of lying here at the mercy of Mary's bathing whims. Another bout with his cravings—not to mention that *cat*—would do him in for sure.

He shot a pensive glance in Mary's direction, wondering when she would go about her morning chores so he could get dressed. Robin and his cohorts had left right after breakfast, but she still sat at the table, staring unblinkingly out the open cabin door.

Something was obviously troubling her, and he wondered if it was her brother's confession about being in love. Shane had seen the way her eyes widened in surprise last night during Robin's declaration. She was in a strange place, with an older brother who was a boy in many ways. Shane understood her concern, but her reaction seemed exaggerated. Why?

Then he remembered her conversation with Tuck and winced. Rodriguez had wounded her inside and out. Any mention of relations between men and women must remind her of what that son of a bitch had done to her.

He held his breath for a moment, then released it slowly, bringing his rage under control before she could notice it. Explaining to her why he was angry would only upset her more. Watching her rise and tie her battered sunbonnet beneath her chin, Shane made a vow to himself. If he accomplished nothing else during his lifetime, he would see Angel Rodriguez pay.

With his miserable life.

Mary dropped her perverted kitten into its box and closed the lid—thank God—then she paused near the door and turned to face Shane. Her eyes looked distant, her brow was creased with worry lines. If only there was something he could do to ease her mind . . .

Like arrest her brother? Shane chose to ignore that nagging voice in the back of his mind. For now.

"I'm going out to gather the eggs," she said, her voice flat and dull. Lifeless. "Robin, Tuck, and Little John went fishing. I'll leave the door open so you can call out if you need anything."

"I'll be fine." Shane gave her what he hoped was an encouraging smile. The last thing he needed was for her to come in before he had on his jeans. Heat burned low, right between his legs, and spread throughout him. He cleared his throat—it didn't help.

Without another word, Mary nodded and left. Shane sat up straight in bed first, allowing his body to get used to the change before moving again. He'd do this one stage at a time until he was on his feet and heading toward his clothes. Hurrying would land his butt on the floor damned fast. He could handle the fall all right, but he'd prefer to do it fully dressed.

Mary Goode had seen enough of his privates already, and he couldn't trust himself not to get hard right before her eyes. Just the thought of her silhouette behind that curtain last night made him shudder and break into a cold sweat.

"Not now, dang it all," he whispered, swinging his legs over the edge of the bunk while strategically keeping the blanket in front of him. He sucked in a sharp breath and bit his lower lip as blood rushed mercilessly to his wound.

Mary had applied a fresh poultice earlier this morning, and Shane noticed now how much healthier his leg looked. No matter how much it still hurt, it was healing. He could do this. He *would* do this.

Summoning his strength and resolve, he pushed to his feet while tucking the quilt around his waist. If he fell this time, he'd make damned sure it wasn't on top of the covers.

He took baby steps, wincing each time his weight came down on his injured leg. By the time he reached the pegs holding his clothes, the stiffness had eased and he thought—maybe—the pain had lessened, too.

Slinging his clothes, gunbelt, and saddlebags over his arm and shoulder, he headed back to the bunk. The shirt he'd been wearing was covered with rusty bloodstains, but he had two more packed. And one thing was for sure—he had to sit down to pull on his jeans. Balancing on one foot wasn't something he'd be able to manage just yet.

But he was on his feet again at last. Smiling through his pain, he limped back toward the bunk, but a faint jingling sound drifted through the open door. *Damn.* He limped faster, which sent sharp pains shooting through his calf.

A few more feet ... The sound of boots hitting the wooden stoop alerted Shane that his visitor wasn't Mary, or any of the Merry Men. None of them owned good leather boots, let alone spurs. A shadow blocked the flow of sunlight, and his blood turned cold.

As he turned toward the door, he made sure his guns were where he could grab them. If the intruder was Rodriguez, Shane had a job to do, and do it he would. *Dead or alive.*

"Well, I'll be," a familiar voice called. "How come you're naked every time I find you?"

"What the . . . ?" Shane looked into the laughing gray eyes of Sam Weathers, his idol and friend. "I am not, you old coot."

"Old? Who are you callin' old, boy?" Sam looked around the cabin. "Do you know where you are?" He lifted one dark eyebrow as he waited for Shane's answer.

"Yeah, I do." Shane looked beyond Sam to make sure no one else was coming, then he sat on the edge of the bunk and pulled his jeans on over the poultice. Once they were fastened, he felt one hell of a lot more secure. There was something about being naked that made him feel vulnerable, just like that time Sam had stolen his clothes back in Redemption to keep him from trying to rescue Jenny. *Didn't work then either.* A smile of remembrance tugged at his mouth as he dug his clean shirt from his saddlebag. Where the devil was his badge? Had it fallen out of his saddlebag back at the clearing?

Or did one of the Merry Men have it? He swallowed hard. He had to find that badge. Fast.

He glanced toward the open door. If he had Sam close it, Mary might get suspicious. "You don't know me and I've lost my memory. Got it?"

Sam chuckled and raked his hand through his hair. "If you say so, but we gotta talk private-like. Soon."

Shane met Sam's somber gaze and nodded.

"What happened?" Sam removed his hat and motioned toward Shane's leg. He walked over to the table and straddled the bench.

"Snake. Got my horse, too."

Shaking his head, Sam rubbed his whiskered jaw, then

shot Shane a sideways glance. "So who do they think you are?"

Shane flashed a crooked grin. "Will Scarlet."

"Shit." Sam chuckled. "Don't that beat all? I ain't read a lot of books in my life, but that's one I remember."

Shane shrugged and sat down again, stretching his leg out beside him on the bunk. "I'm on this case, Sam. You don't know me. I mean that."

Sam sighed and directed his gaze out the cabin door. "Fair enough. I'm on Buck Landen's tail anyway—don't got time for grown men playing Robin Hood." He clenched his fist. "I swear I'm gonna get that bastard this time."

A chill raced through Shane and he thought, for a moment his fever might be returning. But it wasn't that— it was plain, old-fashioned fear. Marshal Sam Weathers had grown downright obsessive about capturing Landen this past year. Shane understood that now, because he felt the same way about Rodriguez.

"Be careful," Shane said. "Landen's a slippery devil."

"Yeah, I know." Sam swung himself around on the bench and faced Shane. "Ain't you wonderin' why I'm here?"

Shane stiffened, noting Sam's badge winking back from the usual place on his vest. The lawman had walked in here like he owned the place, badge and all.

"You've been here before?"

Sam remained silent for several moments, then nodded. "I stop in to check on things now and then."

"They're *wanted.*" The man he considered the greatest lawman to ever wear a badge had known where to find the Merry Men all along. "Why, Sam?"

Sam spread his hands out on the table and stared long and hard at Shane. "I ain't sure I can explain it to you," he said. "Priorities, I reckon. It's somethin' a man's gotta learn for himself, but if you dig real deep and remember everything that happened back in Redemption, you might find your answer. A man—even a lawman—has to pick his battles in this life.''

Since his wife's death, Sam had grown downright philosophical. Sam Weathers had saved Shane from being hanged unjustly. Was that what he meant? Did Sam believe Robin and his Merry Men were innocent? But Shane knew better. They were guilty of stealing, and it was his duty to arrest them and take them to stand trial.

Though it would break Mary's heart . . .

Damn. Guilt and regret pressed down on Shane, and he swallowed hard. Sam was right—they needed to talk privately, but he heard shuffling footsteps outside, and Shane had a disguise to protect. ''Just remember, you don't know me,'' he whispered fiercely.

Sam shrugged and gave a quick nod. He turned to the door, then stood. ''Let me take that basket and pail, Miss Mary,'' he said, hurrying to the door as she stepped through. ''Nice berries, and it looks like your hens have been real busy this spring.''

''Marshal Weathers, what a pleasant surprise,'' Mary said, allowing the lawman to take her basket and set it near the hearth.

Shane was relieved to see her smiling now. He liked seeing her smile.

''I hope you're planning to stay for supper. Robin will be thrilled to see—''

With her fingers on the frayed ribbon of her sunbonnet, Mary stared open-mouthed at Shane. ''You got out of bed again.'' She hurried over to him and pressed her hand to his forehead. ''Will Scarlet, you have the sense of a tadpole. I told you to stay in bed another day at least, and here you—''

Shane grinned. ''Thanks, ma'am, but I couldn't stand it another day.'' The frustration of being a witness to her last bath would remain his secret . . . and his cherished memory. "I'm fine now, thanks to you. The leg'll need more time yet, but I'll cut me a walking stick as soon as I get outside."

"I'll ask Little John to get it for you," she said, her expression growing distant again as she turned away. "Marshal, what brings you to these parts?"

"Same reason as before," he said with a sigh. "Buck Landen."

Mary hung her bonnet on a peg near the door. "I'm happy to report we haven't seen him for over a year."

Shane looked at her tight coil of braids, wishing her hair were down again, like it had been last night. Did Mary try to hide her beauty deliberately? He remembered her vehement denial when he'd told her she was beautiful.

"I don't want to be," she'd said.

Damn Rodriguez's soul to hell.

The truth became painfully clear. Mary Goode hid her beauty from the world because of what that devil had done to her. She couldn't blame herself for that, could she?

Shane drew a deep breath and turned his attention to Sam and Mary's conversation again. Somehow, some way, he had to understand why Sam knowingly allowed the Merry Men to remain free.

"Landen was workin' for Rufus Hopsador for a while," Sam said, his tone sober, his expression sincere. "I think the durn fool was tryin' to go straight, but he ain't no more. Make sure you throw that bolt at night."

"I'd better start supper," she said, her face blazing with shame. She couldn't very well tell the marshal she'd been brutally attacked outside in broad daylight. Angel had said he would kill Robin if she told, and she had every reason to believe him.

Besides, if she told Sam Weathers now, Will would overhear. For some reason, Mary didn't want him to know of her shame. She glanced at him again. He sat there naked above the waist, digging through his saddlebags for something. Frowning, he removed a wrinkled shirt and shook it out, then looked in the bag again.

"Did you lose something?" she asked.

"I'm not sure," Will said quietly. He gave Marshal Weathers a helpless look.

Mary hung the kettle over the small flame, then wiped her hands on her apron. "Marshal, perhaps you know this man from your travels." She was torn. Part of her wanted Will to remember who he was and leave them in peace. But another part of her loved his smile, the way his muscles rippled when he moved, and the music of his deep laughter made her warm inside and out. "Robin— we—call him Will Scarlet, because he remembers nothing before his horse kicked him in the head."

"I don't recollect, ma'am," Marshal Weathers said, looking at Will as he spoke. "You wanted for anything, boy?"

Will's face reddened, and she saw a muscle twitch in his jaw as he shrugged into his clean shirt. "Not that I remember, sir."

"Well, if you do remember, I want you to march your hide across the border to Fort Smith and turn yourself over to Judge Parker." The marshal grinned openly, and Mary couldn't suppress her own. "Tell him Sam Weathers sent you."

"Yes, sir." Will buttoned his shirt, then looked toward his toes. "I owe Miss Goode my life, Marshal. If not for her and her family, I'd be a goner."

"A man never forgets, Will." The marshal sounded sad as he walked over to stare out the door. "Never forget."

Mary uncovered the pot of soaking beans, then dropped in a small piece of salt pork. *Beans, beans, beans.* Sometimes she hated beans. It would be nice to have something special to serve company. But she could bake pies. That was something. After covering the pot, she looked at the marshal. He still stood staring out the door.

She remembered the first time he'd come to Sherwood Forest. Tuck had been suspicious of the man, but they eventually formed an uneasy alliance. Though Mary had feared that Marshal Weathers might have come to take Robin back to that horrid asylum, she soon realized he was a good man who would never do anything to harm them. She told him the truth about why they were here in Indian Territory, and why she could never leave without her grandfather's protection.

Though he'd warned her that times were changing, and that she might not always be able to hide here, as long as they did nothing to break the law, he'd leave them in peace. And he had. In fact, they looked forward to his visits.

"Marshal, how are your wife and son doing?" she asked, remembering how proud he'd been of the new baby.

He looked at her, his smile sad, his eyes weary. "My boy, George, he's just fine, ma'am. Thanks for askin'." He turned his gaze out the door again, and she saw the truth etched across his weathered features. "My missus died right after I was through here last year."

Mary covered the few steps separating them and touched his arm. He turned and looked into her eyes with the most soulful expression she'd ever seen. "I'm so sorry, Marshal," she whispered, choking back her own tears.

"Thanks." He looked outside again. "I'm gonna wander around outside a spell and see if I can spot your brother. I got reason to believe he and his Merry Men might've been up to a little mischief."

"Wha—"

"Nothin' to worry about, Miss Mary." Marshal Weathers smiled, shoved his hat on his head, then stepped outside.

Mary couldn't help wondering what mischief he thought her brother might've been up to. Of course, she had no way of knowing what sort of trouble Robin, Little John, and Tuck might find on one of their trips to town. She only knew that she trusted Little John and Tuck to protect Robin and return him to her safely. Always.

She looked across the room at Will, whose eyes were turned toward the now empty doorway and filled with sympathy. Any man who could feel such genuine emotion for a stranger must be a good man. She definitely had what her mother would've called a soft spot for Will Scarlet. Right or wrong, she cared what happened to him, and, for the time being, she enjoyed his company.

But she feared that her feelings for this strange, wounded man were fast becoming far more than friendship. She closed her eyes for a moment, then opened them to gaze upon his striking features. Even with several days' growth of beard, he was the most handsome man she'd ever seen. Not pretty like Angel Rodriguez—thank heavens—but ruggedly handsome, like a fair-haired Sam Weathers.

Will was kind, friendly, a gentleman in every way that mattered—well, unless she counted his shocking and memorable behavior during his delirium—and she was confident he'd had a fair amount of formal education. Now, on top of all his other attributes, he'd shown compassion for Marshal Weathers.

Yes, in another time and place, if her life were different, Mary could've—*would've*—fallen for a man like Will Scarlet.

If only she could forget . . .

A shudder rippled through her as if someone had turned off the sun's warmth. She hugged herself and turned her attention to sorting the wild raspberries she'd picked behind the henhouse this morning. How fortunate that she'd found so many ripe ones before the birds ate them on a day they had Sam Weathers as their supper guest.

She sat at the table and removed the stems and imperfect berries, popping more than a few into her mouth as she worked. Tuck often said Mary ate more than she picked during berry season. He was right, of course, but they all loved pie. Later in the summer, there would be black-berries, too. Her mouth watered at the prospect.

Anything to keep her mind off her growing feelings for Will and her torturous memories of Angel. Such con-flicting yet distressingly related worries . . .

She worked quickly, trying all the while to concentrate on her task. In fact, she was so engrossed in the beautiful red berries, she was surprised to hear Will slide onto the bench across the table from her. Looking up, she met his gentle gaze and warm smile.

"Can I help?" he asked quietly, reaching out to cover her hand on the edge of the pail.

This recovering Will Scarlet was far more disconcerting than the convalescent who'd been helpless less than twenty-four hours ago. Despite her best efforts, she remembered bathing his feverish body. The way the cloth had slid across his taut skin, the way his muscles rippled beneath the slight pressure, and the shocking size of his . . . his—

No, don't remember that, she chided herself. Too many bad memories haunted her to allow herself the luxury of enjoying the sight of any healthy man.

A quiet but persistent voice in the back of her mind told her this was different. Logically, she knew men and women had loving relationships which included a very physical side. She *knew* how babies were made. Her cheeks burned and she avoided Will's gaze.

Her parents must have had such a relationship, and Robin wanted to with Sunshine. . . .

Barely breathing now, she slipped her hand from beneath Will's, afraid to meet the warmth of his gaze again just yet. "Help yourself," she said, returning to the task of sorting berries without looking at her helper. "You haven't eaten much solid food yet."

He reached into the pail with his large, tanned hand and scooped up a handful of succulent berries. Mary shouldn't look—God help her—but she followed the journey of his hand to his mouth. Grinning at her all the while, he ate several berries.

"Well, now I've eaten solid food, ma'am." His grin widened and his green eyes twinkled.

She couldn't prevent her own smile any more than she could stop herself from breathing. "So you have." She ate a few more berries herself, then decided she had enough sorted for two large pies. "I'll roll out the dough now." She pushed the pail toward him. "There are a few left. Help yourself."

"Thanks."

Mary forcibly withdrew her gaze from Will's mouth as he chewed the berries. For some reason, the shape of his lips disturbed her, but not in an unpleasant way. No, far from it, in fact. Though she tried not to, she remembered—vividly—the kiss he'd bestowed upon her during his delirium. Soft yet firm, and warm—so very, very warm.

Of course, you ninny, he had a fever.

Clearing her throat, she forced her attention to pie making. With her largest wooden bowl, she mixed enough flour, lard, and water for two crusts, then flattened the dough with the rolling pin Tuck had brought her last year. She knew her excitement over the receipt of such a common item would've seemed odd to some, but Tuck had understood.

The little man understood *too* much.

"I like your hair better down," Will said, his voice so low it rumbled through her very bones.

"It's too impractical out here." Mary met his gaze—big mistake. She saw something there, something foreign and exotic. Her heart rolled over in her chest and a strange fluttery sensation spread from her center outward. What she saw burning in Will Scarlet's beautiful green eyes was something she'd never thought to find in any man's eyes.

"You have beautiful hair, Mary," he said in that same buttery voice. "So shiny. I'll bet it's soft, too."

Oh, Lord. The mere thought of Will touching her hair made her heart practically leap into her throat and choke her. She cleared her throat, but it didn't help. The expression in his eyes unhinged her.

He was dangerous. Powerful.

She was weak, unable to keep the wondrous sensations at bay. They'd insinuated themselves into every beat of her heart, every breath she took. She couldn't allow this. She had to find a way to obliterate the consuming shadows.

But this wasn't the lust she'd always perceived in Angel Rodriguez's insolent gaze, and even in the dark eyes of some of the braves who'd stopped at the cabin over the years. No, this was something much greater, and much . . . *purer*. That word seemed odd, but there it was.

She associated what Angel had done to her with filth and terror, and the mere thought made her palms perspire and her breath catch in her throat. The nightmare threatened again, pressing down on her just as that horrible man had. She could almost feel the cold mud sucking at her beneath Angel's rutting weight.

No, not now. Not now . . . With a shudder, she banished the nightmare, though she knew it would return again and again. She'd never be free of the filth and terror. Never.

But all men weren't animals who took what they wanted

whenever they wanted. She drew a deep breath, focusing on this thought. Some men were like Will seemed, and like her beloved brother and father, and Little John's father and cousins. And she knew unequivocally that Henry never treated Ruth that way. Only with love. Good men cherished their wives, as Sam Weathers had cherished his.

Though she grieved for the marshal's loss, remembering the love he'd known with his wife brought joy to her heart, and she knew it must comfort him when he needed it most. Perhaps she would never be completely free of the filth and the terror, but the different sort of desire—yes, desire—she saw burning in the depths of Will's eyes reminded her that most men weren't evil.

Thank you, God. She drew a deep breath and smiled at Will. His eyes flickered in obvious surprise, then he returned her smile and popped another berry into his mouth. The intense desire she'd seen a few minutes ago was diminished now, but when he looked at her she felt wanted and special. Never dirty.

And never, never frightened.

Sam Weathers stared out across the Verdigris Valley, where the lush area Robin Goode called Sherwood Forest appeared as a dark green curve along the river. The spring rains had made this remaining part of Indian Territory look like one of those fancy paintings Judge Parker had in his office.

Sighing, Sam remembered his meeting with the judge last week. Parker had done more to clean up Indian Territory than anyone, but some folks said he was too harsh. Hanging killers was too harsh? The judge had said some politicians in Washington wanted him to step down. Sam spat on the ground, then walked around the side of the cabin.

At thirty-eight, he wasn't old, but sometimes he felt that way. When his wife died, a part of him did, too. Since then, he'd spent way too much time pondering things no man could really understand. Death, life, love . . . At least he knew his boy was safe with his sister in Fort Smith. She'd raise him right.

"You're gettin' soft, Weathers," he muttered, pausing to stare at the cabin belonging to the man the other residents of Sherwood Forest knew only as Friar Tuck.

Sam knew otherwise.

It had taken him years to figure it out, but now he knew Friar Tuck was Ichabod Smith, a famous scientist and professor who'd vanished about ten years ago while traveling across the country with some colleagues. A massive search had been conducted for Smith when he failed to return to his party after a stop in Fort Smith. Eventually, folks decided he must've wandered into the wilderness and died. If he'd been kidnapped and held for ransom, the university sponsoring his research would've heard from the kidnappers.

The way Sam had it figured, Smith had tired of his life and ran away to find something simpler. Well, he'd sure as hell found it here. But Sam knew the man's secret, and he would use it to stop the Merry Men's raiding. Blackmail had its purpose.

Sam walked to Tuck's cabin and knocked. When no one answered—and he'd known they wouldn't—he opened the door and stepped inside, blinking until his eyes adjusted to the dimness.

He gave a low whistle as he looked around the tiny cabin. Various pieces of equipment resembling items he'd seen in doctors' offices, glass vials containing mysterious liquids, and a pile of colorful material occupied one side of the room. The other side obviously belonged to Little John. A small pallet on the floor and a basket were the only belongings the brave had.

Tuck was up to something. A huge pile of fabric, several lengths of stout rope, and all this other stuff didn't add up to anything to Sam, but he trusted his gut. His gut said Tuck didn't do anything without a reason.

Some books sat on a workbench near what Sam figured was the scientist's bed. One was about air currents, another dealt with something scientific Sam couldn't even pronounce, and the third one had an illustration on the cover that made Sam glance back at the pile of fabric in the corner.

"I'll be damned." He noticed a back door and opened it. Poking his head through, he saw a still in the woods. He'd bet money Mary Goode didn't know about that.

He glanced around inside again, then left the cabin and closed the door, knowing what Tuck was up to, but having no idea why. Yet.

He would soon, though, and he'd put a stop to Robin Goode's life as a thief before it was too late. Sam knew Robin had no idea what he did was wrong, and neither did John Runningwolf. Tuck knew, though.

Sam believed the scientist genuinely cared about his little family here, but the fact remained that Tuck was using them to his own advantage. God knew why, but it was true.

The reign of Robin Hood and his Merry Men in Indian Territory was about to end. Sam had to talk to Tuck and play his hand real soon, before Shane made the biggest mistake of his life.

Because all the time Sam had spent pondering death, life, and love had made him too damned wise for his own good. He knew things he didn't want to know, and one look at Mary Goode and Shane Latimer in the same room had said it all. A grin tugged at his lips, and he gave a decisive nod.

Unless that college-educated greenhorn skedaddled real damned fast, Shane and Mary were as good as hitched.

Chapter Eight

Shane had to find a way to catch Sam alone, and unless everybody left again, that seemed unlikely. The Merry Men had returned with their catch, and Robin obviously had a serious case of hero worship for Sam. A condition Shane understood only too well. Who could blame him? But that meant Robin stuck to Sam like they were attached.

Being out of bed and eating real food had already made Shane stronger, but he figured he'd tire easily if he overdid. Still, nothing could drag him from the supper table, even if the food hadn't been tasty. Gathered around the wooden table that occupied the center of the cabin, they ate their fill of fish, cornbread, and beans, then Mary produced two pies so perfect they made Shane's mouth water.

The woman was smart, beautiful, and she could cook, too.

As she cut the first pie into triangles, Shane watched her closely. Her mood was much improved from this morning, and that made her all the more irresistible. Her eyes sparkled, her skin glowed, her smile was easy and frequent. He could watch this Mary all day.

And that scared the hell out of him.

Lusting after her silhouette had been one thing, and despite that damned cat's unholy penchant for his privates, lust was a lot safer predicament than what assailed him now. He swallowed hard as she walked around the table, distributing tin plates filled with pie to each of them.

As she leaned between him and Sam, Shane inhaled deeply. No sickly sweet perfume masked her natural womanly fragrance. It filled his nostrils and warmed him clear to his toes. Though he was exhausted from being out of bed so long, having her near for even an instant aroused him in every way.

She brushed against his upper arm and his breath froze. His heart slammed against his chest like a war drum, and that familiar tightening commenced right between his legs. The buttons at the front of his jeans were one hell of a lot less accommodating than that quilt had been.

The fact that he wanted her the way a man wants a woman was understandable. He could accept that easily enough, and he had enough self-control to survive the physical discomfort, though he had to keep reminding himself.

The fact that her smile and the sound of her voice made him feel as if someone had poured warm honey into his veins, and made his heart swell with something indefinable, was another matter.

A troublesome matter.

She went around the table and took her seat across from him, then placed her napkin in her lap. Robin and Little John dug into their pie like men who hadn't eaten for a week, though they'd just consumed a huge meal. Sam ate slowly, bestowing compliments on the cook, while Tuck sat at the end of the table and stared at, and right through, Shane.

The man's expression redirected Shane's thoughts, which was probably a good thing, considering. However, now wasn't the time for a stare-down with Tuck—too many witnesses, and not enough information. Shane looked across the table at Mary again, trying to mask his suspicions about the location of his missing badge. Was that the reason for Tuck's stare?

Mary smiled as Shane shoved a forkful of pie into his mouth. His throat squeezed shut around the berries and crust, and he washed it down with water. The crust was tender and flaky, but his throat tightened up every time Mary looked at him that way. Yeah, he was in what Jenny would've called *huge* trouble.

"Wonderful pie, ma'am," Shane said.

"Thank you, Will."

Damn, she's smiling again. But he wanted her to smile, to be happy, to never be afraid again. *Enough of that, Latimer.* He was here to arrest her brother and the Merry Men, not fall in love with the outlaw's sister.

Love? *Now where the hell did that come from?* Heat flooded his cheeks and a dull roar filled his ears. He had to regain control of this situation. Fast. His thoughts about Mary Goode were starting to remind him of some of the silly poetry he'd been forced to read in college. Those nonsensical words about love and beauty were even starting to make sense now, and *that* was just too much.

"You look flushed, Will," Mary said, her brow furrowing. "I think you've overdone today."

Sam cleared his throat and Shane shot him a side-glance. The old coot was grinning, almost as if he could read Shane's thoughts.

Shane would rather face another rattler.

Mary rose and walked around the table, pressing her cool hand to his forehead before he could protest. "I'm fine, ma'am," he said, his voice strained and husky even to his ears. "Really."

"Well . . ." She hesitated, then returned to her seat. "You really shouldn't do too much your first day out of bed. Oh, remind me after supper to have you try a pair of Robin's moccasins. I'm sorry we had to cut your boot."

"I'm not." And he meant that. "Better my boot than my leg."

"Or worse," Sam said. "Dyin' from snakebite's a helluva way to go. You're lucky, I'd say."

"Yeah. I'd really appreciate the loan of a pair of moccasins, ma'am. Thank you." Shane couldn't drag his gaze from Mary's, no matter how he tried. He felt Sam's gaze on him again, but he wanted to see the way Mary's eyes twinkled when she smiled. If he looked away, he might miss it.

Damn. Mustering his resolve, he dragged his gaze from her and looked around the table.

"What brings you to Sherwood Forest, Marshal?" Tuck asked, pushing his empty plate away.

Sam nodded in Mary's direction. "Best meal I've had since I last sat at your table, ma'am. Thanks."

Mary blushed and murmured her gratitude as Sam turned his attention back to Tuck. Shane focused on their conversation, but tried not to look directly at the midget. Unfortunately, the most distracting sight in the room was his hostess. He was cursed either way.

"Buck Landen," Sam said finally, folding his arms across his chest. "Seen him lately?"

Shane spared the little man a quick glance, noting the cunning flash through his eyes. Friar Tuck was up to something. Shane could smell it, and he'd bet money Sam did, too. Was Landen the *only* reason Sam had ventured this far into Indian Territory?

Tuck rubbed his silver beard, and lantern light glistened from his bald head. One thing was for sure—that was no halo. Friar Tuck, or whoever he was, couldn't fool Shane

Latimer and Sam Weathers. Well, at least not Sam Weathers.

"Landen . . ." Tuck tilted his head to one side and squinted. "Seems to me we did see him our last trip to Tahlequah."

"We did?" Robin looked up from his second piece of pie.

"Well, perhaps not, but the man I saw definitely had red hair like Landen." Tuck looked around the table without making eye contact with anyone.

Sly little man. Shane wondered what the devil Tuck was up to now.

"Where?" Sam's voice was calm. Too calm.

"Was on the Verdigris, downriver." Tuck pulled his pipe from his pocket and fidgeted with it until Shane wanted to snatch it from him. "Twenty miles or so, I suppose."

Tuck was trying to get rid of Sam. Realization slammed into Shane, but there wasn't a damned thing he could do about it without revealing his identity.

"How long ago was that?" Sam drummed his fingers on the table.

"Two days."

Robin looked from Sam to Tuck, then shook his head and turned his attention back to his pie. Little John seemed oblivious to the conversation. No one here could dispute Tuck's story.

"Well, I reckon I'd better head out tonight then," Sam said.

Shit.

"Lucifer oughta be rested up by now." The lawman swung his leg over the bench and stood. "Thank you again for the fine meal, Miss Mary." He patted his abdomen.

"Marshal, I wish you wouldn't rush off. You're welcome to stay until morning." Mary rose and walked around the table, standing directly behind Shane. "What good will it do to take off after dark anyway? Stay and rest, then get an early start in the morning.''

Shane half-turned on the bench, trying to make eye contact with Sam. He *had* to talk to him before he left. Finally, Sam looked down.

''I reckon you're right about that,'' he said, nodding. ''Thanks for the invite. I'll just bed down in the soddy with Lucifer. That way I can get an early start without disturbin' anyone.''

Having Sam out there would make it easier for Shane to speak privately with him. Sam excused himself after Little John announced he was going to the village for the night, and Tuck stepped outside to smoke his pipe. Mary carried plates to the slop pail and scraped them. Shane followed, leaning on the crude walking stick Little John had brought him, while carrying a stack of plates in his free hand.

''Thank you.'' She stared at him for several moments, then took the plates and turned away.

But not before Shane saw the flash of desire.

Joy and pure terror ripped through him. Part of him wanted to grab her and kiss her, but the voice of reason held him in check. Besides, he knew Mary would be skittish after what Rodriguez had done to her. It would take a lot of patience, a lot of tenderness, and a lot of time to bring her around.

And Shane wanted that job. Badly. He held his breath, staring at the back of her neck as she tended her chores. The fine hairs that had escaped from her coil of braids begged to be touched. How would she react if he were to kiss her right there? Right now?

''Here some moccasins, Will.''

Robin's voice shattered the moment and Shane straightened, reminding himself to breathe. He was getting downright light-headed from lack of air and the rush of blood to his groin.

I need shoes and to talk to Sam. Maybe if he kept playing those words through his mind, he could keep his hands—and his lips—off Mary Goode. She straightened and smiled at her brother. *Then again, maybe not.*

"The nice thing about moccasins is they're soft enough that they'll stretch some." Mary took the soft leather footwear from her brother and held them out to Shane. "These have always been a little too big for Robin. See if they fit you, Will."

"Thanks, ma'am." Shane took the moccasins, then made his way back to the bench. He slipped the soft leather over the foot on his injured leg first, because it was still slightly swollen. If it fit this foot, the other one would be no problem. The leather stretched across his arch snugly, but it would do. He tied the leather strings, then pulled on the other one and stood.

"They'll do. Thank you, Robin." The boy—*no, not a boy*—grinned.

"Welcome, Will Scarlet." Robin took the slop pail from his sister and headed out the door. "Take this to chickens so won't stink. Right back."

Shane was alone again with Mary and more uncomfortable with that situation than ever before. Having watched her bathe last night, and knowing how powerful his hankering had become, he didn't quite know what to say to her now. As soon as Robin returned and Tuck retired for the night, he'd slip out to meet Sam. For now, he was stuck here with a woman who made his blood burn.

"Mary." He wanted—ached—to touch her. "Thanks again for helping me get well."

She stood mere inches from him, gazing up into his eyes with an expression that stole his breath. Shane flexed his fingers several times, but he couldn't prevent himself from reaching out to touch the softness of her cheek with the backs of his fingers.

"You're so beautiful," he whispered.

She bit her lower lip, and lowered her inky lashes to rest against her rosy cheeks. After a moment, she looked up at him again, her expression smoldering with the same fierce need that swept through him.

God, help him.

"Mary . . ." He brushed his thumb across the fullness of her lower lip, but she didn't shy away as he'd feared. Instead, she reached up and captured his hand with hers and turned until her lips were pressed against his palm.

Tingling fingers of need spiraled through Shane, but he held himself back. Guarded. Cautious. He mustn't frighten her. She'd taken this step and nearly waylaid him on the spot, but he would suffer in silence before he'd risk undoing this small progress.

"You're so beautiful," he repeated, still caressing her cheek. Slowly, he eased his hand to the back of her neck, teasing the soft, delicate hairs. He urged her closer cautiously, careful not to exert too much pressure. He wanted her against him willingly. "An angel."

Mary floated on a cloud of sensation. Strange and powerful urges oozed through her as she inched closer to Will. The feel of his callused fingers against the back of her neck sent rivulets of desire trickling down her spine, igniting every inch of her to a fever pitch. She didn't allow herself to think—only to want.

To need.

His breath was a warm caress against her face, and she inhaled his essence. She wanted to smell him, touch him, taste him. Nothing else mattered except finding his lips with her own. Nothing.

She stood on tiptoe to reach his mouth, keeping her trembling hands fisted in the loose fabric of her breeches, not trusting herself to touch him. Only lips. For now.

Hesitating less than an inch from his mouth, she opened her eyes and gazed into his. He took a step, bringing his chest so close to hers she could feel his body heat spanning the short distance. With a sigh, she brought her hands to his shoulders and leaned into him. The shock of feeling his hard length against her was wondrous, and she sought his lips with hers. Seeking. Asking. Giving.

Driven by pure sensation, Mary kissed him and felt him kiss her in turn. His tongue traced the seam of her lips and she shivered, opening her mouth on a gasp. Gently, he urged her closer still, and deepened their kiss. His tongue performed an enticing dance with hers, and she wound her arms around his neck to bring him more fully against her.

So warm. So exciting. Mary's breasts swelled against his solid chest, aching and hungry for his touch. Heat suffused her, dampening her most private place, and urging her to cling to his powerful body.

This was her first *real* kiss. That knowledge made her tingle all over as he placed his other hand around her waist. He stroked her rib cage, gently kneading her as his mouth continued to explore hers. She could kiss him forever like this, because she felt no fear. His embrace was gentle yet passionate, with no hint of violence.

Yes, forever.

"Ooooooh."

Robin's voice made Mary jerk away from Will. She turned to face her brother, stunned to find Tuck at his side. Looking from Robin's wide blue eyes to Tuck's, Mary covered her mouth with her hand. "I . . . I . . ."

"There, there, Mary," Tuck said, clicking his heels together. "No need to apologize." The little man's eyes twinkled merrily. "Though I may have to ask Will if his intentions are honorable."

"Intentions?" Mary looked back over her shoulder and saw Will's wary expression, then faced Tuck again. "Oh." She didn't know what to say. A chill chased itself through her body, and her cheeks burned. "I . . ."

"It was my fault," Will said from behind her, but she didn't dare look at him. "Entirely."

"No, I . . ." What could she say? Mary drew a shuddering breath and searched her brother's face again. He was smiling. *Smiling*. "Robin, I—"

"Like me and Sunshine," he said smugly, his grin widening. "I like kissing."

Tuck cleared his throat and gave a short bow. "I believe I'll retire for the evening." Whistling, he left them.

Robin was still grinning.

Will stepped around Mary, giving her shoulder a squeeze as he turned to face her. "I'm going outside before turning in," he said. "And *I'll* sleep on the floor tonight."

Forcing herself to meet his gaze, Mary held her breath and nodded. The intensity of his gaze sent sparks of renewed longing straight to her womanly core. This man had touched her. Kissed her.

Intimately.

And she hadn't been afraid. She still wasn't, because she knew without a doubt that this was different. So very, very different. "Good night," she whispered.

He winked at her and flashed that lethal grin again. Mary returned his smile shamelessly. Wantonly. For the first time since her nightmare, she felt pretty. She wanted to *be* pretty.

For Will.

Shane looked up at the sky, grateful for the moonlight. This was the first time he'd been outside since arriving, and he'd been worried about finding the outhouse on instinct alone.

Afterward, he scanned the area as far as he could see and spotted a small building he assumed was the soddy Sam had mentioned. Moving slowly with the assistance of his walking stick, he eased into the shadows of the bordering forest to avoid detection. His discussion with Sam had to be completely secret.

The flare of a match startled Shane and he stopped, seeing enough of the man's face in the light to identify it as Tuck's. So much for being able to get to Sam undetected. Shane'd have to try again later.

But as he turned to head back to the cabin, the sound of boots crunching gravel stayed him. He pivoted toward where he'd seen Tuck lighting his pipe and made out the shape of a much taller man.

Sam.

"I'd like a word with you," Sam said to Tuck in a low voice.

Shane swallowed hard, certain no one had seen him. He moved closer through the trees, thankful for the quiet moccasins.

Spying on Sam was low, but Shane figured that might be the only way to find out why the lawman had let the Merry Men remain free. Besides, Shane was already here.

Tuck puffed on his pipe for several silent moments, then said, "Speak your piece, Marshal."

"I know who you are . . . Smith."

More silence. *Smith?*

"I'm listening," Tuck said.

"You're Ichabod Smith, the famous scientist who's been missing for over ten years."

"Famous?" Tuck barked a bitter laugh.

Ichabod Smith? Of course, Shane should've remembered. Smith's disappearance had been in all the newspapers about the time his family moved from Texas to Colorado.

Sam sat on the front stoop of what Shane now recognized as Tuck's cabin, and Tuck—rather, Smith—dropped down beside him. Another few feet in that direction and Shane would've been seen before he ever found

Sam anyway. Then he would've missed this. He turned his attention back to the two men and listened.

"All right, Marshal, so you know who I am." Tuck released a long sigh. "How do you plan to *use* that information?"

Tuck was the brains behind the Merry Men. Shane knew that beyond any doubt, and Sam knew it, too. And Shane was about to find out why his idol had allowed criminals to remain free.

"Pretty simple, really," Sam said, his tone casual and friendly. And disarming. "The Merry Men go into retirement—*permanent* retirement—and I never tell a soul where you are. You can stay dead to the rest of the world, if that's what you really want."

Sam, you slick son of a—

Tuck chuckled quietly. "What makes you think I'm in charge here?"

"I ain't stupid."

"No, you certainly aren't," Tuck allowed. "In fact, you're a lot smarter than you look, Marshal."

"Oh, I ain't finished yet."

Sam's voice was so quiet Shane could barely hear him now, and every instinct screamed that he *must* hear this. He craned his neck, concentrating on every syllable.

Would Sam reveal Shane's identity?

No. Shane trusted that lawman with his life—with good reason. He wouldn't betray Shane. A more honorable man than Sam Weathers had never walked this earth.

Something about all this reminded Shane of Zeke Judson back in Redemption—a man sentenced to hang for executing the murderers of his sister and mother. Zeke hadn't deserved to hang, and Sam had found a way to prevent it. An honorable way. What had the lawman said earlier when Shane had questioned him about Robin and the Merry Men?

"Priorities, I reckon. It's somethin' a man's gotta learn

*for himself, but if you dig real deep and remember every-
thing that happened back in Redemption, you might find
your answer. A man—even a lawman—has to pick his
battles in this life."*

Yes, Shane understood that all too well, but would he
ever be as smart about people as Sam Weathers? Since
Robin and Little John couldn't possibly understand that
what they'd been doing was criminal, how could they be
held responsible? Even so, Shane had been prepared to
arrest them, because it was his duty. Judge Parker would've
decided whether or not to forgive or punish them. But
as long as the stealing stopped, wasn't that all that really
mattered?

Sam was brilliant.

"You're procrastinating, Marshal," Tuck said after
several silent moments.

"Big words won't help you, Smith, and I ain't the only
one who's stallin'."

"Touché, Marshal."

"You recollect a gypsy lady named Fatima?"

Shane recognized that legendary cunning in Sam's
voice now. He was moving in for the kill.

"Quite a looker," Sam said.

"What of her?" Tuck's voice sounded strained now.
Apparently Sam had played his hand well.

"I reckon you know already."

But I don't. Frustration made Shane squeeze his eyes
shut for several seconds. Sam was playing one of his
famous head games with Ichabod Smith, and Shane would
have to wait and get all the details later. *Damn.*

"What is your point, Marshal?" Tuck asked, his voice
laced heavily with irritation. "What price, pray tell, will
your silence cost me?"

"I already told you . . . Tuck."

"That's all?"

"That's all." Sam stood, moonlight flashing off his

badge. "The Merry Men never—and I do mean *never*—commit another crime, and I'll forget I ever laid eyes on Ichabod Smith. Or . . . Adam Bigg."

Adam Bigg? What the—

"Well, well, well." Tuck stood beside Sam, though he didn't even reach the lawman's waist. "You've really done your homework well, Marshal."

"That's a fact."

"I guess I don't have much of a choice."

"That's a fact."

"What if the, uh, Merry Men decide to take off on their own without me, Marshal?"

"Then the world will know where to find you so fast you won't have time to fly away."

"Interesting choice of words." Tuck sighed again. "You're holding me accountable for the Merry Men, no matter what?"

"That's the size of it. Yep."

Shane had no idea who Adam Bigg was, but he'd definitely heard the name Ichabod Smith before. What Shane didn't understand was *why* Smith wanted to remain hidden here in Indian Territory. It made no sense, as he wasn't a wanted man. Then again, maybe this Adam Bigg was. For that matter, how many aliases did Friar Tuck have?

And *why?*

"We got us a deal, Smith?"

Tuck puffed on his pipe, then thrust out his hand. "We do."

"Good, then I'll be on my way at sunup," Sam said, shaking Tuck's hand. "But if I hear tell of *any* more stealin' from the rich and givin' to the poor . . ."

"Understood, Marshal."

"Good enough." Sam nodded and walked away. Tuck stared after him for several moments, then went into his cabin and closed the door.

Shane waited until he felt confident Tuck had turned in for the night, then limped in the general direction he'd seen Sam take. Eventually, he saw the dark shape of another low building against the horizon.

He paused to mop perspiration from his brow. After three days flat on his back, he was weak as a kitten. No, there was nothing weak about Mary's kitten. A sparrow? *Who cares, Latimer?*

And he had a hunch that if he stayed outside too long, Mary or Robin would come looking for him. He needed to talk to Sam and haul his own butt back into the cabin before anyone became suspicious.

Something hard jabbed him in the ribs and a metallic clicking sound followed. A gun hammer being pulled back and cocked.

"Move and you're dead."

Chapter Nine

"Sam, it's me," Shane whispered, though he didn't dare move.

"I know dang well who you are." Sam gouged the gun deeper into Shane's ribs. "You're a low-down sneak, spyin' on me when you knew I'd tell you as soon as I was ready."

Shane knew Sam wouldn't shoot him, but he released a long, slow breath when he heard the hammer ease back into place. "I . . . I'm sorry, Sam." Shane turned to face his mentor and friend. Moonlight hit Sam full in the face now, illuminating the hard set of the lawman's jaw. "I was on my way to find you when I saw Tuck. Next thing I knew, you showed up and started talking. If I'd announced my presence, Tuck would've—"

"Yep, I reckon that's so." Sam holstered his pistol and inclined his head toward the soddy. "C'mon in and have your say. I'm sure you're wonderin' why I—"

"No, I'm not wondering anymore, Sam." Shane limped toward the building and ducked to enter the earthen structure. The pungent aroma of decaying roots and grass mixed with horse assailed his nostrils. Lucifer nickered a greeting.

Shane approached Sam's pitch-black stallion and held his hand toward the beast. "Just me, old boy." He stroked the horse's muzzle, noting another horse and a small pony that must've belonged to Tuck.

Then he turned to face Sam, who filled the open doorway and stood silhouetted against the night sky. "I heard what you told Tuck, and I understand what you're trying to do. And why."

"Good." Sam entered the sod stable and straddled a bench. "Take a load off that leg."

"Good idea." Shane's leg ached, and he slumped down to sit on a saddle. "I understand why you don't want Robin and Little John to go to jail, and after living under their roof the past few days, I'm downright relieved I don't have to arrest any of them."

"But . . . ?"

"I don't understand about Tuck, or Smith, or whoever he is." Shane ran his fingers through his shaggy hair and chuckled. "Why the devil would that little man rather be here, where nobody knows who he is? Unless . . . he's wanted. Is he?"

Sam remained silent for several seconds, then said, "Ichabod Smith ain't wanted."

"But Adam Bigg is?"

"Now who's too dang smart for his own good?" Sam chuckled and leaned closer. "Bigg ain't wanted by the law, but he's definitely *wanted.*"

"By this Fatima I heard you mention?" Shane was still confused, but he had more important things to discuss with Sam.

"Let's just say she's been lookin' for him a long spell." Sam chuckled. "I figure Tuck has his reasons for not wantin' to be found, and as long as he does as he promised, his secret will die with me." The lawman gave Shane an assessing look. "Well, since you don't gotta arrest Robin and his Merry Men, what are you plannin' to do now . . . Will Scarlet?"

Shane drew a deep breath, then released it very slowly. He broke into a cold sweat and his heart gave a decisive thud. "There are things—bad things—going on here I don't think even you know about, Sam."

"And you're gonna tell me about 'em."

"The name Angel Rodriguez mean anything to you?"

Sam gave a low whistle. "That bastard been slinkin' through these parts?"

Shane shared Sam's tension. "Yeah, many times over the years, from what I've been able to learn."

"What the hell would that peckerwood want with the Goodes?" Sam snorted in obvious disbelief. "It ain't like they're rich or nothin'."

Shane gnashed his teeth, then said, "Mary." His voice trembled with barely contained rage; his gut clenched and burned. "He . . . I have reason to believe he . . ."

"Oh, Lord, no."

In the semidarkness, Shane watched Sam's chin drop to his chest, then Sam lurched to his feet and punched the nearest wall of sod. Twice. "Why do bad things happen to good people?" Sam's voice was barely more than a whisper, though his rage and disgust resounded in every syllable. *"Why,* dammit?"

Shane knew Sam didn't expect an answer, and he sure as hell didn't have one anyway. All he had was a plan, though not a very specific one. "I think he'll be back, Sam, and I'm not the only one who thinks that." He vividly remembered Mary's conversation with Tuck. Did she have the gun in her possession now?

Sam went to Lucifer and absently stroked the horse's neck. "And you aim to be here when the bastard shows."

"Will Scarlet does."

"But there ain't no reason for you not to tell them who you are now."

Shane touched the tender spot on his temple. "I've been thinking about that, and I believe it'll be easier to leave things as they are for now." He drew a deep breath, praying he was right. "Will Scarlet will start remembering things little by little, until the time is right to tell them the truth."

Sam remained silent for a few minutes, then gave a single nod. "Good enough."

"Besides . . . my badge is missing."

"Ah, I can only think of one person here who'd want to hide your badge, though I ain't sure why."

"Tuck." Shane rubbed his unshaved chin with thumb and forefinger, the rasping sound filling his head. "It would make more sense for him to confront me with it."

"I reckon he's waitin' to see how much you remember," Sam said thoughtfully. "Or waitin' to see if you never really forgot. Either way, he has your badge to prove to the others you sure as hell ain't Will Scarlet."

"Maybe. Of course, Mary and Tuck realize I'm not Will Scarlet, but Robin and Little John are convinced." Shane didn't want to hurt any of them, but he had to watch his back where Tuck was concerned.

"Tuck's a slippery one, but I got no reason to think he's dangerous." Sam removed his hat and slapped it against his thigh. "Mary Goode is one of the kindest and most generous women I ever met, and I reckon we both want what's best for her."

Shane chewed the inside of his cheek, pondering all the ramifications of doing what was best for Mary. The woman had crawled into a private corner of Shane's heart, and that scared the crap out of him. Other than Jenny and Sam, he hadn't allowed himself to care deeply about anyone since his mother died. It hurt too damned much to let go . . .

"Well, don't we?" Sam urged.

"Yes, Sam." Shane rubbed the back of his neck. "Only the best."

"Good, and makin' sure Rodriguez is stopped is part of that."

"Don't worry, I'll take care of Rodriguez."

"I reckon things'll be changin' for Miss Mary and Robin here in the Territory before long anyway," Sam said. "The government is chompin' at the bit to open the rest of the Territory to settlement, and some of the tribes have sold land to outsiders." He released a ragged sigh. "The government never has given a damn about the Indians or about keepin' promises."

"What's going on, Sam?" Shane remembered Mary's visitors mentioning soldiers, though he still didn't understand all the implications. Sam was right, though— changes were afoot. Big changes. And Shane Latimer intended to make sure Mary and Robin survived those changes.

"You heard what I told Tuck," Sam said, interrupting Shane's thoughts.

"Yes, and I'll make sure there's no more stealing," he vowed. "I'm going to get Rodriguez, Sam. He's going to pay for what he did to Mary."

His beautiful Mary . . . The memory of her sweet lips beneath his made his heart swell with an indefinable emotion, even as the lust for revenge held him in its steely grip. She'd cared for him selflessly, giving all she could to save his miserable hide. He owed her and, more importantly, he *cared* about her.

"I reckon I don't gotta tell you that Rodriguez is wanted dead or alive."

"Nope."

"I didn't think so." Sam turned to face Shane. "I ain't gonna ask what you got planned for that bastard, 'cuz I reckon you'll take care of it, one way or another. I got faith in you, boy.''

Pride filled Shane, and he swallowed the lump in his throat. ''Thanks, Sam. That means a lot to me.''

''I ain't old enough to be your pa, but ever since I first met you and Miss Jenny back in Colorado, you been like kin to me.''

Though Sam's words meant more to Shane than anything he'd heard since his mother's death, he couldn't help wondering why Sam had chosen now to reveal his feelings. ''We feel the same about you, Sam. You've been the big brother I never had. You know that . . .''

''I do.'' Sam cleared his throat and put a hand on Shane's shoulder. ''Keep your head. I can tell you care a lot about Miss Mary, but don't let that turn you soft. Rodriguez is a killer—the worst kind.''

''I won't, Sam.'' Shane sensed finality in Sam's words, and fear shot straight through him. ''Sam, what's wrong? I can tell some—''

''Ah, it's nothin'.'' Sam patted Shane's shoulder and turned toward the door. ''I just been workin' too hard since . . .''

''I know.'' Shane pushed to his feet and stopped in front of Sam. ''You be careful with Landen.'' He put out his hand.

Sam shook Shane's hand, then grabbed him in a bear hug and pounded him on the back. ''Take care, kid,'' Sam said, then released him and stepped away. ''And you do right by Mary Goode, too. Hear?''

Heat flooded Shane's cheeks and he bobbed his head, overcome with emotions he couldn't define. ''Well, I'd best get back before they come looking for me.''

''So long.''

After muttering a farewell, Shane ducked through the low door and limped toward the cabin. A light shone through the small window near the door, and he drew a deep breath of the cool evening air.

He paused a few feet from the door and glanced back toward the soddy. Sam stood near the door, watching. Shane raised his hand and waved, waiting for the older man to wave back before he headed toward the door.

Something about Sam's manner triggered a warning in Shane. It almost seemed as if Sam were saying good-bye forever. *No.* Shane shook off the uneasy feeling and pushed open the cabin door.

Crossing the threshold, he left Shane Latimer outside and again became Will Scarlet. His gaze sought and found Mary the moment he closed the door. She bent down to deposit her kitten in its box, then straightened to face him.

Her hair was down.

Desire coursed through him. Sweet. Fierce. Merciless. His mouth went dry, his palms perspired, and his heart smacked into his chest like a battering ram.

She smiled.

Shane limped toward the table and returned her smile, though it took every ounce of self-restraint to keep himself from grabbing her and kissing her again. And running his fingers through her beautiful, glorious hair . . .

"I was starting to worry. You were gone so long." Her voice poured over him like warm molasses and he shivered.

"Sorry, I . . . I wanted to walk around a bit to test my leg."

"How is it?" She took a step toward him, then hesitated, her eyes wide with genuine concern and something more.

Something terrifying. He swallowed hard. "A little stiff, but better, thanks to you."

"Good." She blushed. "I made up a fresh pallet for

you,'' she said, pointing toward the far corner. ''If you're sure you're ready to give up the bed, that is.''

Oh, he was ready for a lot more than sleeping on the floor. He cleared his throat, forcing himself to nod. ''Yeah, I told you I didn't want to put you out of your bed another night.'' *Though I'd like to join you in yours.*

Mary was a lady. He shouldn't even consider taking her that way, but he couldn't prevent very stimulating images from filling his mind. He grew harder still as he stood there watching her.

Guilty as hell.

Again, she wore the long gray robe, knotted by a frayed sash at her narrow waist. Her hair fell in waves to her waist, full and shiny. She was beautiful all over—he knew too well after witnessing her bath—but it was her hair that beckoned to him. He wanted to touch it so desperately he ached. The satiny strands were long enough to wrap around a man and woman while they made love.

Down, Latimer.

Drawing a deep breath, he scraped his fingers through his hair and turned toward the pallet. Robin snored softly a few feet away. *A chaperon, thank God.* ''Well, I'd best turn in,'' he said.

''Yes, I'm sure you're tired.'' She licked her lips, leaving a silken sheen behind.

God, he wanted to kiss her again. Leaning heavily on his cane, he covered the short distance that separated them and kissed her very gently on the cheek. He withdrew slowly, waiting for some reaction from her.

Hesitantly, she reached out to caress his cheek. ''Good night, Will Scarlet,'' she whispered, then hurried to her bunk and climbed beneath the covers.

Shane reminded himself to breathe again. He looked around the cabin and made sure he had his bearings, then blew out the lamp and went to his pallet.

As he dropped down to the soft blankets, his jeans and

belt pinched his privates so tightly he winced. He was hard. Damned hard. But there was nothing he could—or would—do about it.

"Meow," the kitten said from her wooden box near Shane's feet as he removed his moccasins.

Oh, shut up.

Moonlight stretched across the cabin floor with fingers of silver, linking Mary's bunk with Will's pallet. She lay awake for what seemed like hours, staring toward the corner where she knew he slept. Or did he also lie awake, reliving their delicious kiss in his mind?

She brought her fingertips to her lips and remembered every titillating detail. He'd tasted sweet yet salty and smelled of nothing but lye soap and hickory smoke.

Angel always smelled of sickly sweet bay rum and cigars. The thought sent a chill through her and she shivered, pulling the quilt up against her chin.

Why was she comparing Will to Angel? It seemed almost criminal to do so, yet—good or bad—he was the only other man who'd ever touched her. That nightmare was the only experience she had with which to compare all her new discoveries about Will, about her body, about love.

Forcibly, she banished the memory of Angel's swarthy face and taunting voice. Now only Will's smile filled her mind. She loved the way his eyes crinkled at the corners when he smiled, and his teeth were very slightly—and endearingly—crooked. His hair was golden, the curling tips lighter, as if kissed by the sun.

And the hair covering his muscular chest was even lighter, narrowing to a V below his waist. Shamelessly, she remembered the night she'd bathed him, and how he'd grabbed her and kissed her. How he'd looked with the blanket thrown aside . . .

She swallowed hard, heat coursing through her to settle between her legs. Her breasts swelled against the fabric of her robe, and she yearned to feel Will's body against hers. Yes, his entire body. She'd never expected to experience desire this profoundly, but it was real. Very real.

With Will, she might be able to forget what Angel had done to her. Maybe. Or at least bury it deep enough to keep it from tormenting her every single day. And night.

This night, her dreams would be of Will Scarlet, of his kiss, the excitement she'd felt when he'd first touched her, and how she'd yearned to get closer to that hard ridge at the front of his jeans. She'd felt it throbbing against her abdomen, pulsing with life, yet not threatening her in any way.

She bit her lip to stifle the cry of longing that rose to her throat. Was this love? What else could it be? She wanted to be with Will in every sense of the word.

Would he kiss her again? Would he stay here with her? Forever?

She drifted into a deep slumber, where her dreams dared to cross boundaries she wouldn't have even considered awake. And the face that smiled back at her in her dream world wasn't dark and menacing. No, not at all. The face of her dream lover was fair with startlingly green eyes and a warm smile.

With love, he drove away the darkness and bathed her world in gold.

Shane awakened with the feeling of being watched. Watery sunlight shone through the open shutters. *Not more rain.* Pushing to a sitting position, he found his instincts had been right, as usual. Little John sat only a few feet away at the wooden table, staring at Shane.

"Morning," Shane said quietly, looking across the cabin to Mary's empty bunk. Startled, he lurched to his feet. "Where's Mary?"

"Feed chickens," Little John said. "Before rain comes back. Robin help."

Shane relaxed somewhat, relieved to know Mary's brother had accompanied her. He must've been exhausted not to have heard them rise and leave the cabin. No matter what, he didn't want Mary to be completely alone until Rodriguez was history.

Past history.

Today he would have some sort of memory flash, he decided, stretching and glancing at Little John. The Indian looked worried. "Is something wrong, John?"

The brave turned enough to face Shane and gave a brief nod. Though he seemed slow, the man's eyes spoke of intelligence. Maybe Little John was smarter than Shane had thought. The Indian's difficulty in speaking might have nothing to do with his intelligence, after all.

"Something wrong. Yes," Little John said, the creases in his brow growing even deeper than before. "Father angry."

"Why is he angry?" Could the people of the Indian village know about Rodriguez? No, that didn't make sense. They would've grown angry before this if that were the case. Of course, Shane had no way of knowing how long ago Rodriguez had attacked Mary. "What is it, Little John?"

Little John cupped his hand to his ear and tilted his head toward Shane. "Not hear."

So that was why Little John had difficulty speaking clearly. Shane remembered the Widow Norman, a friend of his grandma's back in Texas who'd heard just well enough to talk, but most folks had trouble understanding her at first. Little John spoke much better than the Widow Norman had, in fact.

"Father angry at . . . at Robin."

Now, *that* really made no sense. Shane raked his fingers through his hair and paced the small cabin. He had to visit the outhouse in a bad way, and he was hell-bent on a bath and a shave today. But first, he would listen to Little John. "Why?"

"Sunshine." Little John rolled his eyes and looked heavenward. "Robin must marry Sunshine."

Uh-oh. Shane rubbed his whiskered jaw as he continued pacing, trying to put the pieces together. He remembered that Walks in Sunshine was the girl—woman?—Robin loved. Oh, yes, and Robin had said he liked to kiss her. Now her father was angry. One kiss could've grown to—

"Oh." Shane froze in front of Little John. "Oh," he repeated louder when Little John tilted his head at a listening angle. "Oh, boy," he added, just for himself. "Robin, you devil." Though this was a serious situation, Shane couldn't prevent his grin.

Little John scowled. "Not funny."

Shane cleared his throat. "No, it definitely isn't funny." He dreaded Mary's reaction. She'd been upset enough about knowing her brother enjoyed kissing Sunshine. Now, it seemed, Robin had done something more. A lot more . . . "Oh, boy."

"Maid Marian not . . . like." Little John sighed again.

"No, that's for sure." Shane looked toward the closed door, then scanned the floor for Katie Calico—far too nice a name for such a vicious beast. He glanced in the box to ensure the cat was locked away, then opened the door. "I'll be back and we'll figure this out together. Don't worry," he told Little John, and the brave merely nodded, dropping his chin into his hand.

"Robin, you really did it this time." Shane paused outside and saw Robin pouring water into an old rusted pan. Mary called out to the chickens from the far side of the henhouse, where Shane couldn't see her. Though his senses were starved for the sight of her, it was for the best. Right now, he needed to talk to Tuck.

On purpose.

Damn, I wish Sam was still here. He'd know how to handle this, though Shane knew the lawman would get one helluva chuckle about it first. Until he realized how serious this truly was, anyway. Like Shane had. Frowning, he visited the outhouse, then went immediately to Tuck's cabin and knocked.

"Enter, enter." The door swung open before Shane was able to follow through. "Ah, Will, good morning."

The midget was in an awfully good mood for someone who'd been threatened last night. *Why* would have to wait, though. First things first.

"Good morning, you got a minute?" Shane had never seen so much stuff crammed into such a small space. The tools of a brilliant scientist in the wilderness?

Tuck motioned toward a chair near an overturned crate, covered with a lamp and a stack of books. "Sit and speak your piece." The little man chuckled and shook his head. "I seem to be in demand these days."

Shane ignored the reference to Sam, since he wasn't supposed to know about that. He cleared his throat and said, "Little John tells me the chief is angry with Robin."

"With Robin?" Tuck frowned and sat on the edge of his bunk. "Continue, please. Why would he be angry with young Robin? Why would anyone? A kinder soul has never walked this land."

"That may be, but apparently he's been more than kind to Little John's sister. Walks in Sunshine, I believe."

"Ho, so the lad . . ." Tuck smiled, then fell silent and shook his head. "This does present a problem, though I can't say I'm particularly surprised. No, not at all."

"No, I suppose not." Shane crossed his arms and chewed his lower lip. "I haven't been here long, and maybe this is none of my business, but—"

"On the contrary, Will," Tuck interrupted. "Robin and Little John have already accepted you as one of them. Don't you know that?"

Shane nodded, his throat feeling unreasonably full and tight. "And you . . . ?"

"I? Well, if I have my wish, you will remain here as long as you make Robin and Mary happy." Tuck smiled, no sign of subterfuge in his expression. "I'm old, Will. They're young."

Regardless of Tuck's past, his motives, or his role in the Merry Men's crime spree, Shane knew without a doubt that Tuck or Ichabod or Adam—whoever the hell he was—cared deeply about the Goodes and Little John. Nobody was perfect, including Shane. Tuck was the right person to talk to about this.

"Like I said before, I'm new here, though I'm right pleased to hear you welcome me. Thank you for that."

"I meant every word, son." Tuck leaned back and crossed his stubby legs at the ankles. "So . . . what to do about young Robin and his lady?"

Shane's face flooded with heat. "Well, I'm just guessing, but the way I figure it, if the girl's father is angry . . ."

"Uh, yes, well." Tuck's face reddened and he grinned again. "By God, I knew the boy had it in him."

Shane couldn't prevent himself from grinning in response. "Yeah, that's a fact."

"But this is no laughing matter." Tuck assumed a somber expression, though his eyes still twinkled mischievously. "The boy has said he loves the girl, so there's only one right thing to do."

Shane nodded, though he winced at the thought of Mary's reaction. "His sister isn't going to like this."

"No, she won't." Tuck looked up at the ceiling and tapped his index finger against his temple. Then he leveled a gaze on Shane that left no room for discussion. "She'll have to accept this, though. It's what Robin wants."

"Yeah, I figured that from what he's said a time or two about the girl."

"Has Mary told you how we all came to be here? Together?"

Shane watched the man's expression for any indication that he was speaking falsely. He wasn't. "Only a little about how their parents died when she was pretty young, and that she brought Robin here so the authorities wouldn't take him away from her."

"Precisely." Tuck stood and walked to the open door, then turned to face Shane, his fists on his hips. "John and I were both incarcerated in that wretched place—a grievous error on the part of the magistrate, I assure you . . ."

Yeah, I'll bet.

"And when Mary rescued Robin, she took us along, too. I don't know what would've happened to either of us if she hadn't come after Robin."

Shane nodded, struck again by Tuck's loyalty to Robin and Mary. The man may have made some mistakes in the past—including leading the Merry Men on several raids—but Tuck's heart was pure when it came to the Goodes.

"I just want you to know how special Robin, John, and Mary are to me." He looked down at the floor, then faced Shane again. "They're the children I never had, I suppose. An old man's foolishness . . ."

"No, I understand," Shane said. "So you'll talk to Mary about Robin and Sunshine?"

"Of course. I've always been here for her, and I shan't let her down now." He appeared thoughtful again, stroking his pointed beard. "If Robin goes to live in the village, I suppose Mary will have to accompany him."

"No." Shane stood, his gaze fixed on Tuck. "She's lived enough of her life in isolation here."

A wily twinkle entered Tuck's small eyes and he smiled. "That's right, son. That's absolutely right."

That man is up to something. Shane nodded, trying to hide his uncertainty about Tuck's motives. The little man definitely had something in mind for Will Scarlet.

And Shane Latimer . . . ?

Chapter Ten

Bartholomew Goode had gone to hell. There was simply no other explanation for the cruel fate that had befallen him. Otherwise, how could he be in a place like Arkansas?

After interviewing practically every person in Fort Smith, he was no closer to finding Mary and Robin than he'd been before leaving England. The postmaster was his last hope.

He withdrew Mary's most recent letter from his vest pocket and passed it to the bespectacled man. "I'm looking for my niece and nephew," he began. "This letter was posted from here."

The man took the envelope and squinted at it. "That don't mean nothin'."

"But—"

"Folks bring mail here from all over the Territory, and letters posted in Tahlequah end up here, too." With a shrug, he gave the envelope back to Bartholomew. "Try the law. Maybe they can help."

Nodding, Bartholomew returned the letter to his pocket

and walked out into the waning sunlight. He was desperate enough to try anything by now, so he dragged his nearly destitute self toward the city jail.

After eight long years of lying in bed, unable to speak, walk, or write, Bartholomew's father had finally passed away in his sleep. While the physician said it was a blessing that the old man no longer had to suffer, Bartholomew found himself in somewhat of a pickle. Though he'd had free access to his father's fortune all this time, thanks to the family solicitor's cooperation, now that the senior Goode was gone, his will went into effect.

And Bartholomew's creditors beat a steady path to his door, demanding long overdue payments.

Unfortunately, the old man had suffered his debilitating stroke immediately after receiving word of his eldest son Lawrence's demise in the wilds of America. Therefore, Lawrence's progeny were the legal heirs to every bloody farthing.

Correction—Lawrence Goode's *missing* progeny.

Bartholomew thought back to all the letters his father had received from Mary over the years, pleading for his help. Had Bartholomew been present instead of exploring in India, he might have been able to find them more easily. Instead, he hadn't learned of the correspondence until after his father's death.

He cleared his throat and tugged on his collar. But now he had no choice but to find the children and persuade them to sign away their rightful inheritance to their adoring uncle. Otherwise, Bartholomew's creditors would ensure the children had no uncle left alive at all. Then where would they be?

Right where they have been all this time, you dolt.

Of course, he would have to see to their care. And he would. He definitely would. Guilt was not an easy companion, and Bartholomew was eager to part company with that pesky little emotion.

He paused on a street corner and gazed at the wanted posters decorating the sheriff's office window. All the outlaws looked alike—bearded, bedraggled, and bad.

But one poster differed from the others. "Robin Hood and his Merry Men?"

Bartholomew moved closer and peered through the glass at the crude sketch of a giant Indian, a dwarf, and an average-sized man with a feather in his cap. *Interesting-looking trio.* It was impossible to see their faces clearly, but their bizarre variations in size certainly set them apart.

Remembrance tugged at him, augmenting his guilt. *The Merry Adventures of Robin Hood* had been his brother's favorite tale, and the reason Lawrence's somewhat obtuse son bore the name Robin.

A woman paused beside him and Bartholomew tipped his hat. She was tall and garbed in garish attire, but when she looked at him, her beauty caught him unaware. She stood there, silently staring at him, and squinting through dark, exotic eyes. Her dusky skin was flawless, despite the striking silver of her hair.

"You've come at last," she said in a sultry voice with the barest trace of a Mediterranean accent.

"Pardon me, madam?" Bartholomew shook his head. "I don't believe we've met." That wasn't true. He knew bloody well they hadn't met, because he would've remembered such a striking creature.

She said, "Wait here, I'll only be a moment." She went into the sheriff's office and returned a moment later with a copy of the wanted poster at which Bartholomew had been staring. "Come."

The woman began to walk away without a backward glance. Bartholomew looked quickly at the poster again, then at her retreating—and delightfully swaying—backside. Clearing his throat, he sprinted after her.

She unlocked a bright turquoise door where a crooked sign read *"Fatima Knows All"* and beckoned for him to accompany her. Somewhat mesmerized, he removed his hat and followed the woman inside. The sweet scent of incense assailed his nostrils. Ah, he hadn't smelled anything like it since leaving India.

"I've been waiting for you," she said, pausing before a round table covered with a red cloth edged with heavy black fringe.

"How could you possibly . . . ?" Of course, this was obviously part of Fatima's ruse. A gypsy? "Ah, I'll bet you say that to all who visit."

The woman's black eyes snapped. "Be seated." She pointed to a small curved chair across the table from her as she lowered herself gracefully into another. "We have a mutual quest." She unfolded the wanted poster and spread it out on the table.

"How do you know my, uh, quest?"

A smirk tugged at her lips. "I am called Fatima. And you are . . . ?"

"Yes, I saw your sign." It was Bartholomew's turn to smirk. "If you know all, then you should already know my name."

Her expression turned thunderous. "I do not know your name, you pompous buffoon," she said, "but I know *why* you've come to Fatima."

Buffoon? "I beg your pardon, but I didn't seek you out, madam." He suppressed his anger and convinced himself to play her game. For now. "Bartholomew Goode, and I have no idea why I agreed to accompany you. Perhaps you could enlighten me . . . ?"

"You seek the Merry Men."

Hearing this second reference to his brother's favorite story jarred Bartholomew, and he swallowed the thick clot of uncertainty in his throat. "What do you mean?"

"Two dollars," Fatima said, folding her arms across her ample bosom. She leaned back in her chair. "Two dollars."

Well, she had him now. He couldn't very well leave without hearing her game. With a sigh, Bartholomew dug two precious American dollars from his pocket and dropped them on the table with a jarring clink. "All right, now please explain."

She leaned forward and retrieved the dollars, deposited them in her deep cleavage, then pointed at the wanted poster. "Look for yourself."

"The Merry Men," he read, then scowled at the gypsy thief. "So we can both read. Bully for us."

"You seek them, as do I." She removed a deck of cards from an intricately carved wooden box. After shuffling, she drew one card and placed it before him. "The Fool."

Bartholomew heaved a weary sigh. "I don't have time for parlor—"

"You." She tapped the card with her index finger. "You are a fool if you believe you don't need me." She shoved the deck toward him. "Draw another card."

Five more minutes, then he was leaving, two dollars poorer and no closer to finding Mary and Robin. He drew a card and turned it up beside the other. "All right, now what?"

"Me." She smiled and arched one brow. "The High Priestess. Together, we will find the Merry Men."

Bartholomew picked up the wanted poster and looked more closely. "Ah, yes, there's a reward." He cleared his throat. "I could use the money, but I have to find my niece and nephew be—"

"Did you *read* the poster, Mr. Goode?"

Bartholomew skimmed over the information until he came to the crude sketch. A giant Indian, a dwarf, and "Robin Hood." Shaking his head, he read more about the outlaws' physical descriptions. "I don't understand."

"The one called Robin Hood is the one you seek," she said emphatically.

Bartholomew frowned and looked again. "It's been many years, and he was much younger then, but I suppose it's possible." It stood to reason that someone with Robin's decided lack of intelligence would immerse himself in a fantasy world. "Yes, yes, it's possible, though I can't tell from the description or this pathetic drawing."

"You must use more than your eyes to see the truth." Fatima leaned closer. "But *I know.*"

"But how do you know *where* to find these outlaws?"

"A marshal interrogated me and I read his thoughts. *He* knew ... and now I do. Alas, I need an escort to venture into the Territory."

"The Territory?" A tingling sensation crept up his spine and danced across his scalp. "What's in this for you?" Somehow, he suspected he would live to regret this.

"The little man," she said in a voice edged with excitement and, perhaps, fury, "is my husband."

Mary couldn't keep her gaze from straying to Will, where he worked side-by-side with Robin and Little John to mend the broken paddock fence. But her mind wasn't on chores as Will slipped his shirt from his broad shoulders and hung it over a fencepost. From her seat on the front stoop, where she was *supposed* to be sewing a patch on Robin's breeches, she ogled Will's physique openly.

"Mercy," she whispered, pulling the needle and thread through the worn fabric. She'd seen every inch of that man while tending his wounds, yet this was quite different.

More exciting. More terrifying.

He swung a mallet, driving a post into the ground, his muscles rippling and flexing with the effort. He didn't seem a bit restricted by his leg or head injury now, though she knew they must still pain him.

Mary bit her lower lip. Would his rapid recovery mean

regaining his memory soon? Though it was selfish of her to hope he never remembered, she feared that if he did he would leave. God help her, but she wanted him to stay.

"He's quite a handsome young man, our Will Scarlet," Tuck said, sitting down beside Mary.

Mary's cheeks blazed with heat, and she forced her attention back to her mending. "He is that, and it's good to see him looking so . . . so healthy."

Tuck laughed loudly, and she couldn't help but join him.

"Very well, so you caught me," she said, casting Tuck a shy smile, then looking at Will again. "I find him pleasant to the eye," she confessed, then turned her gaze on her grinning companion. "Is that so dreadfully wicked?"

Tuck's expression softened. "Child, it's far from wicked." His tone was gentle yet firm. "It's a blessing, and about time, too."

Her eyes stung and she blinked back her tears. Now wasn't the time to allow bad memories to interfere. "Thank you." Though she barely understood her attraction to Will herself, she couldn't deny it any longer. After all, he had kissed her, so he must be feeling something similar toward her.

She hoped.

"It's good to have him here for many reasons." Tuck patted her hand, then turned to look toward the three men. "He's a good influence on Robin and Little John. They need another man to look up to."

Mary heard something in Tuck's tone she didn't like. "Tuck, what's wrong?" She let the mending drop to her lap and turned her full attention on her friend and confidant. "Tell me."

Tuck cleared his throat and fully faced her. "I'm an old man, Mary, and I won't be here forever."

"Don't talk this way. Please . . . ?" Mary couldn't bear to think of losing any of her family. They were all too precious. Though she continued to wait for an answer from her grandfather, as time went by she began to accept that there would never be one.

And, surprisingly, she was relieved. If he were to send for them, she and Robin could return to England, live at Grandfather's estate, be comfortable and protected.

From the likes of Angel Rodriguez.

A shudder rippled through Mary.

But Robin was happy here, though she worried about the lawlessness of Indian Territory. Still, with men like Sam Weathers looking out for them, even Robin should be safe.

A part of her still longed for a different life, but the thought of leaving this one was too painful for words. What to do . . . As long as she had her family and the derringer—which she prayed she would never have to use—she could live her life here in Indian Territory. She could be content.

Content? After Will's kisses, content fell far short of what she really wanted. He was both a blessing and a curse. A thrilling one.

"It's true, child," Tuck continued, startling her.

Had he read her thoughts?

"I'm getting old, and there are other changes coming. Do you understand what I speak of, Mary?"

She shook her head and grabbed her mending, jerked the needle through the fabric again, and stabbed her thumb for her trouble. Pressing her apron against the wound, she directed a side glance in Tuck's direction. "Yes, all right. You mean the talk of soldiers? Ruth and Henry mentioned it when they were here."

"Ruth and Henry are right, Mary. They live in the city where they get news from across the border." Tuck gazed into the distance, then faced her again. "It's a shame to think of this valley being overrun by settlers, but I fear the time is coming. It's already happened to our West.''

Mary chewed her lower lip. ''What will happen to us, Tuck?''

''I don't know, but I doubt you'll be allowed to stay here in Sherwood Forest if Little John's father chooses to sell the land. We're here now only because Chief Runningwolf allows it.'' He gave a wistful sigh and shook his head. ''The government may even force some tribes to sell to settlers. We have no legal claim here, even though it's our home in every way that matters, with or without a deed.'' His eyes looked old and tired. ''Pity. I'll regret leaving this oasis.''

''Leaving?'' She jerked her head around to meet his wary gaze.

''There, there, child,'' he said. ''If the soldiers make us leave, we'll have no choice.''

''Oh, you mean if we should *all* have to go.'' Mary released a shaky breath and lifted her chin a notch. ''Then we'll go to the village. We'll be welcome there.''

''Well, perhaps it's time you considered another sort of life for yourself, Mary.'' Tuck met her gaze steadily, his expression solemn. ''Robin is very happy here in the wilderness. It's as if he were born to it.''

''Yes, with Little John as his brother and mentor, Robin has blossomed here.'' She looked at her brother and smiled. He removed his shirt and hung it on the fence beside Will's. ''He likes Will.''

''We all do, child, though I was suspicious at first. . . .'' Tuck's voice sounded distant. ''Mary, there's something I have to tell you.''

His shift in tone jarred Mary, and she faced him again. ''What is it? Something's wrong.''

''Well, I'm afraid one of those changes is about to happen much sooner than we thought.''

''Tuck?''

"It's warm now that the clouds have burned off." He pulled a handkerchief from his pocket and mopped his brow, then met and held her gaze. "Little John went to the village last night, as you know."

Mary shrugged. "He splits his time equally between here and there. What's so unusual about that?" She knew her tone sounded defensive, but she couldn't help it. She felt threatened. "Tuck, what is it?"

"Robin told me he, uh, mentioned his feelings for Walks in Sunshine to you."

Coldness encircled her heart and Mary's mouth went dry, but she forced herself to nod.

"Apparently . . ."

"Tuck, tell me." Mary squeezed her eyes shut, afraid to face this, then reopened them to meet his gaze. "Just tell me," she whispered.

"From what Little John has shared, it seems his father is . . . angry."

Mary frowned, trying to follow this bizarre conversation. "I don't . . ."

"He's angry with *Robin*, child." Tuck covered her hand with his. "He wants him to marry Sunshine, and I can only think of one reason for him to—"

"Oh." Mary's breath caught in her throat and her stomach lurched. She leapt to her feet, her mending falling to her feet. "No, Robin wouldn't . . . couldn't . . . It can't be, Tuck. There's been a mistake. Robin can't possibly—"

"Yes." Tuck stood and placed his hand on her arm. "It can be. It *is*. Look at me, Mary."

Forcing herself to breathe normally, she met Tuck's gentle gaze. This couldn't be happening. If they made Robin marry Sunshine, he would go live in the village.

Without Mary.

She couldn't protect him if he wasn't here. She'd promised to take care of him. He needed her.

She'd *promised*.

"No." She drew great gulps of air and tried to focus on Tuck's face. "Robin can't marry. He's . . . he's . . ."

"Like Sunshine?" Tuck's gaze was gentle, as was his somewhat sad smile. "They're so much alike, Mary, and they're in love. Surely you can see that in your brother's eyes when he speaks of her."

Guilt pressed down on her, and she couldn't deny Tuck's words. "I promised," she said, faltering. "I don't understand this, Tuck. I never thought . . ."

"I know, child. It's hard, but you must face this for Robin's sake." Tuck gazed into the distance. "Love is a terrible thing to lose."

What would she do? Where would she go? How would she . . . ? "Fine, when he marries Sunshine, I . . . I'll go with him." She sniffled and swallowed the lump of trepidation lodged in her throat. "Though I can't imagine Robin marrying anyone, if that's what he wants, I'll—"

"You will *not* go live in the village," Tuck interrupted. His voice and expression were stern. "Listen to yourself, Mary. It's time to let Robin go. He's a grown man now, and you should have a life of your own—a family of your own."

"Robin is my family, and he'll always be a child."

"No, he's a *man*." Tuck stiffened and his nostrils flared slightly. "Though his mind is like a child's, his body is that of a grown man. With a man's needs." He pinned Mary with his gaze. "Needs he's apparently acted on."

"Oh, dear Lord." Scalding tears filled Mary's eyes, threatening to trickle unheeded down her cheeks. But she wouldn't—couldn't—allow that.

Memories of Angel's attack threatened, but she forcibly banished them. *Not now.* She had to remain strong. For Robin. "I don't understand any of this. It isn't right."

"It isn't right for a man and woman to meet and fall in love? I think you will understand . . . if you'll allow it." Tuck gave a bitter laugh and returned to his seat on the step. "It's ironic, really. I have the mind of a man trapped in the body of a child—after a fashion—and Robin has the body of a man with the mind of a child."

Stunned, Mary resumed her seat beside Tuck, then met his gaze again. She'd never heard him speak of his short stature in such a self-deprecating manner before. In fact, the only time he ever mentioned it was when practical matters required it, such as when he couldn't reach something. Still, his comparison made sense in a twisted way.

"I . . . I guess so." She looked at her brother. He was laughing and joking alongside Will and Little John. A man talking to men. "What am I going to do, Tuck? What will I do without Robin? He's been my whole life. I guess I'm being selfish, though. If this is what he wants . . ."

"It *is* what he wants, Mary." Tuck held out his hands in supplication, then his expression softened again. "You can visit Robin and his wife."

"You'll stay here with me?" she asked, suddenly frightened.

"I've been thinking about the past, Mary." He cocked a brow. "Yes, I've remembered bits and pieces of it for years, but I'm not ready to talk about it. I left some things unfinished which I must rectify. If it isn't already too late . . ."

"Oh." She'd suspected that Tuck must've regained at least some of his memory.

"Even if you move to Tahlequah or Bartlesville— even Fort Smith—where you might find a position," he continued, "you'll be close enough to visit Robin. Remember that. And Robin will be happy in the village. It's practically his second home anyway."

Mary shook her head. The thought of leaving here to find a respectable position and living alone—totally alone—brought a shudder of terror to her heart. She'd always had Robin to care for. Living alone would be . . . unbearable. And what if their grandfather *did* send for them? What then? Would Sunshine go with them to England? Mary couldn't possibly go without Robin.

"I'll stay here," she said, knowing it had to be this way. "Close to Robin."

"That could be an option, if the government will allow it," Tuck said, tilting his head to one side and studying her thoughtfully. "We must ensure that everything is handled properly, of course."

She dabbed at her eyes and met Tuck's suddenly mischievous gaze. "If what's handled properly?"

"Your marriage to Will Scarlet, my dear."

Shane felt like an intruder at the supper table, because he knew from Mary's nervousness that Tuck must've told her about Robin and Sunshine. He shouldn't be here, invading their privacy.

But there was no way in hell he was leaving until he knew Angel Rodriguez could never harm Mary—or anyone else—again.

Clenching and unclenching his fists at his sides, he waited until she finished the blessing; then he reached for his fork. *Concentrate on the food, Latimer.* He had to stop looking at Mary, because she distracted him too danged much.

He had to concentrate on his mission. The case. Rodriguez would wait until he thought she was alone before making his move.

And Shane would be ready.

Tuck cleared his throat and looked around the table. "Robin, I noticed last time we were at the village that you spent a lot of time with Walks in Sunshine," Tuck said, smiling like an indulgent parent.

"Yes." Robin's face reddened, and he looked nervously from Mary to Tuck, then back again. "I told . . . Maid Marian."

It was Mary's turn to blush. "Yes. Yes, you did." She gave her brother an encouraging, though somewhat shaky, smile. "I . . . I didn't react very well then, Robin, but I want you to know I love Sunshine, too. Like a sister."

"Well," Tuck continued in an overly jovial tone, "if young Robin and Sunshine ever marry, she'll be your real sister."

Robin choked on his cornbread, and Shane pounded him on the back until he started breathing again. "You okay there, partner?"

Robin cleared his throat and nodded. "Married?" He looked at Mary again. "Like Mother and Father?"

Mary's blush deepened, but she nodded and smiled nervously. "Just like Mother and Father, Robin."

Her eyes glittered, and Shane feared she would start to cry at any moment. He knew how hard this was for her. "Is . . . that what you want, Robin?" Shane asked, meeting Mary's gaze and relieved she didn't seem angry with him for his interference. "Really?"

Robin pursed his lips into a tight line and looked around the table at them all. Even Little John had abandoned his meal to listen to the conversation.

"Yes," Robin finally said. "Marry Sunshine."

A stifled sob erupted from Mary's throat, and she covered her trembling lips with her hand. Shane ached to gather her into his arms, but he knew that would be unseemly. These people didn't need the likes of him butting into their private business any more than he already had.

Robin rose and patted his sister's shoulder. "Mary, be happy?"

His expression was so filled with hope, even Shane felt a little weepy. "I'm happy for you, Robin," Shane said, and stood to shake his hand. "Congratulations. I can't wait to meet the bride."

"B-bride?" Robin's cheeks blazed with color as he accepted Shane's handshake. "Get married."

"Well, Robin, lad . . ." Tuck winked in Shane's general direction. "You have to ask the girl first."

Little John, Shane, and Tuck all roared with laughter, but Mary only gave her brother a sad smile. Robin folded his arms across his abdomen and lifted his chin, then said, "I did."

"Of course," Tuck said, clearing his throat. "And she said yes, I'm sure."

"Yes." Robin looked at his sister again. "Mary, be happy," he said again, as much command as plea.

Shane fell silent and returned to his chair, again feeling like an intruder. Mary took her brother's hand. "I am happy, Robin, but this will take me a while to get used to." She reached up and cupped her brother's cheek. "If Mother and Father were here, they'd be so p-proud of you. And I'm proud of you, too."

Robin beamed. Shane had never seen anyone look as happy as Robin Goode did at this moment. The boy—man—enveloped his sister in a bear hug and spun her in a circle. Mary laughed, and Shane knew it was the most beautiful sound he'd ever heard. Nothing else even came close.

"So when's the big day?" Tuck asked, turning his attention to his plate. "I, uh, believe the chief would like this to happen soon." He cast Shane a suggestive glance.

Little John gave an emphatic nod. "Full moon."

"But . . ." Mary stepped away from her brother and returned to her place on the bench. "That's next week."

Little John nodded again. "Holy man come then."

Confused, Shane looked from Tuck to Little John, then to Mary. She lowered her lashes, then looked across the table at him. "The priest from the seminary visits the villages at least once a month," she explained with a sigh. "I guess it will have to be next week."

Robin slid onto the bench and looked around the table, then his face split into a huge grin. "No, now."

Tuck and Shane both chuckled, and Mary hid her smile behind her hand. Her cheeks bloomed with color, making her blue eyes sparkle. Shane's chuckle died a quick death as lust shot to his groin with sweet fury. He knew exactly what Robin had meant by "now."

Shane couldn't drag his gaze from Mary's beautiful face. His heart pounded a rhythm as old as time, echoing the insistent throbbing between his legs. This was much more than him needing a woman, and that knowledge scared the hell out of him.

And made him warm all over.

Shit, Latimer.

Yes, he knew damned well what Robin wanted . . . and why. Robin wanted to marry the woman he loved and share her bed every night for the rest of his life. Shane swallowed the lump in his throat, then lifted his gaze from Mary's mouth to her eyes again.

She was staring at him as if she knew his thoughts.

He saw confusion mingled with desire in the depths of her blue eyes. Drawing a shaky breath, he smiled, hoping to ease the tension crackling between them before it killed him on the spot.

Robin, Tuck, and Little John ate in silence for several moments while Shane continued to stare at Mary, mesmerized by the conflicting emotions warring within her, evident in the shifting of color and light in her eyes. Her tongue swept out to moisten her lips, leaving a rosy sheen in its wake.

Shane shuddered from the depths of his soul as the tight knot of yearning brought him to a new level of agony. His gaze traveled down her throat to the collar of her loose shirt, then back again to settle on her mouth.

The fine hairs at his nape seemed to stand on end, and a prickling sensation danced across his scalp. Shifting his gaze, he found Tuck's beady little eyes boring into him. Guilt displaced lust with difficulty as Shane brought himself under control. He cleared his throat and dragged his fingers through his hair.

"I assume you'll live with Sunshine at the village," Tuck said, looking from Shane to Robin. "Or have you decided?"

Robin looked at Mary. "You go, too?"

Mary hesitated, looking around the table at all of them before her gaze rested on her brother's anxious face. "No, Robin," she said, her voice tight with tension. "I'll stay here." She shifted her gaze from Robin to her hands on the table before her. "For now."

"Tuck and Will take care of Mary," Robin said matter-of-factly, then looked at his sister again, his eyes moist and his expression sober. "Come see me?"

Mary gasped, then smiled. "Of course, and you'll bring Sunshine to visit us here. I expect you to spend Christmas here with me, too."

Robin nodded and smiled in open relief. "Tuck and Will take care of Mary," he repeated, turning his questioning gaze on Shane. "For Robin Hood."

Shane nodded. "For now," he said, struggling to keep his voice calm as he contemplated the changes about to take place in Mary's life. Getting rid of Rodriguez suddenly became even more imperative. Except for one pint-sized old man, Mary would be alone here after Shane left. It stood to reason that Little John would return to the village permanently with Robin.

Mary alone? He met her gaze again and found her nervously chewing her lower lip. When she looked up and captured his gaze, Shane gulped, shooting a glance in Tuck's direction. Smirking, the little man tapped his chin with his index finger, looking from Mary to Shane, then back again.

Tuck met Shane's gaze again, arching a questioning

brow. *Holy shit.* The man's thoughts were as clear as if he'd spoken them aloud. Shane had been right—Tuck-Ichabod-Adam-Bigg-Smith had something in mind for him.

That sawed-off runt was a man with a mission. Shane looked at Mary again and swallowed hard.

He was in big trouble.

"Will needs horse," Robin said.

Shane dragged his attention from Tuck and Mary back to Robin. "Yes, I still need a horse. That saddle isn't much good without one." He grinned, though he wanted to gnash his teeth and growl.

"Sing." Little John looked at Shane with complete calm and sincerity. "Sing for horse."

"Ah, I'd almost forgotten." Shane pushed away from the table, relieved to have something take his thoughts away from Mary and the condition of his privates just now. He was in what Sam would've called a bad way. And then some.

Hoping no one noticed the bulge of insistent flesh at the front of his jeans, Shane made his way across the room to the broken guitar. At least he'd be able to hide behind the instrument. He picked it up and sat on the stool near the front door and tuned the guitar as best he could. No telling how old the strings were, but the instrument didn't sound too bad, considering.

He picked a few notes, vaguely aware of the others gathering around. *Sure hope I can remember some real songs.* He strummed his way through a few chords, then picked some scales and runs. Convinced his fingers were limbered up enough, he dredged up the only song he could from his memory and started to hum along. After a few chords, Mary's sweet voice joined his hum. If she recognized the tune as "Amazing Grace," he must not be as bad as he'd feared.

Surprisingly, Tuck joined Mary. Shane cleared his

throat, then started to sing along. Robin and Little John swayed to the music, but didn't sing. Little John's rhythm was slightly off—more evidence of the brave's hearing problem?

After the last verse, Shane met Mary's gaze and found her eyes sparkling and her smile breathtaking. "Thank you, Will. That was wonderful." She patted Robin's shoulder, where he sat on the floor at her feet. "Do you remember Mother singing that song, Robin?"

Robin looked up at his sister and smiled. "Yes."

"Well, you reckon that's good enough to buy me a horse?" Shane raised his voice some for Little John's benefit.

The brave nodded. "Good. Thank you all for the loan of this guitar. I'll take good care of it."

"None of us can play," Tuck said, his dark eyes twinkling. "I think it's only right that it be yours . . . Will."

" 'Cuz you stay here with Mary," Robin added.

With Mary . . . Shane felt fire in his face, and he glanced down at the guitar. Why did this woman affect him so? His gut clenched as he absently strummed disconnected chords. Mary haunted him. Body. Mind.

Heart?

He lifted his gaze and found her smiling approval, and it was as if something slammed into him with all the delicacy of a locomotive. Holding his breath, he continued to watch her, losing himself in the joy and trust he found in her eyes.

The woman had him right where it hurt most.

And felt best.

Chapter Eleven

Mary couldn't refuse Robin when he asked her permission to visit Sunshine after supper, regardless of the impending darkness. No more than an hour of daylight remained when Robin and Little John rode away from Sherwood Forest to announce the news to Sunshine and her family. Because of the looming twilight, Mary gave them her blessing to stay the night.

Her brother was leaving her. She had to accept that, though she'd never expected to . . .

Stop it, Mary. You're being selfish. Tuck was right—Robin wanted this. The little man hadn't accompanied Robin and Little John, and retired to his cabin with a wink, leaving Mary quite alone with Will.

Deliberately, no doubt.

Though no one mentioned the impropriety of her being in the cabin alone with Will—all night—Mary knew it was so. He was no longer an invalid, after all. She would have to send him to Tuck's cabin, whether the little man wished company or not.

Marry Will Scarlet? Tuck's words reverberated through Mary's mind as she carried dirty dishes from the supper table. *Marry him and . . . sleep with him?* Conflicting emotions waged a harrowing battle in her heart and soul. She couldn't deny her attraction, though her fears were equally palpable.

"Here, let me help you with that," Will said, startling her as he carried a stack of plates to the slop bucket.

"No, you said you wanted to visit the river before dark, so go on with you."

Will's expression softened and he held her prisoner with his smoky green eyes. Her flesh tingled beneath his intense scrutiny, and she couldn't help but wonder if she met with his approval. His gaze caressed her, though she felt far from attractive in her usual dowdy attire. Self-consciously, she patted her hair and chewed her lower lip.

"Well, if you won't let me wash dishes, I'll go wash myself," he finally said, rubbing his whiskers. "And shave this ugly mug while there's still enough light to see."

Ugly? He was the handsomest man she'd ever seen, even with several days' growth of golden beard covering his face. From the corner of her eye, she watched him retrieve his razor and other items from his saddlebags.

"Be careful of snakes," she called. "I don't want to have to patch you up again so soon." She smiled over her shoulder, trying to sound—and, she hoped, look—nonchalant. Of course, nothing could be further from the truth.

"Snakes?" He gave an exaggerated shudder. "Perish the thought, fair lady."

Whistling, he left the cabin and Mary released a ragged breath.

Marry Will Scarlet?

art of her thrilled at the prospect, while her mind tried

to consider the practical aspects of such a union. He was
here, after all, and they couldn't very well live together
under the same roof without being married or related by
blood. Marrying Will would solve so many problems,
and—government and God willing—she'd be able to stay
here, close to Robin.

But the fact remained that he had no memory of his
life before his encounter with the rattlesnake and his
horse's kick. What if he already had a wife somewhere,
waiting and worrying?

She'd never forget hearing him call out a woman's
name during his delirium. *Jenny.* Who was she, and what
did she mean to Will? Mary should mention the name to
him and watch his face for a reaction. Besides, asking
him about the woman was the right thing to do. It might
trigger his memory of other things. Everything.

And it might make him leave her.

But she had to at least try. Keeping this secret from
him was wrong, no matter what it cost her in the end.
She hurried through her evening chores and wiped the
scarred wooden table clean. She glanced out the open
door to make sure Will wasn't on his way back to the
cabin yet. Long shadows stretched across the floor when
she lit the lamp and retreated behind the curtain in the
corner to freshen up.

She studied her reflection in the cracked mirror. Her
color was high, which made her eyes brighter than usual.
She bit her lips to make them rosier, then retrieved the
only dress she owned.

What am I doing?

She closed her eyes, praying for guidance and strength,
for she knew exactly what she was doing. Mary Elizabeth
Goode was setting her cap for a man. God help her.

With trembling fingers, she unbuttoned her baggy shirt
and trousers, sponged herself off, then slipped the lavender
broadcloth shirtwaist over her head and fastened the tiny

buttons. When Robin and Tuck had presented her with
the gift for her last birthday, she hadn't known where or
when she'd ever wear it. But suddenly she had two reasons
to wear it. Her brother's wedding . . .

And her first attempt at wooing a suitor.

Dear Lord.

Her hands shook so badly, it was a miracle she managed
the buttons at all. Finally, she closed the last one, then
shrugged as she recklessly reopened the top two. A trickle
of giddy delight lapped through her. Such brazen behavior . . . Even so, it felt right for this occasion.

She loosened her braids, remembering Will's remarks
about her hair, and brushed it vigorously until it shim-
mered in the lamplight. Her reflection looked like someone else entirely. Mary Goode would never wear her hair
loose like this. She looked positively . . . wanton.

Seductive?

What had come over her? She reached for her brush,
intending to rebraid her hair, but hesitated. Looking up,
she met her own gaze in the silver and drew a shaky
breath.

She could do this—she *would* do this. It made sense,
and it was the right thing to do. Robin was beginning a
new life of his own which didn't include her, and if she
wished to remain near him, she would need a husband's
protection.

A bitter laugh escaped her lips, but she quickly silenced
it. How odd that she should need protection, when she'd
always been the protec*tor*. Robin's . . .

No, she wasn't doing this because she needed Will's
protection, though his presence might deter Angel from
bothering her ever again. "Be honest, Mary," she whispered. "You're doing this because you *want* to."

A fierce surge of determination shot through her, and
she threw back her shoulders and lifted her chin. Will
Scarlet was the first man to awaken these urges within

her. Since her parents' deaths, every man beyond her family had either frightened or harmed her.

This might be her only chance. Her *last* chance.

She had no rosewater or anything that smelled pretty enough for Will, not even vanilla extract. She snapped her fingers, remembering the spices Tuck had brought her. She hurried to the small shelf near the hearth and retrieved the can of precious cinnamon. It would smell nice and was almost the same color as her hair, so it wouldn't show too badly. She sprinkled some into her palm, then rubbed her hands together and ran her fingers through her hair, distributing the spicy aroma, careful not to get it in her eyes. Then she returned to her makeshift dressing room and brushed the unusual perfume through her hair.

For good measure, she bit her lips and pinched her cheeks, then stood back to survey the results. For a woman who had deliberately tried to make herself unappealing, she didn't look half bad. Almost pretty, in fact.

The fluttering sensation began in her stomach again, and she held her breath for a few terrifying moments. Will would return soon, and he would know she'd gone to all this trouble for him. How could he not, considering how she'd looked a few minutes ago? Diffidence shoved against her again, but she banished it quickly and cleanly. Now was not the time to permit her insecurities to interfere.

Tuck was right. She should marry Will Scarlet. *God help me.* Girding her resolve, she stepped onto the porch and settled herself on the step to watch the sunset. Arches and streaks of color reached across the sky, painting a picture so lovely it stole her breath. The few clouds mingling with the waning sunlight augmented the colors, prisming into shards of varying shades and degrees.

Perfect. She inhaled deeply of the evening air, allowing her gaze to sweep across the darkening landscape. This special piece of land where prairie met forest had been their haven for eight long years. Would Will remain here with her forever and make it his home, too? Would he tend the land and hunt their food?

Someday, would she bear his children . . . ?

The thought gave her pause, and her hand dropped to her lower abdomen to caress the aching emptiness of her womb. She closed her eyes, remembering for a moment her relief at learning she hadn't conceived during Angel's brutal attack. Fear threatened her conviction with icy fingers as that horrid memory invaded her mind.

Could she ever *be* with a man as a wife should after that? Could she ever be with Will? Unafraid? Unashamed?

She had to try. She *would* try.

Shane thought he'd died and gone to heaven when he crested the rise and saw her sitting there as if part of this starkly beautiful land. The ebbing sunlight spun strands of red-gold fire through her dark hair. Her wonderful hair . . .

Was she waiting for him? Was her hair down for him? His gaze drifted down her length, noting the full skirt spread out around her on the stoop. She lifted her face to the setting sun, and a gentle spring breeze ruffled through her curls.

If God struck him down right here and now, Shane would die knowing he'd experienced the most divine sight a man could ever hope to behold.

"Latimer, you're in a bad way," he whispered, no longer denying the fierce hunger that shot through him. Need purged his soul and cleansed his mind. This wasn't only lust, dammit.

Then what is it, Shane?

"What—" He looked behind him, turned in a circle, scanned the darkening land for the source of the woman's haunting and familiar voice. He'd heard it. Where was she? Then he saw a silver glow in the trees. His eyes blurred, then cleared as he tried—and feared—to identify it.

Yes, Shane, it's me, she said, answering his unspoken question.

"Ma?" His whisper sounded more like a croak as he squeezed his eyes shut, then looked again. The silver glow continued to hover there in the trees. He took a step toward it.

Listen to your heart, Shane, she said, then the ethereal gleam vanished as miraculously as it had appeared.

Stunned, Shane shook his head and blinked several times. He rubbed his eyes and shook his head again to clear it. *Snake venom.* What else could it have been? His mother had been dead five years now.

No, not snake venom. With a shudder, he allowed himself to remember back to the night of her death. She'd come to him in the Redemption jail—rather, her ghost had. If not for that, he wouldn't have known that the smallpox had taken her until days later when Father Salazar broke the news. She must've known that and made certain her only son received word of her passing.

"Ma." And here she'd come to him again when he needed her wisdom, her voice of reason, her love. He squeezed his eyes shut, remembering the unselfish devotion she'd shown her children, even though her marriage had been a living hell.

Shane and Jenny's father had beaten and abused them all—especially their mother—until their uncle murdered him.

A murder Shane had almost hanged for.

Thanks to Sam, he was alive to honor his mother and his sister. He opened his eyes and looked at Mary again as warmth stole through him, attempting to banish every sliver of cold and uncertainty.

Listen to your heart, Shane.

And Shane's heart beat a steady rhythm through his veins, echoing his mother's words over and over again. *Listen to your heart, Shane. . . .*

Mary had touched him in a way no other woman ever had, and he knew this was special. He'd vowed never to marry after watching his father's brutal treatment of his mother, but now he wasn't so sure.

You do right by Mary Goode, Sam had said.

Advice was coming at Shane from all directions. Shaking his head, he drew a deep breath and faced the cabin again. Mary sat staring at the sunset, bathed in shadows and looking more fetching than a woman had a right. His heart gave a decisive flop that sent his blood rushing to his groin quicker than greased lightning.

"You've got no manners at all," he whispered, glancing down at himself. "Mary is a lady."

A lady who made him burn.

Liquid fire pulsed through him, but he squared his shoulders and tried to ignore the insistent throb between his legs. He started toward her slowly, pausing a few feet away to study her. Even in near darkness, he could tell she looked downright edible. He knew she'd taste sweeter than his first ice cream. He swallowed. Hard.

It didn't change things a lick.

"Penny for your thoughts," he whispered, closing the distance between them as she rose.

"Will." Her voice was barely more than a breath on the stillness of dusk. "I . . ."

Lamplight spilled through the open doorway, framing her with a golden halo. "You look like the angel I thought you were the first time I saw you." He reached out to wrap a curl around his index finger. "Your hair . . . I knew it would be soft."

She ducked her head, then looked up at him with a tremulous smile. "You were delirious."

"I'm not now."

"Thank you." Her words floated to him so softly, he barely heard her.

He moved closer, wishing he had a buggy to take her riding, or a restaurant where he could buy her tea. "Mary . . ."

She eased toward him, her breath stirring his senses into an inferno of longing. He ached for her, wanted her.

Needed her.

"Mary . . ."

She stood on the step, bringing her almost to his eye level. He sucked in a rough breath, aiming to free his senses, but her unexpectedly spicy fragrance filled his nostrils and produced a tremor from deep within. It served him right that he'd thought of her as edible earlier, because now his muddled brain thought she smelled just like Grandma's special Sunday cinnamon buns.

And he knew she'd taste even sweeter.

She haunted him with every breath he took, every beat of his heart. Her lips were mere inches from his and he wanted—needed—to taste her. *Now.* Following his desire, he leaned slightly forward, barely brushing her lips with his. A soft moan emerged from her, fueling his hunger until he thought he'd burst into flames right here and now.

Then she stiffened and pulled away. "You'd better put away your things," she said, hurrying into the cabin. Out of reach.

Shane felt as if he'd been gutshot. Drawing great gulps of air into his starving lungs, he summoned enough self-control to get himself up the steps and into the cabin. After returning his razor and clothing to his saddlebag, he turned to find her standing there. Staring. She looked small, vulnerable. He shouldn't press his advantage.

Shouldn't, be damned. No, that wicked voice belonged to his cock, and he reminded himself, with difficulty, who was boss. His body flinched in response, but he chose to ignore the physical anarchy as best he could—piss-poor at best, but a noble fight.

The light was better in here, enabling him to see her much more clearly, but Shane had a crazy urge to take her back outside beneath the stars. "It's warm. Walk with me?"

She blushed and gave a quick nod. "I . . . I'd like that."

Shane offered her his arm and ushered her out the door. They paused on the stoop, and he drew a deep breath. "It sure is pretty here."

"Yes."

He looked down and met her gaze. The three-quarter moon chose that moment to peep over the horizon, bathing her face and the land in silver. She tilted her face toward the moonlight and smiled.

"Not as pretty as you." His voice sounded hoarse, odd even to his ears.

She lowered her lashes, then turned her smile on him. Her smile was both a gift and a curse. Shane couldn't keep his hands to himself a moment longer. He stroked her cheek with the backs of his fingers. "Soft."

"Will, I have something to tell you." Her tremulous voice poured over him.

"I'm listening."

Her smile faded and she bit her lower lip. "I should've told you sooner, but . . . but I didn't really remember it until this evening."

She sounded worried. "What is it, Mary? What's wrong?"

"I . . ." She sighed, then set her lips in a thin line of determination. "You spoke a woman's name while your fever was so high."

Worry sliced through Shane, and he dropped his hands to his sides. "I did?" The last thing he wanted was for Mary to realize he'd been lying about his loss of memory.

He wanted to tell her himself soon. Very soon. "What name?"

"Jenny." Her lower lip trembled, and she cleared her throat. "Who is Jenny, Will? Is she . . . your wife?"

"Jenny?" He ran his fingers through his hair and tried to decide. Should he blurt out the truth now, or a little at a time? *Take it slow, Latimer.* Mary was too special—he couldn't risk hurting or frightening her. Especially not before he figured out his own feelings.

Listen to your heart, Shane.

Well, his heart said to allow "Will Scarlet's" memory to return gradually. This was the perfect opportunity to make his first step toward recovery. And buy Shane enough time to make sure Rodriguez was playing poker with Satan, instead of preying on innocent women. Like Mary.

"Jenny," he echoed. "Jenny." He rubbed his forehead and hoped he looked like a man struggling to remember. "Sister? Yes, she's my *sister,* Mary." He flashed her a grin. "I remembered something. I really remembered."

"Your . . . sister?" She gave him a weak smile. "You're sure? Absolutely sure?"

He rubbed his forehead again, then nodded with a sigh as he met her wary gaze. "I even remember what she looks like, but I still can't remember my name."

"This is wonderful, Will," she said with a decided lack of enthusiasm. "Truly wonderful."

"This is a good sign, I'll bet." He smiled, wanting her to be happy despite her brother's pending marriage. "I'll remember more now."

"Yes, I'm sure you will." She averted her gaze, gripping her hands together tightly. "Then you'll want to go home, wherever that is."

Home? Shane's heart swelled to near bursting. Sure, he missed Jenny and Grandma, but couldn't imagine anywhere without Mary. He wanted to gather her into his arms, to promise her the moon and the stars, to swear he'd never leave. He wanted to touch her, to taste her, to possess her in every way.

"Pretty Mary," he said. "Look at me."

She met his gaze and blinked several times; then her lips suddenly curved into the sweetest smile he'd ever seen. "I don't want to waste a mo-moment," she whispered, a threatening catch in her voice.

God, please don't let her cry.

"Kiss me, Will," she invited. "Kiss me."

And he damned near died.

"We didn't walk very far," he teased, inching closer even as he spoke and trying to sound casual, though he could barely breathe.

Her giggle floated on the evening breeze, surrounding him in a cloud of need so potent it nearly drove him to his knees. He brought his hands to her cheeks, then wove his fingers through her silky hair.

"Sweet."

Mary held her breath as his mouth drew nearer. She wanted him so much she could scarcely breathe or think. By the time Will's mouth found hers, she was desperate. Ravenous. Without hesitation, she parted her lips and welcomed him. He consumed her like a man half-starved—like a lost soul who'd come home at last.

To her.

Though his hands remained gentle, his mouth did not. The urgency of his mouth brought her simmering cravings to a rolling boil, and she returned his kiss with equal fervor. Giving. Taking. Sharing.

Whimpering, she threw her arms around his neck, and his came down around her shoulders, holding her firmly, intimately, against him. Her softness melded against the hard planes and angles of his body, and she knew an incredible hunger for more. Much more.

His hands slid down her back to her waist, and she

Take advantage of this offer to enjoy Zebra's newest line of historical romance novels....Splendor Romances (formerly Lovegrams Historical Romances)- Take our introductory shipment of 4 romance novels -Absolutely Free! (a $19.96 value)

Now you'll be able to savor today's best romance novels without even leaving your home with our convenient and inexpensive home subscription service. Here's what you get for joining:

- 4 BRAND NEW bestselling Splendor Romances delivered to your doorstep every month
- 20% off every title (or almost $4.00 off) with your home subscription
- FREE home delivery
- A FREE monthly newsletter, *Zebra/Pinnacle Romance News* filled with author interviews, member benefits, book previews and more!
- No risks or obligations...you're free to cancel whenever you wish...no questions asked

To get started with your own home subscription, simply complete and return the card provided. You'll receive your FREE introductory shipment of 4 Splendor Romances and then you'll begin to receive monthly shipments of new Zebra Splendor titles. Each shipment will be yours to examine for 10 days and then if you decide to keep the books, you'll pay the preferred home subscriber's price of just $4.00 per title. That's $16 for all 4 books with FREE home delivery! And if you want us to stop sending books, just say the word...it's that simple.

4 FREE books are waiting for you!
Just mail in the certificate below!

If the certificate is missing below, write to:
Splendor Romances, Zebra Home Subscription Service, Inc.,
P.O. Box 5214, Clifton, New Jersey 07015-5214
or call TOLL-FREE 1-888-345-BOOK

SP10B9

FREE BOOK CERTIFICATE

Yes! Please send me 4 Splendor Romances (formerly Zebra Lovegram Historical Romances), ABSOLUTELY FREE! After my introductory shipment, I will be able to preview 4 new Splendor Romances each month FREE for 10 days. Then if I decide to keep them, I will pay the money-saving preferred publisher's price of just $4.00 each... a total of $16.00. That's 20% off the regular publisher's price and there's never any additional charge for shipping and handling. I may return any shipment within 10 days and owe nothing, and I may cancel my subscription at any time. The 4 FREE books will be mine to keep in any case.

Name _____

Address _____ Apt. _____

City _____ State _____ Zip _____

Telephone ( ) _____

Signature _____
(If under 18, parent or guardian must sign.)

Terms and prices subject to change. Orders subject to acceptance by Zebra Home Subscription Service, Inc. .
Zebra Home Subscription Service, Inc. reserves the right to reject or cancel any subscription.

SPLENDOR ROMANCES

ZEBRA HOME SUBSCRIPTION SERVICE, INC.

120 BRIGHTON ROAD

P.O. BOX 5214

CLIFTON, NEW JERSEY 07015-5214

lll..l...lll....ll.l.l.l.l...l.l...ll.l...ll.l.l.l.l

leaned into him, taking his mouth with everything she had, everything she could give. Heavy and aching, her breasts flattened against his chest, and her hips met his completely. Daringly. She hadn't owned a petticoat in years, and as she became aware of the long, hard ridge at the front of his jeans, she was glad.

Once upon a time, she would've fainted or bolted in terror. But this was different.

Will was different.

She couldn't get enough of his warm mouth, his roaming hands. *Closer.* She wanted to feel his skin. All of it. Lost on a wave of sensation unlike anything she'd ever known, Mary entrusted Will with her body . . .

And her heart.

With a guttural growl, he cupped her derriere in his large hands and lifted her up and against him. She broke their kiss on a gasp, her lower body still pressed intimately against his. Powerful pangs of hunger shot from her dark, secret place, spiraling through her without mercy.

She would weep if Will didn't appease her hunger.

"Mary," he murmured against her neck, nuzzling and panting. "Mary."

He kissed her throat, lingering at the indentation near its base to trace tantalizing swirls with his tongue. Shivers of need stuttered along her spine and straight to her bones, which seemed to have turned to nothing more substantial than pudding. His head dipped lower, and the heat of his mouth permeated her dress and found the peak of her breast. His lips closed around the hard, sensitive nub, driving her utterly mad.

"Oh, God, Will," she murmured, lost in a heady wave of relentless longing. What had once seemed dirty now seemed her only salvation. This was Will, and he would never, never hurt her.

He lifted his face to hers again, his eyes glittering

dangerously in the moonlight. "Mary," he said, his voice thick, intense. "I want you."

She swallowed convulsively, trying to summon her conscience. If she denied Will Scarlet tonight, would she lose him forever? She wanted him so much. . . . Her mouth moved, but no words sounded. She knew he'd be gentle, that he'd never hurt her. But she couldn't banish all her doubts, no matter how she tried. Or how desperately she wanted . . .

"Shh." He eased her to the porch, her body sliding down the length of his.

"I . . ." She wanted to invite him to her bed, but the words wouldn't come. "I . . ."

"Shh," he repeated, pressing his finger to her lips. "Not yet, sweet Mary." He rested his forehead against hers and laughed quietly. "You may be the death of me yet, Mary Goode."

"But—"

"Trust me, sweetheart," he said, "I've never wanted any woman as much as I want you right now. Tonight." His voice fell to a rumbling whisper. "But we're going to take this real easy. Real slow."

Realization slammed into Mary, and she pulled away from him, staring into his eyes. "You . . . you know." Her words were barely more than a strangled whisper as icy ribbons of trepidation replaced the heat of passion in her veins. "How . . . how could you know?"

Will brought his hands to her shoulders, and his expression grew solemn. "Yes, Mary, I know." His words were gentle, but ferocity underscored them. "And—"

"How?" A violent shudder erupted from deep within her, and she couldn't prevent it any more than she could have prevented Angel's attack. "How do you know? *Tell* me." Fury and shame blinded her, but she continued to stare at Shane. She had to see his face, to know if he considered her soiled.

Unworthy.

"Please?"

He released a long sigh, massaging her shoulders with his strong hands. "I'm sorry, but while I was laid up in bed, I couldn't help but overhear things."

"Tuck." Misery and shame pressed down against her, driving away everything that had been so wondrous and pleasant a few moments earlier. "You heard us."

Will nodded. "I'm sorry, Mary, I—"

"Don't look at me that way." Even in the dark, she knew without seeing what he thought of her now. "Don't look at me with pity *or* disgust, Will Scarlet. Please, just don't."

"No, that's not—"

"I'm going to bed now. Alone." She pulled free of his embrace and stormed inside, knowing he was right behind her. "You can sleep in Tuck's cabin."

"No, ma'am," he said, his voice tight.

Mary whirled around and saw him buckling his gunbelt around his waist and putting his hat on his head. Was he leaving her? "Excuse me?"

He walked past her without speaking and retrieved the blanket and his saddle, which had served as his pillow. "I'm sleeping on the porch." Without another word, he walked out the door.

Mary followed on wooden legs. "You can't—"

"With all due respect, ma'am, if you think I'm going to Tuck's cabin and leaving you here without protection, you're crazier than me." He dropped the saddle to the porch, then spread the blanket out on the cold, hard front stoop.

"I . . . I'll get you an extra cover." Flabbergasted, Mary went into the cabin and pulled a spare quilt from a shelf behind the corner curtain, then took it to Will. He was stretched out with his head on the saddle, right across the threshold. No one could get inside without climbing over him, and with those pistols strapped to his hips, she knew that was unlikely.

Carefully, she unfolded the quilt and spread it across him, watching it settle over his sinewy frame. A lump formed in her throat, and the strange fluttering in her stomach returned with a vengeance.

"Thank you," she said, hovering in the doorway to watch him.

He tilted back his hat and flashed her a devastating, moon-kissed smile. "You're welcome. Now you'd best bolt that door before I change my mind about ravishing you tonight."

Mary sputtered, unable to form coherent speech, but he pulled the hat low over his eyes and folded his hands across his chest.

" 'Night, Mary," he said quietly. "Sweet dreams."

Utterly speechless, she closed and locked the door. Pressing her backside against the door, she shook her head. The man was positively insane. That blow to his head must've . . .

Then she remembered his words about protecting her, and renewed warmth stole through her like melted butter. She brought her hand to her lips—lips he'd kissed so thoroughly and passionately. She'd been mistaken. Will cared about her and wanted to protect her from harm, but not from pity, and certainly not from disgust.

A smile curved her mouth and she let her head fall back against the closed door with a soft thud. She'd suspected before, but now she knew without reservation.

Maid Marian loved Will Scarlet.

A red glow flared on the tip of his cigar as Angel Rodriguez drew savagely on the thin cheroot clenched between his teeth. Rage made him blind to all but the couple embracing in front of the cabin.

Mary Goode didn't flinch away from the man she called Will Scarlet. She didn't push away his caresses, nor did she avoid his kiss. In fact, she seemed to enjoy it.

Cursing, Angel flung the cigar to the dirt and ground it viciously with the heel of his boot. *"Querida,* you will regret spurning me."* Wicked, bitter laughter poisoned the sweet night air, driving an owl from its perch. The bird of prey spread its dark wings against the moon and flew away, seeking succulent young flesh for its meal.

A craving Angel knew all too well.

"You will all pay. ..."

Chapter Twelve

Ichabod Smith made a few more alterations to the design, then tilted his head to one side, admiring his handiwork. Soon, he would return to the society from which he'd fled so long ago. People would still remember him, of course. He'd been rather well known, though underappreciated.

But would anyone remember Adam Bigg?

Regret rippled through him as he set aside his pencil and stood, banishing such foolish hopes. Why would she want to hear from him after all this time? If she remembered him at all . . .

He turned his attention to the first streaks of dawn spilling between the logs where the chinking had worn away over the winter. Ah, but soon this cabin would sit empty anyway. No need to worry about making repairs now.

He released a long sigh, then headed for the door. His plans were falling into place quite nicely now, with Robin's pending marriage, Little John's return to the bosom of his family, and Mary's promising beau. After all, Ichabod Smith couldn't make his grand return to the world until Tuck ensured his family's safety and happiness.

Especially Mary's. He couldn't bear to see her play the martyr any longer. Though her motives were pure and admirable, denying herself any hope of love and family beyond Robin was too cruel for words. Surely her dead parents would not have wished this upon their only daughter. No, he simply would not allow her sacrifice to continue, and he was confident of success.

With a smug smile, Tuck opened the small wooden box beside his bed and removed a shiny object, admiring the gleaming surface as he read the words inscribed there: *U.S. Marshal.* Will Scarlet definitely wasn't the equivalent of the Sheriff of Nottingham, yet definitely a lawman.

It didn't take a genius, which Ichabod certainly was, to recognize the affection growing between Mary and Will—or whatever his name was. The attraction between those two had become clear the moment that young man opened his eyes and gazed upon Mary's beauty. And it was obvious she returned young Will's feelings.

Yes, all was going quite well. Tuck held the badge up to a shaft of light sparkling with millions of dust motes. This piece of tin could serve many different purposes.

First and most importantly, it assured him that Will wasn't a criminal, thereby making him potentially worthy of Mary. Secondly, keeping the badge hidden removed one possible trigger for Will's memory, if the lad really had amnesia at all. Pretense was a very real, even likely, possibility. After all, Tuck knew all too well how easily one could feign a total loss of memory. Hadn't he done so himself since his memory began to return?

Thirdly, he would use the item in any way necessary to coerce young Will into staying here with Mary, or taking her with him when he left Sherwood Forest.

As his wife.

Whistling the "Wedding March" from *Lohengrin,* Tuck returned the badge to its hiding place, then headed for the door. With any luck at all, he would find Mary and Shane in an exceedingly compromising situation this lovely morning. Still smiling, he left the cabin, stopped at the outhouse, then continued on to Mary's cabin. The young lovers should've had plenty of time by now to cement their liaison. *Yes, indeed.* And Tuck knew in his heart that Will Scarlet would be good to Mary, as she deserved.

Brushing a tear from his eye, he paused at the corner of the cabin and gazed at the pink and coral sunrise. Drawing a deep breath, he quashed the pang of regret he felt each time he thought of leaving this place. It was time—past time—for him to return to the world he'd left behind. Question was, which world? The one he longed for, or the one he'd run away from in the first place?

He pivoted on his heel toward the front of the cabin, took two steps, then froze. The lumpy form stretched out across the front stoop took shape right before his eyes. It even groaned.

"Curses," Tuck whispered. Will should've been wrapped in Mary's loving embrace. With a sigh, Tuck continued his journey with far less enthusiasm, then stopped at the step, his hands fisting at his sides. Why did the young marshal have to prove himself a gentleman? Glowering at the sleeping man, he cleared his throat. Loudly.

Will shoved his hat back from his face, squinting at the pinkening sky. "Mornin'."

Tuck cleared his throat again, deciding to press the issue, even though the evidence wasn't as obvious as he'd hoped. Still, it was possible. "Indeed." He folded his arms and narrowed his gaze. "What proof can you provide that you slept out here all night, Will Scarlet?" He arched one brow. "Since you didn't avail yourself of Little John's empty bunk''—*or the bed of a beautiful woman, young fool*—''I can't help but wonder.''

Will's green eyes darkened as he came fully awake and propped himself up on both elbows. ''First of all, I don't recollect being *invited* to use Little John's bunk, and I . . . I didn't think Mary should be here all night without protection.'' He threw back the covers and patted the gunbelt strapped to his hips. ''And as for proof . . . my word, and Mary's, is all the proof you're going to get.''

The lad was right about Mary needing protection, and Will's efforts on her behalf spoke well of him. Very well, in fact. Tuck had chosen wisely for sweet Mary, not that he'd had other options, but what did that matter? ''Her word is golden, of course, but I'll have to hear the truth from her lips. I shall simply ask the girl myself.''

I'm sure you will, old man. One corner of Shane's mouth tilted upward in a sardonic grin. ''You do that, Friar Tuck. You just do that.''

A sound drifted to Shane's ears as he sat up and scanned the horizon. ''Rider coming.'' He stood and looked toward the river as the horse emerged from the trees. Both hands hovered near his pistols until the figure came close enough to identify. ''It's Sa—er, Marshal Weathers.'' Wondering what would bring Sam back so soon, Shane rolled up his blankets and went down the step to meet his friend.

''Ah, so you've returned, Marshal,'' Tuck said dryly, his displeasure obvious. ''Forget something?''

Sam dismounted, allowing Lucifer's reins to fall to the ground. The well-trained stallion remained stationary. ''Was trackin' Landen, and the trail brought me back upstream,'' Sam said, jerking his head toward the river. ''Landen's got mixed up with another set of fresh tracks right yonder. Thought you might've seen or heard somethin' durin' the night.''

Shane shook his head slowly, concern niggling at him. ''You think Landen met someone?''

"Here?" Tuck added, casting Shane a questioning look.

Thank God I planted my ass right here last night. Shane watched Sam's expression carefully.

"Not here at the cabin, but right close." Sam met Shane's gaze, worry etched across the older man's features. "Maybe Mary or Robin heard something. Or Little John?"

"Robin and Little John spent the night at the village," Tuck said. "Young Will and I were just discussing exactly where *he* spent the night when you arrived, Marshal."

Sam's brow shot upward practically to the brim of his Stetson. "Oh?"

The cabin door squeaked open and they all turned in that direction. Dressed again in her baggy trousers and shirt, but with her hair tied loosely at her nape with a faded ribbon, Mary looked from Tuck, to Sam, to Shane, then quickly back to Sam.

"Oh, what, Marshal?" she asked, her cheeks reddening beneath their gazes, though her expression permitted no misunderstanding of her meaning.

"Uh, well, Miss Mary, I . . ." Sam's neck and face reddened, and he yanked his hat off his head and thumped it against his thigh. "Tuck here just wondered where Will spent the night." The lawman's Adam's apple bobbed up and down in his throat. "That's all. Ma'am."

Tuck flashed Sam a withering look, then faced Mary with an expression of chagrin. "My most humble apologies, Maid Marian," he begged, "but I'm merely protecting your safety and, er, reputation."

It was Mary's turn to arch a brow. "Oh?"

"If you say Will slept out here, ma'am," Sam said quietly, "he did. No harm done." The lawman turned his gaze on Shane again. "Did he? Ma'am?"

Shane wondered how he could possibly look innocent while every detail of the way he'd felt holding and kissing Mary Goode assailed him like a hawk diving for its supper.

Fast. Ruthless. Accurate as hell. He'd awakened hard, as usual, but after a night filled with dreams hot enough to embarrass the most experienced whore in Indian Territory, he knew damned well why he was in such condition this morning. Removing his hat, he clutched it strategically in front of the most awake part of his body.

"Miss Mary?" Sam took a step toward her. "I been up trackin' Landen all night, so I reckon I'm a mite more crotchety than usual this mornin', but I gotta hear you say the word, and nobody'll mention it again." He turned his fiercest gaze on Tuck, then softened it when he looked at Mary again. "Well?"

"Yes, Marshal, Will slept *there* all night . . . to protect me, he said." She pointed down at the porch, then inclined her head almost imperceptibly toward Tuck. "Are *you* satisfied?"

Tuck gave her a sheepish grin and withdrew his handkerchief to mop sweat off his bald head. "Yes, child. Quite."

"Well, I have chores to do, then I'll fix breakfast. You're staying, of course, Marshal." Basket hanging from one arm, she headed toward the henhouse. "If any of you gentlemen would care to tend to the milking, the pail has been scalded and is right inside the door." She didn't miss a step or glance back.

Tuck stomped inside and grabbed the pail. "I'll do the milking," he said, casting Shane a harsh look and poking him in the chest with his stubby finger. "*You* find out who met Buck Landen here last night." Then Tuck headed for the soddy, still mumbling. "If that cow steps on my foot again, we're having beef for supper."

"Bossy old fart," Sam said, watching Tuck's trek to the earthen stable.

Shane chose far more pleasant scenery. Watching the gentle swing of Mary's gait reminded him—painfully— of how it had felt to lift her up and against him last night.

She fit him well. The thought of trying more of her on for size made him swell and throb.

"You sure you slept out here *all* night, boy?"

Shane jerked his gaze from Mary as she disappeared around the corner of the henhouse. With a knot in his gut, he met Sam's half-ornery, half-serious expression. "I'm sure."

Sam cocked his hip to one side and put one booted foot on the step. "But you didn't want to," he said calmly.

Shane swallowed. Hard. "Nope."

Sam wagged his finger. "You're gonna do right by that girl, Latimer, or you'll answer to *me*. And I'll tell that grandma of yours, too. Any part of that you don't understand?"

Shane shook his head, unable to breathe for a few agonizing moments as he brought his physical response to Mary under control. "No questions, Sam." He drew a deep breath and faced the lawman. "Now tell me what's going on with Landen."

Sam's eyes darkened. He leaned closer and lowered his voice. "I've known Landen for more'n ten years now. I've made it my business to know what he eats, what he drinks, which side he sleeps on, and what he smells like." He spat on the ground, then reached into his vest pocket and withdrew the muddy brown stub of a cigar. "And *this* ain't his."

Shane nodded, studying Sam's expression. "Where'd you find it?"

Sam jerked his head toward the river again. "With them fresh tracks I mentioned." The man drew a deep breath. "Now, I don't know that both men was there at the same time, mind you, but they was at the same *place* for sure. Real recent, too."

"You think you know who that cigar belongs to," Shane stated, rather than asked. "Don't you?"

Sam nodded, then dropped the stub back into his vest pocket. "I hope I'm wrong. I really do."

"But . . . ?" Shane's heart raced, and a now familiar sensation flooded his body, deadly and sure. The need for revenge. He *knew*. "Rodriguez."

"That's how I got it figured. I'm sure as hell glad you parked your young ass right here last night." Sam leaned with both hands on his bent knee. "When I first saw that cigar butt and figured it might be his . . ." He released a long, slow breath, then met Shane's gaze. "Well, you know what I thought."

Shane's gut clenched and burned. "Yeah, I know." The words caught in his throat, ensnared by his rage. If Rodriguez were here right now, he could kill him with his bare hands.

"But I saw you sleepin' here and—"

"Now who's spying on who?" Shane grinned, though he felt like breaking something. Rodriguez's neck.

"Question is . . . *why* was that bastard sniffin' around here again?" Sam said.

"We both know why, dammit. Mary." Shane kept his voice low, though he wanted to shout and cuss. "But we don't know why he would be meeting Buck Landen."

"And that's what I aim to find out, pard." Sam straightened and took a few steps away from the cabin, staring toward the thickening trees that stood between them and the Verdigris River. "If Rodriguez saw Robin and John leave, he probably thought Mary was alone last night."

Hearing his own fears put into words made Shane's pulse thunder. A dull roar filled his head as he considered what would've happened if he hadn't been here last night. No words could describe the rage and terror he felt every time he thought of anyone harming Mary.

"What . . . drives a man to do something that low, Sam?" he finally asked, knowing there was no answer to such a question. "Why? And why Mary?"

"I reckon it's a sickness an honorable man can't understand." Sam raked his fingers through his thick, dark hair. "And I don't reckon a man like that cares who he hurts."

"All that matters is that he doesn't do it again."

"That's where you and me come in, Shane. It's our duty to stop the bastard."

"*I'll* stop him."

"I believe you will." Sam shaded his eyes and looked toward the river again. "I still can't figure why that chickenshit bastard would be meetin' up with the likes of Buck Landen." He turned to face Shane again. "Them two's as different as can be, outlaws or no. Just don't make a lick of sense."

"You know, Sam, you're right. It *doesn't* make sense."

"Rodriguez works alone." Sam squinted at him, shoving his hat back on his head. "Maybe their tracks gettin' mixed up yonder was nothin' more than an accident."

"And maybe not." Shane met and held Sam's gaze. "All I know for sure is, I'm not leaving here until Rodriguez is . . . no longer a problem."

Sam nodded. "Fair enough, and I'll pick up Landen's trail again." He patted his abdomen. "But as long as I'm already here, I reckon I oughta take Miss Mary up on that breakfast."

"She's a good cook."

Sam grinned and slapped Shane's back good-naturedly. "She's one helluva lot more'n that, kid, but I reckon you noticed that already."

Shane's ears felt like they would burst into flames of embarrassment at any minute. "Yeah."

"Well, just in case you didn't hear me the first two times, you listen now." He pointed a finger at Shane's nose. "You remember what I said."

Shane didn't ask for a definition. He knew damned well what Sam meant. "I'm confused about Mary, Sam. Real confused."

A knowing look crossed the lawman's weathered face, something like pity. "You're in a bad way."

"Thanks a lot, Sam. How'd I know those would be your exact words?"

" 'Cuz I'm mostly right." Sam shrugged and pounded him on the back. "Just trust your gut, kid. Ain't that what I always say?"

"Yeah." And Shane's mother had told him to trust his heart.

Now if only his gut and heart weren't so damned contrary.

Mary poured coffee into tin cups for Tuck, Will, and Sam, hoping her hands would stop shaking long enough to prevent her pouring it into anyone's lap. But thinking about Will's lap was the last thing she needed right now. She couldn't *stop* thinking about Will's lap . . . and other attributes.

Had she really let him touch her that way? *Oh, yes.* She slid eggs, glistening with grease, onto all their plates. One found its way to the toe of the marshal's boot, oozing yellow yolk over the scarred leather.

"I'm so sorry, Marshal." Mary scraped the egg into an old dented cup for Katie Calico, then wiped the mess off, despite his protests. Her face flamed as she straightened and found all three men staring at her.

Knowingly.

No, they couldn't possibly know. Her wary gaze collided with Will's, and her ability to breathe fled for a few terrifyingly delicious moments.

Did *he* realize why she was so nervous? Why her stomach felt as if a million butterflies were beating their wings against her? Why her hands trembled and her palms perspired? Did he know that she'd lain awake most of the night thinking of him? And that when sleep had finally lowered its soothing hand, her dreams had been about dark, forbidden kisses and caresses?

And more . . . ?

Yes, of course he knew. The expression in his eyes revealed his own need. Remembering his long, hard body pressed ardently against her, she tore her gaze away from the promise in Will's eyes and took the cooled egg to Katie, freeing the kitten from the wooden crate to eat. She stroked the kitten's soft fur, then washed her hands and took her place at the table. The egg would not be missed, as she was far too anxious to eat.

Tuck offered the blessing, then the men dove into eggs, biscuits, and gravy. Conversation flowed between them, but Mary couldn't concentrate on anything but what had happened with Will last night.

After Angel's attack, she thought she'd never want a man that way, but Will had proven those fears false. She wanted *him*. Desperately.

Marry Will Scarlet. Tuck's advice sounded so simple, yet nothing could be further from the truth. Though Will had made her yearn for him, would she be able to follow through? Even if they married, could she ever give herself over to him completely?

Consummately?

". . . a weddin'?" Sam asked.

Mary's attention riveted to the lawman when she heard that word. Then she realized all three men were staring at her. Expectantly.

"Oh . . ." She gave them all a sheepish smile, avoiding Will's dangerous gaze. "Were you speaking to me, Marshal?"

"Tuck here tells me there's gonna be a weddin'."

She opened her mouth, but no sound emerged. Finally, she cleared her throat and said, "Yes." For a terrifying moment, she'd thought Sam meant *her* wedding.

Hers and Will's.

"Well, I'll be. Robin must be proud as a peacock."

Warmth crept up her neck to her cheeks, but Mary managed a nod. She knew the marshal meant well. "Robin loves Sunshine, and this is what he wants," she said quietly. "With her, he'll be happy and . . . and safe. That's all I've ever wanted for him."

She felt Will's gaze on her, but she couldn't look at him now and remain coherent. It was as if his presence robbed her of her sense of reason, her ability to speak and even to breathe. Actually gazing into those summery eyes would reduce her to a babbling fool.

"You're a generous woman, Mary Goode," Sam said, his gray eyes twinkling.

"Thank you, Marshal. It will be hard not having Robin here all the time," she drew a deep breath, "but we'll visit each other often."

"You're plannin' to stay here, then?"

"I am." Mary stiffened, sensing Tuck's eyes on her, but the moment passed and the men finally turned their attention to breakfast again. *Thank God.*

They ate in silence for several minutes as Mary sipped her tea. A prickling sensation at the back of her neck made her swing her gaze toward Will. A mistake. He peered at her over the rim of his cup, his eyes smoldering with unvoiced questions and naked desire.

For her.

She was helpless to do anything more than stare, for his gaze held her captive. Desire skittered down her spine and settled low in her belly, warm and lush and stalwart. A tight knot of longing coiled within her, and she squirmed slightly against the hard wooden bench, but that only aggravated her need.

What he'd awakened in her wouldn't burn itself out, no matter how she wished it. Some decisive action was required, and she knew all too well what that would entail.

If Will kissed her again as he had last night, could she go farther? Could she let him touch her?

There?

The emptiness within her flourished and surged, filling her with a candid sense of urgency. Only Will had ever made her feel this way. Realization spawned deep in her soul and spoke to her mind . . . and to her heart.

Will was the only man who *could* extinguish the fire he alone had kindled. Her body ached, wept, and hungered because of him.

For him.

She drew a deep, calming breath and straightened, averting her eyes as she set aside her cup. There was only one way to find out whether or not she could move beyond the harm inflicted by Angel Rodriguez. Only one way to heal the scars completely.

She met Will's gaze, watched his throat working against his collar, admired the gold-dusted fringe of lashes framing his eyes. Tuck often said that knowledge was power, but knowing, in this situation, was also quite terrifying.

Only one way . . .

"Don't be forgettin' what I said about Miss Mary," Sam muttered, swinging his leg over Lucifer's back and piercing Shane with a stern look.

With his hat pulled low over his eyes, his easy posture in the saddle, and his badge winking in the midday sun, Marshal Weathers looked like the cover of a dime novel. Reminded of the first time he'd seen the man, Shane's heart swelled with admiration. "I will, Sam," he promised.

Sam's expression softened, and a sad smile spread across his leathery face. "Bein' a lawman seems like the work of a loner, but there ain't nothin' better than havin' a warm, lovin' woman waitin' at home."

Shane nodded. "I know you miss her, Sam."

"Miss her?" Sam closed his eyes for a moment, then looked into the distance. "It's like part of me died with her. Yeah, I miss her, but she left me somethin' mighty special." He cleared his throat and faced Shane again. "Well, we both got jobs to do."

Recognizing his friend's need to talk about something else, Shane remembered their combined missions. "Watch your back, Sam. I don't like knowing Rodriguez *and* Landen are out there."

"I know that feelin' well, pard." Sam turned Lucifer toward the river and looked back over his shoulder. "Tell Miss Mary I'll try to make it back for the weddin'. Robin married. Ain't that somethin'?" He pinned Shane with a wily look. "Wonder how long it'll be before there's another weddin' in the Goode family. Looks like a storm's brewin'."

Without another word, Sam rode away, pausing near the trees to wave. Shane returned the salute, continuing to stare long after Sam and Lucifer had vanished into the forest, moving toward the approaching storm.

Another wedding? Shane removed his hat and ran his fingers through his hair. *Another wedding?* Was that where his feelings for Mary were headed?

Listen to your heart.

But his heart was scared shitless, and so was the rest of him. He glanced downward, then amended that thought. No, one part of him wasn't a bit reluctant to pursue Mary Goode, but his feelings for her had grown far beyond physical yearning. Awake or asleep, he couldn't stop thinking about her. Wanting her. Needing her.

Loving her?

Tuck suddenly appeared by Shane's side. "I think I'll ride over to the village and check on Robin and Little John, since you're here." He looked up at Shane and winked. "Wouldn't want to leave Mary here without . . . protection."

Shane had no privacy at all. The whole blamed world knew what he was thinking and feeling. "I'll be here," he said.

"I suspect we'll return by supper. Or maybe not." Whistling, Tuck headed for the soddy, leading his shaggy pony out a few minutes later. The stubby little man climbed onto the fence rail, then slid into the saddle.

Shane watched the pony trot away, Tuck's bald head bobbing up and down. Chuckling to himself, Shane turned and saw Mary standing in the open doorway.

They were alone. *Really* alone.

She smiled, and his insides turned to mush. *You're in one helluva lot more than a bad way, Latimer.*

"Where's Tuck going?" She shaded her eyes and looked toward the disappearing pony. "He didn't mention anything to me."

"He's headed for the village to check on Robin and Little John." Shane took a few steps toward her and rested one foot on the step. "I'm glad you left your hair down this morning." *Was that his voice?* He sounded strange, sort of hoarse.

Her cheeks pinkened and she smiled again, her lips trembling slightly. "Thank you." She looked toward the southwest and frowned. "It looks like a storm brewing."

Shane dragged his gaze away from her sparkling eyes and pink lips—especially her lips—and looked at the distant sky. "It's that time of year." Having grown up in Texas, he was all too familiar with spring storms.

She nodded and frowned. "I hope they don't get caught in it."

"Tuck said they should be back by suppertime." He watched the worry lines smooth away from her forehead, and she smiled again. Had that dimple always been there in her left cheek?

Since when did Shane Latimer notice dimples? *Pitiful. Just pitiful.*

"Then they shall be back by suppertime." Mary gave an emphatic nod just as the wind changed directions. The horizon darkened into a churning wall of clouds. "That looks pretty bad."

Shane couldn't argue that point. He'd seen clouds like that before, and they almost always meant twisters. "Yeah, I'm going to make sure the door to Tuck's cabin is shut."

"Thank you."

The scent of rain reached his nostrils as he ran to the cabin. Rain and something more. Danger. He'd smelled it before.

After securing the shutters and door to Tuck's cabin, Shane headed back toward Mary. Lightning streaked across the sky, followed by rolling thunder. The storm grew closer and more ominous with every second. Clouds roiled, thrusting their towers higher into the sky, even as the darker smudge near the ground loomed lower. More menacing.

He had to get to Mary before the storm reached them. Did they have a cellar? Hazarding another glance at the sky, he broke into a run.

Mary stood in front of the cabin, the wind plastering her baggy shirt against her, outlining the shape of her breasts. All the air rushed out of Shane's lungs in a single blast. He skidded to a halt and stared at her. She cupped her hand to her mouth and shouted into the wind.

"Kitty, kitty, kitty," she called again and again.

"Not that damn cat." But he knew how much the kitten meant to Mary, so he quelled his own dislike of the critter and rushed over to the woman who meant more to him than he was ready to admit. "Where?"

Mary shrugged, her face tense. "Katie bolted out the door and headed toward the trees," she said, shouting to

be heard above the wind. "I . . . I forgot about the door."
Her lower lip trembled. "I lost her, Will. I lost her."

No, Shane wouldn't let her lose her brother *and* her
cat. One loss at a time to deal with was enough. He
gathered Mary into his arms and held her for a few
moments, his heart aching for her. "I'll find your kitten,"
he promised, hoping he wasn't as crazy as he suspected.
"You wait inside."

He lifted her chin and kissed her very gently, then held
her at arm's distance. Otherwise, he couldn't trust himself
not to stay here kissing her instead of searching for that
wretched critter.

She blinked, gazing up at him with large, trusting eyes.
"Thank you." A raindrop hit her right in the face.

"Go inside," he repeated, then ran toward the line of
trees separating the cabin from the river.

He'd never seen such huge raindrops. They struck hard,
soaking his clothes within seconds. The wind whipped
the rain into a torrent; then the sky opened and the rain
came in a solid, blinding sheet instead of individual drops.

Struggling for breath, he pulled his hat lower over
his face and kept running. Lightning struck the ground
somewhere close—too close—but he kept going. He'd
promised Mary. . . .

How would he ever find one small kitten in this tempest?
He had to try. He had to.

The trees offered some shelter from the rain, but lightning shook the ground again to remind him that was false
security. He paused, looking up at the branches. If he
were a kitten, that's where he'd be right about now.

If you were a kitten? Shaking his head in self-disgust,
Shane walked through the forest, shivering when the wind
swept through the trees, ripping new leaves from the
branches. Small bits of hail joined the rain, pelting him
without mercy.

A flash of lightning blinded him, and he staggered

backward to a deafening boom. Shielding his eyes, he tried to focus on the giant hickory in front of him. The trunk was split right down the middle, smoke hissing in the dousing rain.

"Shit."

Then a faint sound drifted to his ears, carried from all directions in the fierce wind. He cocked his head and listened, identifying the muffled meow of Mary's kitten from somewhere overhead.

He searched the branches of several trees, hoping the rain and hail didn't blind him before he was finished. That cat would kill him yet, but all he had to do was remember the look on Mary's face when she'd realized her kitten was gone.

"One more tree," he muttered. The hail stopped, but the wind and rain increased as he paused beneath a blackjack oak and peered into its gnarled branches. Staring down at him from a good twenty feet straight up was the face of a calico kitten. "How the hell'd you get up there?"

Shane shook his head and examined the trunk of the tree. He found a foothold and started up, muttering to himself in the driving rain. This was crazy, but a promise was a promise.

He reached the branch holding the kitten and stretched his hand out toward the varmint. "Here, kitty," he croaked, but the cat just looked at him as if he'd grown two heads. "You flea-bitten, no-account . . ." Gritting his teeth, he drew a deep breath and inched out onto the large branch, praying it would hold. The kitten arched her back and backed away. "Come here, *cat.*"

"Hiss."

That better mean "Yes, sir." Dammit.

The wind suddenly took on an unholy howl, and Shane lifted his gaze. In the distance, he saw what he'd feared. A small twister danced among the tops of the trees.

Heading straight for Mary's cabin.

His blood turned icier than the rain, and he scooted back toward the trunk of the tree. The cat seemed to take the hint and leapt toward him, landing on his back.

"Yeow!"

He slipped, catching hold of the sturdy branch with both hands. Dangling high in the air, he tried to ignore the claws impaling his back. The wind slammed into him, swinging him like a kite in the breeze.

He slipped, almost fell. Struggling and panting, he regained his hold and looked down at the ground, weighing his options. What he saw wasn't what he'd expected. Mary Goode stood there, soaked to the skin and holding her arms upward.

"You can't catch me. Move!"

She scrambled away several feet, and Shane felt the kitten slip, her claws raking him. She scrambled against him until she had a four-footed grip. He envied her those claws about now.

Though Mary was out in the storm with him, Shane was relieved she wasn't in the cabin. He'd lost sight of the twister, but that didn't mean it was gone for good.

"Ready?" he called down, glancing to make sure she was far enough away. He released the branch.

A hot flash of lightning blinded him. The air around him crackled.

And the ground rushed up to meet him.

Chapter Thirteen

A terrified scream tore from Mary's throat and she threw herself to the ground, shielding her eyes. Sparks and bits of bark exploded from the tree, stinging her skin.

She heard a hissing sound and looked up at the mangled tree where Will had been only moments ago. The trunk was split and twisted grotesquely; the branches bowed over to touch the ground on both sides.

Will! Where was he? Panic stole her breath. She hurried to the tree, searching for any sign. Rain continued to lash at her, blurring her vision. Blinking, she wiped savagely at her eyes.

"Meow."

She shoved aside some small branches, and Katie Calico bounded out and cowered against Mary's leg. Ignoring the cat, she dropped to her knees and looked farther under the branches. The kitten started climbing Mary's trouser leg, but she snatched her off and dropped the cat inside her shirt. The damp, frightened, shivering kitten curled against Mary's side where her shirt was tucked into her trousers. More importantly, now the animal was out of the way so Mary could search for Will.

A loud groan drifted out from beneath the leafy prison. Will was alive. Hope swelled in her heart and spurred her to action. "Don't you dare die on me now, Will Scarlet." She shoved the branches aside, revealing Will sprawled facedown in the mire. "You hear me?"

He lifted his face and peered at her. Mud covered everything except the whites of his eyes and his bared teeth. "Where's that damn cat?" he demanded, his tone definitely on the angry side.

"You're not hurt?" Mary asked, relief flooding her and making it nearly impossible not to laugh at his bizarre appearance.

"Nothing but my pride." He crawled out from under the larger branch, wincing as he pushed up onto his knees. "Maybe a few scrapes here and there."

"You ... you're ..." She couldn't hold back any longer. Laughter born as much from relief as everything else bubbled up from her as the rain washed down Will's face in muddy rivulets.

"I'm what?" He still sounded angry. Snarling, as a matter-of-fact.

"Filthy?" She hid her smile behind her hand. "I'm sorry, but—"

"Where's that cat?" he repeated, arching his brows to display even more of his eyes.

Mary patted the lump on her side. "She's quite safe." She met his mud-rimmed gaze and smiled as the rain slowed slightly. "Thanks to you." Slowly, tentatively, she reached out to cup his cheek. "Thank you, Will. You're so brave."

The burn of anger faded from his eyes, replaced by something more feverish. And infinitely more dangerous. He captured her hand with his and planted a muddy kiss in her palm. "Anything for you. Anything ..."

A thrill shot through her and an exquisite ache bloomed again within her. Brighter. Hotter. Stronger. She trembled and brought her other hand to his face and leaned against him. Will's arms went around her, and she felt him kiss the top of her head.

Cold mud oozed between them, but she didn't care. All she wanted was to feel him against her, to grow warm beneath his caresses, to savor his delicious kisses. She tilted her face up to him. The rain had washed away the worst of the mud by the time her lips claimed his.

A growl rumbled up from his throat and into her as she parted her lips and drew his tongue into her mouth the way he'd done hers last night. The wet fabric of her shirt against her breasts abraded their peaks into hard, tingling nubs.

Kneading her back with lazy, luscious strokes, he deepened their kiss until she was little more than a quivering mass in his arms. He brought his hand up to cup her breast, sending even stronger waves of longing through her. She whimpered as his tongue stroked hers intimately, making her long to feel more of him.

All of him.

Only one way.

She knew no fear as he drove her insane tracing tantalizing circles around her breast with his thumb. Gradually, the circles diminished in size until the pad of his thumb finally, deliciously, brushed against her rigid nipple. Somewhere deep inside, she convulsed and cried out for more. Trembling, she clung to him, her arms wrapped around his neck as if she were drowning and he were her only hope.

He was her only hope, her last hope.

Deftly, he released the top two buttons of her shirt and slipped his hand inside against her skin. The feel of his hand against her bare breast made her press her hips against his. The yearning within her burned out of control, and when he rolled her nipple between his thumb and forefinger, she broke their kiss on a gasp.

''Will,'' she whispered, letting her head fall backward as he kissed his way down her throat, to her shoulder.

Lower . . .

A brief image flashed through her mind of a darker head bent down to take, but never to give. She forced her eyes open and looked down at the top of Will's head as he teased her with tiny kisses along the upper curve of her breast.

This is the man I love.

A new and powerful flame ignited in her heart and spread throughout her. This man would never harm her, and though he hadn't yet admitted it, he must love her. He must. The warm glow of love permeated her, chased away the nightmare at last.

For good?

She prayed it was so, and surrendered herself to the joys of this moment. This man. The horror of the past, the taint of the demon who'd hurt her in the worst possible way, didn't matter.

This mattered. The future mattered.

Mary gasped again, stunned by the sight of Will's lips covering her breast. He suckled and kneaded her flesh, sending bursts of torture and wonder through her shocked and pliant body.

''Oh, Will . . .'' she murmured.

He stiffened slightly in her arms and kissed his way back up her throat, lingering where her pulse thundered beneath her skin. ''Mary, sweet Mary,'' he whispered.

A sudden hiss followed by a bronze and white paw sent them both sprawling back in opposite directions. Mary stared in amazement at the angry red streak on Will's chin where Katie had connected.

''Oh.'' She glanced down at the kitten's head peering up through her open shirt. Her wide-open shirt . . . ''Oh.''

Mary clutched the top of her shirt closed, but the kitten's head popped out just beneath her hand.

Will's chuckle surprised her, and she met the heat of his gaze. Her cheeks flamed, but her heart still glowed with the brilliance of new love. "I'm sorry, Will."

His laughter stopped, and his eyes glittered with a feral light. "So am I."

"Oh," she repeated.

"Not about the cat."

"Oh." Her breath caught in her throat and her heart did a flip inside her chest, undoubtedly due to all the butterflies battering her stomach. "Oh."

"You already said that." Still on his knees, he inched toward her, brushing the backs of his fingers along her collarbone, just above where her hand still clutched the fabric of her unbuttoned shirt.

Thunder rumbled in the distance and the sky darkened again. "Looks like another storm," she whispered, wondering where all the air had gone.

His hand fell away and he looked up at the churning clouds. "We'd better make a run for it."

He grabbed her hand as he stood and pulled her to her feet. Mary pulled the kitten from inside her shirt and tucked it under her arm. Before she could close the open buttons, Will dragged her toward the house.

"This one looks worse than the last," he called over the rising wind.

Mary darted a look at the agitated sky and knew Will was right. She ran as fast as she could, knowing he could go much more quickly without her.

Lightning struck nearby, and the earth rumbled beneath their feet. The light took on a sickly greenish cast just as they reached the cabin. A blast of wind slammed into their backs, propelling them through the door.

Trying to catch her breath, she dropped the cat into the crate, then closed the lid. Immediately, her fingers buttoned her damp shirt. She spun around to find Will standing in the open door. When he faced her, she knew what he'd seen without hearing the word.

"You got a cellar, Mary?"

She nodded and hurried to the corner where her curtain hung and pushed it aside, then grabbed a leather latchstring protruding from the floor beside the washtub. Will reached down and helped her lift the heavy door.

A dull roar rumbled from outside, like a train barreling down on them from the sky. Mary's flesh turned icy as shards of fear stabbed her.

"Now, Mary," Will said in an amazingly calm voice. "Right now."

Jerking her common sense free of her terror, she ran across the room and grabbed the lantern and the tin of matches. She handed those to Will, then flung open the crate and grabbed a cowering Katie Calico and tucked her under her arm.

"Now, Mary." Will's calm was gone now, replaced by an urgency that spurred her to action.

He held the cellar door open while she climbed down first and lit the lamp. A shuttered window peered out at ground level at the rear of the cabin, allowing a little light to filter through. Will pulled the cellar door closed as he descended the ladder.

The lamp chased away the shadows, illuminating the few jars of corn remaining from last summer and a dozen or so wrinkled sweet potatoes. She placed the lamp in the corner on the floor. The roar outside grew louder, and the floor above them vibrated in the din.

Something crashed upstairs. Katie yowled and leapt from Mary's arms. Mary met Will's gaze and swallowed hard. "Will, I'm afraid for . . . for Robin and—"

"Shh, they'll be fine at the village."

He held out his arms and she stepped into the protective

circle of his embrace. "Do you think Tuck made it there before . . . ?" she asked.

"He might have gotten wet in the first storm, but I'm sure he beat this one there." Will chuckled quietly. "He's a resourceful old man."

"Yes, he is that." Resting her cheek against his chest, she concentrated on the steady thud of his heart, the warmth of his skin seeping through his damp shirt. Slowly, her trembling ceased, replaced by something powerful and indescribable.

Belonging?

She bit her lower lip, savoring the moment, blotting out the horrible sounds of the storm. Loving Will was right, and she wrapped her arms around his waist and clung to him, no longer afraid.

The shutter over the small window rattled as if someone were yanking at it from outside. An odd tingling sensation crept over Mary, and she lifted her face to gaze at Will. He was looking at the window, too.

"Get down!" He pushed her to the earthen floor and covered her with his body.

The shutter vanished, and a powerful sucking sensation stole the air from her lungs and extinguished the lamp's flame. Sweet potatoes flew toward the missing window, exploding against the earthen cellar wall.

Mary clung to Will. His welcome weight pressed her to the floor.

The din, the sucking, tearing feeling, the suffocating pressure from the lack of air, were all that existed for several terrifying minutes. The destruction ended as suddenly as it had begun, followed by an awesome silence. It ended so suddenly, Mary wondered if she'd gone deaf.

"Is it gone?" She looked up, barely seeing Will's face in the light from the window.

He nodded, then cupped both sides of her face in his large hands. "Mary," he whispered. "We're safe."

His lips met hers in a kiss so sweet it made her sigh. She slipped her hands behind his neck, gently stroking the fine hairs at his nape, wanting to do so much more.

He broke the kiss and rested his forehead against hers. "Mary, I . . . I care about you."

Her heart swelled with love, and she smiled. "I care about you, too, Will."

He flinched.

Why?

"Will, what's—"

Pressing his finger to her lips, he shook his head. "Not here. I—"

Dread oozed through her, and his weight suddenly seemed oppressive, where moments ago it had been comforting. Had he remembered his past? Did he have a wife waiting for him somewhere?

Would he leave her?

He raised himself off her and pulled her to her feet. "I'll explain everything upstairs. We'd better check the damage anyway."

Woodenly, Mary retrieved her cowering kitten from beneath the shelves as Will climbed the ladder. She handed her up to Will, who walked away, then returned for the lamp and matches, then returned again for her.

The look on his face made her shiver, but she took his hand and ascended the ladder anyway. Upstairs, she brushed dust from her clothes and looked at the destruction. Not as bad as she'd feared.

"We got lucky." He placed his hands on her shoulders from behind. "The storm didn't hit directly, but it passed close."

Mary nodded and stepped around the shutter that had blown off the window. Other than a few items strewn about, that was the only damage. The shutter must've been the crash they'd heard.

"Don't worry, I dumped the cat back in her cage." Will opened the door and stepped outside.

His low whistle alerted her that she'd find more damage there. Fearing the worst, she followed him down the steps and looked around. A crooked path of destruction came from the river, where trees had been uprooted. Her gaze followed the twister's disastrous trail to the soddy. The roof was gone, but the structure itself remained. Their cow was out in the pasture, thank heavens, and all the horses were at the village.

"Twister must've danced over the stable, scooted over close to the cabin on the ground, then gone back in the clouds," Will said, pointing. "Could've been a lot worse."

Mary nodded, walking around the side of the building to make sure Tuck's cabin was still there. It was. "Thank you."

He touched her shoulder again and she sighed, savoring the moment. "Now what is it you wanted to tell me?" She had to know if he'd remembered anything.

With a gentle nudge, he turned her to face him and cupped her chin in his hand. "Let's go inside and get you some dry clothes, then we'll talk."

Unwelcome and unwanted, unshed tears stung her eyes, and she feared she was about to lose something—someone—precious. No, she wouldn't lose him. He wanted her body, and that was the only weapon she had to wield. Her source of power. And, Lord help her, she wanted him to touch her again. She had to keep him. She had to do something.

Anything.

Could she use her body? Yes, if it would keep him from leaving her. Now that she'd found him and this wondrous feeling growing in her heart, she couldn't bear to lose them. Robin was leaving, but Will would stay. He had to. He just had to.

Swallowing hard, she banished her fears. She'd found pleasure in his arms earlier, and she knew she could again. Then, and only then, could she put the past behind her for good. Be strong, Mary.

"Will?"

"Not Will."

Shane thought she might faint. He wrapped his arm around her shoulders and guided her back inside, leaving the door open to the rain-kissed air. Another storm was already brewing along the southwestern horizon, and he was worried that Robin and his Merry Men would come home before he'd told Mary what needed telling.

He gazed down into her stricken features. She looked cold and tired. An aching tenderness commenced within him. He cared too damned much, but he couldn't prevent it. "You'd better put on some dry clothes."

She threw up her hands in despair. "Fine. I'll change my clothes, but you'd better start rehearsing what you want to say, because I'm not waiting any longer."

He couldn't prevent a smile from curving his lips. This was the Mary he knew and loved.

Loved?

He had no right to love her. His smile vanished, and he closed his eyes as she ducked behind her flimsy little curtain. He should build her a wall and a door around that corner of the cabin. Opening his eyes, he sucked in a breath. She bent over to remove her soaked breeches, the curves of her sweet bottom outlined against the fabric.

The ability to breathe eluded him for a few memorable moments as he remembered the feel of her in his hands, the taste of her on his tongue. He rubbed his palms together. She'd been so soft. Her breasts . . .

Lightning struck again, but it had nothing to do with the weather. He raked his fingers through his damp curls, wondering briefly where and when he'd lost his hat. Then he could think of nothing but Mary.

That woman was lightning and thunder and sunshine. He'd wanted her—still wanted her. If not for the second storm and that frigging feline, he would've taken her right there in the woods.

And hated himself for it later.

He unbuttoned his shirt and hung it on a peg to dry, tugging at his jeans to relieve some of the pressure against his cock. Didn't help much. He'd been hard more in the last few days than he had in the past year.

Remembering her response when he'd tasted her breast, he knew he could've had her. She was no longer afraid of him, and that was the truly terrifying part of all this. She trusted him—cared about him—and if he hurt her now . . .

Damn.

When she'd called him "Will" out there in the forest, it had been like landing facedown in a mountain stream. He couldn't take her as Will. They'd both end up hating him.

He cared too much about Mary to hurt her that way. She was close to recovering from the damage Rodriguez had inflicted, and Shane couldn't mess that up now.

The curtain opened and he held his breath. She was wearing the pretty dress again with her hair down. Her bare feet peeked out from beneath a ruffle at the hem. He swallowed hard, suspecting she wore absolutely nothing under the dress.

And he wanted to see for himself.

Her hair was loose, hanging in damp ringlets nearly to her waist. "You know you're killing me, slow but sure?" he asked.

Her eyes widened and she licked her lips. "Returning the favor," she whispered, walking slowly toward the door. She closed it, slid the bolt home, then leaned her back against it, devouring him with her eyes. After a moment, she started toward him again.

Shane didn't breathe. He didn't dare.

Pausing directly in front of him, she dropped her gaze to his bare chest.

She took a step forward.

He took a step backward.

"What are you doing?" he asked, glancing over his shoulder when the backs of his knees came up against something solid. Mary's bed. Perfect. He didn't need anything that obvious to give him ideas. He had plenty.

A wicked gleam flashed in her blue eyes and she came closer, raising her hands to his chest.

Holy shit. "Mary?" he squeaked.

"Hmm?" She came full against him, rubbing her hands along his chest and shoulders.

"What . . . what are you doing?"

"You asked me that already."

She was using his own words against him, and he was going to explode right here and now if she didn't stop touching him. Of course, if she did stop, he might just die from deprivation. It was downright unhealthy for a man to walk around hard all the time. Not to mention frustrating as hell.

She looked up at him, her eyes round and shining, her lips moist and inviting. "Why don't you go ahead and tell me what it is you wanted to tell me?"

"Now?" His voice squeaked again.

"Right now." She moistened her lips again. "Right here."

"I . . . I . . ." He closed his eyes and drew a deep breath. "Mary, I don't know if I can with you . . ."

"With me what?"

"Touching me," he breathed.

"Try." Her voice took on a husky quality he hadn't noticed before. "Try . . . real . . . hard."

Hard? Of all the words for her to use . . . Growling, Shane tugged her against him, covering her mouth with his, filling her with his tongue, savoring the pressure of her hips against his throbbing body.

He needed release. No, what he needed was one hell of a lot more than just release.

He needed Mary. Only Mary . . .

She whimpered, entwining her fingers through his hair, holding him against her. She drew his tongue deeper into her mouth where his mated with hers, mimicking what he wanted—desperately—to do with other parts of their bodies. The similarity of the acts unhinged him, producing a groan and a shudder from his very soul.

Clinging to him, kissing him ravenously, Mary brought one hand back to his chest, where she imitated what he'd done to her earlier. No woman had ever bothered with his chest like this before, and Shane liked it. A lot. She rolled his nipple between her fingers, sending ribbons of fire through his veins and straight between his legs.

She was killing him.

He pushed her away, holding her at arm's length as he stared into her passion-glazed eyes. Her breathing labored, her eyes hooded, her lips parted and moist, she had the look of a woman who wanted a man.

A woman who wanted him.

His fingers shook as he released the buttons of her dress. She made no protest, nor did the flame of desire diminish in her beautiful eyes. In fact, as he slipped the dress over the slope of her shoulders, the hungry blaze burned brighter, and he dang near lost himself.

She trembled slightly as a breeze wafted through the window, lifting the curtain. The rumble of thunder heralded the arrival of yet another storm, but Shane knew somehow that the tempest inside the cabin would rival the one brewing outside. Raindrops hit the roof like bullets, slanting in through the window.

"Love me," she whispered, dragging his attention back inside the cabin. "Love me."

Her softly spoken words hit him like the butt of a pistol at the base of his skull. No woman had ever asked him to love her before. Her words threatened his sense of honor and started a chili pepper fire in his groin that promised to incinerate anything in its path, including his so-called honor. He should pretend he hadn't heard her. Instead, he heard a voice—his?—ask if she was sure.

"Yes, Will."

He winced, freezing with the dress halfway down her arms, the fabric hanging from the tips of her breasts to tease and torment him. Swallowing hard, he forced himself to meet her gaze again. He had to give her another chance to change her mind.

"I want you more than I've ever wanted a woman," he said, praying he wouldn't regret these words, "but Will can't make love to you, because he isn't here."

"I want you." She wriggled, and her dress dropped to her waist.

"God, you're so beautiful." Her hair shielded part of her, allowing only a portion of her breasts to peek through. "Mary, I . . . I . . ."

"Touch me." She brought his hand to her breast, biting her lower lip as he cupped and kneaded her delectable flesh.

"Mary . . ."

"Please?" She looked at him with the truth as naked as her breasts. "Please?"

He nodded, leaning close to gaze into her eyes. "My name is Shane." He filled his hands with her breasts, testing their weight. "Call me Shane."

Uncertainty flickered through her eyes, but passion vanquished it. The smile that curved her lips was his undoing. She reached between their bodies and loosened his belt buckle, her small hands trembling against his abdomen. "Touch me . . . Shane."

Hearing his name on her lips shattered his reserve. "Mary, are you—"

"Don't you dare ask me if I'm sure again." With the gleam of determination in her eyes, she released the buttons of his jeans. "I'm more certain of this than anything. I want this. I want you, Shane." She kissed his chest. "Shane." She kissed his shoulder. "Shane." She kissed his nipple.

That did it.

"You're ... about to unharness something wild," he warned, glancing down at her fingers. He brushed his thumbs across her nipples, loving the way her eyes widened and her neck arched. "Once you set him free ..."

She gave him a tremulous smile as the final button popped and his jeans fell open. "I'm pretty green, cowboy," she whispered. "I'm counting on you to teach me ..."

Though her words belied the truth, the slight quiver in her voice reminded Shane of her innocence and the brutality she'd suffered at the hands of another man. He reined himself in as much as he could manage.

He would make love to her—how could he not?—but they'd take it slow and easy at first. Thunder rumbled again and rain came down like they might need an ark. One thing was for sure—they had plenty of time to do this right.

And he would show Mary just how good it could be.

He rolled her nipples between his fingers, and she moaned. Leaning closer, he drew the lobe of her ear into his mouth, and her breasts swelled, filling his hands even more completely. He ached to taste her again.

He shifted his weight from one foot to the other until his jeans fell to the floor around his ankles. In turn, he loosened the last few buttons of her dress, hearing it whisper to the floor. He pulled back enough to watch her changing expression. "I want you to know up front that I won't be able to stop myself if this goes much further."

Her eyes were wide with wonder but not fear as her gaze drifted down the length of him. She brought her hands from his waist to his buttocks, then eased them around to the front. Shane feared he might lose it all right then and there, but he drew a deep breath, tensing while she explored.

"I . . . I don't want you to stop," she breathed, wrapping her hands around him. "It's . . . so big."

"I'll be gentle, Mary." Yes, she was killing him, just as sure as if she'd put a gun to his head. "I promise."

She smiled again, looking a little uncertain now. "I know you will." Tightening her grip on him, she moved closer, her breasts teasing the hair on his chest.

"Mary."

"Does it hurt much?" she asked. "It's so red and swollen."

He laughed, though he felt more like crying. Who would have guessed that Mary Goode could transform herself into a guileless temptress? He was surprised. Not that he was complaining. He cleared his throat and shot her a crooked grin. "It's supposed to look like that, honey, and it doesn't hurt. Exactly. But you can make it feel a lot better." *Or hurt a lot more.*

Her cheeks turned an enchanting shade of pink, and she gave him a shy smile that melted his heart. "I didn't know anything so hard could feel so . . . so soft. Like velvet."

Lord help him, the woman had no idea what she did to him—his body and his heart. "Trust me, sweetheart, at this minute, this here's the hardest thing either of us has ever seen." His voice sounded thick, raspy.

She stroked the length of him, a quizzical expression on her face. Then she lifted her mouth to his and nibbled his lower lip. "I want this." Her voice had a decisive, matter-of-fact quality, despite its slight quaver.

He groaned. He had to give her one more chance to

change her mind, though it might kill him. His fate was in her hands—he glanced down again—literally. Shane held his breath. "Are you sure?" He sounded like a little boy asking for candy, though this sweet was one hell of a lot spicier than any peppermint he'd ever tasted.

Nodding, she shrugged her slender shoulders, her expression seductively innocent.

"Yes, more certain than I've ever been about anything."

Chapter Fourteen

Mary stood before Will—no, Shane—naked and trembling. The ugly demons kept trying to spoil everything, but the magical force between her and this man was more powerful than all the demons and nightmares in the world combined. Nothing could prevent this. *Nothing.*

And that knowledge rocked the foundations of everything she'd believed. This was something she couldn't hide from, nor control to make it fit neatly into the life she'd made for herself.

When she'd first made her decision to seduce Shane, she'd thought of her body as nothing more than a means to hold him here. Ammunition. Now she realized her folly. This was far too masterful for her to command or manipulate. And if their intimacy meant half as much to him as it did to her, he would want to stay.

And if he didn't—God forbid—she would have this precious memory to last a lifetime.

Focusing on the present, rather than the uncertain future, she studied his magnificent body again. His manhood fascinated her, though she'd known a moment's fear at first. Now, each time the nightmare threatened her resolve, she forced herself to gaze upon Shane's face. One look in his eyes was enough to remind her that this was real and good.

It was destiny. Fate.

Yes, a more omnipotent force had brought them here together. Alone. Her father had always said God worked in mysterious ways, though she doubted he'd meant exactly *this* way.

A smile tugged at her lips as she stroked the pulsing, petal-soft length of this man she loved. Engorged and erect, this was how he looked that night when he'd thrown the quilt aside and invited her to wash him.

He looked . . . ready.

Her heart pressed against her throat. A remembered flash of evil invaded her mind, and her courage faltered. Holding her breath, she looked up at Will's—rather, Shane's—face again, drawing strength from the desire in his smoky green eyes. And from the love that swelled in her heart.

He seemed to sense her hesitation, and he moved his hands from her breasts to capture her wrists, drawing them away from his manhood. "Enough of that, sweetheart," he whispered. "A man's only got so much control."

She wasn't entirely certain of his meaning, so she entrusted herself to his methods. "Show me."

His expression tender, he pulled her hands up and draped them around his neck. She clung to him, burying her fingers in his curls. With maddening slowness, he lowered his mouth to hers, nibbling the corners of her mouth, then her lower lip. He tugged it into his mouth, creating a delicious tingle that spread across her face, down her neck, and to her feminine core.

Frustrated, she seized his lips with hers. Groaning, he

deepened the kiss until nothing else mattered except his mouth on hers. She feasted on his singular flavor, gloried in the exotic stroking and parrying of his tongue with hers.

She pressed herself against him, agonizingly aware of their mutual nakedness. Their embrace created a wall of heat unlike anything she'd ever imagined. His coarse chest hair stroked the crests of her breasts, sending rivulets of renewed hunger spiking through her.

The memory of how it had felt to have him kiss and suckle her breast made her shudder with longing. She wanted his mouth on her again.

With a soft moan, he cupped her buttocks and lifted her up and against him, as he had last night, but this time no barriers separated his molten flesh from hers. His hard maleness thrust enticingly against the soft folds of her womanhood. Her arms trembled from a sudden weakness born of a need so fierce it would not be denied.

Even though she didn't understand all the sensations and responses, her body's natural instincts took command. Hungrily, she thrust her hips against his. Aching. Seeking. Wanting.

Realizing *exactly* what her body sought, she broke their kiss, gasping and gazing into his eyes. As breathless as she, he swept her into his arms and turned to place her gently on her bed. He hovered over her, and another shattered fragment of her nightmare loomed over her yet again.

No, please, no.

She squeezed her eyes shut for an instant, trembling as desire battled fear. After a moment, she felt his warm length at her side—*only* his warmth, without pain or fear—and breathed a sigh of relief mingled with a delicious wave of pleasure.

"Look at me, Mary," he said, nuzzling the lobe of her

ear. She felt him shift his position at her side. "Open your eyes."

Obeying, she held her breath, terrified that seeing his face above her would release a flood of horrible memories. She couldn't allow that evil to destroy something beautiful. But all she saw when she focused on his features was tenderness and desire. Joy burst within her, and she smiled.

The heat of his gaze held her prisoner, banishing her trepidation. His lips brushed hers, then journeyed downward, leaving a trail of fire in their wake.

Mary's breath caught, absorbed by a quavering gasp as his kisses moved lower. A deliciously wicked urge to watch his descent took control, and when she lowered her gaze she saw him kissing the slope of her shoulder. Then he turned inward, toward her aching breasts.

A devastating yearning tripped through her. The contrast of his tanned face against the milky whiteness of her breast captivated her. She couldn't have dragged her attention from that wondrous sight even to hide from another twister.

Her breasts looked swollen, hardened, reminding her of Shane's responsive body. Remembering that hard, throbbing part of him brought liquid fire pooling to her loins. She'd never known anything could be like this—so all-powerful, so consuming.

He cupped her breast in his large hand, then covered its cusp with his hot, seeking mouth. Mary found her wayward breath on a second gasp, then it broke into rapid pants that scorched her throat. The fluttering in her belly flowered and unfurled, settling fervently at the apex of her thighs. Craving something more, she writhed inwardly and outwardly.

Shane owned and controlled her destiny. Surge after surge of blistering need took command. She shuddered, wondering if women actually died from a want this mighty.

Then his hand dipped between her legs, fanning the flames that licked at her body, her heart, her soul. He pressed the heel of his hand against her mound, and she thrust upward against him. Bewildered by her body's response, Mary lay very still, watching him abandon her breast to kiss his way down her abdomen. Her heart pounded so hard she could hear it echoing through her head.

He tickled her navel with his tongue, and pleasure oozed through her. Then he pressed his hand against her again and she moaned, wanting more. So much more . . .

She buried her fingers in his golden curls, urging him upward. Gradually, he rose, then claimed her other breast with his mouth as his fingers stroked her slippery woman's flesh.

Then, miraculously, he focused his attention on an incredibly sensitive nub between her thighs. Molten astonishment swirled through her as he stroked and rubbed, seeming to know exactly how to elicit the most maddening response.

She clutched him to her breast as his talented finger continued its delicious invasion of her hot, wet flesh. He rubbed against her in frenzied circles, each rotation pulsing through every fiber of her body.

An astonishing series of convulsions ravaged her body, echoing through her in scalding, staggering eruptions. He relinquished her breast to kiss her mouth again as she squirmed and writhed beneath him. Her every purpose converged on his unrelenting hand and the luscious, wicked things he made her endure and crave. She propelled herself against his palm, dragged her mouth from his, and supplicated in a whimper that was half sob. "Shane . . ."

With a low, guttural growl, he swung himself over her,

covering her full length with his own. He remained poised there for a breathtakingly poignant moment.

Drifting slowly down from the pinnacle he'd given her, she met his gaze and saw his unspoken question. No doubts remained in her, for the love and passion he'd already demonstrated drove the demons away at last.

Forever, she prayed.

Holding his gaze, she eased her hand between their sweat-slickened bodies and found the velvet soft tip of his rigid manhood. "I want you," she whispered. "Inside me." Even as she spoke the words, her womb contracted, encountering an unbearable emptiness. "Please . . . ?"

Their gazes locked, frozen in time. She guided his wide, throbbing tip against her soft folds, biting her lower lip in anticipation and a modicum of fear. Holding her breath, she stroked him against her hot slickness, heard his soft moan mingle with her own. "Love me, Shane."

He pressed inward very slightly, and she wrapped her arms around his back and her legs around his waist. That shift in position brought him deeper into her, and she angled her hips to more fully meet him. Her invitation was clear, and she had no reservations at all. "Love me," she repeated, watching his eyes darken to a smoky green haze.

With a single precise thrust, he filled her.

Incredulous, Mary slapped the rough log wall beside the bunk. She was stunned to her core by the depth, the completeness, the *exquisiteness* of their union.

Recovering somewhat from her incredulity, she focused on his eyes again. She brought her hands to his nape and pulled him down to meet her lips. Her insides clenched around him, holding him tight and deep and sure.

Slowly, he moved against her. Hot, relentless need coiled through her. She broke the kiss to gasp, drawing great gulps of air into her lungs as she met him thrust for thrust.

This was how it was supposed to be.

But only with this man.

She gripped his sweaty back, arching her torso upward. Closer. She couldn't get close enough, though they were locked together as close as a man and woman could be. Deeper, harder, faster, he came into her again and again, driving her closer to the brink of a sweet madness she knew she must find or die. She was a spring, coiling tighter and tighter, about to break free at any moment.

Each precise and powerful thrust pushed her nearer the summit. She knew it was there, just beyond her reach. Closer. Hotter. Higher. She clung to him without fear.

Shane whispered endearments as his loving continued, nudging her further to soar recklessly into an unknown darkness. This was so much more than she'd ever imagined.

Wonderful. Wild. Wicked.

She bridged a threshold into an obscure place where nothing else existed. Every second of his loving unveiled an intense new tier of this special madness.

Thoroughly and inevitably, he reached her very essence again and again. She climbed faster now, tossing her head from side to side, dying just a little with each passing moment.

A dazzling brightness suddenly burst behind her eyes as everything she possessed, everything she was, converged where his body joined hers. She convulsed around him, drew him ever inward, clutched his shoulders to lift her own off the bed. Locked in a lovers' vise, they rocked together in perfect harmony.

My God, *this* was what she'd craved—what she'd missed.

Rapture. Breath eluded her, and she was certain her heart stopped beating as she clung to her lover. Tumultuous spasms coursed through her in one endless, achingly sublime twinkling.

He jerked and groaned, filled her with his molten seed, branded her as his. Mary remained clasped around him as their breathing slowed, their hearts thudding together in a timeless rhythm.

Shane rested his forehead against hers, then kissed her softly on the lips. "You all right?" He raised up on his elbows, gazing into her eyes.

Mary loved him more now than ever. "I'm much better than all right," she said. He smiled, and she brushed a curl from his eye. "That was . . ."

"That was what?" His brow furrowed. "Well?"

"Incredible." Much to her amazement, tears flooded her eyes and spilled onto her face. She wasn't supposed to cry. Crying was for children. "I . . . I'm sorry, I . . ."

"What's wrong?" He frowned, which made her weep even more. "Mary, did I hurt you?"

"No, no," she said, holding him close and burying her cheek against his shoulder. She sniffled and let her head fall back against the bed, smiling through her tears. "I just didn't know how . . . how beautiful it could be."

His eyes widened, then a warm smile curved his mouth. "Beautiful, huh?"

The expression in his eyes said so much more, and Mary held her breath. Waiting. Her need to confess her love for him burned within her, but she waited.

His expression changed, grew more serious, and he nuzzled the side of her neck. "Mary, I've never felt like this before," he whispered.

Hope filled her heart, and she held him in her arms. "Neither have I." That was a beginning, though she desperately wanted more. Everything.

He raised up again, holding her prisoner with the intensity of his gaze. "I was so afraid of hurting you."

"You didn't hurt me." She smiled. "You *healed* me. You showed me what it's like to be treated the way a woman should be treated."

His eyes glazed over and he kissed her so gently she sighed. After a moment, he looked at her again and waggled his eyebrows. "I know a fella who's ready to kick up another ruckus."

Mary laughed, wriggling her hips against him, amazed to feel him growing inside her. "Well, I never . . ."

His answering chuckle was like music. He pressed himself deeper into her, and his laughter dissolved into a moan. This Shane was more relaxed, more playful, less fearful of hurting her. *Thank goodness.*

He entered and withdrew at a leisurely pace, watching her face as if he didn't want to miss anything. She climbed more slowly than before, but knowing her destination empowered her. His rhythm increased and she matched him stroke for stroke, clinging and writhing against him.

Mary reached her completion early, but rather than descending as she had before, multiple explosions ravaged her. One after another, each one more brilliant and shattering than the last, she peaked until it seemed like one perpetual state of enchantment.

And Shane kept on loving her as if he'd never stop. If he didn't stop soon, she'd expire from pure pleasure. But if he did stop, that might kill her, too.

He linked his arms behind her knees and draped them over his shoulders this time, coming into her harder, faster, deeper than ever before. With each stroke, she clenched around him, trying to hold him while the explosions tore her into a million particles of mindless ecstasy. But each time he eluded her and gifted her with even more torturous delight on his return.

His movements changed, more closely resembling the wild man they'd joked about. He delved deeper and remained buried within her longer each time, lifting her body off the bunk to fasten with his.

Mary cried out as Shane came into her in an incredible spasm. His shout of victory mingled with hers, then was smothered by a savage kiss that left her floating slowly back to earth in his arms. Overcome with the enormity of what she'd just experienced, she looked up at him through blurry eyes and said, "I love you, Shane. I love you."

Still breathing hard, he stared down at her without saying a word. As her vision cleared, she saw an expression of guilt cross his face.

She'd rather have been slapped.

You're lower than a snake's belly, Latimer. Shane shouldn't have taken her without telling her everything about his identity. Who he was, what he was, and why he'd come here in the first place.

But once she offered herself to him so sweetly . . .

He rolled to his side and cradled her in his arms, searching for the words that must be said. No woman had ever made him feel this way. He wanted to make love to her every night for the rest of his life. He wanted to walk with her, sleep with her, sing with her, live with her.

But he had to do this right. Before he could tell her he loved her, he had to make sure she knew who and what he was. He pushed himself up on one elbow and gazed down into her eyes. She blinked several times, her expression wary.

She'd trusted him. Dear Lord, he hoped she still trusted him after hearing the truth.

"Mary, I—"

An explosion sounded from outside. "Gunfire." Shane rolled her off the bunk and onto the floor. "Stay down." He retrieved his pistols, then crouched down near the open window. Mary was wrapped in the quilt on the floor, staring at him with wide eyes. "Stay there." She nodded, and he eased up to peer out the window.

The rain had stopped and the sun broke through the clouds, enabling him to see clear to the forest. Nothing moved. He eased himself back down and grabbed his trousers, wiggling into them.

"Who is it?" Mary whispered.

"Didn't see a soul, but I can feel 'em." *Trust your gut*, Sam always said, and right now Shane's gut said someone was out there.

He crawled back to the window, his pistol gripped in his hand. Leaning against the cabin wall, he listened. As quiet as it was, he'd hear anything unusual.

Another blast rent the air and Shane scooted to one side of the window and stood, peering out at an angle. Galloping hoofbeats thundered by and a rock flew through the window, landing with a clatter on the floor. A piece of paper was tied to it with a strip of leather.

Shane's gut said the shooting was only to keep them from seeing the identity of the messenger. More gunshots sounded, then the galloping again. Shane peered out and spotted a tall horse as it thundered toward the trees. The rider was dressed in black and silver, contrasting vividly against the startling white horse.

Out of range now, it was obvious the rider didn't intend to return. Shane glanced at the rock in the middle of the wet floor. No, he wouldn't return yet, but he'd be back sooner or later. Rage and worry plundered through him, but he drew a deep breath to bring himself under control. He didn't want to frighten Mary.

Though Shane had never seen the notorious outlaw in person, he'd heard enough stories and seen enough flyers to recognize the horse and rider immediately, even from a distance. The flashy thief of women's hearts and fortunes was known for always dressing in black and riding a snow white horse.

Angel Rodriguez.

Shane glanced at Mary. He couldn't let Rodriguez— or anyone else—harm her.

"Is he gone?" she asked, rising up off the floor, clutching the quilt to her bare breasts.

"Yeah, he's gone." Shane drew a deep breath and looked out the window again.

"Who was it?"

He shrugged and pointed at the rock. "He left his calling card."

Mary sat on the floor wrapped in the quilt as Shane holstered his pistol and strapped the gunbelt around his hips. Seeing Rodriguez had shaken him—more than he cared to admit. He had to keep a cool head.

He had to protect Mary.

Maintaining a calm front, he grabbed the rock and sat on the bunk. Mary scrambled to her feet, then sat beside him. "What is it?"

"A letter, I imagine." He slipped the leather off the rock and unfurled the damp letter.

"From who?" Her voice took on an edge of worry. "What sort of person would hurl a letter through a window in a barrage of gunfire?"

"A bad one." *You don't know how bad.* Shane squinted at the words. The rain had smeared the ink in places, but the message was clear enough. Rodriguez had pulled out the big guns. "Damn." He wished there were some way to keep this from her, but he couldn't. She had a right to know.

"What is it?" Mary reached for the paper, but Shane held it just out of her reach. "Shane, let me—" Her face blanched and her eyes widened. "Robin. My God, something's happened to Robin."

He put his arm around her shoulders. "Mary, I won't let him get away with this."

"Let *who* get away with *what?*" She lunged for the letter again, and Shane let her grab it this time. With trembling hands, she held the letter in front of her. He knew when she'd reached the signature, because she stifled her sob with her fist against her lips. "Robin. He's got Robin." She looked up at Shane with pleading eyes. "We have to save him. We have to go get him. We have to do whatever he wants."

Whatever he wants . . . ? "Mary, do you *know* what he wants?" He gripped her shoulders, and the letter fluttered to the floor. "He wants *you.*" Shane's voice fell to a rasp as the horror of reality etched itself in his words. "He wants your body, Mary. And your pride."

"He has my brother, Shane." Her voice quivered. "My *brother.*"

"And we'll get him back."

"Alive?" Mary stood and faced Shane, her slender body trembling. *"Alive?"*

He pushed to his feet, swallowing all the doubts and nagging voices at the back of his mind. "Alive," he promised, and prayed to God he really could bring Robin back to Mary unharmed. "First we have to make sure he really has him. Could be bluffing."

Her lower lip trembled, but she swiped angrily at her eyes with a corner of the quilt. When she met his gaze again, determination gave her blue eyes a hard glint.

Now was the time, Shane realized. She needed him, and he couldn't hide behind feigned amnesia any longer. "Mary, you need the law to go after Rodriguez. He's a dangerous criminal." He placed his hands on her shoulders.

"I know better than anyone how *dangerous* he is." Her voice dripped acid; then she sucked in a huge breath and nodded. "That's why we have to save Robin *now.* He warned me that he'd go after Robin if . . ."

Shane gathered her against him, and her arms went around his waist, but she didn't remain there long. After a few moments, she pulled back and stared at his face as if she'd just realized something.

"Yes, we need the law," she said. "Sam Weathers can't have gotten far in the st—"

"Mary," he said quietly. "My name is Shane Latimer . . . and I'm a United States Marshal, too."

Confusion flitted across her face, replaced by suspicion. "Sam must have . . . No." She shook her head. "Just how long have you remembered?"

Shane drew a sharp breath. "I never forgot."

Chapter Fifteen

Mary's hand smacked Shane's cheek with a resounding, but far from satisfying, crack.

"You lied to me." Her voice was nothing more than a hoarse whisper, the words nearly gagging her. "You *lied.*"

A muscle twitched in his jaw and he closed his eyes, making no effort to touch the angry red handprint on his cheek. "I deserved that," he said, his voice flat, emotionless.

She couldn't tell from his reaction if he was riddled with guilt or merely upset that he'd been caught. Either way, she'd been deceived. "Lies. All lies." Traitorous, scalding tears struggled to spill from her eyes, and he reached for her. She stepped back, holding up her hands to ward off an attack. "Don't touch me."

"I'm sorry."

Unflinchingly, she met his gaze. The expression in his eyes staggered her. He looked as miserable as she felt. *Good.* She quickly recovered herself as much as possible, then lifted her chin, refusing to acknowledge that he might actually regret his deceit.

No matter how much she hoped. . . .

"Nothing matters right now but finding Robin," she said, forcing her voice to sound far stronger and steadier than she felt.

He nodded. "Fair enough."

"Marshal Latimer, I'm going to get dressed now." Keeping the quilt clutched around her, she walked toward her private corner. "I suggest you determine how we're going to rescue my brother." She paused and turned to face him. "Because if you don't . . . *I will.*"

"Mary, please—"

"Don't. Not now." She whirled around and retreated to her corner, jerking the curtain shut. Several huge breaths quelled her rising nausea and vanquished more threatening tears. For now.

She'd given her body to a man who'd lied to her. Staring at the cracked mirror, Mary saw herself for what she truly was.

A fallen woman.

She dropped the quilt to the floor. *Silly woman, it isn't as if you were a virgin.*

But being raped had been against her will. Today's events hadn't. That made her no better than Sassy Sally, though Mary hadn't been paid for her favors.

Exhausted, she grabbed her clean shirt and pulled it on, trying not to remember all the ways and places Shane had touched her. Her memory of the paradise she'd discovered in his arms was now tainted. She should've known . . . Angrily, she buttoned her shirt and finished dressing. She brushed her hair and braided it tightly, wrapping it around her head and securing it with pins.

"You have beautiful hair," he'd said.

Her hair was no concern of his.

Banishing his words from her mind, she was relieved

to find water in the basin. The discovery gave her pause. Shane's touch hadn't made her long for a bath as that other encounter had. Still, it had been wrong. A mistake.

She splashed her face with cool water, dried it, then looked at herself again. The sadness in her reflection was certainly appropriate. She'd lost the only man she would ever love—yes, love, though she hated to admit it even to herself. And her brother's life was in danger.

If he wasn't already dead.

God, no. Please, no. She couldn't bear to lose Robin, too. A powerful shudder rippled through her, and she drew another deep breath. She didn't have time to cry. Eight years ago, she'd realized tears were for children. How could she have allowed herself to forget the pain and determination that had fueled her resolve to rescue Robin then?

Now she would rescue him again, and she would use any means necessary. An image of Angel Rodriguez's face as he'd prepared himself to ravage her appeared in her mind. Her belly roiled and her flesh turned frigid.

She straightened and ruthlessly dismissed her fears. Nothing mattered beyond saving Robin. *Nothing.* And her virtue was nothing more than a worthless memory now anyway. Lost. Gone.

Along with her heart.

With a sniffle, she grabbed her moccasins and shoved the curtain aside. Shane still stood where she'd left him, his jeans and gunbelt hanging low on his lean hips. He looked dangerously handsome. Miserable. *He should.*

She tore her gaze away and sat on the wooden bench to put on her moccasins. Once they were secured, she looked up at Shane again. "Well? What have you decided?"

He bent down and retrieved Angel Rodriguez's note from the floor, then cleared his throat. "This says to meet

him at the nearest tributary to the north. I take it you
know the place?"

Mary nodded. "And I know what the letter says, Marshal. Right now I want to know *how* you're going to save
my brother."

Still shirtless, he looped his thumb through the waistband of his jeans, reminding Mary of what they'd shared
such a short while ago. She closed her eyes to gather
her wits. "I think you should put on a shirt," she said,
reopening her eyes.

"Mary, I wanted to tell you before we—"

"But you didn't."

His smile was sad, rueful. "You didn't give me much
of a chance."

Embarrassment warmed her cheeks as she remembered
how she'd thrown herself at him. "A momentary lapse
in judgment, I assure you." She cleared her throat, narrowing her focus to what must take precedence. "I don't
wish to discuss my . . . my mistake ever again."

"Mistake? The only mistake was mine. I should've
told you the truth first, then made love to you."

"Is that what you call it?" Bitter laughter tripped over
her tongue, its madness surprising even her.

"Yeah, that's what I call it." He came toward her and
straddled the bench beside her. "Mary, we have to discuss
what happened between us today . . . no matter what you
want to call it."

"No, we do not."

"What if . . ." He reached for her hand and held it,
despite her repeated attempts to break free. "Look at me,
Mary."

Hot and cold at the same time, she obeyed. And regretted it. Something she'd longed to see earlier now blazed
in his eyes, but she couldn't bear to hear the words. Not
now. "Don't." Her throat convulsed.

He pinned her with his gaze, so intense it burned through

one layer of her resistance and threatened the protective shell she'd worked valiantly to erect around her heart. "Don't hurt me again," she whispered.

"I would never deliberately hurt you," he said, his voice thick and raspy. *"Never."* His eyes glistened as if he, too, fought against tears. "Mary, what if . . ."

"What?" She drew a shuddering breath and held it. "Just say whatever it is and get it over with."

He flinched as if she'd struck him again. "I deserve that, too."

"Yes, you do." God help her, but she couldn't rescue her gaze from his, no matter how she tried. Her words sounded brave. Tough. But inside, her heart splintered into a thousand woeful pieces.

He squeezed her hand and pressed it to his chest. The steady thud of his heart beneath the warmth of his skin reverberated through her hand and straight to her bones. "Shane, please . . ."

"All right." He drew a deep breath, but didn't release her hand. Staring intently into her eyes, he asked, "What if there's a child?"

Shock ricocheted through her at his words, replaced a second later with wonder. *What if there's a child?* She finally succeeded in freeing her gaze from his and looked down at her hand pressed to his bare chest. She'd always wanted a child of her own. Then she'd never have to be alone. . . . Resolve laced heavily with hope settled in her heart, and she lifted her chin a notch to look at Shane.

The daughter of missionaries had fallen very far. She would actually *welcome* a child out of wedlock.

"Is it . . . possible?" She hated herself for expressing her naiveté aloud.

"We did everything right to make one." His voice was gentle, his eyes smoldering, his smile warm.

Mary girded her resolve and squared her shoulders.

"Well, if there is a child, then I'll become a mother."
Her false bravado contradicted her true feelings.

"If there's a child," Shane said steadily, "*I'll* be the father."

Mary tore her hand from his grasp and stood, turning her back on him. "I see no reason to borrow trouble," she said, struggling to maintain some semblance of composure. "I'll worry about that *if* it happens."

And it will be my secret.

He stood behind her, the heat of his body radiating through the back of her shirt and targeting her heart. *God help me.* She kept her back straight, though she wanted to bury her face in her hands and weep. She didn't tremble, though her heart and soul quivered as if caught in a wild stampede. She didn't turn around to look at his face, though she longed to do just that.

He touched her shoulder—she stepped away. "I'm going to the village," she said in careful, precise syllables—anything to mask her turmoil. "If you're going with me, you'd better get dressed."

"All right."

She heard him walk across the room to get a shirt and seized the opportunity to escape for a little while. "I'll wait outside."

Shane whirled around and grabbed her arm just as she reached the door. "No, Mary, I don't want you going outside alone."

With her lips pressed tightly together, she stared at his hand on her arm. He held his shirt—the one she'd been unable to get the bloodstains out of—in his other hand. Shane's blood. No matter how he'd hurt her, she prayed he would never be so seriously injured again. She cared, though she was loath to admit it even to herself.

"Did you hear me, Mary?"

"This is my home and I'll be fine." Her words sounded unconvincing even to her own ears.

He tightened his grip, an internal battle playing itself out across his handsome face. "We haven't talked about what Rodriguez did to you, Mary," he said, his voice fierce, his nostrils flaring, "but I figure it must've happened right here. In your home. Where you say you'll be fine."

Revulsion swept through her, and she swallowed the lump of terror lodged in her throat. "Not . . . not in here," she said so quietly she wasn't sure he'd heard her. She would've burned the cabin to the ground if that nightmare had occurred here. "You have the distinction of being the only man who's ever hurt me *inside* this cabin."

His hand dropped away, and a flash of misery appeared in his eyes, replaced just as quickly with anger. "You have every right to be mad at me, but you have no right to endanger yourself out of stubborn pride."

She lifted her chin and met his gaze unwaveringly. "I beg your pardon, Marshal, but *you* have no right to tell me how to behave."

He acknowledged her remark with a grudging nod. "Maybe not, but you owe it to Robin to take care of yourself." He drew a deep breath through his nose and released it through his mouth. "Rodriguez is a killer . . . and worse, Mary. You know that better than anybody, and you aren't going outside alone." He raked her with his gaze. "Even if I have to hog-tie you."

"Very well," she said through clenched teeth. "Then at least have the decency to dress yourself. And, by all means, *do* wear your badge." She tapped her cheek and looked at the ceiling. "Which reminds me, I can't wait to hear *why* you felt it necessary to pretend you couldn't remember your own name. Or was that merely a ruse to get me into bed, Marshal? Did you have some reason to believe I wouldn't bed a lawman?"

"Sarcasm doesn't become you, Mary." His jaw

twitching, he tugged on his shirt and buttoned it. "I'd love to oblige you, ma'am, but someone stole my badge."

"Stole it? Why?"

"You ask a lot of questions." Shane shrugged, then sat on the bunk to pull on the soft moccasins, securing them over his jeans just below his knees. "I reckon it must've been Friar Tuck."

"Why would he do something like that?" Mary frowned, wondering why Tuck had encouraged Robin's proclamation that Shane be Will Scarlet in the first place. Nothing made sense anymore. "Never mind, it doesn't matter. If you're really a marshal, then it's your duty to save Robin."

Shane nodded and stood, tucking his shirttail into his waistband. "Yes, ma'am, it sure is." He strode over to her and stood close.

Too close.

Towering over her, he added, "And it's my duty to protect *you,* too, whether you want it or not."

He leaned toward her, bringing his face within inches of hers. A rush of anticipation filtered through her, but indignance overruled. "Don't you dare."

"Don't I dare what?" His rumbling voice compelled her to meet the challenge that glittered in his eyes. "Kiss you?"

The intensity of his gaze pilfered all the air from around them, and Mary feared she might faint. "No man who lies to me will ever kiss me. Again." She gasped for air, forcibly quelling the blatant desire attempting to overshadow her much-deserved outrage.

"I didn't want to," he whispered, his expression softening. "I only wanted to . . ."

"To what?"

He reached out and cupped her cheek, brushing his thumb across her lips. "To love you, Mary."

And arrest your brother, Shane added silently. He'd

made one hell of a mess out of this case. Some marshal he was turning out to be. Not only had he come after outlaws who weren't the kind who needed arresting, but he'd mangled his chances with the only woman outside his family who'd ever meant anything to him.

And she meant a lot.

"Don't you dare speak to me of love." Her eyes widened and she stood there, staring at him. After several moments so silent he could hear their combined heartbeats, she tore her gaze from his.

"Let's go," she said, shoving a battered sunbonnet over her braids and tying it beneath her chin. "It's not far, but we're on foot."

"Rain seems to have stopped, at least." He spotted the guitar leaning against the wall and grabbed it. "Guess today's as good as any."

"Tell me, Marshal," she said as they stepped out into the watery sunlight, "once you have a new horse, will you be leaving us?"

He grinned and drew a deep breath. "The rain sure made it smell good out here."

"You didn't answer my question."

"Nope, I didn't." Shane crooked his elbow toward her and waited. She simply stared at it as if she had no idea what to do with it. Of course, he knew better. After a moment, he dropped his arm to his side and released his breath in a loud whoosh. "Have it your way."

"I intend to." She started walking toward the forest.

Shane shook his head and slung the guitar strap over his shoulder so the instrument hung against his back. He caught up with her after a few long strides. "Where's the village?"

"Across the river and downstream a ways."

"And the tributary is upstream?"

She nodded, keeping her nose pointed straight ahead, the bonnet shading her eyes.

"How do we get across the river after all that rain?"

"You'll see."

Reminds me of Jenny in a snit. Shane fell into an awkward silence at her side, aching to take her hand in his. Frustrated, he concentrated on the scenery while constantly checking to make sure they weren't being watched. There was no sign of Rodriguez or anyone else, for that matter.

He and Mary were completely alone.

For all the good that would do him now. . . .

The violent storms had left everything clean and fresh. The grass and trees—those that hadn't met with the business end of a twister—were at least thirty shades of green. A perfect day.

Though he'd liked it better during the storm.

Somehow, he had to make Mary forgive him. He'd resisted letting things get out of hand, and he'd tried to tell her who he was, but . . .

Ah, hell, Latimer. The woman made every reasonable thought flee his mind faster than lightning had destroyed that tree. He raked his fingers through his hair and cursed his missing hat again.

He only knew three things for sure right now. First and most important, he would return Robin Goode to the bosom of his family.

But thinking about Mary's bosom was dangerous.

Even so, he couldn't prevent the image from exploding in his memory. As if she were beneath him this moment, he saw her curving upward to meet him, her breasts bared and glistening with perspiration . . .

Damn.

He was thinking with his cock again. That insolent part of him flinched in response, but he gnashed his teeth and tried to ignore it.

Venturing a glance at her profile, he not only saw her naked beneath him, he felt her, tasted her, smelled her . . .

"No." He didn't realize until she looked at him that he'd spoken aloud.

"What?"

"Nothing." He cleared his throat and looked along both sides of the riverbank.

"Did you see something?" Mary looked around them, too, and back over her shoulder.

"No, just thinking out loud." The river twisted and meandered along, then widened.

The rocks dug into the soles of his feet. "These moccasins aren't much better than going barefoot."

She almost smiled. "Tenderfoot."

Shane chuckled. "With all due respect, ma'am, I'm used to good boots."

"And I'm used to honesty."

No point in arguing that point, he decided.

The bank changed from rocky to sandy around the next bend. A raft was tied to a tree there, and a length of stout rope stretched from one side of the river to the other.

"River's up, but probably a lot worse downstream," Mary said, pointing to the raft. "Tuck designed the ferry for us shortly after we settled here, and Little John helped Robin build it."

Shane smiled. "It's a good design."

Mary tilted her head and stared up and into his eyes. "How do you know?"

His cheeks warmed and he rubbed the back of his neck. "I studied stuff like this in college."

"You went to college?" Distinct surprise widened her eyes. "Oh, well, that explains it then."

Narrowing his gaze, he held her gaze as they paused near the raft. "Explains what?"

Her lips twitched and she cleared her throat. "Never mind."

So now she was playing games with him. Shane sighed and reached for the rope holding the sturdy raft of logs tied together with lengths of rope and leather. It was large enough to hold a couple of horses and men, but not a wagon. Good to know, because he fully intended to have a horse on their return trip.

"How come the raft is still here when everybody else is across the river at the village?"

"There are three rafts," she explained. "Two of them are already across the river."

"Ah, good planning." A leather harness was looped over the rope and would keep the raft from breaking loose and escaping on the river's swift current. The engineering impressed him, but that made perfect sense, since the famous Ichabod Smith had designed the ferry.

Once Mary was seated on the logs, Shane released the rope holding the raft in place. The current tugged, but the ropes held.

"The river's moving a lot faster after the storm," Mary said quietly, though she didn't seem worried.

He made no comment and positioned the long pole he'd found tied to the edge of the raft against the river bottom. Slowly, he walked the length of the raft, pushing against the bottom to propel them toward the opposite bank. The leather harness slid along the sturdy rope as he repeated the action again and again.

They were more than halfway across when he saw the white stallion again. In that moment, Shane knew fear like he'd never imagined. "Mary, lie down."

She glanced upstream, then obeyed without argument. *Thank God.* They were stuck out here in the middle of the danged river like sitting ducks. But the black-clad outlaw merely sat on his horse, watching them.

"Is Robin with him?" Mary whispered.

"No, he's alone." Shane felt Rodriguez's hatred even from this distance.

And he returned it tenfold.

"God, please let Robin be all right," Mary prayed, her voice trembling.

Her words cleaved into Shane. He *would* save her brother.

He continued to propel the raft, though he didn't remove his gaze from Rodriguez. As the raft bumped against the sandbar on the opposite side, he released a sigh and leapt into the water to pull the raft onto the bank.

"C'mon, Mary," he said, grabbing her hand as she stood, and helping her off the raft. "Get to the trees quick."

Again, she surprised him by not questioning him. He secured the raft, then joined her. They both stared at Rodriguez, who remained as still as a statue, making no effort to draw his pistols.

Finally, the outlaw cupped his hand to his mouth and called, *"Mañana."* Then he tipped his silver-studded hat and whirled his horse away from the river, disappearing into the trees.

"What does *mañana* mean?" Mary asked, her voice trembling.

"Tomorrow."

They remained silent for several moments after Rodriguez had left. "Let's go," Shane said, holding his hand out to Mary again and waiting for her reaction.

With a nod, she slipped her small hand into his, her eyes moist and trusting.

Something twisted in his chest and his throat felt tight and thick. He ached to gather her into his arms and declare himself to her right here. Right now.

But first he had to save Robin Hood from a villain one hell of a lot more menacing than the Sheriff of Nottingham. Then, and only then, could he woo Maid Marian and beg her forgiveness.

"Show me the way, Mary," he said softly, wondering if she recognized the double entendre.

She blinked once. Twice. Then she nodded and started walking away from the river. They emerged from the trees and climbed a long, sloping hill choked with wildflowers of every color and shape.

At the crest of the hill, she paused and drew a deep breath. "I always think I can see the whole world from up here," she said reverently. "It's so beautiful."

Shane followed her gaze to the valley below. The Indian village sat at another bend in the river, though he could see from here why she'd chosen this route. The way the Verdigris snaked its way through the valley, it would've taken hours to reach the village by following it.

A gentle breeze lifted his hair and he turned to look at her. He wished her hair were down, blowing freely. Somehow, he would earn Mary's forgiveness. That strange sensation in his chest increased like something warm and liquid flowing against his heart.

Yeah, you got it bad, Latimer.

Suddenly, she turned to face him, holding him prisoner with her gaze. "Who's Jenny?"

Her question surprised him, and he chuckled, but the insistence in her eyes quieted him. "I already answered that question, Mary."

"Will Scarlet did, but Shane Latimer hasn't."

"Jennifer Mae Latimer."

A look of horror crossed her face, and he knew what she was thinking. He squeezed her hand in what he hoped was a reassuring gesture. "She's my baby sister, Mary. Not my wife."

"Oh." Her cheeks bloomed with color, then she looked away. "Well, let's go find out what the others know about Robin."

"At least grass and wildflowers are easier on a man's feet," Shane said, painfully reminded of his duty. He kept Mary's hand in his as they made their way down the hill toward the village. Any hope he'd harbored of finding Robin safely at the village had vanished with Rodriguez's most recent appearance. The outlaw must've known where they were headed. And why.

Rodriguez really had Robin. *Damn.* Shane could only pray that he would find Mary's brother.

Alive.

Chapter Sixteen

Please let Robin be all right. The prayer ran through Mary's mind again and again to the rhythm of her footsteps.

After seeing Angel across the river, her hopes of finding Robin safely at the village seemed futile. Even so, without absolute proof, she refused to accept that he'd been kidnapped.

Mañana.

Angel must've known where they were headed, and why. Since he'd made no effort to stop them . . .

Unmindful of where she stepped, she stumbled over a clump of wild violets. Shane thrust his arm in front of her and wrapped it around her waist, saving her from tumbling down the hill.

She gasped when he pulled her against him and stared down at her with a look that stole her breath. His beautiful green eyes beheld her with a possessive tenderness she couldn't deny. His expression tunneled into her, threatening to breach the crumbling barrier around her heart.

God help her, but she wanted to surrender, to lay her head against his chest, to allow his strength to support and surround her now when she needed it most. She wanted to let down her guard and *cry* until there were no tears left to shed.

But crying was for children. Mary girded her resolve and drew a deep breath.

Besides, he'd *lied* to her. She couldn't trust him.

Then why did she?

He reached up to touch her cheek with his callused fingertips, rough yet gentle at the same time. "Don't cry."

"I . . . I never cry." Mary tried to summon the mettle and resolve necessary to pull away. She shouldn't let Shane touch her, though his quiet strength comforted her. Why were her feelings for this man so conflicted?

Because he lied.

Motivated by the reminder of his transgression, she pulled herself free of his embrace. "I'm all right." She cleared her throat and faced the village. "Let's go. Maybe Robin's there . . ."

Shane's expression wavered between pity and tenderness, chipping away even more at Mary's shield. She couldn't allow that. Later, after Robin was safe again, she would face her feelings for Marshal Shane Latimer once and for all. *Not now.* She couldn't think straight with Robin in jeopardy.

Her brother would be fine. Anything else was . . . unthinkable.

She set a swift pace down the hill, more determined than ever to reach the village. Also, the sooner she and Shane were among other people, the easier it would be to keep her distance from him. He was simply too appealing, too irresistible, and *she* was far too vulnerable.

Shane remained blessedly silent as they entered the village, a mishmash of rough cabins and tepees—evidence of the aimless blending of two worlds. Mary looked around, trying to spot Robin, Tuck, or Little John. Finally, Little John emerged from a cabin, and she ran to him, noticing the absence of the children who'd left the village with their parents over the years. Only Little John's family remained, and their three younger sons had moved away as well.

"Little John, where's Robin?" she asked, grabbing his arm.

A look of confusion crossed the brave's face as he looked quizzically from Mary to Shane, then back. "Robin go home."

Mary shook her head violently. "He didn't come home, Little John. Where could he be? Where . . . ?" She'd so hoped to find him here, no matter how unlikely.

Shane put an arm around Mary's shaking shoulders and cleared his throat. "John," he said loudly. "Robin didn't come home. Did he leave before the storm or after? And where's Tuck?"

"After storm. Tuck, too." Little John turned toward the hill Mary and Shane had just traversed and pointed between it and the river. "They go short way."

"Where? Which way?" Shane tightened his hold around Mary. "Not over the hill?"

"No. Shorter." He pointed again.

An aging woman with silver hair and a face as wrinkled as a molasses cookie stepped around Little John. "Maid Marian, come."

Mary glanced at Shane. "This is White Dove, Little John's mother. Her husband is Chief Runningwolf."

"Come," White Dove repeated. "Hawk and your man will find Robin. You stay. We go talk to Walks in Sunshine about the wedding."

Mary drew a steadying breath, knowing White Dove made sense, but she couldn't bring herself to remain behind. "I can't. I must go with Hawk."

"Hawk?" Shane echoed, scratching his head.

"Indian name." Little John indicated himself by placing his hand on his own chest. "We go now."

White Dove sighed, but gave a knowing nod. "Go, child, find your brother."

Shane slid the guitar strap over his head and handed the instrument to White Dove. "Would you please keep this for me, ma'am?"

"White Dove, this is Shane Latimer," Mary said quietly, watching for some reaction from Little John. The brave appeared not to have heard the new name for the man he called Will Scarlet. "He's a lawman."

"White man law," White Dove said, but not distastefully. She narrowed her gaze and stared thoughtfully at Shane, taking the guitar in her hands. "You are good man. This is in your eyes. Find Robin Hood for Maid Marian and Walks in Sunshine."

Shane's throat worked visibly. "I'll do my best, ma'am."

"Come. We go." Little John took off in the direction he'd pointed to earlier. Mary had to run to keep up with his long strides, and had no choice but to accept Shane's arm for support. He helped keep her upright and propelled her along at a faster pace. She could tell he was trying hard not to limp on his sore feet.

The trail forked, one way leading over the top of the hill where Mary and Shane had come only a few minutes ago. The other twisted off toward the river through the trees. They didn't slow their pace until they reached the dark, cool shade along the river. Little John paused and looked around, his breathing normal.

Mary and Shane were both winded, but she didn't take her gaze off Little John. He scrutinized the riverbank with a solemn expression, turning periodically to search another area.

The forest was so dense near the water, Mary had no

difficulty understanding why Angel might have chosen this spot for an ambush. *Oh, Robin . . .*

A soft nicker sounded from the trees, but Little John didn't react. Shane moved slowly toward the sound, releasing Mary's hand as if that would convince her to remain behind.

Never. She followed a few feet behind, swallowing hard when Shane slid the leather loop from the butt of his pistol. The horse nickered again. It sounded familiar, if that was possible. A moment later, Tuck's pony stepped into the open.

Riderless.

"Oh, no." Mary moved beyond the pony and Shane, into the denser shade. "Tuck? Robin?"

Her throat squeezed around the mass of misery lodged there as she walked slowly through the trees, calling their names. *Please let them be all right,* she prayed, struggling against the threatening tears.

Shane and Little John joined her in the trees, walking slowly, surveying the twisted clumps of tree roots and mud as they went. The stagnant air was imbued with the pungent perfume of molding earth and rotting leaves. No birds stirred; the silence was unearthly. Frightening.

A low moan rose up, seemingly from the earth itself. Shane froze, holding his hand up as he, too, listened. "Shh."

Could it have been an animal of some kind? Mary's heart thundered in her ears as she strained to hear the sound again. It came louder this time. "I think it's Tuck."

"Tuck, where are you?" Shane shouted.

"Here."

Mary bolted toward the voice, stopping a few feet away and gasping in shock. Tuck was tied to a tree with his own suspenders. "Where's Robin?"

Little John went behind the tree and freed Tuck. The little man staggered, gripping his head with both hands as he regained his balance. He pulled his suspenders over his shoulders and shook his head as if to clear it.

"A man jumped us as we were heading toward the raft," Tuck said.

"Rodriguez," Shane said.

Tuck shot Mary a questioning glance. "Mary . . . ?"

She nodded, and her lower lip trembled. Meeting Tuck's worried gaze, she noticed the dark bruise on the top of his bald head. "You're hurt."

"It's nothing." Tuck turned to Shane. "Will, what happened?"

"He's not Will Scarlet." Mary drew a deep breath, girding her resolve. "He's Shane Latimer, a United States Marshal." Remembering what Shane had said about his badge, she tilted her head to one side. "But maybe you already knew that."

Red crept up Tuck's neck, across his face, and over his scalp. "I, uh . . . didn't know his name, child."

"It doesn't matter now," Shane said, stepping forward. "Finding Robin is all that matters."

Thankful of the reminder, Mary released a long sigh. "Angel Rodriguez threw a . . . a rock with a letter tied to it into the cabin after the storm."

"The same one he used on my head, no doubt." Tuck's expression sobered. "You're sure it was Rodriguez?"

"Yeah, we're sure," Shane said. "I saw him riding away, then later at the riverbank. He was watching us cross the river."

"What happened, Tuck?" Mary asked. "Please remember everything you possibly can. We have to save Robin."

"He jumped us from behind and clubbed my skull before I could get a good look at him." Tuck rubbed the lump on his head gingerly. "I came to when I heard you calling and found myself tied to that tree. I figured Robin might have gone for help, since his horse was gone, too."

"Wait a minute, something doesn't add up," Shane said, looking toward the river. "How can Rodriguez have jumped you two on this side of the river, then gotten back across without using one of your rafts?"

Mary untied her bonnet strings. "There's a narrow place to ford upriver, near the tributary he mentioned in the note."

"We need to head back to the cabin and figure out how to rescue Robin," Shane said, moving toward Tuck's pony. "I'm going to need a horse, though. Better go do some pretty singing first."

They walked in silence until they emerged from the trees. Little John paused, staring at the village, then he looked down at Tuck. His expression was one Mary had seen before.

"Make haste, men," Little John said, a baritone impersonation of something Robin had said at least a thousand times over the years.

Tuck met Little John's gaze soberly, his dark eyes glittering. "Indeed," he said, turning toward Shane. "We need Will Scarlet now . . . and Shane Latimer. Are you in or not?"

"I . . . I'm not sure." Shane shook his head and shrugged. "What are you talking about?"

Tuck stood at attention and looked off into the distance. "Regardless of what Sam Weathers or anyone else says . . ."

Mary looked from Tuck to Little John, to Shane, who appeared as bewildered as she. "What *are* you talking about?"

"I got a hunch." Chuckling, Shane shook his head. "Go on, little man. I'm listening."

Tuck looked up at Little John and gave an emphatic nod, then he faced Shane and Mary. With his hands on his hips, he looked like a politician about to deliver an oration.

"The Merry Men must ride again."

Sam's gonna kill me. "I'm in," Shane heard himself say, then he looked at Mary's stunned expression. "To save Robin from that bastard, I'll *be* Will Scarlet and Shane Latimer at the same damn time."

Her eyes glistened and she nodded. "Let's go get you a horse, and I'll see if I can borrow one, too."

Shane grabbed her arm. "You're staying here."

Mary lifted her chin a notch and glowered in his direction. "We already established that you have no right to tell me what do, Marshal."

"Will Scarlet." He flashed her a grin, and her expression softened.

"My still . . ." Tuck said thoughtfully, stealing their attention from the ongoing argument. He turned his gaze on Shane. "Do you think we can convince Rodriguez to bring Robin to the cabin instead of us going there?"

"Not a chance, and this isn't the time for a drink, little man." Shane released a long sigh. "As soon as I get a horse, I'm going to check out the area where the exchange is supposed to take place."

"I don't want a drink, young fool. Alcohol is a combustible liquid for which I have other plans." Tuck narrowed his eyes. "Tell me, exactly what does Rodriguez want in exchange for Robin's safe return?"

Shane inclined his head toward Mary. "I think you know the answer to that," he said, his voice laced with the flavor of his barely contained rage.

"That son of a bitch." Tuck took Mary's hand. "Obviously, there will be no exchange, child. We'll find another way."

Mary made no response, which worried Shane far more than if she'd argued the issue. "Yeah, we'll find another way." He patted the butt of his pistol. "Rodriguez is going to meet his Maker."

Mary's eyes flashed. "Yes, he is," she said, her voice flat. Emotionless.

Shane shook it off. She wouldn't do anything foolish. Would she?

I promised to take care of Robin, she'd said.

Damn. Now he had to rescue a man who thought he was Robin Hood and keep Maid Marian from playing martyr while he was at it. This really was a job for Shane Latimer and Will Scarlet combined. All he needed now was Sam Weathers.

"Make haste, men," Little John said and started walking toward the village again.

Jerked back to the present, Shane followed the Indian and offered Mary his arm. When she didn't take it, he shot her a side glance. She had her nose in the air, her chin thrust out, and walked with her arms in an exaggerated swing.

She was definitely up to something.

He sought out Tuck and realized that he, too, was staring at Mary with a furrowed brow. Maybe, just maybe, between the two of them they could keep her from doing something heroic and dangerous.

Why'd he have to go and fall for such a hardheaded female?

Listen to your heart, Shane.

His mother had picked the worst possible time to haunt him. As they reached the edge of the village, he finally acknowledged the truth banging around in his head and heart.

His mother had chosen the *best* possible time to haunt him. He needed a swift kick in the butt—or three—and, dead or alive, she was the best person for the job.

Right or wrong, smart or foolish, easy or difficult, Mary Goode was the only woman for him. His heart warmed at the thought, even as his head gave him a none-too-gentle mental shove for being such a damned sissy about the whole thing.

I'm in love with Mary Goode.

There, he'd admitted it to himself. Now all he had to do was rescue her brother, save her from doing something foolish, get rid of Angel Rodriguez once and for all . . .

And tell the woman how he felt.

Little John led them to the center of the village, where a large charred area indicated many fires had burned over the years. On this mild spring day, only a few hot embers remained.

"Wait here," the Indian said.

"We don't have much daylight left," Tuck said, looking west.

"Yeah, but we'll explain to John's father that we're in a hurry here." Shane rubbed the back of his neck.

"If anything has happened to Robin," Tuck said, his voice thick with emotion, "I'll never forgive myself."

"It's not your fault." Shane patted the shorter man on the back. "Rodriguez was determined to do this, and there wasn't anything you could've done to stop him."

"But *I* could have," Mary said, avoiding Shane's gaze. "It's my fault, because I angered him enough to . . . to do this horrible thing."

Shane reached for her, but she evaded him and turned to Tuck instead. "You know what he did to me," she said quietly. Wretchedly.

"Mary, please don't do this to yourself." Tuck's voice faded to a mere whisper. "Don't, child."

"You . . . you know what he did," she repeated.

"Yes, I know."

"And . . ."

"Mary, this isn't your fault," Shane said, aching to take her in his arms. He couldn't bear her pain. Why didn't she cry? Any other woman would, but not Mary. She was too strong sometimes for her own damned good.

Somehow, he had to make this right. He *had* to. "Rodriguez attacked you."

She nodded, and when she met Shane's gaze, her expression nearly killed him on the spot. She really blamed herself for everything. *Everything.*

"He said . . ."

"Child, don't," Tuck said, squeezing his eyes tightly shut. "Please, don't."

"He said I made him do it."

Rage slithered through Shane like an insidious snake. He'd never known hatred like this, but he had to maintain control.

"Mary, nobody made him do anything," Shane said quietly, though he wanted to yell and kick and hit something. He reached for her and placed his hand on her shoulder, watching the way she trembled at his touch. But it wasn't a tremor of fright. This was a tremor of longing, evident by the way she closed her eyes, the almost euphoric expression that softened her lips, the yearning in her sigh.

Emboldened, Shane massaged her shoulder. "He's been cheating women out of their hearts, their fortunes, their virtue, and their bodies for over ten years."

She nodded. "I suspected he was wanted."

"Dead or alive."

He met Tuck's gaze then, and the old man looked from Shane to Mary, then back. "Did the storm do any particular damage at Sherwood Forest?" His tone was casual, but his expression demanding. It was clear his question had another meaning entirely.

The little guy's a mind reader.

"Lightning hit a couple of trees," Shane said, "and a twister took the roof off the stable."

Tuck gave a curt nod. "I think you know what sort of damage I mean."

"I do, and I figure that's between me and Mary." Shane met and held the little man's gaze.

"And those who care about her," Tuck said, his voice too low for anyone else to hear. He arched a quizzical brow, breaking eye contact with Shane to look at Mary. "And I'm sure this one was a perfect gentleman."

Mary's face flared crimson and she looked down at her feet. "We need to get to Robin," she said, pacing. "What's taking so long?"

"Well, well, well." Tuck folded his arms, and a knowing smile parted his lips. "I believe there may be two weddings in the family."

Mary gasped and walked to the far side of the fire pit. She chewed her nails and continued to pace.

"Well, Marshal?" Tuck stroked his silver beard as he waited for an answer.

"Mary and I will discuss things once Robin is safe at home again." Shane raked his fingers through his hair. *Damn.* The little guy was joining Sam Weathers and Shane's mother.

You do right by Mary Goode.

Listen to your heart, Shane.

Enough!

"Yes, we certainly will discuss it," Tuck said, tilting his head to one side. "I'll admit, Marshal, that I'm eager to see Mary married, but I'm even more eager to see her *happy* and safe."

Shane swallowed hard. "Getting rid of Rodriguez will go a long way toward keeping her safe." He made a fist at his side. "A long way."

"That it will." Tuck looked toward the cabin. "Well, here comes Little John with his father."

Shane noticed the chief was nearly as tall as his son. John's—rather, Hawk's—father wore white man's clothes with an Indian headdress. *Peculiar.*

"Chief Runningwolf is a fair man," Tuck said, turning back to Shane. "He'll see to it you have a horse."

Mary rejoined them, and White Dove appeared beside her husband with Shane's guitar. The chief stopped before Shane and inclined his head. "I am Runningwolf, chief of the People."

"Pleased to meet you, sir. I'm, uh, Shane Will Scarlet Latimer." With a sheepish grin, Shane thrust out his hand, which the chief took in a sturdy handshake. "I take it Little John—er, Hawk—told you about our predicament?" Though he hated to rush things, time was critical.

With a nod, Runningwolf reached for the guitar, then held it out toward Shane. "You make music?"

"Some call it that." Shane grinned and took the instrument. He slipped the strap over his head and put his right foot on a large rock, bringing the guitar to the proper level. Slowly, he plucked the strings and tuned it as best he could, then strummed a few chords.

He glanced at Mary and flashed her what he hoped was an encouraging smile. God willing, her brother would sleep in his own bed tomorrow night, then next week there'd be a wedding.

One wedding?

Think about it later, Latimer. He cleared his throat and lapsed into "Amazing Grace" again, since there hadn't been enough time for him to rehearse any other songs. The chief smiled, and his wife swayed to the gentle rhythm. As he finished the last verse, Shane turned to Mary and saw her shining eyes.

Sighing, he turned to the chief. The older man's leathery face crinkled even more in a wide smile. He held up two fingers.

"What?" Shane turned to Tuck, who nodded toward the chief.

"I believe he wants you to have two horses."

"Good," Mary said, stepping forward. "I'll take one of them."

"Wild mustang not for white woman," Chief Runningwolf said with an emphatic nod.

Shane couldn't resist the urge to peek at Mary, remembering what they'd shared. Tuck cleared his throat, dragging Shane's attention to him. The little man's expression could only be described as shocked. Pleasantly so.

Damn.

"Two horses and you bring Robin home for wedding," the chief said, his tone leaving no doubt that Robin's safety was part of the bargain.

"I'll do my best, sir." Shane meant every word, and he prayed he could pull off this miracle. "I don't suppose you got a stout pair of boots lying around somewhere, too."

The chief arched a silver brow. "You do not like soft moccasins?"

Shane shook his head. "My feet are killing me."

"I have white man's boots Lone Eagle brought from town," the chief said. "I prefer my moccasins. You are welcome to boots, if they will help you return the man my daughter will marry."

"Lone Eagle is Henry," Mary explained. "He and Ruth brought me the kitten."

"Ah, I guess I'll have to thank him then." Shane would rather return the kitten, but Mary loved it.

The chief sent White Dove after the boots and Little John after the horses. "My sons have taken white man's names," the chief said while they waited. "All the young people of our village have moved away, except Sunshine and Hawk. Lone Eagle wishes us to move to town with him, and White Dove misses the sounds of children. Our youngest sons go to college in Tahlequah. It is lonely here."

Mary's eyes widened. "But—"

"First thing to worry about," Shane said steadily, "is getting Robin back safe and sound."

"Yes, of course." Mary chewed her lower lip.

Shane leaned close to Chief Runningwolf and whispered, "If you decide to sell, tell me first, please."

The chief nodded, assessing Shane with his wise old eyes.

White Dove returned with the boots a few minutes later, and Shane removed the moccasins, then slid his feet into the boots. "They're perfect," he lied gratefully. Though they were too big, they'd protect his bruised feet.

White Dove held out her hand. "You take these, Shane Will Scarlet Latimer. You might need them."

Shane opened his hand and took the small wrinkled berries. "What are they?"

"Spring purge."

Why was the woman giving him these? "I don't—"

"Use them wisely."

"Ah, yes. I see," Tuck said with a knowing smile. "I do believe I might be able to enhance their, uh, effect with a few embellishments I've been saving for just such a, uh, special occasion."

"Wait, I sure as hell don't need a spring purge," Shane said, his face flaming again. "What in tarnation are you trying to—"

"Not for you, young fool," Tuck said, a wicked gleam in his eye. "The purgative is for a certain outlaw, who'll suffer a major . . . inconvenience if we need to use these. I have another plan, but we'll take those, just in case."

"Ah, I get it, and you'll tell me about this other plan on the way back to the cabin." Shane glanced at Mary, whose cheeks were still fiery red, then he met the chief's twinkling dark eyes. "I don't know about you, Chief, but I'd just as soon shoot the man."

White Dove chuckled. "The bad man will wish you had."

Chapter Seventeen

"I'm going with you," Mary announced as she cleared the dishes from the table and tried to avoid Shane's probing gaze. "We have enough horses now, so there's no reason we all shouldn't go."

"Mary, I have to agree with Will. I mean, Shane," Tuck said. "It isn't safe. You should stay here . . . with the derringer loaded."

She shuddered, trying not to think about the time they'd already wasted. Was Robin hurt? Cold? Hungry? Frightened?

Alive?

But of course, they had to wait until dark. "He's my brother and I'm going. And I think we should take that scarecrow Robin made, too."

"Whatever for?" Tuck demanded.

"A decoy," Shane answered, giving Mary an approving nod. "Smart." He drummed his fingers on the table, then rose and walked to the open door. He stood there for several moments, staring toward the sunset, then finally turned to face her.

Mary's breath caught at the sight of him standing there, tall and proud and magnificent. The sunset provided a fitting backdrop for this handsome man.

She longed to touch him, to hold and be held, to murmur words of love. Her throat felt thick and tight, and a warm knot commenced low in her belly.

"That horse is half wild," he said quietly, his expression unreadable. "But if you insist on coming along, then I reckon that's the way of it."

"I do." She lifted her chin. "I know how to ride a horse."

He arched his brow so slightly she suspected that no one but she noticed. Dragging in a deep breath, she squared her shoulders.

Shane looked at Tuck and Little John before she could read his expression. "All right, Professor, do you have your snake oil and bombs ready to go?"

Tuck gave a wicked chuckle. "Indeed, though I doubt we'll need the purgative."

"And how are we going to get Rodriguez to drink this special treat, if we do need it?"

Little John looked up at Shane. "I make noise and bad man follow."

"Carefully," Mary interjected. She knew better than anyone how much Robin meant to Little John. They were brothers in every way that mattered.

"Careful," Little John echoed.

"All right, then what?" Shane asked Tuck.

Though they'd been over this at least fifty times, Mary understood the necessity of making certain everybody remembered their roles.

"Well, if the bombs don't do the trick, I'll slip the potion into the bastard's—er, into Rodriguez's beverage of choice."

"You were right the first time," Mary said, rubbing her upper arms to ward off a chill that had nothing to do with the evening air. "But . . . have any of you considered that *I* should be the one to distract him?" All three men gawked at her as if she'd grown an extra nose. "He's more apt to follow me than anyone."

"Imagine that." Sarcasm gave Shane's voice a hard edge. "He'd like nothing better than to drag you off into the trees, Mary."

She dropped her gaze, struggling to compose herself. Bile burned her throat, and her stomach roiled more violently than the twister had earlier. Being touched by Angel Rodriguez was her worst nightmare over and over again.

No, she realized, drawing a deep, fortifying breath. It was her *second* worst nightmare. Losing her brother was the worst. The same evil man was responsible for both.

She lifted her gaze to look from Tuck to Shane. "But you won't let him harm me, and we all know this is the most . . . effective way to distract him."

A muscle twitched in Shane's jaw, and Tuck stood to pace before the hearth, his cold pipe clutched in his hand. Little John sat at the table, obviously unaware of the not-so-subliminal messages passing between the others.

Shane turned his back on her as the sun dipped below the horizon. Dark shadows bathed the land beyond him. When he finally turned to face her again, she saw more in his expression than she'd expected. Compassion, determination, a deep yearning, and—she hoped—acceptance.

"Rodriguez will be expecting us at dawn," Shane said, rubbing the beard stubble on his chin. "Maybe we can catch him by surprise and rescue Robin tonight."

"This is preposterous," Tuck said, whirling around to face Shane, his fists on his hips. "I will not allow you to endanger Mary."

Shane's lips pulled into a thin line, then he said, "Endangering Mary is the last thing I want, Tuck." He looked across the room at her, his eyes shining, his expression tender. "And we aren't going to endanger her, because she's staying put."

"What . . . did you say?" she asked, shocked by his refusal. Until now, Shane Latimer had proven himself a man willing to listen to reason.

"I said endangering you is the last thing I—"

"I don't believe anyone asked your permission, Marshal." Mary eased herself onto the bench at the table, fury and determination writhing inside her as if they had a life of their own.

She *would* save Robin, no matter what.

"Ahem." Tuck pounded Little John on the back. "I believe you need some fresh air and I need to smoke."

"Not need fresh air," Little John said. "Stay here."

"You *need* fresh air." Tuck practically dragged the giant Indian out the door with him. "And I'm going to teach you to make bombs."

"Boom?" Little John asked.

"Yes, big booms," Tuck said, chuckling as he left the cabin.

Mary remained motionless, dumbstruck. She shouldn't have mentioned going with them. He might try to stop her, and she couldn't allow that. She'd trusted him.

But what about his lies?

"Mary, look at me," he said.

She heard the door close, and he crossed the room to sit beside her. He cupped her chin in his hands. "Look at me, Mary."

Her gaze narrowed, she turned to face him, lifting her gaze to his. *Why do I let myself care about you?* His eyes blazed with emotion. Nameless emotion. But she couldn't allow that to sway her. Robin came first.

"You can't go anywhere near Rodriguez," he said quietly. "Do you understand me, Mary?"

Her breath came in short bursts as she struggled between

fury and the love she felt for this man. He only wanted to protect her, but by protecting her, he could be sentencing her brother to God knew what horrors.

"I hear you," she said stoically, "but I don't understand."

"Don't you remember what he did to you? What he'll do to you again if he gets the chance? I'm not giving him that chance, Mary." Something glowed in his gaze that stole her breath. "Never."

"You have no right to fight my battles for me unless I invite you to do so." She drew a deep breath, jerking her chin from his hand, her voice dropping to a fierce whisper. "And if you think I've forgotten what he . . . he did to me, you're very mistaken, Marshal. I live with that memory every day of my life."

He stared at her in silence, his expression wary. "Just stay here, Mary," he said, rising. "That's the best way for you to help your brother."

"So you say." She stood, too, her back erect, her fists clenched at her sides.

His eyes darkened, and she watched him battle his rage in silence. "So I say."

Silence stretched between them, and he took a step closer. Mary held her breath, simultaneously praying he'd touch her and praying he'd leave her. He pressed a finger to her lips. "I care about you, Mary."

"I didn't ask you to." Her head ached, and those pesky tears threatened to escape, but she brought them under control with a deep breath and pure willpower. Tears were for children—not grown women with responsibilities. "I promised to protect my brother. And I will."

"And I promised to protect every law-abiding citizen," Shane whispered, his nostrils flaring slightly, "whether they want me to or not."

Their gazes clashed and held. He reached for her and

pulled her against him, precipitating a whimper from deep in her traitorous heart.

Mary squirmed in a feeble attempt to free herself from Shane's embrace. "Let me go."

"No." His breath fanned her face, warm and compelling. "I don't know why, but you make me burn, Mary Goode, and until I figure out why, I aim to make sure you stay safe."

His words struck a chord deep within her and she blinked. "You lied to me."

He nodded, his green eyes blazing like twin emeralds. "I had good reason."

She squirmed again, but he held her fast, the heat of his body seeping through her clothing and straight to her bones. That treacherous boneless feeling crept through her, but she battled it.

And lost.

"Tell me why you lied to me," she demanded, fighting to remain focused.

He stroked her hair, inciting a riot of need deep within her. Though she could utter words to deny her desire for this bewildering and complex man, she couldn't prevent the surge of hunger his touch created within her. Heat coiled low in her belly and spread throughout her perfidious body.

God help her, she *wanted* him to kiss her again. And more.

"Tell me why you lied," she repeated, her voice deep and throaty.

"Promise me you'll listen to everything before you get mad?"

"Why will I get angry, Marshal?"

"Why do you have to be so danged pretty *and* stubborn?" His golden lashes veiled his eyes as he lowered his lips to hers. She didn't even try to avoid his kiss.

None of the tenderness he'd shown her earlier was

present now, but she still didn't fear this man. Though he'd lied to her, she knew he wouldn't harm her. His tongue forged its way between her lips, laying claim to the darkest recesses of her mouth.

He sought, plundered, gave, but he didn't punish. Knowing he would never harm her empowered Mary, freed her to savor the exotic tumult of his kiss.

She bowed her body against his, her softness yielding to his hardness. Her curves flowed counter to the rigid planes and angles of his magnificent body, making her yearn to fit herself even more closely—intimately—against him.

He broke their kiss, nibbled the corners of her mouth, planted tiny kisses along her jaw to the lobe of her ear.

"I want you," he whispered.

Oh, God, she wanted him, too, but she could not succumb to her wanton nature now. Robin came first. He *must* come first.

"No, please." She jerked her hands free. Struggling against the onslaught of savage need tearing through her heart, body, and soul, she stalked to the hearth. "We're wasting time now. Tell me why you lied."

She felt him behind her before he touched her, then his hands came to rest on both her shoulders. Desperately, she wanted to turn into his embrace, to allow him to protect her.

But she couldn't.

She'd promised to protect Robin, and now Angel had stolen him from her. Memories of the others who'd taken Robin away to that asylum so many years ago surged through her. That nightmare had returned with a vengeance.

Releasing an exasperated sigh, she whirled around to face him. "Tell me why you lied and get it over with."

He dropped his hands to his sides. "After Little John

brought me here, two things disappeared from my saddle-bags.''

''Your badge and . . . ?''

''A wanted poster.''

''Of Angel Rodriguez?'' Mary shuddered, wishing they could turn back the clock and undo the damage.

''No.'' Shane ran his fingers through his wild, golden curls, then met her gaze again. ''Robin Hood and his ragtag crew of Merry Men.''

''What?'' Mary laughed, but it sounded false even to her ears. ''What nonsense are you talking about now?''

''The truth.'' Shane looped a thumb through his belt loop. ''You promised to listen.''

''I *am* listening.'' She tilted her head to one side. ''Are you suggesting that my brother is an outlaw?''

He sighed, then gave a curt nod. ''Robin, Tuck, and Little John are wanted men, and I came here to arrest them all.''

''That's preposterous.'' Mary pressed her fingertips to her temples. ''Finish this nonsense so we can go rescue my brother from a *real* outlaw.''

''That's right, Mary,'' Shane said quietly, his voice intense yet soothing. A moment later, his hands were on her shoulders again. ''Rodriguez is the real outlaw, and Robin and Little John were simply misguided.''

''And Tuck . . . ?''

''The brains behind the Merry Men.''

''What?'' Mary tried to pull away again, but Shane's hands on her shoulders held her fast. ''Tuck is not a criminal.''

''Maybe not before he came here, but since then he's been the brains behind Robin Hood and his Merry Men.''

Shock numbed her and a low roar commenced in her ears. ''All right, tell me what kind of crimes these *danger-ous* outlaws supposedly committed.''

''Stealing from the rich and giving to the poor,'' Shane

said with a grin. "Keeping just enough to clothe and feed all of you. What else?"

Mary almost laughed. Much as she wanted to deny the whole thing, a kernel of truth prevented her from doing so. Her brother stealing from the rich and giving to the poor sounded so . . . Robin. "What changed your mind about arresting them? Or have you changed it?"

"Oh, I've definitely changed it." Shane massaged her shoulders, his gentleness seeping into her. "The outlaw's pretty sister turned my head."

"Shane . . ." Her voice held a warning tone, though warmth stole through her at his words. "I'm serious."

"So am I." He sighed, and his expression sobered again. "Sam straightened everything out by confronting Tuck."

"Ah, so he knew, too." She tilted her head back and met Shane's gaze, wondering why men felt compelled to keep secrets from women under the guise of protection. "And what happened after that?"

"Tuck agreed that the Merry Men would never commit another crime, and I stayed on to . . ."

"To what?"

One corner of his mouth lifted and he quirked a brow. "To woo Maid Marian?"

"You can do better than that, Marshal."

"That's a half-truth," he admitted, bringing his hands up to cup her face. His expression hardened, and anger sparked in his eyes. "I stayed to catch Angel Rodriguez, Mary. I stayed to kill that bastard so he could never hurt you, or anyone else, again."

And *that,* she knew, was the truth. "Oh."

"While I waited to catch Rodriguez, I got to know two women—Maid Marian and Mary Goode." He smiled sadly. "And I came to know and respect men who were supposedly outlaws. Men I came here to arrest."

Torment tinged his words, and Mary loved him more

now than ever. "And I came to know and respect Will Scarlet," she said, her voice trembling.

He arched his other brow.

"And Shane Latimer," she added.

A quiet knock sounded at the door, answered by a loud meow from Katie's box. Mary sighed. "Time to rescue Robin Hood, Will Scarlet."

He nodded and went to answer the door, leaving Mary to stare after him in wonder.

Tuck strolled in and handed something shiny to Shane. "You might want this tonight."

Shane took the object and stared down at it, then closed his hand around it. "My badge." He sighed and shoved it into the front pocket of his jeans. "Tonight . . . I'm Will Scarlet."

Mary drew a deep breath. She'd worry about her feelings for Shane Latimer—and his for her?—after Robin was safe again. She knew what she had to do, and though it involved keeping secrets from Shane, Tuck, and Little John, she would do anything necessary to save Robin.

This would be like saving her brother from the devil himself.

The original fallen angel.

"Why the bloody hell did I let you talk me into this?" Bartholomew Goode asked for at least the thousandth time, shooting Fatima a derisive glance. "Why, I ask you?"

"Silence, Bartholomew." Fatima dismounted and tied her horse to a tree, waving for him to follow.

With an exasperated sigh, Bartholomew swung his leg over his rented horse and dropped to the ground. He was tired, cold, hungry, thirsty, and in desperate need of a bath. "It's dark now. Can we please st—"

"Silence," she hissed, peering through the trees.

Angry retort poised on his lips, Bartholomew caught sight of a flickering orange glow. Pushing aside a branch, he peered down at the campsite. The aroma of coffee and beans wafted up to his nostrils, and he drew an appreciative breath.

A lone figure lounged beside the fire, tipping a bottle to his lips for a long drink. The firelight gleamed against the man's dark hair and illuminated countless silver studs on various parts of his attire.

"Who is he?" Bartholomew whispered.

"Don't know." Fatima pointed beyond the fire's friendly circle. "There."

Peering into the semidarkness where the clearing met the trees again, Bartholomew made out the lone figure standing before a tree. He squinted. No, tied to the tree.

"Hmm."

"Do you recognize him?" Fatima whispered.

"The outlaw?" Bartholomew shook his head.

"No, fool, the other one."

"If you call me fool once more, madam—"

"I am sorry, Bartholomew."

Moonlight broke through the clouds and chose that particular moment to shine down on her silver hair. Bartholomew's breath froze as he gazed on her ethereal beauty. Though he'd found her striking before, he now found her captivating.

No, bewitching.

"Bartholomew, is that your nephew or not?"

"What?" He shook himself and cleared his throat quietly. Parting the branches again, he looked at the poor sap slumped against the ropes. A cockeyed cap boasting a droopy feather covered the lad's head. "I would say that's the infamous 'Robin Hood,' but I can't see his face well enough to tell if it's my nephew."

"They are one and the same."

Bartholomew had seen enough evidence of Fatima's

gifts by now to believe her. He made the mistake of looking at her again. Her hair practically glowed in the moonlight. Silver on silver. Ah, he wanted so very much to touch it.

To touch her . . .

A throaty chuckle floated to him on the evening breeze. "You like Fatima," she said quietly. She looked at him through veiled lashes. "You *want* to show me how much beast there is in a gentleman, but you forget something important."

Bartholomew couldn't breathe. The woman wove her spell around him and through him, sucking the air from the sky and sending all his blood below his belt.

Smiling, she reached over and pushed his chin until his gaping mouth closed. "First, we have a quest to complete. Remember? And—please do not forget this again—I am a married woman."

Ah, yes, married. He nodded numbly, then shook his head in self-contradiction. "Yes, quite." Discomfited, he looked toward the fire again. The dark man stood and took another swig from the bottle. Bartholomew could use a stiff drink about now, though he'd much prefer a snifter of his father's special Napoleon brandy.

"He is evil," Fatima said, her voice low and filled with concern. "Very evil."

The man definitely fit Bartholomew's standard description of evil. "What are we going to do about him?" Even a man in his distracted state knew they had to free "Robin Hood" before they'd know whether or not he was truly Robin Goode.

"Evil," Fatima repeated. "Kill him."

"Pardon me?" Bartholomew whirled around to face her, but she continued to glower through the trees at the outlaw. "I have no intention of killing anyone, madam."

She shot him a quick glance, then looked back to the

fire and shrugged. "Then I'll—" A small gasp sounded from her throat. "There."

Bartholomew turned his attention back to the fire. A third figure appeared in the trees opposite from the captive. She seemed to be . . . offering herself to the outlaw. "My God," he breathed.

"You know her?" Fatima grabbed his arm. "Is it . . . ?"

Bartholomew nodded slowly. "She's the image of Elizabeth. Like seeing a ghost . . ."

"Elizabeth?"

"My brother's wife—rather, deceased wife."

"Then she is your niece?"

"Yes," Bartholomew whispered, swallowing the lump of trepidation trying to crowd his guilt for supremacy.

"Then 'Robin Hood' is your nephew."

"Yes, but why is my niece with that outlaw?"

Mary held her breath as she approached Angel Rodriguez. He hadn't seen her yet, and neither had anyone else, thank goodness. She'd tied her horse in the trees far from Shane, Little John, and Tuck.

Casting furtive glances toward her brother, she stepped partially into the open to make certain Angel saw her. *God, let Robin be all right.* She couldn't tell if her brother was unconscious, asleep, or . . .

She refused to consider anything worse. After all, there would be no reason for Angel to keep Robin tied to a tree if—

No!

"Querida," Angel said, jerking Mary's attention back to him. "You've come early."

She drew a deep breath, forcing her trembling to cease. "Yes, I . . ." She'd rehearsed her speech so well, but now she couldn't remember any of it. "I've come to offer myself in exchange for Robin."

Angel staggered toward her, a nearly empty bottle clutched in his hand.

He's drunk.

He waggled his finger from side to side, pausing directly in front of her. "Not now, *querida.* I said *mañana.*"

Mary backed into the trees, praying Shane wouldn't see or hear her. With trembling fingers, she reached for the ribbon holding her hair at her nape and released it, giving her head a little shake to loosen the tendrils. "I couldn't wait," she whispered, hoping she sounded convincing.

His gaze narrowed, he tilted his head to the side as he followed her into the trees. "For what?" Menace tinged his words as he reached out to lift a curl between his fingers. "For me?"

"Y-yes." She drew great gulps of air, praying for strength and a great big miracle. "For you."

"*Por qué?* Why should I believe you now?" He moved closer. "I saw you with the golden-haired one."

His liquor-tainted breath enveloped her in a noxious cloud, but Mary refused to back away. She tilted her chin and met Angel's obsidian gaze. "You want me."

The moon allowed her to see the feral gleam in his eyes. He chuckled low and came closer, dropping the liquor bottle to the muddy ground with a soft thud. "*Yo te quiero.*"

His arm snaked out and encircled her waist, pulling her hard against him. Nausea rose in her throat, but she forcibly quelled it, casting another surreptitious glance at her brother.

He still hadn't moved.

"*Show* me you want me," Angel whispered, his breath fanning her face and prompting her nausea to return. "Show me now."

"Not here," she said, her voice surprisingly steady. "Someplace where Robin can't see us."

Angel arched a brow. "Angel Rodriguez is no fool."

Mary feigned a pout. "I can't show you where my brother might see." She leaned backward slightly, releasing the buttons at the top of her shirt. "Come with me."

He looked around the camp, then gave a shrug. "Don't try anything, *querida,*" he warned. "Your brother will pay for your foolishness with his life."

"I want to go away with you, Angel," she lied. "You promised to show me Mexico City."

A wicked smile pulled at his lips. "It's about time, *querida.* I will dress you in gold and silk."

Mary forced herself not to scream as he yanked her to him, brandishing his erection like a weapon. Bile threatened to gag her, and her heart performed an Irish jig. Darkness wavered just out of reach, encouraging her to abandon this insanity and surrender to unconsciousness.

No, Robin needed her.

Angel kept his arm around her waist as he staggered toward the trees, farther from Robin, thank goodness. Mary could only pray that Shane would free Robin before Angel could . . .

She focused on the cold steel of Tuck's derringer tucked inside her moccasin. It was loaded, and she would use it. There was no question about it.

Angel Rodriguez would die, not only for what he'd done to her, but for what he'd done to her brother as well. Mary had never considered killing anyone before, but she accepted the knowledge with cold certainty that she *would* kill Angel Rodriguez.

He staggered against her, and she nearly fell beneath his weight. The thought of him covering her again chilled her blood to ice. But the memory of his earlier attack strengthened rather than weakened her, and she pushed him back to an upright position.

"I would not have consumed so much tequila if I'd

known you were coming.'' His words slurred slightly, his English precise and slow.

Emboldened by his display of weakness, Mary squared her shoulders and made sure he was completely stable before loosening her grip on his arm. Touching him made her want to scream, and she did so inside. Repeatedly. Though there was nothing she could do to prevent his arm from snaking its way around her waist again.

Please let Robin be all right, she prayed again as Angel dragged her into the trees. He seemed suddenly stronger, more threatening.

More dangerous.

He whirled her around to face him within the shelter of the trees, reaching for the front of her loose shirt. Mary held her breath as he fumbled with the buttons.

"Jesús." He grabbed the front of her shirt with both hands and ripped it open, sending buttons flying in every direction.

The horrifying memories she'd held barely in check flooded her mind, filled her with the all too familiar terror. Last time he'd used a knife to strip away her protective clothing, but he was even more dangerous now.

Because he had Robin.

He pulled her against him again with one hand and grabbed her exposed breast with his other. Shock recoiled through Mary, and a shudder dawned from her very soul. She couldn't let him do this to her again.

She *wouldn't* let him do this to her again.

"Slow down," she purred, praying her fear didn't reveal itself in her tremulous voice. "We have all night."

"Do we, *querida*?" He kneaded her flesh with his rough hand, then bent toward her.

Mary arched backward, hoping she didn't appear unwilling. Instead of kissing her mouth, he pressed his lips against her pulse at the base of her throat.

An explosion rent the air, and Angel froze. Mary's heart pressed against her stomach. *Tuck's bombs.*

"You betrayed me, *querida.*" Angel pulled back his hand to strike her.

Another explosion sounded from the clearing, and Mary could no longer restrain her screams. She screamed through the explosion, then continued screaming.

"Shut up, *puta.*" Angel shook her.

Mary struggled to break free, but Angel pushed her against a tree. She reached for her moccasin, visualizing the derringer in her hand. It would gleam in the moonlight. She would aim it at his black heart.

She would squeeze the trigger . . .

Panting, Angel fumbled with the buttons of her breeches. "You going to give Angel what you promised, then I kill your imbecile brother with my bare hands."

Mary screamed again, jerked back to the present. Angel's words were terrifying, but his promise to kill Robin assured Mary her brother was still alive. She squirmed and strained, desperate to reach her gun, but Angel's weight held her pinned to the oak tree.

Surely Shane would hear her screams.

"Unhand her!" an outraged male voice commanded.

Bewildered, Mary was barely cognizant of the beefy hands dragging Angel from her. She fell sideways with an undignified plop, her shirt gaping open.

A silver-haired woman appeared, more beautiful than anyone Mary had ever seen. She couldn't be real.

Mary couldn't think. She leapt to her feet as the large man dragged Angel aside. A loud thud reached her ears, followed by a quiet rustle.

"He won't wake up for a long while," the man said, appearing beside the silver-haired creature.

The man's English accent triggered memories of warmth and comfort, and Mary stared at him, transfixed. "Who are you?"

The woman draped a shawl around Mary's shoulders. "Come."

"No. My brother—"

"He is safe. Come."

The man swooped her into his arms and ran through the trees with the woman. Clutching the shawl around herself, Mary screamed again, wondering what nightmare she'd encountered now. But Robin was alive.

They crested a hill and she looked back at Angel's camp. Smoke curled upward from Tuck's bombs. A figure still slumped against the ropes, but from this distance, she couldn't be sure.

Was it Robin or the scarecrow?

Chapter Eighteen

Shane cut Robin loose and tied the scarecrow wearing Robin's hat to the tree. The stench of Tuck's smoldering bombs permeated the campground with a noxious cloud. The little man seemed to be enjoying his job. Considering what Rodriguez had done to Mary, Shane understood that only too well.

Tuck stuffed a rag into another half-filled bottle of corn liquor, then lit the rag with a match and hurled it into the clearing. The explosion made more noise than anything else, but sent shards of glass flying. Pity Rodriguez wasn't in camp to appreciate their efforts.

Shane would find him once Robin was safe. Then the bastard would answer for his crimes. One more explosion, then Shane froze, his blood chilled through.

Was that a woman's scream?

Another shrill cry filled the night, sending a shudder through Shane. "Mary," he whispered, glancing at Tuck, who'd also paused to listen. "Mary."

"Maybe it's an animal," Tuck reasoned, though the

tone of his voice made it clear even he didn't believe that.

Shane continued to stare across the clearing, squinting toward the trees where he'd seen Rodriguez vanish mere moments ago. Surely Mary hadn't . . .

Oh, God.

He remembered the fierce glint in her eyes, the stubborn thrust of her chin. When they'd left to come after Robin, he'd heard her slide the bolt home. He'd been confident she would remain safely at the cabin with Tuck's derringer until they brought Robin home to her.

The night had grown quiet now. Too quiet.

Shane stole a glance at Robin. He was badly bruised and tired, but not seriously injured. His left eye was swollen shut, and Shane vowed to make Rodriguez pay for that, too, though the bastard was already slated to pay the ultimate price for his crime against Mary.

Pity it couldn't be more. . . .

Shane had only known such hatred once in his life— for his father. Angel Rodriguez was about to join the old man in hell where they both belonged.

"See?" Tuck said nervously. "It was no—"

Another scream reached them, louder and more terrified than the others. Keeping near the trees, Shane maneuvered himself around the campsite. He almost fell over Rodriguez, sprawled facedown in the mud.

"What the hell?" Shane stooped beside Rodriguez and checked for a pulse. The bastard was still alive. For now. Pity Shane wasn't cold-blooded enough to finish the job this way. But he had to look the devil in the eyes to kill him.

First, he had to find Mary. He'd heard her scream. Where was she? Icy fingers of fear spiked through Shane, and he leapt to his feet, hurrying farther into the trees. "Mary?"

He searched the area as thoroughly as possible in the moonlight. Then he searched again. "Mary?"

Where was she? Was she unconscious? Hurt?

Dead?

She had to be all right. He'd never forgive himself if anything happened to her. He should've known she wouldn't stay behind. Dammit, he should've tied her up for her own good.

"Mary!"

"Shane, where is she?" Tuck appeared at his side. The smaller man grabbed his arm. "What happened? I saw Rodriguez."

Dread settled over Shane, reminding him of his time in the Redemption jail, where he'd awaited execution for his father's murder. "I don't know, Tuck." Helplessness pressed down on him. "God help me."

"She has to be here. We both heard her." Tuck cupped his hands to his mouth and shouted, too.

Desperate, Shane returned to where he'd left Rodriguez.

He was gone.

Sweat trickled down his face and into his eyes. Where the hell was Mary? Did Rodriguez have her?

Tuck came up behind him. "Maybe she returned to the cabin." The smaller man approached the area where Rodriguez had been. "My God. Where's . . ." Tuck stomped around the area, kicking at shrubs and searching as frantically as Shane had. "He was here. Right *here*. I should've killed him."

"We both should've."

"Could he have Mary?"

Silently, Shane rose, clenching his fists at his sides. "I'm going to find the bastard. And kill him."

"There's nothing more we can do in the dark."

There was plenty Shane could—and would—do in the dark, but he intended to send Robin and the others back to the cabin first. He'd promised to return Mary's brother safely, and he would.

But at what price?

Swallowing his fear, Shane followed Tuck back to their horses. He glanced at Robin, slumped over the animal's neck. "Take him home, Tuck."

Shane looked back toward the clearing, his gut coiling into a burning knot of fear and rage. "Mary," he called again, and an owl hooted in the distance.

"Maid Marian here?" Little John asked. "Where?"

Shane shook his head. "I wish I knew." Swinging his leg over his saddle, he grabbed the reins of the horse bearing Robin and handed them to Little John. "Return Robin Hood and Friar Tuck to Sherwood Forest, Little John."

"What about you, young fool?" Tuck asked knowingly, but without an inkling of disapproval.

"Will Scarlet won't return without Maid Marian." Shane held Tuck's gaze for several moments, and he remembered the old man's words about Mary and Robin being the children he'd never had. His throat felt full and tight. "I'll find her, Tuck. I swear."

"If anyone can . . ." Tuck sighed and rode ahead of Little John.

Shane backed into the trees and sat frozen in the saddle, watching the dying campfire. Rodriguez's supplies were here. Searching for Mary and the outlaw in the dark was futile, so Shane would wait for the bastard to return, with or without Mary.

Earlier, he'd thought himself incapable of killing an unconscious man in cold blood, but now he wasn't so sure about that. Executing Angel Rodriguez wouldn't have been murder.

It would've been justice.

Shane checked his pistols. And waited.

Rodriguez would soon be begging for death.

* * *

At least no shots were fired. Mary hoped that meant Shane had saved her brother without anyone being hurt. She still didn't know who the strangers were, or whether they'd rescued her or abducted her, for that matter.

For some strange reason, she felt safe in their presence. Besides, if they hadn't come along when they did, she—

Unthinkable.

"Which way is your home?" the man asked, his English accent reminding her again of happy, long-ago times. He placed her on the horse behind the woman. "We'll take you there."

"I need to check on my brother," Mary argued.

"He is safe," the woman insisted again. "We go now."

Mary stared long and hard at the woman's back in the moonlight. She seemed so sincere Mary believed her. Surely Shane and the others were taking Robin home even now. The only way to find out was to go see for herself. With a sigh, she gave the strange man directions to the cabin in Sherwood Forest.

Riding double with the silver-haired woman, Mary studied the man in the moonlight. There was something vaguely familiar about him, though his accent had probably triggered the thought.

They rode in silence to Sherwood Forest, and Mary told them to put their horses in the roofless soddy. There was no sign of the others, and her heart ached with the need to see them all here safely again.

Was Robin hurt? Was he even alive?

This had been an excruciatingly long day, but it was far from over. Without hesitation, she invited the strange couple into the cabin and lit the lamp. Then she left them and went behind her private curtain to change into an untorn shirt. If only she had enough time and privacy to bathe after suffering—briefly, thank God—Angel's loathsome touch.

When she emerged, she returned the woman's colorful shawl and looked at the strange couple. At last, she could see them both clearly. The woman was incredibly beautiful and much younger than her silver hair suggested. The man was . . .

Familiar. Yes, very familiar. "Who are you?" she asked, watching him remove his hat and drag his fingers through dark hair with streaks of gray at the temples. She swallowed the lump in her throat as suspicion dawned. "You look like . . ."

He smiled. "Like your father?"

Mary's knees buckled, and she grabbed the table's edge for support. The woman came to her at once and slipped an arm around her waist.

"Tell her now, Bartholomew," the woman said, easing Mary to the wooden bench. "I am called Fatima, and I will prepare food. You rest."

Numbly, Mary stared at the man. He sat across the table from her, a sheepish expression on his distinguished face. "Bartholomew?" she repeated.

The man nodded. "Bartholomew Goode. Your uncle."

A loud roar filled Mary's ears, and the room spun madly. Groaning, she rested her forehead in her hands until the spinning ceased and her rising nausea abated. "My . . . my uncle?"

He sighed. "Yes, and I can't tell you how hard it's been locating you."

Fatima cleared her throat loudly as she bent to stir the hot embers in the hearth into a small blaze.

Bartholomew's face reddened beneath his whiskers. "And without Fatima's help, I'd still be searching."

Mary wavered between surprise and anger, then remembered her brother and looked at Fatima. "You said my brother is safe. How do you know that?"

"Fatima knows." The woman shrugged and looked in the pot. "Beans. They'll do." She stirred the pot without looking at Mary, obviously unwilling to discuss her mysterious "knowing" any further.

Mary stood, uncertain how to talk to her uncle. She knew he spoke the truth, because the physical resemblance between him and her father was undeniable. Why had he come *now?*

Feeling steadier now, she went to the door and gazed out at the dark night. Frogs and crickets sang, an owl hooted, but no human or horse sounds reached her ears. The moon outshone most of the stars and bathed the land in a blanket of spun silver, though it would soon set and leave only blackness in its wake.

Where were they?

She felt her uncle's presence behind her, but she didn't turn to face him. Unshed tears stung her eyes, and her heart played the rhythm of her turmoil. Nothing mattered but having the men she loved return to Sherwood Forest safely. *Nothing.*

"If Fatima says Robin is safe, he is," Bartholomew said quietly. "Mary, I would've come sooner, but—"

"Why didn't you?" She turned slowly to face him, shocked again by his resemblance to her long-dead father. "I wrote and wrote and wrote and . . ." Scalding tears threatened, but she quelled them. She would *not* cry. "Why?"

If her grandfather or uncle had sent for them years ago when she'd first written, Robin would be safe now. They'd be at Briarwood in England, warm, fed, together.

And she never would have met Shane Latimer.

Her heart turned over and pressed against her constricting throat. She breathed deeply and brought herself under control, then lifted her chin to await her uncle's response.

"I . . ." Bartholomew shrugged and held his hands

toward her beseechingly. "My father—your grandfather—suffered a debilitating stroke upon learning of your parents' deaths, Mary."

"I wrote letters," she whispered, trying to grasp this bizarre turn of events. "Dozens of letters."

"Letters that weren't opened until six months ago, Mary." Her uncle looked down at the floor, then met her gaze again with an expression so wretched, she almost regretted her harsh words. Almost.

"For the past seven years I've been in India and exploring parts of Africa," he explained. "I didn't see any of your letters, because my father's loyal servant tucked them away unopened. When I returned to Briarwood after my father died, I found and opened them. I read every single one, Mary. I'm so sorry."

"Oh." Their grandfather was dead. Mary drew a deep breath, then released it very slowly. "I'm sorry."

"No, I'm the one who's sorry." Bartholomew's sad eyes were the same shade of hazel as her father's. "Your grandfather never spoke or moved again under his own power after his stroke, Mary. The wit and wisdom that made him who he was vanished long ago, which was the main reason I spent so much time abroad."

"I see." Mary resisted the urge to look outside again. She would hear their approach before she saw them anyway. "Where *are* they?"

"They will come soon," Fatima said, putting tin plates on the table. "Very soon."

"How . . . . ?" Mary stared long and hard at the mysterious woman.

"Fatima knows things." The woman shrugged and tilted her head to the side. "Ah, they come now. Won't Adam be surprised?" She patted her hair and smoothed her split riding skirt, then rearranged her bright paisley shawl to display a generous amount of cleavage.

"Adam?" Mary shook her head, not bothering to tell

Fatima that she knew no such person. The blessed sound of hoofbeats reached her ears, and she forgot everything except setting eyes on her brother and the man she loved again.

Little John came toward the cabin, and she saw shadows as someone took their horses to the soddy. Mary strained to count the horses, to identify the men, but failed. It was simply too dark. As Little John drew closer, she realized he was carrying Robin.

"He's hurt." She rushed out into the darkness and met Little John in front of the cabin. "How bad?"

"Robin Hood all right," her brother said weakly. "Maid Marian home, too."

"Yes, Robin," Mary said, her voice breaking, "I'm home. Bring him inside, please, Little John." *Thank you, God. Thank you, God.*

Little John seemed unaffected by the sight of strangers in the cabin. He stepped around Bartholomew and placed the man's nephew on the bunk nearest the hearth.

Mary dropped to her knees beside the bunk. "Lie still and let me make sure nothing's broken."

"Nothing broken," Robin said. "Eye hurts."

His eye was nearly swollen shut and he had a jagged gash on his eyebrow. *Damn Angel Rodriguez to hell.* Mary never cursed, but now certainly seemed the time to learn. "I don't have any ice, but I'll get a cool cloth to clean that."

The moment she stood, Fatima appeared at her side with a basin of fresh water and a cloth. With only a passing thought for the woman's intuition, Mary thanked her.

Robin pushed up onto his elbows and squinted through his one good eye. "Who that?"

Before Mary could answer, their uncle came to her other side and smiled down at Robin. "Do you remember me, young man?"

Robin's mouth fell open and he stared in fascination. Finally, he nodded and said, "Uncle Bot."

Mary looked from her uncle to her brother. Robin was six years older than she, and it made sense that he would remember their uncle better than she did. Despite his slowness, Robin Goode had an outstanding memory.

"Uncle Bot," she repeated, remembering that they'd both called their uncle by that special name because Robin couldn't pronounce Bartholomew then, and she was fairly certain he wouldn't be able to now. "Yes, I remember."

She cleaned Robin's wound, then rinsed the cloth and placed it gently against his entire eye. "Keep that there for a while."

Robin nodded, still staring at his uncle. "Uncle Bot," he said almost reverently.

"Yes, lad," the man said quietly, his voice hoarse with emotion. "I've come to take you and Mary home."

"This home," Robin said emphatically, thrusting out his jaw. "You stay here."

God, why now? Mary bit her lower lip, wanting desperately to change the subject. They could discuss the future later. She heard shuffling at the door and left her brother's side to greet Tuck and Shane.

"Shane," she said, her heart plummeting when she found only Tuck on the stoop. "Where's Shane?"

The old man sighed. "Thank heavens you're safe. We looked everywhere for you. What possessed you to—"

"Where's Shane?" Mary repeated, looking beyond Tuck and into the cloying darkness.

"He's not here, child." Tuck stepped into the crowded little cabin and stared at Bartholomew. "Who's he?"

"Never mind, just tell me where Shane is." Mary grabbed Tuck's arms and terror ripped through her. "Is he—?"

"No, no, he's searching for a brave but foolish girl by

the name of Mary. Do you know her?'' Tuck patted her hand and pointed at Bartholomew. ''Who is that man?''

''Uncle Bot,'' Robin said, swinging his legs over the side of his bunk.

''Uncle?'' Tuck echoed, turning his wary gaze on Mary again. ''Really?''

''Our father's brother.'' She couldn't stop thinking about Shane out there in the dark. Alone. With Rodriguez. ''Are you sure Shane's all right?''

''He was fine when we left him, Mary, and once he has daylight, he'll track you right back here.'' Tuck gave Mary an indulgent smile. ''If he isn't here by midmorning, I'll go find him myself, child.''

Tuck squeezed her hand, then approached Bartholomew. ''Pray tell, what took you so long to come for your orphaned niece and nephew, Mr. Goode?''

Tuck placed his fists on his hips and glowered up at the much larger man in the same manner with which he'd greeted Mary the first time they met eight years ago. *So much courage in such a small package.*

She had to believe this man who'd been like a father to them. If he said Shane was safe, then he was.

For now.

''It's a long story,'' Bartholomew said with a weary sigh.

''Sit and eat something.'' Mary moved around Tuck to stand beside her uncle, trying not to think about Shane or Angel or going home to England or *anything.* ''I'm sure Uncle Bot will explain everything.''

''Uncle *Bot?*'' Tuck arched a speculative brow.

''Short for Bartholomew,'' Mary explained, looking around for Fatima. ''I don't remember having this many people in here at the same time before.'' Of course, that wasn't quite true, but her uncle and Little John were larger than the average man. If Shane were here, too ... *But he will be.*

He had to come back.

If she'd remained here as he'd asked, he would be here now. Guilt pressed down on her, but she shoved it aside. She had distracted Angel enough to allow Shane and the others to rescue her brother. She knew in her heart that was true.

And she prayed Shane would come home to her, so she could thank him properly. Warmth oozed through her at the prospect, but she reminded herself she had guests.

Turning her attention to the present, Mary looked around the cabin again for Fatima. "Where did she go?"

"She?" Tuck arched the other brow. "Did you lose that infernal kitten again?"

Bartholomew and Little John both stepped aside and Fatima came forward, looking even more exotic and stunning than before. A knowing smile curved her ruby lips, and a mischievous gleam danced in her dark eyes.

"Meow," she said.

Small, courageous Friar Tuck gave a mighty gasp, then his eyes rolled backward and he toppled like a felled tree.

Shane watched Rodriguez stagger back into his camp. The outlaw tilted the bottle of tainted tequila and drained its contents. He turned it upside down and shook it, then muttered a curse in Spanish. He hurled the empty bottle against a tall oak, where it shattered into hundreds of splinters.

With only his fury to warm him, Shane waited. Rodriguez staggered over and pissed on the ground, then the desperado yanked the hat off the scarecrow and shook his head, still muttering in Spanish as he returned to his campfire and landed facedown on his bedroll. It wouldn't take the outlaw long to fall into a deep, drunken slumber.

Then Shane would pay him a little visit.

The moon dipped below the horizon and stars burst

into brilliance in the inky sky. He watched them twinkling, brighter and more numerous with every passing second. A shooting star arced before him and he made a wish.

Please, let Mary be safe.

The only light in the small clearing was from the dying embers of the campfire. No movement came from the bedroll as Shane swung his leg over the horse's back and eased himself to the ground.

He stood there for countless minutes, watching the sleeping bastard who'd raped Mary, kidnapped her brother, and possibly harmed her yet again. Dear God, how else could her disappearance be explained?

Shane drew a shuddering breath and took a step toward the outlaw. Dried leaves and twigs snapped beneath his oversized boots and he paused, waiting to ensure his nemesis wouldn't awaken.

Rodriguez snored.

Drawing his pistol, Shane continued toward the bedroll. He paused right beside the drunken bastard and took aim with both hands.

Pure hate simmered from the darkest corners of his soul. Last time he'd felt this way toward another human, Shane had been barely twenty years old. Though he hadn't killed his father, he could have. The last time the old man had beaten Ma was destined to be his last, but someone else had saved Shane the trouble.

He'd hated. He'd vowed to kill. But he hadn't.

Now, here he stood with the law on his side. *Dead or alive.* He could choose to snuff out this bastard's miserable life, collect the reward, and never look back. Justice would be well served. Mary and Robin would be avenged.

And Shane would have killed in cold blood.

He swallowed hard. Sweat trickled down his temples, to his neck, into the open collar of his shirt. The silence pressed down on him, rivaling his nagging conscience for supremacy.

He wanted to kill Angel Rodriguez because of what he'd done to Mary. It was the *wanting* that stopped Shane from pulling the trigger now.

Taking human life—no matter how vile—by choice was wrong. Plain, old-fashioned wrong. But if Rodriguez so much as looked like he planned to run, that would change things considerably.

Do it, you filthy bastard. Run, fight back—make me have to kill you.

Shane kicked him in the ribs. Twice. Three times. "Wake up, you swine."

Another snore.

He hooked the toe of his boot beneath the bedroll and flipped it over, occupant and all. Groaning, his enemy came awake and looked up at Shane with a grimace. "Go away, gringo. You got what you wanted."

"Not quite, Rodriguez." Shane struggled to keep his rage under control long enough to get the answers he needed. "There's one more thing I want."

Rodriguez seemed surprisingly sober as he stared up at Shane. "What do you want, gringo?"

"Revenge."

The outlaw chuckled. "What did I ever do to you, *amigo*?"

"I'm sure as hell not your *amigo*." Shane pulled back the hammer. "You raped Mary Goode and kidnapped her brother."

Rodriguez showed no fear, though the campfire's glow illuminated his black eyes, fixed on the barrel of Shane's pistol. "Rape, *amigo*? Is that what the *puta* called it?"

Shane swallowed hard, wishing he was the type who could simply pull the trigger and have his revenge. No matter what, he wouldn't—couldn't—let this depraved scum go free.

"Where's Mary?"

"How should I—" The Mexican stopped midsentence,

and a wheezing chuckle erupted from deep in his diaphragm. "Ah, so the bitch ran away from her big gringo knight in shining armor."

"You want to die real bad, don't you, Rodriguez?" Shane remained steady, poised to pull the trigger if his prisoner so much as flinched the wrong way. "Tell me where she is, you bastard."

Rodriguez fell back, laughing uproariously and thrashing around on the ground. Shane was no fool. That thrashing was nothing but a distraction so Rodriguez could get to his gun. As predicted, the villain went for his weapon, but Shane was faster. He brought his boot heel down hard on Rodriguez's gun hand.

"I asked you a question," Shane said quietly. Menacingly. "My patience is wearing thin."

"I do not know."

"Not laughing now, eh, *bandito*?" Shane gouged his boot harder against the outlaw's forearm. "Answer me."

"I do not know."

"Not good enough."

"We were there in the trees, *amigo*." Rodriguez chuckled again. "She was all over me, tearing off her clothes, begging me to take her there in the mud like the *puta* she is."

He's only trying to rile you, Latimer. And doing a fine job of it, too. "Then what happened?" he asked blandly. It would never do to allow Rodriguez to know how much Mary meant to Shane.

"Someone intruded."

"What?" Tuck and Little John had been with Robin. "Who?"

"A silver-haired *mujer* and another gringo."

Shane had to find Mary, and right now he had no choice but to believe this low-life. "Who were they?"

"No more."

"This Colt says you're going to tell me a whole lo

more, Rodriguez.'' Shane swallowed hard. ''You want
to argue with a bullet?''

''You won't shoot me.'' Rodriguez looked down at
Shane's boot on his hand. ''My hand, *amigo*.''

Keeping his pistol aimed at the villain's black heart,
Shane kicked Rodriguez's gun out of reach. ''Don't try
anything stupid.''

The outlaw's dark eyes twinkled in the waning firelight
as Shane eased his foot off the man's hand. ''Now tell
me where they took Mary,'' Shane said. ''Otherwise, I
intend to collect the bounty on your head.''

''Dead or alive, eh, *amigo*?'' Rodriguez rubbed his
bruised hand, chuckling quietly. ''I tell you about the
puta . . . for a price.''

So that was his game. ''You aren't going to need money
where you're going.''

''Ah, but you are mistaken, gringo.'' The desperado
tilted his head back and grinned. ''I will live long and
need *mucho dinero*.''

''Roll over.'' Rodriguez shrugged, but obeyed, then
Shane tied the outlaw's hands behind his back. ''Now
get up.''

Obviously still under the influence of tequila, it took
Rodriguez several minutes to stand without the assistance
of his hands. Swaying, the man finally stood before Shane,
but the wicked light still gleamed in the villain's eyes.

Now Shane had two reasons not to execute the bastard—his pesky conscience and finding Mary—and he
didn't like it at all. He would get answers.

One way or another.

Remembering one of Sam's tricks, Shane deftly released Rodriguez's belt, and the outlaw's black dungarees
fell around his ankles.

''What is this, gringo?'' Rodriguez narrowed his gaze,
and deep creases lined his brow.

Let the bastard think whatever he wanted. Shane didn't

care about anything but finding Mary. "Kick off the boots and step out of your jeans."

"*Qué?*"

"Now." Shane fired a shot near Rodriguez's feet. Dust and gravel flew, but he didn't even blink.

Muttering to himself, Rodriguez obeyed and kicked his breeches away. The outlaw opened his mouth as if to speak, then a grimace twisted his features. "*Dios mio.*" With a low moan, he doubled over. More groaning commenced, then he drew several deep breaths, finally lifting his head to gaze at Shane with a pleading expression. "*Estómago.*"

"Bad tequila?" *Serves Rodriguez right.*

"*Dios.*"

"Move into the trees." Shane weaved his pistol in that direction. "Toward the river."

Rodriguez obeyed and Shane followed, loosening the coiled rope from his belt. The outlaw groaned again and leaned against a tree.

Shane moved cautiously behind the outlaw, then yanked Rodriguez against the giant hickory and wrapped the rope around him several times before tying it securely.

"What are you doing?" Rodriguez asked.

Shane turned and waited. "Getting answers." He holstered his pistol and withdrew the knife his grandfather had given him many years ago.

"You going to cut Angel, *gringo*?"

Trust your gut, Sam always said, and Shane would use whatever means necessary to find Mary. "Yep."

"If I die . . ."

"Justice will have been served," Shane finished.

Rodriguez groaned again. "*Por favor.*"

"Please?" Shane barked a derisive laugh. "That's a switch, Rodriguez." He moved closer and slipped the point of his knife beneath each of the silver conchas adorning the outlaw's black shirt. They popped like corn hitting a hot skillet.

"Why'd you do that, *amigo*?"

The outlaw's obvious regret at having his clothing ruined gave Shane more ideas. He returned to the campfire and retrieved Rodriguez's fancy boots, hat, belt, and studded breeches.

"*Dios.*"

"You said that already, and I don't reckon God's feeling real sympathetic toward you about now." Shane stood a safe distance from Rodriguez and dropped the clothing into a pile. Streaks of pink illuminated the sky. *Dawn.* Soon he could start searching for Mary's trail.

Mary. He had to find her.

Shane lifted the black hat and used his knife to send the silver studs flying. One of them struck Rodriguez's forehead.

"Wait!" Grunting and panting, Rodriguez stared through the dim light of dawn, his expression imploring. "Leave my things alone, *amigo*, and I tell you all."

What would Sam do? Shane rubbed his chin, then leaned against a nearby tree, staring at the pitiful sight before him. "Nope, you got it backward, *amigo*." It was Shane's turn to chuckle as he popped silver conchas off Rodriguez's belt.

"Ah, *gringo*, you ruined my beautiful belt."

"You can stop me, Rodriguez," Shane said, his voice low, daunting as he held the outlaw's hat between two fingertips.

"I don't—"

"Tell me where Mary is." One concha flew at Rodriguez's head.

"Stop first."

A second concha ricocheted off the tree and fell at the bandit's feet. "Answers first."

"Don't—"

Shane dropped the hat and lunged for Rodriguez, pressing the point of his knife against the bastard's throat. "You tell me where Mary Goode is now, Rodriguez."

The bandit's throat worked, but no words emerged.

Shane pressed the blade harder against the oily skin until a pinprick of blood oozed around it.

"Or I'll use this knife on you instead."

Chapter Nineteen

Despite her exhaustion, Mary slept fitfully. Her dreams wavered between lush and exotic memories of Shane to nightmares of Angel Rodriguez. Terror awakened her at least six times before she abandoned her bed for good.

Shane would come home soon. Convinced of this, Mary swung her feet to the floor and rose, looking toward the door. Wondering . . .

She faced the hearth, but hesitated. Finding Fatima seated at her table startled her at first, then memories of last night flooded to the forefront of her mind. Her uncle was here; Robin was safe. She renewed her belief in both miracles by peering at her uncle's sleeping form on the floor beside Robin's bunk.

"Uncle Bot" had read to Robin last night from *The Merry Adventures of Robin Hood,* and his voice so reminded Mary of her father's that she'd wept silently throughout. Before they'd turned in for the night, the older man had reminded them that he was here to take them home.

Home? As happy as she was to see their uncle again—and it was clear Robin shared her joy—*this* was their home now. All these years of praying for someone to come for them, and now . . .

And now, all Mary wanted was to keep her brother safe and happy, and—*dear God, it's true*—to spend her life with Shane. To be his wife. To bear his children. Nothing more.

Nothing less.

Please, let it be so.

Admitting these facts to herself sapped every ounce of strength from her body, but she forced herself to function. She had to, and she had to keep believing that Shane would come home.

Sighing, she went to the table. "Good morning," she whispered. Tuck's wife. His *wife*. And the little man hadn't denied it after he'd recovered from his initial shock of seeing her.

"Good morning," Fatima said. Her silver hair hung in one long braid down her back, and in the light of dawn, her age was more evident. "I fear I shocked all of you last night with my, uh, revelation."

"Yes, you could say that." Mary helped herself to the tea the woman had already prepared. "We had no idea Tuck was married."

Fatima smiled wanly and took a sip of tea. "It seems Adam forgot as well."

"Adam?"

She nodded. "Adam Bigg, my husband."

Bigg? As she pondered the irony of Tuck's surname, Mary's gaze darted to the door several times. With the shutter still missing from the storm, she could hear every sound from outside. Unfortunately, none of them signaled Shane's arrival.

Convinced he would return soon—anything else was

unacceptable—she sipped the bracing tea and peered at Fatima over her cup's rim. "What happened?"

"With Adam?" Fatima shrugged. "I remember the day I first met him. He came to my show—I remained with the carnival after my first husband died—and afterward Adam asked me to tell his fortune."

Though Mary loved Tuck dearly, she couldn't help but wonder about a woman like Fatima actually marrying someone of Tuck's stature. "Did you . . . love him?" The question was crass, but Mary needed to know. She couldn't bear to see Tuck hurt.

Again, that beautiful fleeting smile appeared on Fatima's face. "Very much. He was warm and witty and wise, and he made me smile inside for the first time in many years." She gazed into her cup for several moments, then looked up again. "I believe Adam left without knowing how much I loved him."

Mary mulled this over in silence. Shane had left last night after hearing her say she loved him. Why hadn't she told him sooner? This morning, all her reasons for keeping her feelings secret seemed trivial. "Why did Tuck, er, Adam leave?"

Fatima rose and refilled her cup, then resumed her seat. "The carnival owner accused him of stealing the payroll."

"Tuck wouldn't—" Then Mary remembered what Shane had told her about the Merry Men. She bit her lower lip and met Fatima's gaze. "Would he?"

Fatima sighed. "I don't know, though I've consulted the cards many times."

"Cards?"

"Yes. I will read yours for you when I am more at peace inside." She pressed her hand over her heart. "Now I am too distracted."

Mary nodded, though she had no idea what Fatima meant about reading cards. "How long were you and . . . Adam together?"

"Eight months." Fatima stirred her tea slowly, staring into the dark swirling liquid. "The happiest eight months of my life, Mary. He may be small in size, but he's big of heart."

Mary sniffled. "I know that better than anyone."

Fatima gave her an assessing gaze. "Yes, I suppose you do."

"I just can't understand why he would leave you." Mary shook her head. "The Tuck I know would never have done anything like that."

"Perhaps he did steal the carnival payroll."

Despite Tuck's supposed activities with the Merry Men, Mary couldn't accept that he would've stolen the carnival payroll and left Fatima without a very good reason. "No, I don't believe it."

Fatima's lips twitched, then one corner quirked upward. "Neither do I."

"What did you do when he disappeared?"

"I searched, asked questions, and the sheriff asked more questions. The carnival was on the road in Kansas at the time." Fatima's brow furrowed, and her dark eyes flashed angrily. "Though I cannot prove it, I believe the carnival owner took the payroll himself, then cast blame on Adam. The owner had asked me to become his mistress before Adam came into my life."

"Ah." Mary's sheltered life had left her ill-prepared to comprehend the world beyond Sherwood Forest. "If Tuck, I mean Adam, leaves Indian Territory, will he be arrested?"

Fatima shook her head. "I repaid every cent with the understanding that my husband would not be accused when he returned. Hope can be a very powerful force, and I never gave up hoping for his return."

Mary looked toward the door again. "I pray you're right about hope," she whispered.

Fatima gave Mary's hand a squeeze. "You love your young man very much."

Scalding tears filled Mary's eyes, but she blinked them back. They filled her throat and stung her nose, but she wouldn't cry. Not now. Not ever. She nodded, then looked again at the silver-haired woman. "More than anything, but I didn't tell him enough."

"He knows." Fatima reached across the table. "Finish your tea and give me your cup."

Puzzled, Mary took one last sip, then passed her empty cup to Fatima. "Why?"

"I wish to read the tea leaves." The mysterious woman offered no further explanation as she stared intently into the container. After several moments, she looked up and gasped. She reached for Mary's hand and turned it over, trailing her oval fingernail along the creases in Mary's palm. "You are with child," she whispered fervently.

Mary's heart climbed to her throat. Shock, then joy, burst within her, followed just as quickly by disbelief. "Even if that were true," she said quietly, hoping Robin and her uncle wouldn't overhear this conversation, "it's far too soon to know." But if hope was as powerful as Fatima had said, then perhaps it would prove true.

Fatima's eyes twinkled. "Not always." She released Mary's hand and leaned back in her chair. "I knew immediately."

Mary blinked, studying her new friend. She'd missed having another woman to share things with—things men didn't, and couldn't, understand. "You have a child?"

Fatima nodded slowly, and her eyes grew moist. "Yes. He's at school now, near my sister's home. He's very handsome and wise." She drew a sharp breath. "Like his father."

"Oh." Mary's eyes widened as she considered the implication. "You mean . . . ? How old is your son?"

"Adam turned eight only three months ago."

"Adam?" *Eight years.* "That's how long we've been here." It all made sense. Tuck disappeared from southern Kansas, and that was where Mary found him in the asylum eight years ago.

"You think I'm too old to have a child so young." Fatima's gentle expression belied the harshness of her words. "I thought so, too."

Mary couldn't prevent her answering smile. This woman was unusual but delightful. "Wait." She met and held Fatima's gaze. "Does . . . does Tuck know?"

"Does Tuck know what?"

Mary gasped and turned toward Tuck's voice. "I . . ." She looked anxiously at Fatima. "I . . . I need to visit the necessary house."

"Don't leave because of me," Tuck said to Mary, though his gaze never left Fatima.

A groan sounded from the corner, followed by the rustle of blankets. "Wake up, Robin," Bartholomew said as he sat up and patted his nephew's leg. "We're going fishing or something."

Bartholomew met Mary's gaze, and she realized he'd overheard far more of their conversation than she would've liked. Had he heard Fatima's prediction about a child? Did it matter? Mary would cherish Shane's child under any circumstances.

Bartholomew looked toward Fatima with a longing gaze, tinged with open regret. Perhaps he hadn't heard that part, after all, but it was clear her uncle was more than a little fond of Fatima.

Love in the springtime.

Mary sighed and realized she was still wearing her clothes from yesterday. She'd clean up later for Shane. *Yes, for Shane.* Right now, she wanted to give Tuck and Fatima as much privacy as possible.

"No need for you all to run off," Tuck said. "Fatima and I will go to my cabin to talk. It's time I put the past to rest." He held his crooked arm out to his wife, and she eyed him warily, then rose and looped her fingers around his elbow.

Though Fatima towered over her husband, Mary thought they made a handsome couple. Of course, knowing how much Fatima loved him went a long way toward forming that impression. She gave Fatima an encouraging smile as they passed.

"What a remarkable woman," Bartholomew said as the door closed.

"Yes, she certainly is." Mary turned to Robin. "How are you this morning?"

"Fine," he said, standing. His eye wasn't as swollen now, but the discoloration was much worse. "Go see Sunshine."

"Is Sunshine a pet?" Bartholomew asked, looking from Mary to Robin, then back again.

Mary laughed. "No, but speaking of animals, Robin, since you're feeling better . . ."

Robin sighed and scratched his head. "I lost my hat."

"Bossy won't mind."

"Bossy?" Bartholomew asked, lifting his eyebrows. "Sunshine and Bossy?"

Robin laughed, and Mary's heart swelled with love and pride. "Bossy is our cow," she explained.

"Oh, I see." Uncle Bartholomew slipped his jacket on over his wrinkled clothes. "I'm afraid my appearance might frighten the poor beast."

"Nah." Robin put on an older hat and retrieved the scalded milk pail from its customary peg near the door. "To Bossy, then Sunshine."

"Sunshine?" Bartholomew donned his small round hat—much like the one her father had worn—then stepped out onto the porch.

Mary stood in the doorway, watching her brother lead her uncle to the soddy, chattering the entire time. Robin was home and safe, and next week he would marry Walks in Sunshine.

Shane had kept his promise to return her brother safely.

Now he had to return himself to her safely. He just *had* to.

The sound of an approaching horse jarred Mary from her thoughts. *Let it be Shane.* She hurried down the steps, shading her eyes against the bright morning sun.

As the lone rider came nearer, Mary's hopes plummeted. The tall horse was black, and a white hat covered the man's head. Shane had left here last night on a roan mare, and he'd lost his hat in the twister.

Then she recognized the man as Sam Weathers. Talons of fear tore through her. "Dear God." Was Marshal Weathers coming to give them bad news about Shane? Her mouth went dry and her stomach fluttered. She plucked nervously at her sleeve. And waited.

If only she'd told Shane she loved him sooner . . .

"Mornin', Miss Mary. I'm headed to Hopsador's, and thought I'd make sure everything's all right here first." Sam tipped his hat to Mary.

He didn't know about Shane. Mary breathed a small sigh of relief. "Good morning, Marshal."

She glanced at Robin as he released Bossy into the pasture. The three men came toward the house. Little John carried the milk pail, not spilling a drop. He never did. The Indian set the pail inside, then joined the others to stare expectantly at Sam Weathers.

Sam greeted Little John and Robin, then narrowed his gaze when it fell on Bartholomew. "Got company, I see."

"Uncle Bot," Robin announced, beaming.

"This is our uncle from England, Bartholomew Goode," Mary announced, and as Sam dismounted and shook her uncle's hand, she held her breath. She didn't feel like being polite right now. She wanted to scream.

The moment Sam turned toward her, she said, "Shane has disappeared, Marshal."

Surprise flashed in the marshal's eyes, then he nodded. "So he told you who he is."

"Yes, and I don't care," Mary said.

Robin tugged on Mary's sleeve, a quizzical expression on his bruised face. "Who Shane?"

"Will Scarlet's real name is Shane Latimer," Mary said quickly, then pinned Marshal Weathers with her gaze. "And I love him."

Sam Weathers cleared his throat and his cheeks reddened as he removed his hat. "That's right fine, ma'am, 'cuz I reckon he feels the same way about you."

"I pray he does." Ignoring her uncle's questioning gaze, Mary remained focused on the marshal. "I believe Angel Rodriguez may have . . ." She bit her lower lip. "We have to find him, Marshal."

"What's Rodriguez got to do with this?" The lawman's voice lowered and his expression grew solemn. "Somethin's happened here. What?"

Mary drew a deep breath, then said, "Angel kidnapped Robin and we went to rescue him last night."

"Boom," Little John said.

"What?" Marshal Weathers frowned and shook his head. "Never mind, just tell me what happened."

"I . . . I distracted Angel while the others rescued Robin."

"Distracted?" The marshal's voice was deadly. "I see, and I'll bet Shane didn't cotton to that much. Then what happened?"

"I'm afraid Fatima and I came to Mary's aid and inadvertently led the young man to believe she'd met with foul play," Bartholomew explained.

"Fatima's here?" The lawman raised his eyebrows and chuckled. "I reckon old Tuck's gettin' his come-uppance."

''You knew?'' Mary asked, then quickly shook her head. ''I don't care, we can discuss that later. After I left with Uncle Bartholomew and Fatima, according to Tuck, Angel disappeared, too. Shane stayed behind to search for . . . for me.'' She grabbed the lawman's arm in both her hands, wishing, for once, she could allow her tears to escape. ''Please, Marshal, bring him back to me, so I . . . I can tell him I love him.''

Marshal Weathers hugged her, and Mary almost broke. For eight long years, she had rarely permitted herself to shed a single tear, even after Angel's attack, but now . . .

''Allow me, Marshal.'' Bartholomew described the area, and Sam immediately knew where they meant. He gave Mary a stern look. ''You stay here and stay safe,'' he said.

''Go see Sunshine,'' Robin said.

Sam Weathers looked soberly at Bartholomew Goode. ''You got a gun, Englishman?''

Bartholomew stiffened. ''I do.''

''And you know how to use it?''

''Proficiently, sir.''

''Take it and use it on anybody Robin or John tell you to.''

''I shall, sir, but would someone please tell me who Sunshine is?''

''At full moon,'' Robin explained, beaming with pride, ''Sunshine be my wife.''

''Wife?'' Bartholomew shot Mary a look of alarm, then ducked into the cabin and returned, buckling a holster around his hips. ''Wife, Robin? Truly?''

''You take Robin and Little John to the village, but leave the horses,'' Sam said, rubbing his whiskered chin with his thumb and forefinger. ''If anybody shows up here, I want them to think there's a full house.''

''Capital idea,'' Uncle Bartholomew said.

''We stay all night,'' Robin announced.

"Wait, I—" Mary bit her lower lip to silence her protests. If Angel came after one of them again, it would be her, not Robin. The farther her brother was from Sherwood Forest, the safer he would be. "Give Sunshine my love."

"I will." Robin kissed Mary on the cheek.

"What about breakfast?" She cupped her brother's cheek in her hand.

"We eat at village."

"I'll find Shane, Miss Mary." Sam swung his leg over the stallion's back. He sat there, looking down at Mary with a solemn expression. "You got a gun, Miss Mary?"

"Tuck's derringer."

"Keep it with you."

"I will, Marshal."

"Fatima and her long-lost husband still around?" One corner of Sam's mouth quirked upward. "I would like to have seen the look on his face . . ."

"They're in Tuck's cabin." Impatience nagged Mary. "Please, find him for me, Marshal."

"I will." Sam gave his horse a nudge. "C'mon, Lucifer."

"Mary come see Sunshine, too?" Robin asked, touching her arm.

She met her brother's gaze and saw worry etched across his innocent features. He obviously sensed that Angel Rodriguez was a threat to her, though she prayed Robin would never know exactly what that monster had done.

"I need to stay here and wait for Shane, Robin," she said. "You heard the marshal. Besides, I have Tuck's derringer. I'll be fine."

He hugged her and Mary held him tight. So much had happened to them both in a very short time, yet their love for each other would never change. "You be careful, Robin Hood," she whispered, pulling away when their uncle rejoined them.

Bartholomew cleared his throat. "Mary, we need to talk after—"

"I know, and we will," she said. "Go meet Sunshine."

Bartholomew kissed her cheek, then turned to face Robin and Little John. Mary watched the threesome walk away, her throat working convulsively. She went inside and put on her moccasins, tucked the derringer inside, then did her morning chores. Once the chickens were fed, she went back to the cabin and stared forlornly toward the forest.

Come home to me, Shane. Could he come back? Was he lying hurt out there somewhere? Or dead? Or perhaps he'd decided he didn't want to see her again. . . .

She closed her eyes and remembered his kindness, the tenderness he'd shown her when they made love, his vow to bring Robin home safely. He *would* return if at all possible.

Only death could keep him away.

Her hand dropped to her lower abdomen as she recalled Fatima's words.

If Shane's child now grew within Mary's womb, then he would never die. He would live on through their child.

And in her heart.

Shane gouged the point of his knife into the fine leather of Rodriguez's fancy boot. The outlaw cursed and moaned. The knife pierced the leather of the other one; then Shane dropped the ruined boots to the ground with the growing pile of destroyed finery.

"Looks like I'm out of clothes to destroy," he said thoughtfully, tilting the blade of his knife so the sunlight glinted off it just right. He eyed Rodriguez. "Guess it's your turn now."

"Ah, *amigo,*" Rodriguez said wearily, "I am so tired."

"Yep, it's been a long night." Shane held the knife

upward, then wiped it on his sleeve. He came toward Rodriguez again and grabbed a handful of the Mexican's shiny black hair. "Did I mention that I lived awhile with the Comanche?" He sawed through the hair, then held the cut ends out in front of Rodriguez's widening eyes.

"I kill you, gringo."

"Tsk, tsk, tsk." Shane shook his head and whacked off another handful of hair. "Doesn't appear to me that you're in much of a position to kill anybody right now, Rodriguez."

Shane eyed his handiwork. "Hmm, I reckon it could be a mite shorter in front." With that, he planted his elbow against the bandit's throat and scraped the blade along Rodriguez's scalp. "There, only a little blood. I should've taken up barbering." He stepped back and held more hair up in front of the outlaw's face.

A roar erupted from Rodriguez's throat as Shane dropped the hairs to the ground. "I'm still waiting for you to tell me where Mary is," Shane said calmly, though he'd exhausted all patience hours ago. "Or do you want me to take a little more hair . . . and a lot more scalp? *Amigo?*"

All he wanted at this moment was to hold Mary in his arms and to tell her how much he loved her. Yes, loved her. He'd been a fool not to tell her before, but now that Robin was safe and Rodriguez was in custody, nothing else mattered except Mary.

Listen to your heart, Shane, his mother had said.

And his heart said it was time for Shane Latimer to get hitched. Lord help him.

Mary had to be safe.

He tucked away his knife and drew one pistol. Holding it up where Rodriguez could see what he was doing, he emptied the chambers and pocketed the bullets. He held one piece of lead up to the early morning sunlight, then pretended to slide it into a chamber. Instead, he slyly dropped it into his shirt pocket.

Whistling quietly, Shane spun the chamber. "Wonder where that bullet is." He turned the pistol toward Rodriguez and squeezed the trigger.

Click.

The outlaw quaked in terror as Shane came closer and pressed the cold steel against Rodriguez's temple. "Tell me where she is, damn you."

Click.

"That's two, Rodriguez," Shane said calmly. "There's four chambers left, and any one of them could have the bullet. Tell me *now.*" His voice fell to a ragged whisper, and he gouged the barrel harder into the bastard's temple.

Click.

Something wet hit Shane's boot and he glanced down. "Rodriguez, I believe you pissed yourself."

Click.

Rodriguez whimpered and trembled against the ropes that bound him. "You kill me, gringo, you never find your *puta.*"

Click.

"One shot left, Rodriguez." Shane rubbed the smooth steel against the outlaw's temple. "It's your choice. Talk . . . or die."

"The . . . the man and woman said they would sell Mary."

Shane squinted at the pitiful sight of the immaculate Angel Rodriguez caked with mud and sweat. "To who and where?" He gouged the barrel against the villain again to remind him. "One chamber, Rodriguez. One bullet."

"Muskogee." The outlaw wheezed as Shane pressed against his throat with his elbow. "White . . . slaver."

Shane's blood chilled and a shudder passed through him.

"A name, Rodriguez. Give me a name."

"White slaver in Muskogee. No name." Rodriguez met Shane's gaze. "Now let me go, *amigo*."

"You haven't told me enough to help me find Mary." Shane prayed Rodriguez was lying. Sweet Mary sold into slavery . . . He'd rather kill her himself than have her suffer that way. "I don't believe you." He didn't *want* to believe this.

Rodriguez sighed. "I speak the truth."

"The slaver's name." Shane was so damned tired he could barely see, and now this chickenshit bandit was telling tall tales to get him riled.

And it was working.

Rodriguez furrowed his brow as if trying to remember, but something about the man's expression didn't ring true. It struck Shane as suddenly as that lightning almost had, and with far more accuracy. "You're lying."

"Would I lie to you, *amigo?*" Rodriguez gave a weary sigh. "With your pistol at my head?"

"There's a price for your life, Rodriguez." Shane pulled back the hammer.

"Wait!"

"You got sixty seconds, Rodriguez. Start talking."

"The slaver's name is Buck Landen."

Sam's old nemesis. Shane searched his mind, but couldn't remember anything about Landen being involved in white slavery. "You're still lying."

"No, Landen has a hideout north of Muskogee, in the bluffs overlooking the river."

Shane knew the area. At least that much rang true. "Go on, I'm listening."

"Slavers meet him there and take the women downriver to New Orleans, then they," Rodriguez paused to draw a breath, "board ship for Mexico."

"Why should I believe you?"

"It is the truth."

"You're running out of time."

"Fifteen seconds, but if you piss me off once more . . ."

"*Qué?*"

Shane leaned closer. "Then time's the one thing you won't have. *Amigo.*"

A familiar metallic click sounded behind Shane, and he stopped breathing. Rodriguez always worked alone. But if that was the case, who the hell was fixing to shoot Shane in the back?

He straightened very slowly, watching Rodriguez's expression of surprise. The bandit obviously hadn't been expecting anyone. That could be either good or bad, and Shane suspected he was about to find out which.

"Turn around real slow," a strange voice ordered.

Shane obeyed. He couldn't help Mary if he managed to get himself shot.

The tall, gangly man had a full head of wild red curls. Shane studied the intruder's face, partially covered with a scraggly beard. He'd seen that face before many times on wanted posters.

Only one outlaw had hair like that. It was his most distinguishing feature. Shane knew without a doubt that he was staring into the wily eyes of the notorious and elusive Buck Landen.

"I heard my name," Landen said. "I wanna know *why?*"

"Rodriguez here's been telling tales."

Keeping his gun on Shane, Landen darted a glance at Rodriguez. "You don't got no britches."

"*Dios.*" Rodriguez looked up at the sky and shook his head. "This gringo stole them."

"You some kinda pree-vert?" Landen asked, smirking.

"Nope."

"Drop that pistol."

Shane dropped the empty pistol to the ground, wondering if he was fast enough to take Buck Landen with his other *loaded* one. Considering the outlaw already had his gun in hand, that was unlikely as hell. Shane inclined his head toward Rodriguez. "He's the pervert."

"You're a couple of sorry bastards." Landen chuckled, then glowered at Rodriguez. "I heard you say my name. Why?"

"You are . . . Buck Landen?" Rodriguez asked, rolling his eyes. *"Dios,* can this day get any worse?"

"Trust me, it can," Shane said, not taking his gaze off Landen's gun, "and it will." He had to find Mary. "Rodriguez here says you're a white slaver, Landen. That so?"

The redheaded bandit gave an ominous chuckle. "That's a good one. I reckon I've done purt near everythin' else, though." He looked down at Rodriguez again, his moment of good humor vanishing. "Why you tellin' lies about me, Mexican?"

"Forgive me, but I only wished to win my freedom," Rodriguez said smoothly. "Surely a man of your, uh, reputation can *comprende?* The gringo had unfair advantage."

"Yep, it looked that way to me." Landen chuckled again. "I been known to spin a yarn or two for that same reason."

"Then perhaps," Rodriguez continued, "you could see your way clear to cut me free, *señor?"*

"Not so fast." Landen returned his attention to Shane. "Who are you?"

Shane hesitated for only a moment. "Will Scarlet."

Landen squinted and tilted his head to one side. "You a lawman?"

"I don't remember." Leaving his badge in his pocket had been a wise move. So far.

"You smell like a lawman. You know Sam Weathers?"

Shane hesitated, wondering if the truth would hurt or help.

"Oh, he knows the big lawman," Rodriguez said. "I saw them talking at the Goodes' cabin."

So much for deciding myself. Shane shrugged. "What of it?"

Landen looked crazed as his gaze darted around as if looking for someone or something. "Weathers here? That lawman's been pesterin' the hell outta me for years. Can't go straight no matter what, with that one on my tail."

"Sam's not here." *Unfortunately.* Landen was obviously terrified of Sam Weathers, and for good reason. "I'm taking Angel Rodriguez in for the bounty, Landen. You gonna try and stop me?"

"I sure as hell am."

"Please, *amigo,* cut these ropes?"

"You, Will Scarlet, back up against that there tree," Landen ordered, pointing toward a giant oak with the barrel of his gun. "Don't try nothin'." The outlaw reached forward and pulled Shane's remaining pistol from his holster and threw it into the trees behind him.

Keeping the gun on Shane, Landen retrieved a knife from his belt and sawed through the rope holding Rodriguez's hands. Once his hands were loose, Rodriguez freed himself from the rope tied to the tree.

Landen returned to Shane. "I'm meetin' someone here today," Landen said. "You two take your argument someplace else."

"Wait," Rodriguez said. *"Por favor,* keep your gun on this one for *un momento."*

"Hurry the hell up about it." Landen kept his gun on Shane.

Rodriguez staggered toward his campsite, returning a few minutes later wearing another pair of pants. He slid into his cut boots and waved his pistol in Shane's face. *"Gracias, amigo."*

Landen shrugged. "Don't let my name cross your lips again. Hear?"

"As you wish, *amigo.*"

The redheaded outlaw turned and walked away, leaving Shane staring into the barrel of Angel Rodriguez's gun. Shane figured he'd been a lot better off in front of Landen's, if that were possible.

"You were right about one thing, *amigo,*" Rodriguez said, leering.

"What's that?" Shane asked, trying to buy time while he figured out how to get out of this mess.

"Time, *amigo.*" Rodriguez leaned into Shane's face and chuckled. "One of us is out of time, but it is not me. I feel much better now, but not as good as I will when I have your *puta* moaning beneath me again."

Shane lunged for Rodriguez's pistol. He held the outlaw's wrist and slammed the back of his hand against a tree. Rodriguez loosened his grip, and the weapon fell to the ground.

The outlaw and Shane both dove for the gun. Shane wrapped his hand around the butt of the pistol. As he swung his arm around, anticipating justice at last, Rodriguez smashed a rock against the top of Shane's head.

Pain exploded. Blood trickled across his forehead. The ground opened up and swallowed him into a yawning, groping pit.

Of blackness.

Chapter Twenty

Mary watched and waited all morning. Midday, Tuck and Fatima finally emerged from his cabin.

Glowing.

What had caused their mutual glow was so evident that Mary's cheeks flamed the moment she saw them. Tuck had obviously not only regained his memory, but had embraced his past. Literally.

"No sign of Shane?" Tuck asked.

"No." Mary's voice caught and her eyes burned, but she refused to cry. That wouldn't help Shane. Besides, crying was for children . . .

"I have much to tell you, Mary, but I'm going to search for Shane first."

Mary cleared her throat and drew a steadying breath. "No. Marshal Weathers came."

"Ah, good. I'm glad Sam is on the job." Tuck motioned toward the table. "Can we talk now?"

With Katie Calico in her arms, Mary nodded, needing something to occupy her mind. She sat facing the open door, hoping for a glimpse of Shane riding toward the cabin. Absently, she stroked Katie, drawing some comfort from the kitten's contented purring.

"Fatima told me she explained our, er, relationship to you."

"She's your wife." Mary smiled weakly, her heart elsewhere. "And I can see that you love each other very much."

Tuck's face reddened and he gave her a sheepish grin. "More than I ever realized." He took Fatima's hand and kissed the back of her knuckles. "I have a son, Mary. A son!" The old man's voice cracked and his eyes glistened threateningly.

"I know." Mary's heart swelled with love for this little man, who'd been such an important part of her life. "I'm happy for you, Tuck."

"My husband has told me what happened, and I insisted he tell you everything as well." Fatima gave her husband an encouraging smile.

Tuck sighed, patted his wife's hand, then met Mary's gaze. "My name isn't Tuck, which I'm sure you've always known, nor is it Adam Bigg."

"Not Adam Bigg?" Frowning, Mary looked from Fatima to Tuck. "I don't understand."

"Neither did I," Fatima said.

"When I met Fatima, I was traveling with a group from the university where I taught physics."

"University? Physics?" Stunned, Mary shook her head. "Amazing."

"My real name was—is—Ichabod Smith." Tuck waited for a few moments. "That name means nothing to you?"

"No, should it?" Mary studied Tuck's expression. He was being completely sincere. Of that she was certain. "Please, tell me about Ichabod Smith."

"I was a professor of physics at Zurich Polytechnic Institute in Switzerland."

"Switzerland?"

Tuck nodded. "A group of us traveled to America in the spring of 1887."

"A year before I found you," Mary interjected.

"More like eighteen months, actually," he said, smiling sadly. "I was born in Boston, and all my life I'd dreamed of seeing the West. Alas, a small man like myself had few options—then or now, I'm sure. The world, after all, was not designed for adults the height of ten-year-old children."

"I'm sorry."

"No, don't be." Tuck smiled. "I've had a good life, Mary." He turned to Fatima again. "And it's bound to be even better now."

"I'm happy for you," Mary said, and meant it. She looked toward the door again, longing to hear the sound of hoofbeats. Shane would come back for her. He *would*. Then she could tell him she loved him.

"Mary, don't worry so," Fatima said, reaching across the table to cover her hand. "Your young man will return for you."

"You . . . you know?"

Sadness filled Fatima's dark eyes. "I've had no vision, dear, but I have hope. Like you."

Mary nodded and met Tuck's gaze again. "Tell me how you met Fatima," she said, needing to know almost as much as she needed to keep her mind occupied. "And why you became Adam Bigg."

"I spent much of my life abroad, receiving my education, then teaching later," Tuck continued. "I knew the moment I set foot in America again that I wanted to stay, and I longed to have my own laboratory where I could conduct research and make wondrous discoveries."

"I still don't understand."

A wan smile curved his lips beneath his silver beard. "I spent most of my adult life teaching others to go forth and make discoveries which would change the world."

"And that's what you wanted to do," Mary said. "Why didn't you?"

"My parents discovered my superior intelligence and tried to enroll me in various American colleges." He heaved a weary sigh. "It broke my mother's heart when Harvard turned me down. They were prepared to accept me until they saw me for the first time."

Mary's heart broke for the young man Tuck had once been. She understood all too well how his mother must have felt, for didn't Mary harbor similar hopes and fears for Robin? "How narrow-minded of them."

"Indeed." Tuck held up a finger. "But . . . if they'd accepted me, I might never have gone to Europe, or traveled here . . . or met either of you."

Fatima kissed his cheek. "Tell her everything, Adam."

"Not Ichabod?"

Fatima wrinkled her nose. "I prefer Adam."

Tuck's cheeks reddened, but his eyes glowed with love. "Whatever you wish, my dear." He turned to face Mary again. "I applied for a grant from a foundation years before returning to America. My hope was to establish a laboratory here where I could work on an incandescent light."

Mary wrinkled her brow and shook her head. "What's that?"

"Material that glows without consuming itself," he explained. "My dream was to make it practical enough to use in homes and businesses."

Mary leaned closer. She'd read about such modern conveniences in newspapers Henry and Ruth Runningwolf had brought to her on numerous occasions. Reading about them and actually seeing them were far different, however. "What happened?"

"The foundation gave the grant to another man who was a little younger and a lot taller." He pressed his lips into a thin line. "You've heard of Thomas Edison, I presume?"

"I've read about him. Yes."

"He received the grant, made the discovery, and has received all the glory." Tuck shrugged. "I carried that bitterness in my heart for many years, and when I saw the opportunity to run away from my life and start a new one, I did."

"I see." Mary glanced at Fatima. "Then you met Fatima."

"Correct." He smiled again. "And what a fortuitous happenstance that was."

"I understand your wanting a new life," Mary said, shaking her head, "but I still don't understand why you used a fictitious name." She met Fatima's gaze. "Especially with the woman you loved."

"I wanted to leave Ichabod Smith, the brilliant scientist and professor, far behind," he explained, then drew a deep breath. "I fear I was still suffering from my jealousy of Edison. It was wrong. I should have merely resigned my position and married Fatima as Ichabod Smith."

"I prefer Adam Bigg," Fatima repeated. "But I love Ichabod, too."

The woman's statement reminded Mary of Shane's being Will Scarlet, too. Her heart constricted and her throat burned as she struggled against tears. After a moment, she recovered herself.

"The world searched for Ichabod Smith," he explained. "But no one knew or cared about Adam Bigg."

"We care," Mary said, meeting Fatima's gaze. She faced Tuck again. "How did you happen to leave Fatima and end up in the asylum with Robin?"

His eyes flashed with anger. "I only remember part of

what happened, but enough to know I was the victim of foul play."

"Go on," Mary urged. "I'm listening."

"The carnival owner lusted after Fatima and wanted me out of the way."

"Certainly not love." Fatima made a delicate snorting sound.

"No, definitely not." Tuck stroked his beard as he spoke, something he often did when agitated. "He had someone jump me late one night—at least, I believe that's who was responsible—and the next thing I knew, I awakened in a boxcar on a westbound train in southern Kansas."

"If that man weren't already dead, I'd kill him myself," Fatima said, anger sparking in her eyes.

"He's dead?" Tuck asked.

"Yes."

"Good," Tuck said, nodding.

"So how did you end up in that horrible place with Robin?" Mary asked again, though in her heart she thanked God Tuck had been there with Robin and Little John. "And how did you lose your memory?"

"There was a terrible train wreck." Tuck shuddered, and perspiration beaded his brow and bald pate. "I was seriously injured, and after I awakened, I remembered nothing of Ichabod, Adam"—he looked at Fatima—"or my lovely wife."

Silent tears streamed down Fatima's face. "I wish I'd been there for you."

Tuck patted her hand again and leaned toward Mary. "The doctors and authorities put me in that asylum, where I recovered from my injuries but didn't regain my memory." He barked a derisive laugh and shook his head. "After all, where else would they put someone like me? Someone *different?*"

"Like Robin." Mary could barely breathe, remembering that horrible place, the babies behind iron bars, the rows of closed doors harboring people whom society didn't want to even try to understand. She brought her fist to her mouth and bit her knuckles. "Dear God."

"Potentially a living hell, to be sure," Tuck whispered. "Little John was brought in after I'd recovered physically, though I still hadn't regained my memory. He'd broken his leg and was taken there to recover. I'm still not certain why he'd ventured so far north."

Mary drew a deep breath. "Of course, I know how Robin ended up in that awful place." She slowly shook her head. "I'll never forget how frightened I was when I recovered from my illness and learned he was . . . was gone."

Tuck reached for Mary's hand. "I know, child, especially after losing both your parents."

Mary nodded and squeezed his hand before releasing it and rising. She walked woodenly to the door, stroking the kitten in her arms as she stared out the window. "I came here because I didn't know where else to go," she said, remembering aloud. "Little John showed us the way."

"You were such a strong child." Tuck appeared at her side and patted her shoulder. "The burdens you carried were far too great for such a young heart."

Mary couldn't argue that point. "I'm sorry you were taken from Fatima—very sorry." She turned and met Tuck's gaze. "But I'm very, very glad you were there for Robin. And me."

"Everything happens for a reason," Fatima said quietly, joining them by the window. "You needed Tuck and he needed you. Though I grieved after he left, I had our son to comfort me, and I am strong. For a while, you needed him far more than we did."

"You and Mary are the strongest women I've ever known," Tuck said, taking his wife's hand. "I remembered everything eventually, though it took years. By the time I remembered you, my love, I feared you would have forgotten me. Thank you for not forgetting, Fatima.''

The silver-haired woman nodded, her lower lip quivering. ''I knew you were alive, Adam, and I started having visions about the character of Robin Hood and his Merry Men.'' She laughed quietly. ''At first, I thought it was because I'd read the story to our son, but the visions were too powerful. Once I saw the illustrations, I sensed the truth. At least, part of it.''

''Will you . . .'' Mary swallowed convulsively. ''Will you leave us, Tuck?''

His eyes glittered. ''For a short while,'' he said. ''I want to bring Fatima and our son here to live. With your permission, that is.''

''Permission?'' Mary gave Tuck an indulgent smile. ''You really are an old fool if you think you need my permission.''

He gave a joyous laugh, then grew sober as he looked out the window. ''We'll wait until after Robin's wedding,'' he said, then turned to face her again with a determined set to his jaw.

''And yours.''

Darkness fell and Mary was thankful that Robin, Little John, and Uncle Bartholomew had remained in the village. She didn't permit herself to dwell on the bad things that could have happened, because she knew in her heart that they were safe.

If only she could be as certain about Shane.

''We'll stay here in the cabin with you tonight,'' Tuck said after supper.

''No, you won't. You and your wife need your, uh, privacy.'' Mary's face flamed with heat. ''Besides, I have the derringer and I'll bolt the door. Now that you've

repaired the broken shutter, I'll be fine. You have nothing
to worry about.''

"Mary, Rodriguez might still be—''

"Tuck, I have your derringer, and you showed me how
to use it. Remember?''

Mary didn't tell them she craved her privacy right now.
She wanted time alone to summon and cherish her memories of Shane's lovemaking, and—*please, God*—if he
should return tonight, she wanted him all to herself.

Fatima seemed to sense Mary's need for solitude, and
she encouraged her husband to accompany her back to
his cabin. Once the door closed behind them, Mary heard
Tuck's voice telling her to throw the bolt.

Smiling at the old man's protectiveness, Mary slid the
bolt into place. "All right, now go,'' she said in a voice
that belied the agony rumbling through her. "Good
night.''

"Good night,'' Tuck and Fatima called back.

Mary listened until she was certain they were gone,
then trudged to the table and slumped onto the bench.
Wearily, she stared into the dying fire. The evening was
mild; she wouldn't need another log tonight.

Come home to me, Shane. Tears stung her eyes, but
still she held them at bay. *Come home.*

Exhaustion ebbed through her, and she rested her forehead against her arms. Gradually, sleep claimed her and
images of Shane filled her dreams—his special smile, the
way his eyes lit up when he looked at her, the gentleness
of his fiery touch.

Something reached into her slumber and relentlessly
plucked her from the pleasant dream. Startled awake,
Mary sat up straight and stared into the hearth, where
only embers glowed among the ashes now. She must've
been asleep for hours in this position. The kink in her neck
confirmed that, and she reached behind her to massage it
as she rose.

She stretched, then turned toward her bunk, dousing the lamp as she went. Eager to escape again into her dreams, she flopped down belly first. Worry had sapped her strength.

A soft knocking caught her just as she began to fall asleep. Disoriented, Mary pushed herself upright and listened. Had her brother and Uncle Bartholomew returned so late?

Shane.

Her heart slammed into her ribs as she hurried to the door. And froze. What if it wasn't Shane or Robin on the other side?

"Mary?" The whisper was so weak, she couldn't possibly identify it. "Help . . . me."

"Shane?" she called, holding her breath.

"Help . . . me."

She tried to peer through the slit Little John had put in the door for her, but the moon hadn't yet risen. She could see nothing. She had no choice. Shane could be out there, hurt and bleeding.

Dying.

Swallowing hard, she removed her moccasins and withdrew the derringer, holding it so tightly her hand trembled. She slid the bolt slowly, praying with every inch that she wasn't making a dangerous mistake.

A deadly mistake.

The door opened slowly and she backed away, holding the tiny pistol in both hands. "Who . . . who is it?"

The man kicked open the door and lunged into the cabin. Mary leapt backward, still clutching the old pistol. The cabin was too dark. If only she hadn't put out the lamp on her way to bed.

"Shane?" *God, please let it be Shane.*

The door closed with a squeak and a decisive click. The man slid the bolt home. Shane would talk to her, wouldn't he? Mary backed into the corner, aiming toward the dark shifting form near the door. If she spoke again, the intruder might be able to follow the sound of her voice.

An evil chuckle permeated the cabin. Mary's skin turned frigid. She stopped breathing.

"Ah, *querida*," he said, no longer whispering, "we are alone."

If Angel was standing here in her cabin, then where was Shane? Dread settled over her, piercing her heart with agonizing precision.

Shane was dead.

Unshed tears gathered and singed her eyes and nose, her pulse thrummed in her ears with a deafening roar. Her belly clenched with agony, her throat seized with terror, her heart shattered with grief.

She struggled against the urge to scream. That would only help Angel locate her in the darkness, and Tuck would never hear her with both cabins closed for the night.

What would Shane have done? Mary drew a shaky breath, trying desperately not to sob. He would've remained still and quiet until the intruder grew close enough for him to shoot.

What other choice did she have? Motionless, she stood with her back pressed against the corner farthest from the door. The only light came from the dying embers in the hearth.

The clock struck once, then resumed its steady tick-tock. She'd lost track of Angel's shadow, but was almost certain he no longer lingered near the door. Darkness was both her friend and her enemy.

Oh, God, Shane . . . Mary bit her lower lip to silence her unspoken prayers. If the man she loved was truly dead, then his baby became even more important. She would do anything to protect Shane's unborn child.

And herself.

A solid thunk reached her ears.

"Dios."

There he was, near the table. Able to focus on his dark shape against the glowing embers in the hearth, she turned slightly to aim the pistol more accurately. This time, she wouldn't look away.

"Come, *querida,*" Angel said in a singsong voice that made her cringe inwardly and outwardly. *"Yo te quiero,* and I will make it good. *Muy bien."*

Mary understood almost no Spanish, and she was glad. If she'd grasped his meaning, she might grow angry enough to scream. Resolute silence was her only hope.

Two softer thunks reached her ears. She had no idea what the sounds meant, but she maintained her silent vigil. Praying. She had to see him clearly enough first. Then she had to pull the trigger.

The thought of killing Angel Rodriguez brought her no remorse. In fact—God forgive her—she would enjoy this revenge. *An eye for an eye . . .*

Another soft sound came from the same area, followed by a slight swish. Mary strained her eyes through the darkness. She'd lost him again to the shadows. Where was he?

The swish came again, and she searched the room frantically for any movement. The fine hairs at her nape stood on end, her flesh tingled. He was close.

Too close.

Holding her breath again, Mary discerned another swishing sound and realized Angel was on the floor. She envisioned him on his belly like the snake he was, slithering toward her with evil intent.

The derringer held two shots. She lowered her aim when she heard another swishing sound. Slowly, steadily, she squeezed the trigger.

The explosion made her leap to the side. She heard

Angel's curse, followed by a scrambling sound. He grabbed both her ankles and jerked.

Mary fell backward, the derringer slipping from her grasp to clatter across the floor. Angel hauled her toward him with a powerful tug.

Twisting, she tried to free herself, but he held her tight. He pulled once more on her ankles, simultaneously lunging forward to land atop her.

The screams Mary had withheld now broke free with a vengeance. She screamed and screamed until Angel backhanded her. Her ears rang, and the metallic taste of her own blood filled her mouth.

She had to protect Shane's unborn child. Charged with that mission, she jammed her knee into her attacker's groin. He cursed again, pinning her arms in place with his powerful hands.

The Angel Rodriguez she knew had always been immaculately groomed. Tonight, he reeked of stale liquor, sweat, and human excrement. Bile rose to her throat as he tried to capture her mouth with his. She jerked her head from side to side, avoiding contact.

"Mine, *querida*," he whispered, his breath enveloping her in a pernicious cloud. "You shot me, now I take what's mine."

So her bullet had struck, but not well enough to help. "No." Mary tried to lift her knee again, but he had her pinned too tightly to the floor. She couldn't move at all, but she took solace in the knowledge that he couldn't take advantage of his position without compromising his hold on her. "No," she repeated, forcing her voice to sound calm and firm.

"*Sí.*" His menacing chuckle filled her ears. "Your gringo is dead, *querida*." He slipped his hand between their bodies and pinched her nipple. "All mine."

Shane dead . . . She died a little inside at those words, praying this evil man was lying. Angel continued to grope and knead her flesh, but she remained stoic beneath him. She refused to even display her disgust. This, she knew, would enrage him.

Savagely, he yanked the fabric of her shirt to one side, exposing her breast. His weight bore down on her so viciously she could barely breathe, let alone move.

Mary eased her arm from beneath him while he busied himself with her breast. She felt nothing but the cold certainty that this monster would soon be dead.

By her hand.

He was distracted—deranged, she realized—when her trembling fingers found the smooth butt of his pistol. As she'd hoped, his slight shift enabled her to move enough to find his weapon.

Filled with purpose, she slid the gun from his holster in one graceful motion. Though everything seemed to move at a torpid pace, in reality it must have happened swiftly.

He flinched when she gouged his own weapon into his ribs. Mary pulled the trigger without hesitation, the explosion resonating through her head, her bones, her very soul.

Angel jerked spasmodically. Warm, sticky blood spurted from his chest, drenching her neck and torso. She shoved him away and rolled from beneath him, aiming the pistol toward him again as she stood.

Rage, terror, and a perverse sense of triumph roiled through her with all the finesse of another twister. Mary's breath rasped through her throat, her heart fluttered and raced, and hatred suffused her.

He'd raped her. Repeatedly. He'd murdered the man she loved. Obsessed with her need for justice and retribution, she pulled the trigger again. He'd kidnapped Robin. She pulled the trigger again.

The sound of splintering wood reached her ears, but she couldn't stop squeezing the trigger. The explosions ceased and only the ineffectual clicking of empty chambers filled the cabin.

"Mary, he's dead."

The gentle words barely penetrated her daze. She tried to struggle back from the madness that had consumed her, but pulled the trigger again. Once. Twice.

Someone wrapped a hand around her wrist. Mary looked toward the newcomer, seeing nothing but darkness. Then a match flared from behind him as someone lit the lantern.

The carnage at her feet was bathed in an insidious golden glow. Someone gasped from across the room, and Mary jerked her gaze toward the sound. Fatima. Tuck. Sam. They stood there staring at her, their eyes round with horror.

Then she shifted her gaze to the man who still held her wrists in his strong hands. The lamp's golden glow flowed around him, leaving no doubt as to his identity. The expression in his eyes was part pity, part worry.

Then the floor rushed up to meet her.

Chapter Twenty-one

Shane caught Mary as she fell, thankful that she regained consciousness almost immediately. He stared into her glazed eyes, praying he could bring her back from this madness. He'd seen a woman react this way once before, after she'd killed her drunk and abusive husband with a butcher knife. Having seen his own mother beaten by her husband, Shane hadn't questioned the woman's right to eliminate the threat. Unfortunately, that woman never recovered from the madness that had pushed her over the edge.

Mary would.

"Mary, it's Shane. You're safe." He eased the empty revolver from her grasp and dropped it to the floor. She didn't even flinch at the loud clatter. "Mary?"

She blinked once. Twice. Finally, she met his gaze, and her face crumpled. Her mouth formed a perfect circle as reality obviously paid her a sudden visit. Gasping, she stepped into his embrace. Wild shudders racked her lithe form, but Shane simply held her, stroked her hair, massaged her back with soothing strokes.

Fatima threw a wool blanket over what remained of Angel Rodriguez, and Shane urged Mary to walk toward the door. He wanted her out of here, away from the aftermath of her self-defense.

Thank God she was safe.

Shane paused near the door and released the buckle of his holster with one hand, then handed his gun to Sam. "We'll be back soon," he said. "And I won't need this."

Sam inclined his head toward Rodriguez. "You take up barberin'?" Though his words were light, his tone was sober.

"Yeah, but just once."

"Good enough." Sam gave Shane's shoulder a squeeze.

Tuck's worried expression softened, though his eyes burned with determination. "This . . . mess shall be gone before you return."

"Thank you."

When he stepped outside with Mary, Shane's breath caught in his throat as he remembered hearing the first shot. He'd leapt from the saddle before his horse stopped. Finding the door bolted, he and Sam had kicked it down as the final shots were fired.

Mary was so quiet. She should cry. Now that he thought about it, he couldn't remember ever seeing her cry more than once. Worried, he swept her into his arms, knowing what he had to do.

Thankful for the warm night, he carried her to the river and walked into the water. She clung to him as the river's gentle current flowed around them, bathing the vile blood of Angel Rodriguez from her skin and clothing.

And, Shane prayed, from her soul.

Mary eased herself down his body until her feet touched the river bottom. The water was waist deep on him and came almost to her shoulders. She looked up at him as the moon rose, bathing her in silver. Without speaking, she lowered herself under the water, then rose and came full against him.

"Thank you," she whispered. "Thank you." Pressing her head against his shoulder, she clung to him.

"Did . . ." Shane swallowed hard. Though Mary's clothing had been intact, for the most part, when he found her, he needed to know how badly Angel had wounded her. "Did he hurt you again, Mary?"

"He . . . he tried." Her voice broke and she drew a shuddering breath. "But I *killed* him. I always knew I would."

"Yes, you did." Shane stroked her hair. "He can never harm you or Robin or anyone else again."

"I was so . . . so frightened."

"You're safe now." Shane sighed, thanking God again and again for this miracle. "I love you, Mary Goode." He held her and kissed the top of her head. "Marry me."

Maybe his timing was wrong, but it felt right. The past was past. The future was theirs to embrace, and he didn't plan to waste a moment. "Marry me," he repeated.

She tilted her head back, and a slow smile curved her lips. "When?"

He chuckled quietly, gazing into her eyes. "Does that mean yes?"

"Yes, yes, yes."

He lifted her and spun her in a circle. She laughed joyously, and he prayed he would hear that sound at least a million times in this lifetime and the next.

"When?" she repeated when he lowered her to her feet again. "When?"

"The full moon." Shane bent toward her mouth, brushing his lips to hers as he spoke. "Next week with Robin and Sunshine."

"Yes. Oh, yes."

He kissed her soundly, rejoicing at her open response.

Angel's attack had left no lingering scars on her person or her beautiful heart. His sweet Mary was unharmed, whole.

And his.

She shivered in the cold water, and he lifted her into his arms again, carrying her to the bank. As he lowered her to her feet, she clung to him, claiming his lips in a kiss so sweet it danged near made his teeth ache. Ah, but what a delicious ache it was.

"I love you, Shane Latimer," she whispered.

"And I love you, Mary Goode." He held her close, relishing the steady thud of her heart against his.

"What about Will Scarlet?"

"He's in love with some woman named Maid Marian," he teased. "Hopeless case."

Her laughter was like music.

"And what about Maid Marian?" His voice grew husky as he nuzzled the side of her neck. "Hmm?"

Mary gasped, letting her head fall to the side, exposing more of her tender skin to his seeking lips. "She's in love with Will Scarlet. Hopeless case."

"I'm happy for them, but I'm even happier for us." He licked river water from her skin, nipped her jaw, sucked her tender earlobe into his mouth.

"Love me, Shane," she murmured. "Here. Now."

She didn't have to ask twice.

He slipped her torn, damp shirt from her shoulders and dropped it to the ground as she opened the buttons of his and pressed the tips of her tantalizing breasts to his bare chest. He released his breath in a long, slow whoosh. "Woman, you make me burn."

"Mmm." She unbuckled his belt and deftly worked the buttons at his fly until his jeans gaped open below the waist. "Barn door's open," she said, her voice laced with a seductive huskiness that seeped through him.

Shane held his breath as she slid her hands beneath the

waistband of his jeans, pressing her palms against his hips. "Slow down, you're ahead of me." He could barely speak, let alone unfasten her breeches. Finally, after much fumbling, he managed to slip the wet garment down her hips.

Her breeches slid to her ankles and she stepped out of them. "Now who's ahead?" she whispered, pushing his jeans downward. The damp fabric clung tenaciously.

Shane flinched when the waistband of his jeans caught on the part of him that wanted her almost as much as his heart did. "Whoa, hold on there." He quickly adjusted himself so his jeans fell away, baring his heated flesh to the cool night air. "You cold, sweetheart?"

"Not anymore." She pressed herself against his full length, stroking his hips and buttocks with her soft hands until he moaned. "You like that?"

"Yes," he breathed, capturing her mouth in a hard, demanding kiss. He drank from her lips, filled her with his tongue, sought and gave in turn.

God, how he loved her. He filled his hands with her delectable breasts. Her husky groan overflowed into him like good bourbon—smooth and smoky and satisfying. Her arms encircled him like velvet ribbons as he brushed his thumbs against her rigid nipples. A shudder of longing rippled through him.

He relinquished her mouth to explore new territory, nibbling and kissing her cheek, her jaw, her throat. Tarrying at the curve of her shoulder, he traced tiny circles against her flesh with his tongue. Mary buried her fingers in the hair at his nape and pulled him closer, her head falling backward, baring her flesh to his hungry lips.

Shane cupped her breast, lowering his mouth to its peak. He flicked his tongue against her, savoring the raw, needy sound that erupted from her.

Empowered, he drew her deeply into his mouth. Nothing could taste sweeter. She was a tiny morsel, but she was as perfect as any woman could be. Because she was his. *His*.

That knowledge humbled him. How and why Lady Luck had smiled on him, he'd never know. But he really was the luckiest of men. Blessed, his grandma would say.

Mary made small purring sounds from deep in her throat that pierced his heart as sure as Cupid's arrow. She lifted one leg and hooked it behind his, brushing her silken calf along the back of his knee.

He pulled back, gasping for air. "I want you," he muttered.

"Yes. Now."

"Soon." Dropping to his knees before her, he kissed his way down her torso, tickled her navel with his tongue, cupped her bottom in his hands. "Sweet," he whispered, exploring lower. The curling hair between her thighs tickled his nose and tongue, driving him mad with the need to savor her.

She stiffened, and he reminded himself that she couldn't possibly have experienced anything like this before. "I want to taste you, Mary. All of you."

And he did.

She moaned, and her legs trembled as he explored and tasted at his leisure. He kept one arm around her body and parted her velvet folds with the fingers of his other hand.

"Mercy," she whispered. The next moment, her body convulsed and tightened around his fingers, and he knew she'd found her release. Her knees buckled, and he rolled, pulling her along to land on top of him.

Mary lay motionless along his full length, her breathing heavy, her heart beating against his chest. "I didn't know," she murmured, sliding her legs down his torso.

"I love you, Mary," he said. "All of you."

She pushed upward, bracing herself with her arms

against the ground above both his shoulders. Her glorious hair cloaked them within a soft, damp veil. "I love you, too, Shane." She kissed him softly. "So much."

He caught her breasts in his hands and urged her closer, encircling her nipple with his tongue. He nipped, then suckled until she writhed against him and brought her knees forward to rise above him. She lifted herself up and back until she straddled him.

Afraid to contemplate her position lest he explode immediately, he groaned. Dipping his fingers between her thighs, he again found her honeyed core. Mary gasped and lowered herself over him, enfolding his throbbing body within hers.

He found the sensitive nub between her legs and massaged it. In response, she clenched around him like a hot velvet glove. "Mary."

She gave a throaty laugh, and clenched the vise around his body and his heart even more tightly. He was at her mercy and he *liked* it. She could do anything she wanted with him now.

And he sure as hell hoped she wanted plenty.

He thrust himself upward, deep and hard. She leaned back and pressed downward in shimmering complement to his movements. Desire spewed through him in a piercing, blistering flash. Her body fused with his, thrust for daring thrust.

Bathed in moonlight, he watched her ride him. It would never be enough, he realized.

"Oh, Shane," she whispered into the night.

Her head lolled to one side, then backward as she took all he could give. The impact of her completion possessed him, drew him ever inward, drained him of his very essence. He held nothing back, gave and took ruthlessly as he spilled himself into her.

Branding her as she had branded him.

* * *

"Are you ready, my dear?"

Mary looked up at her uncle and nodded. She wore the lavender dress, because it was the only one she owned, but also because it had been a gift from Tuck, Robin, and Little John. And because she'd worn it the night she set out to seduce Will Scarlet.

Smiling, she looked down the path of wildflowers to where her brother now stood holding Walks in Sunshine's hand. Little John stood with them, serving as Robin's best man.

On the somewhat befuddled Father Fitzpatrick's other side, Shane stood like a beautiful bronze god. Mary's breath caught when she met his gaze. Even from this distance, she felt his love pouring over her. She was the luckiest woman on earth.

Freshly shaven, tall and proud, Sam Weathers stood at Shane's side, his ever-present Stetson clutched in his hands. He'd appeared again at just the right moment to stand up with the boy he'd rescued once upon a time in Colorado.

"Come, child. They're waiting." Tuck took her left arm while Uncle Bartholomew took the right. With two men to give away the bride, Mary literally floated toward the man she loved.

She reached the specially constructed arbor of wild-flowers and took Shane's hand. Warmth washed over her as his green eyes beheld her. She felt truly beautiful, wanted, and loved.

Tuck left them and escorted Fatima to the altar as well, determined that they be remarried under his legal name, even though his lovely gypsy had made it known she intended to call him Adam forever. They made a handsome couple, despite their drastic differences in height. Their honeymoon would be spent fetching their son from a private school in Little Rock. Afterward, they would return to Sherwood Forest as a family.

Mary couldn't imagine anything more perfect.

Clearing his throat, Father Fitzpatrick looked from one couple, to the other, to the other and rolled his eyes. "This is a challenge," he said with a smile, "but God works in mysterious ways."

Her father's favorite saying . . .

Joy swelled in Mary's heart as the ceremony commenced. Father Fitzpatrick pronounced each couple husband and wife separately. Mary cherished Sunshine's shy smile as her brother kissed his bride on the cheek. Robin was happy and in love. Their parents would've been so proud.

Then the priest pronounced Fatima and Ichabod Smith husband and wife. The bride bent down to kiss her groom without hesitation, and there was nothing shy or chaste about it. Mary blushed and looked away, meeting her man's smoldering gaze.

"I pronounce you husband and wife," Father Fitzpatrick announced. "What God hath joined together, let no man put asunder."

Smiling, Mary welcomed her husband's kiss, as she always would. Warmth and love surrounded her, and all was right with the world. The ceremony ended and the feast began. White Dove had prepared various roasted meats, and Fatima had baked a cake lovely enough to make angels weep.

Tuck had promised a surprise later, and he looked anxiously toward the trees along the riverbank on several occasions throughout the afternoon's festivities. Mary had no idea what the old man was up to, but she was certain it would be interesting and memorable.

They dined outside on a cloth-covered slab table Little John had constructed for the occasion. Overcome with joy, Mary barely tasted a thing. Besides, her hunger was

for what awaited her on her wedding night. Meeting
Shane's gaze, she knew he shared her appetite.

After the wedding supper, Sam stood and cleared his
throat. He held three rolled documents in his hand, each
one tied with a ribbon. "I got somethin' here for Little
John Runningwolf, Ichabod Tuck Adam Bigg Smith, and
Robin Hood Goode." Grinning, Sam passed the papers
to the appropriate owners.

Robin opened his and stared at it. "Read this, Mary,"
he said, holding it out to her. Though he could read simple
words and write his name, he was unable to read anything
complex, let alone understand it.

Mary unfurled the paper and cleared her throat. She
read the words silently first, holding the document so
Shane could read it at the same time. They looked at each
other and smiled, then looked at Sam.

"When did you have time to do this?" Shane asked
his friend and mentor. "Thank you."

"Rode hell for leather to Fort Smith and back again.
Judge Parker owed me a favor or two." Sam shrugged.
"You're all mighty welcome."

"What is it?" Robin asked impatiently.

Tuck laughed when he read his, then gave Sam a solemn
look. "Thank you, my friend."

"What is it?" Robin demanded more forcefully.

"What?" Little John asked as well.

"Pardons," Sam said, "for Robin Hood and his Merry
Men. You ain't wanted no more."

Though the documents held little meaning to Robin or
Little John, they both seemed pleased. Mary offered to
keep Robin and Little John's papers in a safe place, and
they readily relinquished them.

"Thank you, Sam," she said, smiling at his bashful
grin.

"That's the first time you ever called me Sam, ma'am."

Mary laughed. "You're family now, so do you suppose you could call me Mary without the Miss?"

"I'd like that, ma'am—er, Mary."

"One more thing," Shane said, glancing at the chief.

Runningwolf stood, wearing his ceremonial headdress. He painted an awesome portrait against the clear blue sky, and a hawk chose that moment to glide behind him. Melancholy threatened Mary's joy. Runningwolf's way of life was dying. The fact that all the able-bodied young people had left the village was proof of that.

"The soldiers told us this land is ours to do with as we please," the chief said, taking his wife's hand in his. "It pleased us well for many years, but now it pleases us to sell this land to our new brother." He looked at Shane. "He promises to respect the land, to leave the village intact for our visits, and to provide a home here for Robin and Walks in Sunshine. He also promises to respect our burial ground, and to allow us to return when we enter the spirit world."

Stunned, Mary met her husband's gaze. "How did you . . . ?"

"There was a reward, Mary," Shane said quietly. "It's yours, but I thought you'd like to use it for—"

"Yes." She didn't want to think about the horrors of the past, but it seemed somehow appropriate that the death of evil could spawn the birth of good. "Yes, thank you."

"And your uncle wants to help," Shane said. "Does this make you happy, Mary?"

"Very happy." She cleared her throat, suddenly quite full. "Does this mean Sherwood Forest will be our home forever?"

"Forever."

Robin cheered while Tuck applauded and Little John grinned.

Mary kissed her husband soundly, then turned to Chief

Runningwolf. "Thank you, my friend. After Little John brought us here, you welcomed us. You *saved* us."

"We were pleased to welcome Maid Marian, Robin Hood, and Friar Tuck." The chief appeared wistful. "White Dove wishes to live near our firstborn and his family now, but we could never take Robin from this land. It is in his heart." He held his hand to his heart and heaved a weary sigh. "I am old and tired, but we shall return often."

"Please, do." Mary faced her uncle, who'd made no secret about his reason for coming here. "And you, Uncle Bot? Will you stay here with us?"

"I was hoping you'd ask, Mary." His voice cracked and he nodded. "I came here because of guilt born of greed. But you and Robin are my family." He looked around the gathering. "You all are now. There's nothing left for me in England, and this land"—he drew a deep breath as if sampling the air—"it calls to me. With your permission, and Robin's, I'll instruct Father's solicitor to sell Briarwood, pay my debts—if I may?"

Mary nodded.

"Thank you. And then he can send the balance to you." Bartholomew looked around the table. "There should be plenty of money left to build sound homes for you all. We can turn this into a real ranch—buy good stock, build fences, barns . . ."

"And a laboratory?" Tuck asked, grinning and rubbing his hands together.

Bartholomew gave a robust laugh. "Why not?" He gave Mary a wistful smile. "There are many things at Briarwood that belonged to your parents. I'll arrange to have them shipped here. I know the cradle that once held Robin, then you later, is still there. Oh, and there are multiple copies of a certain book." He grinned.

"Good." Robin nodded.

"I'd like that, Uncle Bot," Mary said, smiling. "Thank you."

"My pleasure, Mary. Truly." Bartholomew gave Fatima a sad smile. "Ah, if only you had a sister just like you."

A mischievous gleam danced in the gypsy's eyes. "Be careful what you wish for, Bartholomew," she said, "because I do."

They all laughed, and Mary marveled at the joy and love surrounding her now. "This is how it should be."

Shane gave her hand a squeeze. "How it will always be."

Tuck rose and tucked his pardon into his vest pocket, then turned to look toward the trees again. "My dear?"

"You will release my sons from bondage now, Friar Tuck?" Chief Runningwolf asked, his eyes twinkling.

"I shall, and I thank you for loaning them to me for the afternoon." Tuck sighed dramatically. "Otherwise, our carriage would've floated away without us."

"What in tarnation . . . ?" Sam rose, staring toward the trees, his hand hovering over his pistol.

"You won't be needing that, Marshal," Tuck said with a chuckle. "Thank you all for the wonderful wedding, but my bride and I have a son waiting for us. We'll be back."

Mary stood beside Shane and looked toward the river. Something bright rose above the trees where Tuck had been staring all afternoon. "What is it?"

Sam and Shane exchanged glances. "I reckon it's a . . . ."

"A what, Sam?" Mary walked around the table, still holding her husband's hand and dragging him along. "Shane, what is it?"

He flashed her a grin. "I remember seeing some real interesting books in Tuck's cabin one day." He pointed toward the object as Tuck and Fatima disappeared into the trees. "Let's wait and see."

A series of roars sounded from the trees, and Little John's youngest brothers emerged at a dead run. One of them leaped into the air and released a whoop of delight.

Father Fitzpatrick crossed himself and muttered a prayer as the mysterious object grew right before their eyes. After a few moments, it rose into the sky.

Mary held her breath, clutching Shane's hand tightly. "Mercy."

Higher and larger, it lifted into the beautiful blue sky. Mesmerized, Mary gasped when the entire object came into view.

"It's a hot-air balloon," Uncle Bartholomew said, shading his eyes to watch its ascent. "The old fellow must've made it, and coated the fabric with a substance I'm sure he also concocted himself. Amazing."

Mary's throat clogged as she identified fabric shaped like women's undergarments. "I think I see some things that weren't given to the poor," she muttered for Shane's ears alone. A basket, much smaller than the balloon itself, hung beneath it. She focused on it and saw a flame. Tuck and Fatima waved down at them.

"Is it safe?" she asked, holding her breath.

"Oh, perfectly," Uncle Bartholomew said, admiration entering his voice. "The balloon is made of, uh, silk, and the fire will heat the air and make the balloon rise. Tuck controls the altitude by adjusting the flame. That's the roaring sound you keep hearing."

Mary squinted. "It looks like the fabric is shaped into letters on this side."

"Yep, it sure does." Sam donned his hat and tilted his head back. "Says 'Sherwood Forest or Bust.'"

"That is one incredible man," Uncle Bartholomew said, shaking his head in wonder.

"A brilliant scientist, actually," Mary said proudly, as her absolute faith in Tuck vanquished her fears.

"Me fly," Robin said, holding his bride's hand.

"No," Sunshine said, shaking her head emphatically.

"Yes." Robin looked at her with an all-too-familiar stubborn set to his jaw. "Sunshine, too."

"No," she repeated, stomping her foot.

Robin stared at her for several silent moments, and everyone present fluctuated between watching the balloon and the newlyweds' first argument. Finally, Sunshine smiled and planted a kiss on her husband's mouth.

"No," Sunshine repeated quietly after the kiss.

Robin's cheeks pinkened and he grinned. "All right."

Bartholomew and Sam chuckled quietly, as did Sunshine's parents. Shane smiled at Mary and wiped a tear from her cheek. He held it up to the sunlight. "Beautiful," he whispered, then turned to gaze into her eyes. "Almost the first tear I've seen you shed, though you've been through enough to make anyone cry more."

Mary touched her husband's cheek as the protective layer she'd constructed around her heart many years ago yielded beneath the onslaught of his love. Tears she should've shed eight years ago now slipped freely down her cheeks, though she smiled as she wept. "I love you, Shane Latimer."

"And I love you, Mary Latimer."

"Mmm, I like that." Sniffling, she leaned closer to whisper. "But what about that rogue, Will Scarlet?"

Shane touched his forehead to hers. "He still loves that temptress, Maid Marian."

"I hope they'll be very happy together."

"An absolute certainty."

"That's one of the things I love about you."

"What?"

"The way you talk like a cowboy and a man with a college education at the same time."

"Hmm. I may be a rancher part of the time, Mary, but I'm still a lawman. You know that, don't you?"

"Yes, I never expected you to give that up, Shane."

Heat radiated from Shane's eyes and filled her with thoughts of their wedding night as they watched the balloon drift away. She pressed her hand to his chest. "I think Maid Marian and Will Scarlet deserve a honeymoon of their own." Desire oozed through her as his green eyes darkened and devoured her.

Shane cleared his throat and slipped his arms around her waist. "They have to wait their turn."

The timbre of his voice rumbled through her, inciting and igniting her needs. "Oh?"

"Marshal and Mrs. Latimer get theirs first."

Sam Weathers cleared his throat. Twice. Mary turned to face the older man, her face flooded with liquid fire.

"I reckon your folks are mighty proud of all of you," he said humbly.

Didn't Sam realize their parents were dead? Mary looked up at Shane, confused. Her husband gave her a gentle smile, then faced Sam.

"They are, Sam." He nodded slowly. "They are."

"But . . ."

"They're here, Mary," Shane said gently but firmly. "Always have been—always will be."

"Yes," Uncle Bartholomew said quietly, pulling a handkerchief from his pocket to dab at his eyes. "Lawrence and Elizabeth live on through you and Robin."

Understanding eased through Mary, and she wondered why she'd never seen this before. It was so simple and so true. Hadn't she felt her parents' love every day of their eight years here in Indian Territory? Yes, every day.

Every person ever loved by another human heart lived forever.

She touched her husband's cheek again. "Forever."

Epilogue

February, 1897

"I think you'd better let them in before they break down the door," Shane said, smiling at Fatima. He'd never been as proud in his entire life as he was at this moment.

"Yes, it's time." Fatima swung open the door, admitting Tuck, Little John, Robin, Bartholomew, and nine-year-old Adam.

They gathered around the bed, their eyes wide and mouths agape.

"Twins?" Tuck grinned and pounded Shane on the back. "Well done, son."

"What about me?" Mary asked, smiling.

Tuck's face flushed. "You, my dear, are magnificent."

Mary looked radiant as she surveyed the group. "Shane, aren't you going to introduce our sons to their family?"

Shane cleared his throat and turned slightly to present the bundle in his arms to his Uncle Robin. He folded back the corner of the blanket to display the screaming infant's face. "This noisy one," he announced over the din, "is Samuel Lawrence Latimer."

"After Sam, and Robin and Mary's father," Tuck said.

"And do you know who this is, Robin Hood?" Mary asked her brother.

"Who?" Tuck asked, putting one fist on his hip and the other around young Adam's shoulders.

Robin bobbed his head and took Sunshine's hand in his. "Will Scarlet Latimer."

Put a Little Romance in Your Life With
Fern Michaels

__Dear Emily	0-8217-5676-1	$6.99US/$8.50CAN
__Sara's Song	0-8217-5856-X	$6.99US/$8.50CAN
__Wish List	0-8217-5228-6	$6.99US/$7.99CAN
__Vegas Rich	0-8217-5594-3	$6.99US/$8.50CAN
__Vegas Heat	0-8217-5758-X	$6.99US/$8.50CAN
__Vegas Sunrise	1-55817-5983-3	$6.99US/$8.50CAN
__Whitefire	0-8217-5638-9	$6.99US/$8.50CAN